IRON HERETICS MC: ST. LOUIS

MICHELLE FROST

Warning: This book is meant for mature readers. It contains graphic violence, sexual content, attempted sexual assault, homophobic language, mentions of drug use, and domestic violence.

HERETIC

her·e·tic /ˈherəˌtik/
a person holding an opinion at odds with what is generally accepted.

IRON HERETICS UNIVERSE

Recommended Reading Order

When I began writing Cold Light, I hadn't realized the world and characters that book would spawn, and the Heretics found their way into several projects before I was able to give them an official start of their own. Below, I've listed the titles in the order I recommend them to be read. However, ***Disrupt*** can be read as a stand alone if you'd like to start there. Enjoy!

1. Cold Light (Iron Heretics MC Prequels #1)
2. Discord: An Iron Heretics Short Story
3. Make No Mistake (Iron Heretics MC Prequels #2)
4. Disrupt (Iron Heretics #1)
5. Disarm (Iron Heretics #2)
6. Discordant (Iron Heretics #3)
7. Dissent (Iron Heretics #4)

DISRUPT

Iron Heretics MC #1

PROLOGUE

Mace

One Year Ago

The door cracked open. Half a pale face and one dark eye appeared in the sliver of light coming from inside the apartment. Well, pale except for the multi-colored bruises surrounding his eye and trailing down his jaw bone.

"Pax?" I asked, keeping my voice low like I was trying not to spook a cornered animal. "I'm Mace." He scanned over my face, taking in the evidence of my own injuries—the sling my right arm was in and the butterfly strips holding together several cuts on my face and neck. Pipsqueak, my friend Lex and Arden's puppy, let out a little yipping bark from his place beside my feet and pulled on the leash as he snuck his nose through the crack in the door. Pax's eyes went wide and dropped to the puppy. He pulled the door open wide and knelt, gathering Pip's wiggling gray body into his arms and holding him close.

A small smile lit up his bruised face before he moved his eyes back to me. He licked his lips. "You can come in."

"Thanks," I said, walking inside and letting go of Pip's leash. "Lex wanted me to tell you he appreciates you being willing to watch this little guy until Arden's on his feet again."

"Of course." He shut the door before his eyes came back to mine. "Arden's my family."

"I know he thinks of you that way, as well." I took a step farther into the apartment. It was an open floor plan with the living room, dining room and kitchen all making up the main room, and there was a short hallway leading off to the right. When I turned back, Pax was watching me with wary eyes. He had Pip's lease held in one hand and the puppy stopped sniffing around to lift up onto his hind legs, pressing his front paws against Pax's leg. Pax leaned down to lift him and as he stood back up, a pained grimace pinched his face and his skin went pale.

"Are you okay?"

"I'm fine," he said through gritted teeth.

I moved forward, wrapping my good arm around Pip and lifting him out of Pax's. I set the puppy on the floor and unclipped his leash before laying it on the coffee table. "You don't look fine," I started to say as my eyes zeroed in on the red stain seeping into his T-shirt at the top of his shoulder. "You need help bandaging that?" I asked with a nod toward the spreading bloodstain.

Pax brought his hand up and gently touched the spot with another wince and scowled at the red stained fingers when he pulled his hand away. When he opened his mouth, I thought for sure he was going to argue with me or tell me to fuck off, but instead he let out a tired sigh. "That would be great, actually."

Turning toward the hallway, he motioned for me to follow him and led us to the door on the left. His bathroom was small, but tidy, with a dark wooden vanity cabinet and bright colored beach themed decorations on the white walls. He glanced back at me, his dark eyes vulnerable and a little bit scared, like maybe he was regretting taking a biker up on an offer to administer first aid. But just as quickly, he pulled his shirt over his head with a rough exhale like even that basic movement had pained him. When I saw his back, I was surprised he was able to move at all, and I exhaled roughly myself. "Shit. Pax... Have you had a doctor look at these?"

He nodded. "Yeah, Vivian has one that makes house calls and is, you know, discreet."

Scanning over the multiple gashes covering the otherwise pristine skin of his back, a deep boiling rage started to fill my gut. Not wanting to make him any more uncomfortable than he already was, I turned to the sink and got the hot water going. "Where are your washcloths?"

"In the small linen closet across the hall."

I turned and took the two steps to get out of the bathroom and across the hall, pulling open the slim door there. I grabbed a couple neatly folded washcloths and a towel before stepping back into the bathroom. Pax was shaking. I could see his tremble even before I touched him.

"I know you don't know me," I said to him in a gentle voice. "But I won't hurt you. And I promise you, I'm going to find the man that did this." I doused one of the washcloths in the hot stream of water. After wringing it out, I gently started to clean the blood away from the gash that had reopened on his shoulder blade. He didn't wince, but that tremble got the slightest bit harder. "And I promise you, he's never going to touch you again."

CHAPTER ONE

Mace

"I thought you had the night off?" a voice I knew well asked from behind me. Turning, I already had a smile in place for Vivian Sinclair, owner of the nightclub we were standing in and Iron Heretics MC business partner. Vivian was a beautiful woman with fire red hair and a temper to match. She'd also have the exact information I was looking for.

"You know me, Viv. Couldn't stay away." I stepped closer to the corner booth—her preferred one—with its silver threaded cushions and shot her a wink.

Wrinkling her nose at the nickname, she motioned for me to take a seat, then lifted her eyes and nodded to the bartender. "Apparently not."

Viv watched me as I slid into the horseshoe shaped bench on the opposite side of the table from her. I made sure to keep my cocky smirk in place. It had become an essential part of my armor—the same as my Kevlar vest or the glock resting in the shoulder holster beneath my right arm. At the moment, it was a cover for my impatience for this pit stop to be over so I could locate my target for the evening. I let my eyes sweep the room, but there was no sign of the one dark head of hair I was hoping to find.

A tall pilsner glass was set on the table in front of me. With a nod to the server that delivered it, I slipped my fingers around the cool glass and took a long drink. It was my preferred lager, because of course it was. Vivian missed nothing. She also couldn't leave anything alone—not the beer that would have been perfectly acceptable out of a bottle, not the men she groomed to be in her employ, and certainly not anyone who set eyes on one of them. *Spritz* was a well-oiled machine and no one had any illusions about who kept the wheels turning.

"Looking for someone?" Vivian's lips pulled into a little smile that she hid behind her own glass. Scotch, if I had to guess. The crystal it was sitting in glinted in the low light.

Fuck it. I didn't feel like playing coy. "Yeah, I am. Is Pax working tonight?" I'd texted him earlier, but hadn't gotten a response. That usually meant he was asleep or already at work. Or flat out ignoring me. That last one grated on my nerves. Not that he did it very often, but he'd been in a valley for a while now, between the torture last year and the damn Devil's Rage MC guys coming in here and stirring up trouble at the beginning of the year. He sometimes tended to deal with it by shutting out the world.

There wasn't even a flicker of surprise, and her eyes stayed glued to my face as she set her drink back on the table. "He's downstairs."

Something violent erupted in my gut. Pax didn't work downstairs anymore. Hadn't for almost a year, and the thought of him down there now had rage and jealousy I had no business feeling clawing at my insides. "What the fuck is he doing downstairs?" My voice came out low and menacing, so I didn't blame the bodyguard watching Vivian tonight when he took a step forward. Vivian waved him off. He wasn't a Heretic, but he knew who I was. Since the Iron Heretics had partnered with Viv as *Spritz's* security team, we vetted all her personal security as well.

She raised two elegant eyebrows at me, like I'd both behaved exactly as she'd expected and had baffled her at the same time. "*That's* not what I meant by downstairs."

"What did you mean?"

"He's behind the bar."

STEPPING OFF THE ELEVATOR, I MADE MY WAY DOWN THE dim corridor that led to the *other* half of *Spritz's* business—an exclusive brothel that catered to a select clientele. Namely, gay men. Powerful, well-connected gay men, most of which had no wish for exposure. Vivian offered a discreet buffet of tantalizing morsels, along with a fully stocked bar, as long as a person was willing to pay for the privilege and play by the rules. After a rigorous screening process, of course. One that I'd helped implement after what happened to Pax last year at the hands of a supposed "client."

When I reached the thick, black metal door at the end of the corridor, I opened a concealed panel to the right of it and input my code. The door clicked open and before I'd taken another step, I was staring down the barrel of a Rock Island 1911 9mm. I remembered the day Cleave had picked out that gun.

"Dude, you're supposed to be off tonight," our Road Captain said, lowering the weapon and lifting his hand to speak into the mic at his wrist. "Cancel that. It's just Mace."

I knew the answer would come through the ear piece I could see in his right ear.

"Who's on tonight?" I asked, stepping fully inside and securing the door. The area we were standing in was a type of foyer—the place where clients handed over their coats, cell-phones, and were patted down before entering the lounge and play areas beyond. It didn't exist before the Heretics took over security here, and the thought of the things that could have walked right through the old door made my skin crawl.

"Axel is backstage. Eben and Riot are inside." Cleave holstered his gun and stepped behind the slim counter that held security monitors.

"You didn't see me coming?" I nodded toward the screens.

"I'd just finished doing a search when the door opened." On the weekends, we had two people manning this room, but on slower traffic nights, usually one was more than enough.

I nodded. He'd done exactly what he should have. Cleave was good that way, steadfast and reliable. Plus with his imposing stature and serious demeanor, he was perfect for this job. Scare people at the door and they tended to behave.

"So what brings you in tonight?" Cleave sat on the stool behind the counter and leaned forward, resting his elbows on the sleek black top. "Or should I say, who?" He cocked one black eyebrow at me and smirked. Jesus, was everyone going to bust my balls tonight?

"You're an asshole," I told him and motioned toward the door to the lounge. "You gonna let me through or should I use my own code again?"

"Are you carrying a cellphone or any concealed weapons?"

I narrowed my eyes. "What do you think?"

He laughed and pulled out a black plastic basket before walking back around the counter and holding it out to me. "Rules are rules."

Reaching under my leather jacket, I removed my glock from my shoulder holster, then pulled my cell out of my jeans pocket. After tossing the phone into the basket, I dropped the magazine out of the glock and pulled back the slide to eject the round I'd already chambered, then placed all of it in the basket. "Happy?"

He eyed me for a moment. I knew he was doing it just to fuck with me because I was such a stickler about making sure no one walked through that door with something that could hurt one of the boys or another client. I also knew that he knew that wasn't the only weapon on my person.

"Yep." He reached over and punched a code into the number pad beside the interior door. "And tell Pax I said hi."

With a nod, I walked through the now open door and into the most exclusive club in the city. The whole room was done in muted metal tones—silver, gold, bronze—with thin metal chains hanging together to form curtains, dividing the large space into cozy seating areas and hiding the doors that hid more...interesting activities. There were several small groups taking advantage of the groupings of plush chairs and couches, drinking and talking and enjoying the scantily clad men roaming about. They all wore something metallic themed—actual chainmail or all manner of metal toned underwear.

A gorgeous little redhead, Leith, skipped over to me before I took another step. He was a newer addition, a total flirt, and quite the brat to hear Pax tell it. With his stunning blue eyes and freckled skin, he damn near had his pick of anyone who walked through the door. Not so long ago, that would have included me, but the fire I'd always had for hook-ups had dimmed since the shitstorm at Lex's cabin a few months back.

"Mace!" Leith threw his arms around my neck and kissed my cheek. He was in a silver jockstrap tonight, his truly luscious ass exposed for the viewing pleasure of all the hungry eyes in the room.

"Hi, sweetheart," I said, patting him on the back. I gently

disentangled myself and lifted his hand to press a kiss to his knuckles. He giggled and blushed. "How's the night?"

"Boring," he said with a pout, which quickly morphed into a sexy smile as he lowered his lashes. "But only if you're not here to play?"

I could see the bar on the other side of the room. A huge dark wooden semi-circle surrounded by metal barstools. Pax was standing behind it, pouring a drink with his dark eyes locked on me. I tore my eyes from my target and dropped them down to Leith's azure ones and told him the same thing I always said, "Not tonight, darlin'."

"Someday, Mace, you're going to give me a different answer."

I chuckled. "Someday." With one more kiss to the back of his hand, I excused myself and made my way to one of the metal bar stools in front of Pax. Eben, another Heretics member working security tonight, nodded at me from his position in the corner and I returned it before letting my eyes fall on the man in front of me.

"No parasitic growth this evening?" Pax lowered his eyes and his voice. He dropped a cherry into the drink he'd been pouring and turned to hand it to the server waiting at the end of the bar.

"The night's still young." I smirked when he rolled his eyes. Bronze boy shorts pulled tight over his plump ass as he moved, grabbing two rocks glasses and a bottle of bourbon. In the low light the color blended with his skin, making him look nude besides the dark leather harness weaving around his shoulders and over his chest. I had the sudden urge to lean over and grip the metal ring holding the straps together and haul him over the bar and into my lap. It had been that way since the moment I met him. There was no one in my life that I'd ever wanted to just cuddle except for Pax. Don't get me wrong, I wanted to fuck him too, but seeing the dark circles under his eyes and how the muscles he worked so hard for were losing their definition apparently brought out every nuturing instinct I had.

It didn't help that I genuinely liked the guy, either.

He shook his head and poured two finger's worth of liquor into the glasses before setting one in front of me and the other off to the side for a server to collect. "What brings you in? Work?"

I held his eyes and picked up the glass, taking a slow sip. The hot burn of alcohol slithered through my chest before settling its dark warmth in my stomach. "You. And you'd know that if you checked your texts. Can you take a break?"

The scowl he shot my way only made me smirk harder. I downed the rest of the bourbon while he went to tell his fellow bartender he'd be back in a bit.

CHAPTER TWO

Pax

C risp, cool night air enveloped me as soon as I pushed open the door leading to the roof. After the brutal winter we'd had, spring was struggling to take hold and even this late in May, the nights were still pretty chilly. It was a slow enough night that my fellow bartender had been happy to send me on break and collect all the tips for himself. I'd slipped into the track pants and hoodie I'd worn over my work uniform, when Mace said it would be best if we had this conversation where we wouldn't be disturbed. I could feel Mace behind me like his presence was a physical force pressing against me. He'd been quiet as we made our way through the underground tunnel that led to the apartment building Vivian owned and where most of us *Spritz* employees lived, all the way up the elevator ride to the fifth floor and the stairs that led to this door.

I could have taken him to my apartment, but that seemed dangerous. Most people would probably think coming to an isolated place with the Sergeant-at-Arms from an Iron Heretics MC chapter was dangerous, *period*, but Mace had never been a danger to me *that* way, though. Ever since we met, we'd been skirting the line between flirting and actually doing something about the attraction that I was positive wasn't just one-sided. The danger lay in me liking the way he looked at me a little too much, while knowing that he looked at everyone that way. Mace had never had a relationship in his life—not a real one—and while we would probably be a match made in fuck-buddy heaven, I'd been trying to save myself from that particular scenario for as long as possible.

I hadn't taken clients since I was tortured for information about a member of Mace's club last year. Hadn't had sex at all, actually. Sometimes I thought I'd rather not have my next foray between the sheets be as just another notch in someone's bedpost, and sometimes I thought maybe it would be better that way. It's not like I was the poster boy for healthy relationships and at least I trusted Mace. The decision to stop being an escort, a prostitute, at *Spritz* had been an easy one. I couldn't imagine allowing myself to be that vulnerable with a man I didn't really know ever again.

"You're thinking awfully hard," Mace said, leaning his elbow on the ledge surrounding the outside of the building. His green eyes were locked on my face. He had a layer of dark stubble on his jawline and his chin-length dark hair was tucked behind his ears. He'd cut it recently, and I did my best to ignore the thought it might have been because of how much I'd teased him about his man bun.

The familiar sounds of the city drifted up from the streets below. I crossed my arms and rested my elbows on the ledge, close enough to him that I could feel the heat from his body. He stepped closer, his chest brushing my shoulder and I turned my face to look at him. I really liked that he was a couple inches taller than me. "What did you want to talk about?" I had a feeling I knew and it was turning my empty stomach sour. I should have eaten before my shift, but despite my sleep being restless, I couldn't find the energy or motivation to drag myself out of bed for a minute longer than it took me to shower, dress, and get over to *Spritz*. That was becoming a habit I wasn't sure how to break. Before...everything...I was always up by midday—running errands, cleaning, hitting the gym—and now I just, couldn't.

On cue, my stomach rumbled and Mace's brows scrunched together.

"Have you had dinner?"

"No."

"How long a break can you take?"

I huffed a laugh. "You're not feeding me dinner."

Mace's eyelids lowered and his signature smirk curled up one side of his lips. "Oh, I think you'd let me if I asked *just* right."

"You're ridiculous." I turned my face away from him as heat infused my cheeks.

"Pax." He moved even closer and damn, if the warmth of his solid chest pressed against my side didn't feel like a balm.

"I'll grab something before I go back," I told the darkness around us instead of looking back at him. There was a security light attached by the door, but here on the edge, with no moon to speak of, we were shrouded in shadow. I hoped that meant that he missed my blush.

"Alright. You going to kick my ass if I ask for evidence of that?"

A low chuckle spilled out of my throat. Even when I'd been lifting weights and working out faithfully, there was no reality where I could kick Mace's ass. "Maybe."

He nudged me, bumping his chest against my arm. "Okay." He sighed. "I need to show you something and I just need you to say yes or no." Mace reached into the inner pocket of his jacket and pulled out a folded picture. From the back, it looked like any innocent 4x6 that you could have developed at your choice of grocery or drug store anywhere. It wasn't that, though. He'd promised me this. Promised me that the man that had hurt me would pay for it. At the time, those words were one of the only things holding together all my broken pieces, but on some level, I hadn't truly believed him. Almost a year later and there was no room for doubt anymore. The look on his face told me all I needed to know.

He was going to keep his promise.

My stomach clenched. Unfolding my arms, I gripped the ledge, bracing myself and letting the cold bite of stone ground me in the here and now. A year later and I was still afraid. Afraid that a mere glimpse at the piece of paper he was holding would send me careening back to that night. I visited it enough in my nightmares. I didn't want to have to live it in my waking hours too.

When his voice came, it was low, soft. "I'm sorry. If you don't want to look—"

I shook my head. "I don't, but I will."

He nodded. "I want you to understand something, Pax. This man, he's a monster, but he's also a professional. Finding him wasn't easy, even with some very powerful help. There was *no way* you could have known what he was up to."

I nodded, appreciating his words more than I could say. Pulling in a deep breath, I let go of the ledge and turned to Mace. "Okay. Show me."

His eyes stayed on my face when he turned the picture around. He held it so the security light illuminated it completely, and for a moment, I lost my breath.

"It's him."

I turned my face away, back out into the night, staring off into the darkness and letting my eyes skip from window to window on all the buildings lining both sides of the street beyond. I wasn't really seeing them though, my mind was locked onto the image of dark blond hair, blue eyes, and the kind of smile that belonged on the boy next door. The kind that led lambs to slaughter.

The flick of a zippo lighter brought my gaze back to Mace. He'd taken a couple steps back from me and was holding the picture on one corner as he lit the other with the flame from a silver lighter with a wolf's head engraved on the side.

Fire caught and spread, making the paper—making *his* face—twist and curl, writhing in its death throes as the picture was eaten away. When the flames got close to his fingers, Mace let go and what was left of the photo floated to the ground. We both watched for a moment, letting the fire turn the photo to ash. Mace stepped on the still glowing fibers, stomping them out with the thick sole of his motorcycle boot.

Then he reached for me.

I went willingly, letting him pull me in and wrap me in his long arms. My arms were trapped between us, so I burrowed into him, pressing my nose against the henley shirt covering his chest and inhaling deeply. He smelled of leather and deodorant and laundry soap. The scruff on his chin tickled my temple and as the seconds ticked by, I realized that I was okay. I'd been so afraid that seeing even an image of him would bring it all crashing back after I'd worked so hard to stuff it down, but it hadn't. Instead, it felt like relief. Like the vice that had been squeezing my chest for the last year was suddenly released and I could breathe again.

"He's never going to touch you again," Mace whispered, his lips ruffling the hair above my ear and echoing the same promise he'd made me a year ago when I'd been freshly bruised and broken.

I nodded, pulling back enough to see his face. "I know." Leaning in, I brushed my lips against his, then took a quick step back. His green eyes were locked on mine—surprise and pleasure written in the depths of them.

"What was that for?" he asked with a tilt of his head.

"Just to say thank you."

"You don't need to thank me." He smiled and stepped forward, wrapping an arm around my shoulders and guiding us back toward the door. "Now, let's go find you some food."

CHAPTER THREE

Mace

A fucking year. And it had taken all of that year, every favor I had, and offering a favor to Rick Morgan to find the bastard. Morgan, who was thrilled to help as soon as he named his terms, had been the reason I finally knew where the asshole was. Rick wasn't what I'd call a friend, or a nice guy, but he was useful. Lex Campbell—Heretic Nomad, my former lover, and current boyfriend of Pax's bestie, Arden—had worked for Rick for eight years after I'd trained him to be a sniper, and after Rick had helped us when Arden had been taken, I'd done some work for Rick, as well, to repay that debt.

Contract killing—that's the work Rick dealt in, and he was excellent at finding people that didn't want to be found because he had contacts all over the world. I'd pay my debt to him happily once I put this fucker to rest once and for all. I didn't know his real name, but he used the alias Vector and he wasn't convinced yet, but he was drawing some of the last breaths he'd ever take.

Although, it seemed he was starting to get the idea.

"You haven't got the balls," Vector sneered at me from

where he was tied to a metal chair in the middle of what used to be a restaurant kitchen. Blood dripped from a cut above his eye and his dark blond hair glistened with sweat. I wasn't usually one to actually get my hands dirty when I set out to kill a man. I'd been a sniper in the Marines and typically preferred a quick, clean kill from behind the scope of my rifle. This guy though... I couldn't see his face without remembering the bruises on Pax's skin and the gashes covering his back. This guy deserved every hit I'd rained on his face and every second I made him sit in that chair knowing there was nothing he could do to change his fate.

Rick had finally helped me track him down to a small town outside of Dallas. I'd followed him for a few days, and although he was careful, I'd managed to grab him the night before. It hadn't been easy, and I'd probably have bruises for days, but watching him wake up, trussed up and not knowing where he was had been worth it.

"I think the only balls on the line around here are yours," I answered, snapping open the leather strap from around the handle of my knife and pulling it out of its sheath. I gave him credit. Where I assumed most men would beg or bargain, he simply looked at me.

"You're not an up-close killer, Mace," he said, startling me when he used my name. "What? You think I don't know you? You think I don't know about your whole organization? I study my targets. I have to assume you're here because of the boy. He had the most wonderful screams." He laughed, a dark, ugly sound full of twisted joy that turned my stomach. I stepped forward and leaned down, stopping only inches from his face and placed the tip of my knife directly over his heart.

"You're right," I said, staring him directly in his eyes. "This isn't my normal style. I'm much more comfortable behind the scope of my rifle, but I do know what you did to Pax, and I'm happy to make an exception this time."

"Well, faggot got some balls after all. Go ahead and do what you gotta do, but I promise you this, it won't be the end of his suffering."

"He'll take solace in the fact you're ash in the ground. You were dead the moment you touched him." He opened his mouth to spit some other venom at me, but I'd heard enough. I slammed my knife forward.

———

A GRATEFUL SMILE PULLED AT MY LIPS AS I ACCEPTED THE beer Lex was holding out to me. "Thanks, man." It was good to be back home. Back in Heretic territory where I knew my brothers were watching my back and I could watch theirs.

Lex settled across the fire pit from me. We were at his cabin outside of Gnaw Bone, Missouri, a tiny little town with only a single four-way stop and a handful of businesses to its name. One of my favorite diners was among them, though. Lex and Arden spent their time here when Lex wasn't out doing runs as part of the Nomad chapter in our club. While the Nomads had a Prez and a VP, they were more or less free agents, able to be called on by any Heretics chapter that needed an extra pair of hands or if they needed someone from the outside to come in and clean up a mess.

Which suited Lex perfectly. I knew he hated leaving Arden behind, but Arden took it all in stride. While Lex was away, he stayed at his apartment in the building next to *Spritz* and worked at the club. Like Pax, Arden didn't work the floor in the lounge anymore, but he still danced because he loved it and was absolutely beautiful on stage.

I'd sent Lex a message as soon as I'd gotten back in town, and he'd insisted I come out to the cabin for dinner. Since I'd moved to the city, I'd never thought of owning a place anywhere else, but sitting there with a crackling fire, a cold beer in my hand, and a full sky of stars starting to emerge overhead, I could see the appeal. It was a great place to unwind after a job.

Especially, it seemed, if you had someone to share it with.

I shook my head. These thoughts kept creeping into my brain. All my life, I'd known that locking myself down in a committed relationship wasn't for me. Not after the shit I'd seen. But more and more, I found myself wondering what it'd be like to come home to someone every night. To know there was someone who actually knew me waiting to let me lose myself in them when I came off the kind of job I'd just been on. Looking at the peace etched into every line of Lex's face, I'd say it was definitely working out alright for him.

My friend took a long pull of his own beer and leaned forward, resting his elbows on his knees. He'd grown into a fucking gorgeous man. Tall and solidly built—he'd been trying to talk me into doing Crossfit with him since he'd moved back—with dark brown hair and eyes. He'd been sexy as a spitfire eighteen year old, but pushing thirty was a good look for him.

"What's that smirk?" he asked, eyes narrowing in my direction while he scratched his beard.

I shook my head and took a drink of my own. "Just reminiscing."

Lex raised an eyebrow.

"You know, thinking about how pretty you used to be."

A deep chuckle tumbled out of Lex's mouth. "Fuck you."

"I think Arden might protest, but I'm down." I smirked when he rolled his eyes. Sometimes the cycle of our relationship felt strange to me—from fuck buddies to near radio silence for eight years to probably best friends. Arden was a lucky man and I was just grateful to have Lex back in my life despite the circumstances surrounding his return. Last summer, I'd failed him. Failed to keep Arden safe and gotten the shit kicked out of me and thrown right through a window at the back of the cabin. Lex never blamed me, but those scars still lingered.

"Now you look like you're planning a funeral." Lex's voice brought me back to the present. "You alright, man? The job give you trouble?"

"Just tired I guess." I downed the rest of my beer. "The job was smooth."

Lex's dark eyes held mine. "Good. Needed to be done."

I couldn't agree more. The look on Pax's face alone when I'd held up that photo would have been enough to send me after that fucker. The sound of one of the ATVs Lex and Arden used to get from their garage out by the road back to the cabin filled the quiet clearing. A moment later, headlights illuminated the trees from the front of the house, then the engine went quiet. Lex and I both stood, ready to go help Arden carry our dinners into the house—he'd already been gone to pick them up from the diner when I got there—but then laughter reached us and Arden walked around the corner of the porch, a plastic bag in one hand and Pax beside him.

"Hey, guys!" Arden said, bouncing down the steps and lifting on his toes to plant a kiss on Lex's mouth. "You wanna eat inside or out here?"

My eyes wandered to Pax, who was still standing on the porch. He looked hesitant which I didn't like at all. I hadn't seen him since I'd gotten back, and even though I wasn't sure what my next move should be where he was concerned, that didn't mean I didn't *want* to see him. Judging by the way my stomach had swooped when he'd come into view, I definitely *did* want.

"Don't I get a kiss?" I joked, thinking they'd assume I meant from Arden, but I kept my eyes on Pax's, smiling when he blushed. Arden pulled back from his man and arched one elegant blond brow at me before coming over and kissing my cheek. "Thanks, sweetheart."

"You're welcome." Arden smiled wide. "Now, food! Out here or inside?"

"Out here, I think," Lex said. He lifted one hand to his mouth and let out a loud whistle. "Pip! Dinner time!"

Their gray pitbull had been out playing in the trees, but only a moment after Lex's call, I could hear paws hitting the ground at a run. Arden handed off the bags to Lex and dropped into a crouch. A second later, Pip came barreling out of the woods and went straight to Arden's open arms, licking his face and nearly knocking him on his ass.

"Easy, boy," Lex admonished, setting the bags of food on the picnic table.

While they pet Pip, I took a couple steps toward the porch where Pax was standing. He looked good, but still so tired. I wondered if he'd been sleeping at all.

"Hey, stranger," I said, walking right up onto the bottom step and holding up my hand in offering. "You wanna join us?" I felt it all the way down into the soles of my feet when he slipped his hand into mine.

CHAPTER FOUR

Pax

I was going to kill my best friend. Not because I didn't want to see Mace. I did. But he could have warned a guy. Instead, I'd been struck dumb by the sight of Mace standing beside the fire in his dark jeans and hunter green henley. He had it pushed up his forearms, showing off all their sexy, corded muscle. Then he'd smiled at me, and my brain had flashed to the one perfect second I'd spent with my lips pressed against his. All that was tangled up with the mess of feelings that I was still trying to work through from knowing the reason I hadn't seen him for the last couple of weeks had everything to do with that photo he'd burned to ash.

The relief pulsing through me at seeing him alive and well left me lightheaded and made up for every sleepless night I'd had since the last time I saw him. If Mace was here with a smile on his face then a man was dead. Dead because he'd hurt me. Dead because the reliable man in front of me made me a promise when I was at my weakest, and he'd kept it. It was a lot to take in, and part of me thought I should be swimming in guilt. The only guilt I felt was that I didn't feel guilty at all.

Mace's thumb brushed over the back of my hand, and he stepped up a couple more steps until he was only one below me.

"You okay?"

I tilted my chin down and met his eyes. His gaze was heavy, filled with questions beyond the simple one he'd asked.

"Yeah, I think so," I answered in a whisper. Arden and Lex weren't actively paying attention to us, but the connection stretching between us in that moment felt personal, private, and I didn't want to share it.

Mace smiled. "Good. You hungry?"

Suddenly, I was. "Starving."

"Then come on." He lifted my hand and pressed a kiss to my knuckles, then led me down the steps. As soon as my feet hit the ground, Pip pulled against the hand Arden had on his collar and my best friend let him go.

"Hey, boy." Letting go of Mace's hand, I dropped to my knees and let the now eighty pound dog lick my chin while I gave him all the pets. "I've missed you."

Pip barked at me and then took off running, making zigzagging circles all around the yard.

"Zoomies!" Arden laughed, watching him. He walked over to me. "Help me bring out drinks?"

"Sure."

Mace had walked over to the table and was helping Lex unload all the carry-out boxes of food. He glanced at me as Arden and I made our way up onto the porch and through the back door. The moment it closed behind us, Arden turned on me.

"I think you've been holding out on me," he said, hands on his hips and a little pout on his lips.

I rolled my eyes. Dramatic was my best friend's middle name. "I really haven't. You're reading too much into it. He made me a promise and he kept it. End of story."

Arden narrowed his gray eyes. "Is it though? Do you want it to be? Because what I just saw looked more like opening credits."

With a sigh, I walked over to the fridge and pulled it open. "You know things have been a little rough for me since everything happened last year, and I just...I don't think I can let myself—" I cut off not knowing exactly what I wanted to say. Be that open? Be that vulnerable? Trust that much? Neither one of us were relationship people, but I was afraid even something casual with him could ruin me. Mace's attention was addictive, and I really didn't need to let myself get hooked. "It doesn't matter. It's just a bad idea."

"I don't know if you noticed, but things have been a little rough for him too." Arden's hand landed gently on my shoulder, turning me so we were facing each other. His eyes were shiny. "I hate that so many people got hurt because of me and I don't mean to push. I just want you guys to be happy."

I sighed again and wrapped my arms around him, tucking his head under my chin. "I know, and none of that guilt nonsense. None of what went down was your fault. I know you know that." It had been right here in this kitchen where the men had come to kidnap Arden and nearly killed Mace in the process. They did kill one Heretic. A man named Damon. Both of them had been here watching over Arden while Lex chased down a lead on Arden's uncle. The same uncle who'd gotten some of his information from the man who'd tortured me because I'd broken and given it to him.

We stood there quietly for a moment until Arden whispered, "You don't get to feel guilty, either."

Tears stung my eyes as I nodded.

Arden pulled back and looked at me. "How have you been doing? No bullshit."

"I'm... I'm getting by. It's getting better. It really is. The last couple weeks haven't been great, but..." I shrugged.

"Would you...would you like to maybe come sit in a therapy session with me?"

I took a step back and Arden held up his hands. "No pressure, okay. I just wanted to put the offer out there."

Letting out a long breath, I nodded. "Thank you. I can't make any promises, but I'll think about it." What I wanted to say was hell no, but I wouldn't. He was trying to help and I got that. No one more than me wanted to get back to being the fun guy who loved flirting, and sex, and spending hours in the gym. Looking back, I honestly didn't know how I'd ever had energy for it all. My body had been my crowning jewel— the proof of my hard work, the proof that I was thriving. I was still muscular and lean now, but the definition I'd worked so hard for was diminished. Back then, I'd not only happily taken clients in the lounge, but enjoyed fooling around on the regular with several of my co-workers or anyone who caught my fancy. Now, I hadn't had sex since it happened.

The back door opened and Lex stepped inside. "You guys alright?"

Arden smiled and went to him. Lex opened his arms without pause, drawing his lover close and holding him protectively. I envied them. Envied how easy it seemed. Dropping my eyes, I turned back to the fridge and grabbed a couple bottles each of water and beer.

IT WAS AFTER MIDNIGHT WHEN LEX DOUSED THE FIRE AND we all went inside. There was no point in Arden driving me back to the city now so I decided to sleep there and go back the next day. Apparently, Mace and Lex both needed to go to the Heretics' clubhouse the next day for a meeting, and Arden was dancing at *Spritz*, so we'd all chosen to call it a night.

Since I'd stayed there several times, I helped myself to a pillow and blanket from the linen closet downstairs. There was a spare bedroom, and several air mattresses they'd gotten for their New Year's party that I could have blown up, but the big sectional couch in the living room would work just fine.

Lex had locked up and set the security system before him, Arden, and Pip had trooped upstairs. Their bedroom door click seemed loud in the quiet house.

I'd just settled on the couch under the blanket in my boxer briefs and T-shirt when the guest bathroom door opened and Mace stepped out. He'd taken off his boots by the back door and his Iron Heretics vest was hanging on the back of one of the dining room chairs.

"You know," he said, coming to stand by the couch and looking down at me. "There's a perfectly good bed upstairs."

"I know. You can have it."

"Did I mention it's a big bed?" He sat down on the edge of the couch cushion, the warmth of his hip seeping through onto mine. "Big enough for say, two grown men."

I couldn't stop the chuckle that tumbled out of me. "Want to sleep with me that bad, do you?"

Mace pursed his lips. "I think we both know the thought has crossed my mind, and in this case, yes. I do want to sleep with you. Just sleep."

My heart was thudding in my chest. I'd always been a touchy-feely guy, or I used to be, and the thought of sleeping wrapped up with someone—*with Mace*—was so fucking tempting and everything I'd been telling myself all night that I needed to stay away from. We'd had a nice dinner, light and fun with no talk of work or biker business, just friends enjoying each other's company. I'd needed that. Some part of me thought I needed this too—to take his hand and let him lead me up those stairs. "Thanks, but I'm good here."

If he was disappointed, he hid it well.

"Good night, Pax."

"Good night." I watched him climb the stairs. A door opened and I waited, holding my breath, to hear it click closed. It didn't. Blood roared in my ears. The need to get off this couch and follow him became a gnawing monster in my gut. Before I could change my mind, I slipped from beneath the blanket. I was two steps from the spare bedroom door when my survival instincts kicked in, screaming at me to abort, but it was too late.

Mace looked up from his phone and a soft smile stretched across his lips. He was leaning shirtless against the headboard, the comforter pooled around his waist. Vivid tattoos were scattered over his torso. I couldn't tear my eyes away from a set of realistic looking claw marks covering his rib cage. Setting his phone aside, he reached over and flipped the covers down on the far side of the bed, then brought his eyes back to mine. The green of them was startling, even in the low light from the bedside lamp.

This was a crossroads. We'd been walking on an edge for a while now, and I knew if I crawled into that bed with him it was one step closer to tumbling over the side completely.

I stepped into the room, feeling unbearably shy, and shut the door behind me. My eyes stayed glued to him and he stayed still, like he thought any sudden movement would have me bolting. He might have been right. With a deep breath, I walked around the side of the bed and slipped under the covers.

The lamp clicked off, then Mace was sliding down, settling under the covers on his back. We lay in the quiet dark for a moment, a single slant of moonlight from between the curtains the only light in the room.

The blankets rustled and calloused fingers found my shoulder. I jolted at the touch and then feeling silly, chuckled at myself. I swore I could feel his answering smile in the dark.

"Come here." The words were whisper soft and washed over me, dispelling my doubt and quieting the pounding in my head. Sliding over, I pressed myself against him, resting my head on his chest and draping an arm over his stomach.

The arm he'd held out for me wrapped around my back. He snuggled closer, resting his other hand on my arm and pressing his lips to the top of my head.

"Sleep, Pax."

I pressed my hand over the claw marks covering his ribs and closed my eyes.

CHAPTER FIVE

Mace

The clubhouse was packed. Calix, our chapter President, had called for a full meeting. I made my way to the table, exchanging greetings with all the guys as I went. Pulling out my seat, I caught the eye of a Prospect across the room and pointed toward the coffee pot. Being the Sergeant-at-Arms meant that I sat to the President's right hand. Settling in, I looked around and was happy to see all of my brothers talking and laughing amongst each other. It was nice to have a meeting that wasn't centered around some emergency or to discuss retaliation.

The Prospect, Zach, placed a cup of coffee in front of me, and I gave him a nod. He seemed like a good kid and I hoped he made it through. Breathing in the rich aroma, I took a sip and let my mind wander back to that morning. Pax and I had shifted in our sleep and somehow ended up with my back pressed to his chest. It was a strange sensation to wake up being the little spoon, but I couldn't say that I hated it. With my position in the club and the upbringing that I often tried to overcome, feeling like I was in a weaker position wasn't a wonderfully comfortable situation. In my mind, I knew that being held that way didn't make me weak—didn't make anyone weak. I just wasn't used to it.

Any misgivings I had about being cradled in Pax's arms ultimately had been overshadowed by the hot line of his body against mine, the erection I had felt nestled against my ass, and the way his arms had held me in such a sure grip even in his sleep. It was the first night I could remember in a long time not having woken during the night. When Lex had tapped on the spare bedroom door to let me know he was ready to go, I'd groaned to myself because the last thing I'd wanted to do was move, but I'd gently extricated myself from Pax's hold and with a scribbled note and a quick kiss to his temple, I'd slipped out of the room.

"Take your seats, gentlemen," Riot said as he came into the room. Our Vice President was a mountain of a man, and while he appeared larger than life—from the dreads on his head down to biceps that were the size of my thighs—he was one of the quietest, most serious men I'd ever met, but his voice held such authority that everyone stopped to listen when he spoke. I honestly wasn't sure if I'd ever seen him smile.

The members who were officers in the chapter sat around the table, and the rest in extra chairs around the edges of the room. We called this room our chapel. The table was large and heavy—made of the same dark wood as the gavel that sat at the head in front of the President's chair. Everyone finished taking their seats. Across from me at the President's left was Riot, beside him, Axel, who was our acting Treasurer. The rest of the table was filled out by Cleave, our Road Captain, Eben Vanos who was moving up the ranks, and our most senior member, Barrett.

Calix entered last and moved to sit beside me at the head of the table.

"I appreciate you coming in today, guys," Calix said in his

gravelly voice, picking up the gavel and slamming it once on the table before setting it down again. "For once, this meeting is mostly a check-in. Things have been quiet the last couple of months, but I don't want that to turn into complacency. The Devil's Rage MC, who we all know have had it out for us since I took over, seem to be having some type of internal beef. Which means they've been focused inward, but we all know it won't stay that way."

I understood Calix's concern. We hadn't seen much from the Devil's for a while, but the last stunt they'd pulled had lasting effects. First, several of them had come to *Spritz* just before New Year's shouting homophobic slurs, knocking over tables and chairs, and disrupting the flow of business. But worse, one of the assholes had grabbed Pax by the arm and tried to drag him outside. Luckily, Riot and Axel had been on the floor that night and had stopped them only moments after they'd put their hands on Pax.

He seemed okay about it, but I knew it had shaken him up and brought back memories from when Vector had hurt him the year before. A slow smile spread over my face thinking about how that bastard would never hurt anyone, especially Pax, again.

"That smile makes me think your side job went as expected?" Calix said, his black eyes trained on me.

"It did."

"Excellent," he said with a dark smile to match my own before he turned his attention back to the table. "Stay sharp. All your schedules have been updated. Those working the event tonight, Mace is on point. Let's make sure our clients and their guests leave happy."

THE SMELL OF SWEAT AND BOOZE WAS HEAVY IN THE AIR.
Aside from our legitimate security business, we hosted illegal
fights around the city—MMA, boxing, and occasionally bare
knuckle, depending on the client. On occasion we set up the
fight events on our own, but more often for clients wealthy
enough to pay the fee to have such an event at one of their
private parties. On top of that fee, we also got a cut of the
betting pool, and it was usually always a win-win situation for
everyone. Well, except for the guy who lost, but even he got a
purse.

This particular fight was one of our regular customers.
Some money guru guy, who owned a large farm outside of
the city. To call it a farm was probably simplifying things a
bit. The small patch of land in southern Illinois with its
little herd of cattle and rusted tractor in the side yard was a
farm. The barn we were currently standing in was nicer
than the house I grew up in. The wooden slat floors were
clean and large area rugs had been situated around the
metal fight cage erected in the center of the open space.
The ceiling was high with exposed beams and inset lighting.
Two bars had been set up, one on either side of the cage
against the wall, and servers, mostly from *Spritz,* were circu-
lating—taking orders and fetching drinks—while others
simply held trays loaded with glasses of champagne up for
the taking.

Their uniforms for this evening were quite different from
what they wore at the club. Black slacks and shoes, white
dress shirt tucked in under a sharp black vest and tie. Pax had
his shirt sleeves rolled up to his elbows in a neat cuff. He
looked sharp, and I'd be lying if I said I wasn't distracted
every time I caught sight of his ass in those pants as he
moved through the crowd. I was stationed in one corner of
the large room and the other three were covered by Riot,
Axel, and Cleave. Eben was on the door tonight. Us Heretics

were in similar attire to the servers—we lacked the vests but wore suit coats. It was easier to hide our guns that way.

As my eyes continued to scan the crowd, I caught sight of Pax coming my way. Instead of the champagne he'd been distributing, he had several short, clear plastic punch glasses on his tray. He caught my eye when he broke out of the crowd.

"Thought you might be thirsty," he said holding the tray toward me.

I picked up one of the glasses and took a long sip of the ice water. "Thank you," I said, holding his eyes, enjoying the way a bit of pink filled his cheeks. "How'd you sleep?"

He looked down for a moment before lifting his eyes back to mine. "Honestly?"

I nodded.

"Better than I have in a long time."

Warmth filled my chest, and I couldn't stop the spread of a slow smile across my face. "That could be an open invitation, you know?"

He looked at me for a long moment without saying anything. I wanted to ask what he was thinking because Pax was good at hiding what he was actually feeling. It seemed like the kind of skill that a person developed in his former profession. It was also the kind of skill someone developed when wearing your emotions on your sleeve could get you beaten or worse. I didn't begrudge him for hiding things from me because I wasn't entitled to how he felt about anything, but I hoped he trusted me enough to share, anyway.

I knew we weren't quite on that level, and it surprised the hell out of me how much I really wanted us to be. How much I wanted him to know that he could trust me, that opening himself up with me wasn't a danger to him. And wasn't that a kick in the balls? Since when was I ready to settle in with someone? Ready to wade into someone else's emotional baggage and potentially allow them to witness mine? I didn't know when it happened, but apparently Pax was the key to tripping up all the rules I had for myself, and all the ways I had looked at relationships before.

"I'll think about it," Pax said quietly. "I just don't know if I can handle the weight of someone else's expectations right now."

With a nod, I finished my water and replaced the cup on his tray. "I understand that, and there's no pressure here, okay? I think you know this is all new territory for me. But I'm here. I want to be here for you. With you."

That got me a small smile which I couldn't help but return. Static sounded in my ear a moment before Axel's voice came through my comm, "A person could die of thirst over here while you two make moon eyes at each other."

I ducked my head and chuckled before glancing back up and catching the puzzled look on Pax's face. "Axel is apparently about to perish from dehydration," I said, pointing to my earpiece.

The little blush Pax had been sporting turned even darker as my smile got bigger.

"Well, we wouldn't want that," he said, taking a small step back.

I wanted to reach out and touch him so badly, but this wasn't the place, so I settled for shooting him a wink and letting my eyes linger on him as he disappeared back into the crowd, making his way across the room. Lifting my wrist to my mouth, I pressed my mic. "You're an asshole."

I couldn't hear their laughter, but I could see the smirks on each of the three other men positioned in the corners around the room. With a little shake of my head, I settled back into my ready position—feet shoulder width apart, knees loose, and my hands clasped in front of me while my eyes scanned over the crowd. Lifting my wrist again, I pressed the communicator. "Eben, check in."

A moment later, Eben's voice filled my ear, "All's quiet. Waiting on a few stragglers."

"Good. Keep me updated. The fight should be starting soon."

"Understood."

This party was invitation only, and typically those invitations went to rich assholes in various social circles that preferred a little blood with their entertainment. There were different gyms around that we pulled opposing fighters from, but the Heretics liked to be on the winning side of things, and all of our fighters came from the Heretics' owned gym in Sand Lake. Jebidiah Campbell, Lex's dad, was the President of that chapter and operated the gym, producing top-notch fighters looking to cut their teeth and make some money in the illegal fight circuit.

A few moments later, several more guests stepped into the room and Eben said his list had been cleared. On my signal, Zach, the Prospect we had watching the fighter's changing rooms, let them know that we were ready to begin and sent the announcer out. I kept my eyes scanning the room as the announcer stepped into the cage, and in a booming voice, riled up the spectators as he gave stats for each of the fighters.

The crowd placed last bets and some wandered over to the bars to refresh their cocktails as the excitement in the room ramped up for the show. Some thumping rock music poured through the speakers that we'd set up as the fighters made their way to the cage. These parties demanded the whole production, right down to the little details.

As the fighters came out, their progression wasn't where I kept my eyes. More than once we'd seen fights break out in the crowd when too much drink in the volatile atmosphere—not to mention the potential for large amounts of money to change hands—sent people to a breaking point. Unfortunately, a few years back, we'd lost a Heretic when a guest pulled a knife on another guest and he'd stepped in to stop the fight. Chris Vanos, Eben's brother, had been fatally stabbed. His death had led to more rules and tighter reigns about who was let into our events and what they were allowed to bring into the building.

The music died out as the fighters squared off. When the bell rang, the fighters launched themselves at each other, clinching in the center of the cage, each vying for the upper hand and determined to put on a good show for their audience. It wasn't a bare knuckle fight, but the men wore very small gloves and there were very few rules.

One of the fighters broke away and threw a flurry of punches. The other fighter blocked and they bounced from foot to foot, dancing around the cage and looking for an opening. As soon as they found it, one of them shot in for a takedown, and just as the fighter hit the mat with a smack, the side door of the barn burst open and all hell broke loose.

CHAPTER SIX

Pax

I managed to get around the rest of the perimeter delivering water to all of the Heretics guys before the fight started. I knew once the fighters were in the cage, most everyone would be so focused on them that they wouldn't be worried about us, and it was usually the time that we went around the edges of the crowd and collected any trash or took orders when someone flagged us down.

I stole a glance at Mace in his position in the corner. He looked sexy as hell in his suit with his dark hair pulled back in a low ponytail and the black wired earpiece fitted over the top of his ear. I saw him so often in the more casual security attire for *Spritz* or in his Iron Heretics vest that it was easy to forget how well he cleaned up for events like this.

Not all fights required a suit and tie, though. Depending on the location and clientele, some of these parties let me double the nightly income that I made at *Spritz* working the bar or serving. When the opportunity came up, I usually tried to be on staff for them.

My heart was still buzzing from the wink Mace had given me and from him telling me that we should sleep together again. I wasn't lying when I told him that the night before had been some of the best sleep I'd had in a long time. It was also shocking how much better I felt being well rested. When I'd first woken up alone, a pang of disappointment had settled in my gut. It was alleviated fairly quickly when I saw the scrap of paper on the nightstand. It hadn't been any flowery or fancy words, not that I expected them from Mace, and that was okay. I wasn't one for sappy nonsense myself, but simply knowing he'd thought to leave a note soothed my disappointment and made my heart race all over again. The note had said, *Good morning beautiful. I'll see you later.* As simple as it was, it sent my stomach fluttering like a teenager with a crush.

We were walking in dangerous territory. I knew that. I'd known it the moment I slipped into the bed. If I were being honest with myself, I would say I'd known it for much longer, possibly since a busted up and bruised Mace had stepped into my apartment with Pip all those months ago.

The fight was in full swing now, pulling all the spectators' eyes to the cage. I made my way over to one of the makeshift bars, tossing some trash into one of the receptacles there when the side door, not five feet down from me, burst open. The tray in my hands clattered to the floor as several men in dark hoodies and ski masks burst into the room with baseball bats in their hands.

Chaos erupted as people screamed when the men charged forward. I felt frozen, my feet rooted to the floor in fear. One of the men who'd rushed toward the crowd swung his bat, knocking a beer bottle out of someone's hand before the masked man lowered the bat and used his shoulder to ram into the person, knocking them and two other people to the ground.

The other men were swarming around the room, and I could hear the Heretics barking orders as they rushed in to protect the crowd and stop the intruders. The man who'd just knocked over those people turned and locked his eyes on mine. The kind of terror I hadn't known in months leached every rational thought from my head. I wanted to shrink in on myself and disappear, to hide, to run, but I was frozen where I stood.

He approached quickly, and I saw him grip the bat with both hands and raise it above his head. I lifted my arms to protect my head, but the blow never came. Peeking out, I was met with the sight of a broad back in a black suit. The baseball bat the man had been wielding was on the floor, and Mace had one of the man's arms locked behind his back. He slammed the masked man face down onto the bar before he wrenched his other arm back and pulled a set of zip-tie cuffs out of his back pocket. He secured them quickly and then put the man face down on the floor.

"Don't move," Mace barked at the man, then lifted his wrist to his mouth to use the communicator there. "Report."

I don't know what was said back to him through his earpiece, but I could see that people were running to the exit. The cage was empty, but it didn't seem like the intruders were causing any more havoc. As a matter of fact, I couldn't see them at all, and I wondered if the other Heretics had subdued them much the same way Mace had done this one.

He stood abruptly and turned to me, green eyes sweeping over my face and down my body.

"I'm okay," I heard myself say, even though I didn't feel like my mouth was connected to my body. Mace's hands landed on either side of my face, and he tilted my chin up, searching my eyes.

He nodded and lifted his wrist back to his mouth. "Prospect! I need you at the bar on the left." He looked back down at me. "I want you to get behind the bar and stay there while I make sure they're all captured, okay?"

I nodded quickly, not wanting to keep him from his job, but also not wanting him to leave. I pressed my hand to one of his against my face, and much like I'd done that night on the roof, popped up on my toes and pressed my lips quickly to his. He kissed me back, hard, for just a moment and then he let go, stepping back and nodding toward the bar.

The Prospect ran over, one of the ball bats in his hands, and nodded at Mace.

"Watch him," Mace said, motioning to the man on the floor. He looked over at me with a wink before turning and rushing off to get the situation under control.

———

WITH MY ADRENALINE CRASH, I FELL ASLEEP AS SOON AS Mace closed the door to his truck. When I woke up, the truck was stopped in a dark parking lot. There was a large building sitting in front of us, and as my eyes adjusted to the dim light, I saw the fence spanning the perimeter around the building and the parking lot. We were at the Heretics' clubhouse.

I swiveled my head toward the driver seat. Mace was there looking back at me. He'd taken off his suit jacket and tie, leaving the top button of his dress shirt open. His sleeves were rolled up to his elbows, and the dark leather of his shoulder holster stood out in stark contrast to his white dress shirt.

The only sound as we sat watching each other was the ticking of the cooling engine.

"I thought maybe you could stay here with me tonight," Mace said quietly. He reached across the console and brushed one finger across the back of my hand. The gentle touch was like a spark, igniting a fire in me.

"But if not, no worries. I'll take you home."

"I think..." I licked my lips and tried to shake the last remnants of fog from my brain. "I think I'd like to stay." I turned my hand over and his fingers brushed across my palm, sending a pleasant tingle through my body before he threaded them between my own.

"Good," Mace said, voice sounding rough. He slid his hand out of mine and opened the truck door. I squinted my eyes against the dome light until darkness fell again when his door closed. Before I'd even reached for my handle, Mace had already made it around the truck and was opening my door. I took his offered hand and climbed down, wobbling a little when my feet hit the pavement, my legs like jelly.

"Easy," he said, wrapping a steadying arm around me. "You crashed hard."

Shame burned my cheeks and hollowed out my stomach. I suddenly wanted to pull away from him, and find somewhere to hide. I hated feeling like this, feeling weak, feeling like I needed someone to take care of me. I hadn't needed anyone in my life. From my time in the system, to the time I ran away, squatting in abandoned houses and buildings, but I'd always taken care of myself. And I'd been in more situations like what happened tonight than I'd like to recall, but ever since that bastard Vector had tied me down and beaten me, had made me give him information betraying my best friend, nothing had quite been the same.

I didn't know how Mace knew, if I'd tensed up or if he could just read me better than anyone ever, but the arm he had around me tightened.

"I'm feeling the effects pretty heavily myself," he said. "Like I could lay down and sleep for a week."

"Was everyone okay?" After he told me to hide behind the bar, things got a little fuzzy. I knew that the Heretics had handled the situation quickly and efficiently, but I also knew that a lot of the guests had fled the scene, and that a couple of the masked men had gotten away—running as soon as they'd realized it wasn't such an easy target. At least, that's what I thought. I wasn't sure what they'd been after in the first place. Perhaps the money? The purse for the winner of an event like that was probably worth the effort to a thief, not to mention the potential money and jewelry they could've lifted from the crowd if the Heretics weren't so good at their jobs.

"A few bumps and bruises, but nothing major." Mace's voice was tight like he was measuring his words. Measuring what to tell me which made me wonder if the attack had been less random and more club oriented than I thought. When we reached the door of the clubhouse, Mace produced a set of keys and let us inside. It was well after midnight, but there were lights on in several rooms that we passed in the main hallway and hushed voices filtered through at least one of the doors.

"Am I keeping you from work?" I asked as he led me to a set of stairs.

"Nothing that can't be handled in the morning."

That should have been a satisfying answer, but I found myself wanting to press. What was the work I was keeping him from? Who had those men really been? I wondered if he and I were in a real relationship, if those were things that he would tell me or would this be the norm?

I tried to let it go, because we weren't in a relationship and it wasn't my business to ask. We were friends, and while we may have been moving in that direction, we weren't there yet.

Mace led me up the stairs and we took a left at the top. There were four doors in this hallway. He went to the last on the right and opened it with a key.

"It's not the Ritz," Mace said as he pushed open the door and flicked on the lights. "But it's home."

The room was spacious with light gray walls, dark hardwood flooring, and two big windows—one on each of the outside walls making up the corner of the building. There was a kitchenette just inside the door to the left, and a large flatscreen TV in the corner between the windows with a loveseat angled in front of it. His bed was to the right and two doors were on the wall beside it.

Mace closed and locked the door behind me, then slipped off his shoes and picked them up, putting them in a shoe rack to the right of the door, so I did the same.

"The bathroom is over there." Mace pointed at one of the doors. "Are you hungry? Or want something to drink?"

I pulled my eyes away from taking in all the little details of his room, including a set of shelves beside the bed that were filled with books and knickknacks. "I'll take a beer if you have one," I said, giving into my curiosity and walking toward the shelves. What I thought had been knickknacks were actually little wooden figurines. Mostly animals. They were all intricately detailed. One, a little dog which looked so much like Pip that I had to pick it up and have a closer look.

"What do you think?" Mace asked from right behind my shoulder, making me jump. After my heart settled, I gently placed the little wooden dog back on the shelf and turned to look at him.

He smirked and handed me a beer. The cold bottle felt good in my hand and I lifted it to my lips, suddenly parched. Mace watched me as he took a drink of his own.

"Sure you don't want some food? I make a mean fried bologna sandwich."

"I can't say that I've ever had a fried bologna sandwich," I said, trying not to scrunch my nose. It didn't exactly sound appealing, but the look on Mace's face said I was crazy.

"Oh, we gotta fix that."

He turned and went back to the kitchenette, rummaging

in the fridge and setting a pan to heat on the stove. At the first sizzle in the pan, my stomach grumbled and I decided that maybe fried bologna was going to be the best thing that ever happened to me.

"Where did you get these figurines?"

Mace glanced back over his shoulder at me from where he was slicing a tomato on a cutting board on the counter. "I made them. I like working with my hands." He winked and turned back to the tomato while my cheeks tried to match its color.

"They're amazing." I picked up another one, this one a wolf carved to look like he was in a full run, much like one of the tattoos on Mace's chest. It was on his left pec, a heartbeat with the sketch of a running wolf. It wasn't anything more than thin black lines, but I grew warmer thinking about how I'd rested my cheek on it the night before. I hoped that was exactly how I'd fall asleep again tonight when we finally made our way to the bed.

"It's ready." Mace walked over to the small two-seater table positioned underneath one of the windows and set one plate down on one side as he slid into the chair on the other with his own.

I walked over to join him, secretly pleased at the domesticity of it all. I wasn't much of a cook myself, burning even the simplest of things, and other than Arden, I couldn't remember the last time someone had cooked for me.

I picked up my sandwich and took a tentative bite much to Mace's amusement. Surprise lit up my features at the burst of flavors on my tongue—the hearty crust of the bread, the creamy coolness of the mayonnaise, the acid bite of the tomato, and the crisply seared goodness of the bologna. I never would've guessed that something so simple could be so good. When I lifted my eyes back to Mace, he was smirking at me.

"It's good, right?" Mace asked, taking a large bite from his own sandwich, chewing for a moment before speaking again. "Growing up, we were pretty poor and I ate so much of this that you would think I'd be sick of it by now. I don't eat it all the time, but it certainly hits the spot."

A thread of soothing warmth wrapped around my heart. As far as I knew, other than with Lex, Mace didn't share much of himself. It was all smirks and the charming mask he showed the world. Suddenly, I wanted more.

"You said that you made the wooden figurines?"

Mace nodded, picking up his napkin and wiping his mouth before crumpling it in his fist. "Yep. Woodwork is probably the only valuable thing my father ever taught me."

"I never knew my father or my mother. There wasn't anyone for me until Vivian and Arden." I didn't know why I'd said that. Maybe because it felt fair to give a little of myself after he'd shared with me.

"As bad as my home life was sometimes, I can't imagine what that was like. My mom's gone now, and I don't speak to my father, but at least I know who they are."

"People always say, *you can't miss what you never had*." I shook my head. "That's a lie."

He reached across the small table and took my hand. I squeezed his fingers. There was a warmth in his eyes that eased all those old hurts, and I honestly didn't know how to deal with that. Intimacy wasn't something I'd had much of in my life. Sex, sure. But real intimacy? No. I slipped my fingers out of his and went back to my sandwich.

"Thank you for..." I trailed off, a self-deprecating chuckle escaping me. "Saving me and feeding me." Sucking in a deep breath, I blew it out slowly and reached for my beer.

He smiled at me and I could tell that he got it. "Anytime, sweetheart."

We finished our sandwiches and beers, and even though

Mace said he'd do the dishes in the morning, we stood side by side at the sink washing and drying. There was only one skillet and two plates, but I felt better getting to help with something. I think he could tell I was fading fast as my eyes kept drooping and conversation had ground to a halt.

"If you want to take a shower, there are towels and things in the cabinet beside the sink, and I can get you something to sleep in."

"That would be great," I said, standing up and unbuttoning my shirt. Mace went to his dresser and pulled out a pair of red boxer briefs and a black tank top. He turned and handed them to me.

"Will these do?"

"Perfect. Thank you."

Mace stepped in front of me, pressing the palm of his hand to the side of my neck and using his thumb to tilt my chin up. "You don't have anything to thank me for." He leaned down slowly, leaving me plenty of time to pull away, but I didn't want to. His lips moved over mine in a slow kiss, so warm and soft that I let myself get lost in it. He pulled back and rested his forehead against mine.

"I need to run downstairs, but I won't be gone long. Enjoy your shower and you're welcome to anything in here you want, okay?" He stood up enough to meet my eyes. "Make yourself at home."

"Okay."

He pressed one more kiss to my lips and turned for the door.

CHAPTER SEVEN

Mace

Now that Pax was safely tucked away in my room, I needed to go check on the situation downstairs. I made my way quickly through the main hall toward the back of the converted warehouse that we Heretics used for our clubhouse. I opened the door to what used to be the warehouse's shipping and receiving department and now served as our garage.

Three of the men who had disrupted the fight were on their knees in the middle of one of the large bays with their hands tied behind their backs and their mouths covered in duct tape. Riot, Axel, and Cleave were standing off to one side, talking amongst themselves. They all looked up as I approached and widened their circle to include me.

"Is Pax okay?" Axel asked. The big, bald man had a soft spot for all the boys from *Spritz*. Arden had even started calling him Daddy Axel, almost as a joke, but I often got the feeling it was probably true.

"He's okay. He's up in my apartment getting ready for bed."

Cleave and Axel both raised an eyebrow at me before Cleave said, "Not like you to have sleepovers."

Not wanting to get into it, and not seeing how it was any of their business, I simply said, "First time for everything. Now, what do we know about these three? They give you anything?"

Riot folded his massive arms over his chest. "They're Devil's."

"Are you fucking serious?" I shot my eyes over to the men still kneeling, none of them looked particularly familiar, but I couldn't say I knew the face of every Devil in town. "Are they trying to start a fucking war? Aren't they in the middle of some upheaval of their own?"

"That's been our understanding," Riot replied. "Calix is out of town this weekend, but I let him know what's going on. He said he'll leave it in our hands how to handle cleanup."

The four of us looked at each other, and I could tell that we all had no interest in provoking a war ourselves, but we also couldn't let the attack on the party go unanswered. I held Riot's gaze, and he gave me a small nod, letting me know it was okay for me to make the call.

"No permanent damage," I said, looking from Cleave to Axel. "But make sure they're feeling it for a few days." They both nodded. "Let's deliver them to the front of the Devil's clubhouse at dawn."

Riot offered me his hand and I clasped it, pulling him in and clapping him on the back with my other hand. I shared the same embrace with Cleave and Axel, knowing I could trust them to get the job done, and turned to head back up to my room and Pax.

I just left him a few minutes ago, but it was so strange to think that he was there sitting at my table, using my shower, and that he would be sleeping in my bed. I liked it. I liked it a lot more than I'd ever imagined feeling about someone in my space. The word *relationship* had never had positive connotations in my life, but after nearly twenty years of nothing but hookups and fuck buddies, I was beginning to wonder if maybe I should give it a shot. Sometimes it seemed like parts of me that I'd never let factor into the equation—namely, my heart—had already made the decision where Pax was concerned. I guess it said a lot that I wasn't fighting harder against it, or hell, that I wasn't fighting it at all.

I cracked open the door to my room quietly in case Pax was already asleep. The room was silent, the only light inside coming from a crack in the bathroom door and the slits in the blinds showing a Pax-sized lump on the right side of my bed. I locked the door behind me, and after taking off my shoes, made my way across the room to the bathroom.

The mirror was still fogged over, and the humid air inside my shower stall was a warm mix of my own body wash and Pax's scent. Soaping up quickly, I ignored my painfully erect cock, deciding it was creepy to masturbate while the object of my lust was asleep in the next room. I smirked, thinking how Pax would probably call me a dork or roll his eyes. Thinking about him, warm and sleepy in my bed, had me hurrying along, rinsing the soap from my body and giving my hair a fast wash. Once I was out, I dried quickly and wrapped a towel around my waist. Clicking off the light, I made my way out into the bedroom. Moonlight slanted through the gaps in the blinds turning the darkness to pale blue and giving me enough light to see to find a pair of boxer briefs in my dresser.

Just as I dropped my towel, the rustle of blankets sounded behind me.

"Mace?"

I turned to look at him, boxer briefs still in my hand. He

was sitting up, hair messy and eyes squinted, with the comforter pooled in his lap. He hadn't worn the tank top I'd given him. His bronzed skin looked pale, washed out by the moon.

"It's just me," I said, bending over to slide on my underwear.

"You don't have to do that... I mean, if you don't want to."

Our gazes held. "You sure?"

Even from across the room, I could hear his shaky exhale. " Yeah, I'm sure."

Taking him at his word, I turned and put the briefs back in the drawer, then made my way over to the bed. My heart was thumping in my chest, and any blood in my body that hadn't already migrated south was heading there now. Just the thought of being skin to skin with Pax was enough to have a pool of warmth spreading in my belly and my balls drawing up tight. I slid under the covers, and he moved toward me even before I reached for him. I slipped my arm around his waist, letting my hand wander from his shoulder blades where I could still feel the rough edges of his scars, down the dip of his spine onto his cotton covered ass. It was no mistake I'd handed him the red boxer briefs. I bet they looked sexy as hell with his tan skin and dark hair.

My lips found his and I plunged my tongue inside, thrusting deep and savoring his taste. Something crazed cracked open in me, wanting to devour him and commit every second to memory in case I wasn't ever allowed this delicacy again. Pax moaned, the rumble of it vibrating from his chest into mine. He slid his arms around me, fingers clutching my back, holding on with the same sort of wild desperation that I was feeling.

I slid a leg between his, grinding my thigh up against his balls. He tore his mouth from mine, a shaky breath stuttering out of him. "Mace," he groaned, humping against my thigh and digging his fingers further into the skin of my back.

"I've got you. I've got you, Pax," I told him, slipping my hand beneath the waistband of his underwear and pushing them down his legs. He kicked them off and we crashed together again, skin to skin. I rolled us, putting Pax on his back as I settled between his legs, keeping our mouths fused together.

He kissed me with the ferocity of someone who'd been waiting to do it a long time, and I knew that my kisses matched his vigor. Lining up our hips, I pressed against him. Our cocks slid against each other, hard and leaking between us.

He gasped, tearing his mouth away from mine and throwing his head back, so I did it again and again. He planted his feet on the bed and with both hands gripped my ass, pulling me harder against him as he thrust up to meet me. We set a hard, inevitable rhythm that had me seeing stars every time our matched movements brought our bodies together.

"Fuck, Mace. That's so goddamn good," Pax panted against my mouth.

"Are you gonna come for me?"

When he whined, I increased my pace, grinding down hard and dropping my head to suck a mark at the juncture of his neck and shoulder. Pax's rhythm faltered and his body went tense beneath me as gasping breath filled my ear and the hot shot of his cum splattered my chest. I pulled back, not wanting to miss a moment of it.

He was fucking beautiful as he came, eyes clenched shut and mouth open. I thrust against him again as my own orgasm ripped through me, blanking my mind out in pleasure and sending my load out to mix with Pax's between us.

With arms like jelly, I collapsed on top of him. "Sorry," I

panted and started to lift myself, but he snaked his arms around my back and hooked his legs over my thighs.

"Stay for a minute," he whispered.

"I'll stay as long as you like."

His eyes were wide, totally black in the pale light of the room. I kept mine open as I kissed him and wrapped him back up in my arms.

CHAPTER EIGHT

Pax

"What is that?" Arden asked the moment I opened my door. "Paxton Neace, who has been giving you hickeys?"

It'd been two days since Mace and I had slept together in his bed, and he'd left quite the love bite on the top of my shoulder. I wanted to be mad about it, but I hadn't stopped him and honestly, it had felt amazing in the moment. There was also a part of me that liked the thought that Mace had marked me...possibly as his.

Arden was standing in front of me, hands on his hips with that questioning look still on his face. I shot him a smile and stepped out into the hall, closing my apartment door and locking it. We were supposed to be meeting JJ and Cody for lunch. It was something we'd tried to do at least once a month, and this was the first time in several months that I hadn't thought about canceling and was honestly looking forward to being out in public and with my friends.

"So, you and Mace finally pulled your heads out of your asses?"

"Who said anything about Mace?"

Arden shot me a look that said I wasn't fooling anyone and that I could take my shit and shove it. I rolled my eyes. "I wouldn't say we've pulled our heads out of our asses exactly, but—"

Arden squealed, cutting me off and jumping up and down in the hall and grabbing my hand. "I knew it! I knew it! You guys have been fucking meant to be from the very beginning!"

Fighting the smile on my face was pointless, so I didn't even try and let my lips stretch wide. It felt good to be excited about something and especially good to be excited with my best friend.

"Oh my God, look at that smile. You have to tell me everything!" Arden looped his arm through mine as we made our way down the front steps and out onto the sidewalk. We turned right for the two block trek to the little bistro where JJ and Cody were probably already waiting for us.

"There's not much to tell, honestly," I said to him while we waited for the light to change at the crosswalk. "It just kind of happened."

Arden huffed. "What do you mean it just kind of happened? I need details! Who kissed who first? How were things the next day? Why hasn't he proposed?"

A loud bark of laughter sprang out of me, and I shook my head. "Okay, okay. Technically, I kissed him first—"

"Oh, I like it! Take what you want!"

I could feel my cheeks getting hot, but still the happy smile wouldn't wipe off my face. "And yeah we fooled around, *obviously*, and the next morning was perfect." I knew my voice had that stupid dreamy quality that I so often made fun of others for, but it was like I couldn't help myself.

Waking up that next morning with Mace in his bed *had* been perfect. He'd kissed me good morning, while bright sunlight filled the room through the large windows, and then made us coffee and breakfast. We'd taken a shower together, each taking turns washing the other, and after a pair of hand-jobs he'd loaned me some sweats and a T-shirt before driving me back to *Spritz* in his truck.

It'd all been so domestic—right down to the kiss goodbye—but it was still hard for me to believe it was real. Because I'd never had that, never had a real home life, never had a real boyfriend. I still didn't know if that was what Mace was, but I felt like it was where we were headed. I'd been so afraid of it, but now that it'd happened, I decided I wasn't going to be afraid anymore. Or at least I wasn't going to let it hold me back, because Arden was right, I did want Mace. I wanted him to be mine, and for me to be his, and he'd given me no reason not to trust that that was what he wanted, as well.

We made it to the restaurant to find Cody and JJ already seated at a table in the corner by the windows. As we made our way over, they both stood to give us a hug. Cody squeezed me tight, and I could tell that he saw the hickey, but he was too sweet to say anything, so he only gave me a little smile before settling back in his seat. He and Eben had been together since New Year's, and while I hadn't been in the best headspace when I'd met him, he'd easily become a good friend.

JJ arched a brow at me and pulled me in for a hug. He was a singer in a locally famous band and stood out in the earth-toned bistro with his electric-blue tipped hair. He was also dating Cleave, the Iron Heretics Road Captain. "I'm guessing someone had a good night last night?" JJ asked as we all took our seats.

"Night before last, actually, but yes, it was a very good night," I said with a conspiratorial smile.

Arden plopped his elbows on the table with his chin in his hands. "And now he's going to tell us all about it."

We all laughed, and I gave in, sharing a couple details about my first time with Mace and just how happy I was.

LUNCH HAD STRETCHED ON INTO THE AFTERNOON, BUT IT had been a good feeling to be out with my friends, joking, laughing, and catching up on all the things that had been going on with each of us. Arden left with JJ and Cody after I assured him I was fine to walk back by myself. It was a warm sunny afternoon and Mace was supposed to be coming to meet me at my apartment. I'd mentioned wanting to get back into weightlifting, so he'd asked if I'd like to go to the gym together.

I thought that was a great idea as long as we spent as much time lifting weights as we did flirting. I smiled to myself, breathing in the city air and enjoying the sunshine on my face. The two block walk breezed by and before I knew it, I was rounding the corner of my apartment building. Just as the building's entrance came into view, Leith and a tall man in a baseball cap stepped off the bottom step. Leith waved and shot me a smug little smile that told me the man with him was probably a booty call. I glanced at him and for a moment, the world froze. Dark blond hair was half-hidden under a baseball cap, and as they turned away, I only caught a glimpse of his profile, but the sharp edge of his cheekbone and straight line of his nose looked so much like the man who'd assaulted me my knees got weak.

I was seeing ghosts, I knew that. The man who'd hurt me was dead, and this was just someone who resembled him—probably some completely innocent guy—but my first instinct was to scream for Leith to get away from him and run. I pressed a hand against my chest over my rampaging heart and looked the way they'd gone, but they'd already disappeared around the opposite corner.

I took a deep breath and let my wobbly legs collapse, sending me to my ass on the steps of the building. I propped my elbows on my knees, put my forehead in my hands, and breathed in and out until I felt myself settling down. I had no idea how long I sat there like that.

"Pax?"

Mace's voice startled me and I looked up, the sudden movement making my head spin.

"Hey, easy, are you okay?" Mace knelt in front of me, hands grasping my wrists and eyes searching my face. I threw myself forward, wrapping my arms around his shoulders and burying my face in his neck. I felt his balance teeter, but he righted himself and held me back just as tightly.

"Pax, you need to tell me what happened. Are you hurt?"

I shook my head, sucking in the scent of him, burying my nose against the leather of his Iron Heretics vest. I was safe, Mace was here, and even if that man was still alive, I knew he'd never touch me again because this man wouldn't give him the chance.

"No, I'm not hurt. I just..." My voice came out in a raspy croak. I felt so stupid now for seeing things that weren't there. "I saw something that freaked me out. I'm really fine."

Mace scrunched his brows together. "What did you see?"

Tears stung my eyes as humiliation made my whole body feel hot. "Just someone who reminded me of...you know." I shrugged, the hollow pit in my stomach spreading.

Gentle fingers brushed over my cheeks, wiping away tears I hadn't realized I'd let loose. "I wish you'd have called me." His green eyes were dark, filled with worry and so soft I wanted to cry all over again.

I looked down and noticed the gym bag on the step beside his feet. "Shit, I ruined our plans."

He shook his head. "No, you didn't, because my only real plan was to spend the afternoon with you. The gym will still be there tomorrow. Now, come on, let's get you inside and out of the sun."

"Okay." I took a deep breath and let him pull me to my feet.

CHAPTER NINE

Mace

I pulled the truck up to the curb in front of Pax's apartment building. It had been a couple weeks since he'd gotten so upset right there on those very steps, and even though he hadn't had another episode like that, at least not one he'd told me about, I was still worried for him. He admitted to me that he felt weak and ashamed at the way he still got scared sometimes, and I told him exactly what I thought—that he was one of the strongest people I'd ever met. I spent the night with him that night, cooking dinner, watching a movie, and just holding him. Other than him still being shaken up, it was one of the best nights of my life; I wanted more of them.

The door to the apartment building opened and Pax and Arden came out, headed toward me. It wasn't lost on me that Pax had never been on the back of my bike, something I fully intended to change and quickly, but for today, since Lex was out of town on Nomad business with Stone, the truck it was. We were headed to Eben and Cody's housewarming party, and I could see that the boys hadn't spared any expense in gifts. Both of them had a giant gift bag and another wrapped present. Pax pulled open the passenger door and the smaller door that led to the back bench seat.

"Hey. What did you guys do, buy out the store?" They both laughed, loading their gifts into the back seat behind me, and then Arden climbed up to sit behind the passenger seat, pulling the door closed.

"Only half of it," Arden said, leaning over so he could look in the rearview mirror to check his hair.

Pax hopped up into the passenger seat and without pause, leaned over and pressed a quick kiss against my lips. "Hey, thanks for driving us."

I gave him the look that told him he was being silly, and then waited until they buckled up before pulling us out into traffic.

"Speaking of gifts, is yours in the back?" Arden asked from his seat.

I chuckled and patted my vest. "Nope, it's right here. A handy-dandy Home Depot gift card."

They both chuckled and started chattering away about how happy they were for Cody, Eben's boyfriend. He was a relatively new addition to our lives as they'd only gotten together at the beginning of the year, but he fit right in, and Eben was completely gone for Cody. This would be their first home together since Cody had lived with JJ in his townhouse before this. First, Lex got himself all partnered up and moved Arden into his cabin, and now, Eben was playing house, too. Cleave and JJ were together, and seemed happier for it, but Cleave still chose to live in his room at the clubhouse, and JJ was back on the market for another roommate.

Apparently, all the happy couples had passed the Kool-Aid on to me, I thought, casting my eyes over to a smiling Pax riding shotgun. We were off to a good start, and there was still a lot to learn about each other, but it shocked me how important he already was to me.

The biker life wasn't for everyone, and sometimes club business took precedence over everything else in my life, but that was before Pax. Family was important to the club. Partners were important. Pax and I'd been friends for a year, and while we'd only been something more for a few weeks, it had already settled into me. This thing between us, it felt permanent and more significant than anything else in my life.

I maneuvered us through the residential neighborhood where Eben and Cody's new house was. We turned onto their street and there was no missing their house with all the bikes lining one side of the road. I drove down and turned around, coming back and parking on the opposite side of the street. We all climbed out, gathering up gifts and making our way to the front door. Cody opened it before we had a chance to knock, and Arden and Pax nearly knocked me out of the way to get through and hug their friend.

I stepped inside, closing the door behind me, and after the boys released Cody, I hugged him myself. "Congrats on the new house. It's beautiful."

"Thank you," Cody said. "There's food and drinks in the kitchen which is back through the arch, and Eben set up a badminton net in the backyard if you guys want to play."

"That sounds fun." Arden started moving farther into the house, talking to Cody. Pax turned to follow them, but stopped and came back to me.

"Did you want to come outside or..."

"I'm going to make my way around, but don't let me stop you. Go have a good time." I stepped into his space, pulling him to me, pressing a quick kiss against his mouth. "I'll come find you soon."

A small, private smile lit Pax's face. Then he was off after Arden and Cody, and I headed toward the kitchen.

Most of my fellow Heretics were gathered around the kitchen island with some form of libation or another in front of them. Eben set his beer down on the counter and walked over to me, offering me his hand and pulling me in for a back-slapping hug.

"Thanks for coming, man," he said, pulling back with my hand still firmly gripped in his. "Cody and I appreciate it."

"Of course. Wouldn't miss the chance to see your new digs. And I'm pretty sure Pax and Arden needed my truck just to get all the gifts they bought for Cody over here."

Most everyone laughed, and Calix gave me a nod from his place at the end of the island, his back to the large picture window overlooking the backyard. "Things are going well with your boy, I take it?"

I walked over and slipped onto the stool beside Calix, one of the Prospects in the room automatically going to the refrigerator to get me a beer. "Real good." I picked up the bottle and twisted off the cap before clinking my bottle against Calix's and taking a long pull.

"That's good to hear," Calix said after taking a long drink of his own. The President wasn't the most talkative guy, but he always managed to have an eye and ear on everything.

"We still haven't seen any backlash from the Devil's?"

"None. Quite frankly, that makes me a little nervous." Calix rested his arms on the island and glanced around at the others. "Let's not worry about business today. We're here to celebrate because our little Eben's growing up."

"Hell yeah, he is," Axel said, standing up and putting Eben in a headlock. "I swear it was just yesterday this little shit was in a Prospect vest."

I chuckled and took in the razzing they were giving Eben while letting my eyes drift over Calix's shoulder to the window. The badminton court was set up in the middle of the backyard, and with this house being on a corner lot, I could see the street beyond. Cody and Pax stood on one side of the net with rackets in their hands while Arden and JJ were on the other. Arden had the birdie in his hand and looked like he was preparing to serve when I noticed someone walking down the sidewalk, then turning up into the yard.

When I caught sight of what he was wearing and the insignia on his vest, I shot to my feet as ice poured into my veins. "There's a fucking Devil in the backyard."

"What?" Eben shoved his way from between Axel and Cleave where they'd still been giving him a hard time and ran for the door. I was hot on his heels, and I could hear the others behind me. All I'd been able to tell was that the Devil had something in his hand, but I didn't know what.

My gun was in my hand before I cleared the door.

"Pax! Arden!" I shouted, running forward to get myself between them and the fucking member of the Devil's Rage MC who'd decided to make a house call. Pax's head swiveled my way, then quickly back as he realized we had a party crasher. I could see my brothers on either side of me fanning out and putting themselves between our partners and potential danger.

The moment I stepped in front of Pax, I felt him settle in behind me, watching the Devil. I glanced over to where Arden had been playing and found Axel covering him. Cleave was with JJ and Eben with Cody. We all had our guns trained on the intruder.

Calix stood in the center of the badminton court, one hand resting casually on the net and the other loose at his side. "What are you doing here, Holden?"

I glanced at Axel out of my peripheral. He looked as confused as me. I had no clue who this guy was, but our President seemed to.

Holden, apparently, slowly lowered the expensive looking bottle of alcohol to the ground and held up his hands. "I didn't come here to start anything. I'm unarmed." He lifted the edges of his vest, showing he wasn't wearing a shoulder rig.

"Take it off."

With a nod and no sudden movements, Holden pulled the vest off and turned around so we could see he didn't have a gun at his back, either.

Seemingly satisfied, Calix said, "Lower your weapons. We don't want Eben and Cody's new neighbors to think this is the kind of scene they can expect on their peaceful street." He glanced at me. "Pat him down."

Slipping my gun back into my shoulder holster, I turned my head and looked at Pax. "Go to Cleave, okay?"

He nodded, but the hand he had fisted in my vest gripped tighter for a moment before he let me go. I approached Holden slowly. He lifted his arms out to the sides and I made quick work of checking him for weapons. "He's clear," I said, taking a step back.

The other Heretics had moved closer and it looked like Pax, Arden, JJ, and Cody weren't in the yard anymore. Good. We formed a semi-circle around Holden with Calix at its center.

"I'll ask you one more time, what are you doing here Holden?" Calix's voice was ice cold and had the lethal edge he reserved for when some truly dangerous shit was about to go down.

Holden swallowed as his eyes swept over all of us. "I came to offer apologies for the behavior of some of our former members and to let you know our leadership has changed." He slipped his vest back on.

My eyes immediately dropped to the patches on his chest. *President* sat on the right side just above his Devil's Rage patch.

"And you thought this warranted a home visit?"

"Calix, look, I'm sorry about showing up here and

disturbing the party. I just wanted to apologize and say that the Devil's Rage isn't looking to engage in any sort of war with the Heretics. We want a truce."

Calix was quiet for a moment, and it felt like we were all holding our breath. "We'll take it to our table and vote because that's what a real MC does. Now get the fuck out of here."

Muscles in Holden's jaw clenched, but he nodded, then turned and walked away.

We stood there until the rumbling of a motorcycle starting and pulling away reached us.

"That took some fucking balls, man," Cleave said, looking out at the street like Holden might come roaring back any second.

Calix let out a long breath. "Yeah. Eben, my apologies."

"It's not your fault, Prez. He probably thought since my piece of shit father was a Devil that coming here to make his apologies was somehow the right thing to do."

"Let's get back inside," I said, not trusting Holden and wanting to get back to Pax. Either way, I turned and went, leaving the others to fall in behind me.

CHAPTER TEN

Pax

S *pritz* was packed. I was working the main floor of the club tonight instead of the lounge downstairs, serving drinks and trying to avoid getting my ass groped. I made my way over to the bar after delivering the latest round of refills to my tables, and went down to the end where the bartender set out servers drink orders on thick black mats.

My steps slowed when I saw Leith was standing there, elbows on the edge of the bar and a small tray tucked under his arm. Not seeing any way to escape without being rude, I settled in beside him to wait on my order.

"Hey, Pax," he said, shooting me a little smile and turning his head to leer in the direction where Mace was positioned off one side of the dance floor.

Things had felt more concrete between Mace and I in the last couple of weeks, but we still hadn't had a real conversation about what we were to each other now—if we were anything. I rolled my eyes at myself. I was being ridiculous. I knew we were something, and I hadn't seen Mace so much as look at another man the way he used to since the first time I kissed him. It was just our lack of communication and Leith being a brat that was putting these thoughts in my head.

"Hey, Leith. How's your night?"

"Could be worse. Could be better." He waggled his eyebrows at me.

His face was so silly I couldn't help but chuckle. He was one of the newest *Spritz* employees, and I wasn't sure of his background, but I knew Vivian typically chose guys who could use a leg up in life. Most of the time that meant the people coming in were quiet, or kept to themselves, or had a prickly exterior designed to protect them from anyone getting to their vulnerable hearts underneath. I knew something about that last one, and I wondered sometimes if Leith's bratty routine was just his form of armor.

"Speaking of," I said, as casually as possible. "Were you headed out on a hot date the other day?"

"Why, you jealous?"

It'd been stupid of me to even ask. Whoever the guy Leith was seeing was, he didn't deserve my suspicion just because he reminded me of Vector. I huffed. "Never mind, I was just trying to make conversation."

Something...*earnest* flashed across Leith's face. "Sorry, it wasn't exactly a date. I mean, we've seen each other a couple times, but we were going for coffee."

I watched him for a moment, and when the ridiculous smirk he always wore didn't come back, I nodded. "That sounds nice. I hope that works out for you."

He laughed, and I think it was the most genuine sound I'd ever heard come out of his mouth. "Well, not looking to marry the guy, but you're right. It was nice, but I don't have plans to see him again. How are things with you and Mace?"

I knew the smile stretching across my face was sappy as shit, but I couldn't stop it. "Things are good."

We both laughed.

"I can see that," Leith said. "I'd be lying if I said I wasn't a smidgen jealous, he's gorgeous. I mean, I don't think I've met a Heretic yet that isn't, but there's something about that long hair."

"He is very pretty to look at," I agreed, letting my eyes wander over to Mace. The black T-shirt with Security imprinted over his left pec and across his shoulders was pulled tight against the defined muscle in his chest and arms, and his long hair Leith was so fond of was pulled back in a low ponytail. His beard was freshly trimmed and quite frankly, he looked damn good enough to eat.

Leith set his tray on the bar and lifted a hand to fan himself. "Jesus, I'm surprised that stare didn't set him on fire. Guess I'll have to turn my sights elsewhere."

I made a dramatic sweep of my hand, encompassing the whole of the club. "I can't imagine where you'd find an eligible gay man."

Leith smirked. "This is true."

The bartender working on drinks for servers set several down at the same time with the ticket sitting beside them and shot us a wink before getting back to work.

"That's me," Leith said, loading up his tray with the drinks.

When he looked back at me, he seemed almost shy. "It was good chatting with you, Pax."

"You too, Leith."

He walked away, leaving me by myself at the end of the bar. I let my gaze wander around and my eyes landed on Vivian in her preferred booth. She had a smile on her face and raised her glass in my direction as if to salute me. I assumed for talking with Leith. I knew he'd been having a hard time fitting in, even though he mostly brought it on himself, but I was one of the employees who had been here the longest, and it should have been my duty all along to help him get settled.

I'd be sure to pay more attention to that in the future. I moved my eyes from Vivian over to Mace to find him looking back at me for just a moment. It was hard to see his expression, but I could have sworn he shot me a wink before his eyes started scanning the crowd again. I smiled to myself and loaded up the drinks the bartender brought me.

———

THE REST OF MY SHIFT WENT BY SMOOTHLY. JUST AFTER two a.m. when I was done for the night, I took my sweaty, tired self down to the tunnel that led to my apartment building, which most of us lovingly called *Spritz Villa*. I hadn't seen Mace since earlier and figured he had club business to deal with tonight. When I opened the door to the building, I found an equally tired looking Mace leaning against the wall beside the elevators and looking straight at me.

"I thought you were already gone for the night," I said, making my way over to him. He reached down and pressed the up button for the elevator and then opened his arms for me.

Without hesitation, I walked into them, wrapping my arms around his waist and tilting my chin up until he smiled and pressed his lips to mine.

"Is it okay that I waited for you? I was going to head back to the clubhouse and get some sleep, but I thought maybe I'd stay with you instead."

It was more than okay with me, and I tried to show him that, raising up on my toes and pressing my mouth to his again while I slid my arms up from his sides and over his shoulders, pulling him closer, and getting one hand tangled in the loose strands of his hair.

He groaned against me, opening his mouth and thrusting his tongue against mine. We kissed like that until the elevator door slid open. Mace pulled back and chuckled when I tried to chase him. He took my hand, leading me into the elevator and hitting the button for my floor.

We stood against the back wall as the elevator climbed, his arm around my shoulders. "You sure you don't mind me inviting myself to stay?"

"I don't mind at all. Honestly."

When the elevator opened, we made our way to my door. Mace had been over several times since we started seeing each other, but I always thought about that first time when he'd shown up as bruised and beaten up as I was, and even with his own injuries, had insisted on taking care of me. I unlocked my apartment, letting us inside, thankful for the rush of cool air from the air conditioner. I turned to ask Mace if he wanted something to eat, only for him to seal his lips over mine again. His strong calloused hands slipped around me and slid down my back to my ass, gripping tight and pulling our groins together.

He ground against me, the hard length of him making it obvious that food was the last thing on his mind. We pulled back with a gasp, and he pressed a quick succession of chaste kisses against my still open mouth.

"How about a shower? Then food."

I didn't have enough brain cells working to speak after his absolutely drugging kisses, so I simply nodded and led us to the bathroom. It was as tiny and cramped as it always was, but Mace didn't seem to mind. He stripped me first, and then himself, before getting the hot water going and herding me into the shower.

"You're on a mission tonight." I laughed as the warm spray hammered my back.

"Maybe I missed you." As soon as he said it, those green eyes I was so fond of bounced around the small space before landing on the shower head. It was detachable, and Mace pulled it down, then gripped my chin to tilt my head back so he could rinse my hair. After it was soaked and slicked back from my face, he rinsed his own before finally bringing his eyes back to mine. "Besides, is it so wrong for a man to know exactly what he wants?" He arched a dark eyebrow at me and reached over my shoulder to replace the shower head and grab the shampoo bottle.

I pulled the bottle from his hands, squirted a generous dollop into my palm before setting the bottle back on the shelf and rubbing my hands together. I slid my hands into Mace's hair, letting my fingers swirl and rub at his scalp. He groaned, letting his head fall forward. We were so cramped together in my tiny shower that the action made our foreheads touch. Leaning in, I took his mouth in a quick kiss, then used my grip on his hair to pull his head back so the soap wouldn't run into his eyes. "There's nothing wrong with it." I shrugged. "I guess it still catches me by surprise sometimes that it's me you seem to want."

Opening his eyes, Mace pulled the shampoo bottle down again and washed my hair the same way I'd washed his. We didn't speak while we rinsed our hair and started soaping the rest of ourselves. I'd turned to replace the shower head once we were cleaned and rinsed, my back to Mace's chest before he spoke again.

"I don't know why it surprises you," Mace said quietly, his hands gliding over the slick skin of my stomach as he wrapped his arms around me. "Since I laid eyes on you the first time, I haven't wanted anyone else."

It felt like my heart floated up with the steam lingering above our heads, and I wasn't sure that my tiny shower could contain all the emotions that were rampaging through me like they could burst forth at any second. "I want you too."

Mace kissed my neck and reached out to turn off the water while his other hand slid down, making my breath catch a second before he wrapped his fingers around the hard length of me. His breath was hot on my ear. "You want to make me yours tonight? Fuck me with this beautiful cock?"

He turned me around so I was facing him and smiled, a honey-sweet stretch of his lips, like he could tell he'd just short-circuited my brain.

"Fuck, yes," I breathed, getting my hands on him and slamming my mouth over his.

We haphazardly dried each other. Mace took the towel from my hands and lifted his arms, rubbing it vigorously over his longer hair. I put his distraction to good use and latched onto his nipple, just beneath the running wolf tattoo, and sucked hard.

He stumbled back, his shoulders hitting the wall and a groan escaping him. "Jesus fuck, Pax!"

I smiled around my mouthful, lapping at his hardened nub with my tongue and running my fingers over the cut furrows of his abs until I got to what I really wanted. Gripping his cock, I stroked him slow, thumbing his slit, then sliding lower to cup his balls and run my fingers over his taint.

I'd been with a lot of men—*a lot of men*—mostly for work, but fewer for pleasure, and I could already tell that not any one of them would hold a candle to Mace. His hips pushed forward, moving fast and sliding himself through my grip, but I tsked and pulled my hand and mouth away from him.

He actually whined.

"Oh no, you don't get to come yet. Not until I'm buried in your ass."

He huffed a laugh. "I knew you'd be a bossy shit the moment I told you I wanted you to top me."

I leaned into him, relishing in the fresh scent of our bodies and the heat of his skin. "Is that a problem?"

Mace snorted. "Hell no. I love it. I know I'm the *big bad biker*, but when things get horizontal, I love it all—fucking, being fucked—whether I'm playing the dominant role or not."

"I can totally see you being a toppy bottom."

"Not tonight, apparently."

"No," I said, my lips finding his again and pressing my tongue in slow and deep. We were both panting before I pulled back. "Not tonight."

CHAPTER ELEVEN

Mace

Pax was absolutely owning my body. He'd taken me to his room and lain me out in the middle of his bed, kissing me in that deep, searching way that made me want to rip my heart out of my chest and present it in humble offering. It was moments like these, when his mouth was moving possessively over mine, that I realized just how enormously fucked I was. I also realized just how much I didn't care. Not as long as I got Pax out of the deal.

Pulling back from my lips, he nipped at my jaw and slithered down, his delectable ass in the air, kissing and sucking at my throat.

"Pax," I said, because I couldn't be quiet. "Goddamn, you're so fucking sexy." I watched him arch his back, plumping the curves of his ass to a perfect display, because he knew exactly what he was doing. "If you don't get inside me, I'm going to change my mind and—" Every word in my head turned to mush. He'd swooped down, smooth as fucking silk, and sucked my cock down to the root. Raising up, he licked around my head before sliding back down again and again until I was mindlessly babbling his name and so close to blowing there was no way I was going to be able to hold off.

Popping off, a shit-eating grin pulled at Pax's lips as he gripped the base of my cock. "You were saying?"

"Oh, fuck you," I rasped, still trying to remember my name.

"No, definitely fuck you." He chuckled, low, pulling at the massive pool of desire in my belly and making pre-cum ooze out of my slit. He leaned over and dug around in the night-stand before dropping a bottle of lube on the bed and ripping open a condom. After sheathing himself in the latex, he popped open the lube and drizzled some on his cock, stroking until he threw his head back and moaned. Then, poured some onto his fingers.

Gripping my leg, he lifted it up and rested it on his shoulder. A cool lubed finger probed at my hole. I sighed when he slipped it in, pumping in and out before adding a second.

"Come on," I said, so turned on my skin felt hot and too tight for my body.

He looked up at me, dark eyes serious, before lining himself up and pressing in slowly.

I took a deep breath, loving the burning pressure of Pax stretching my ass open. He moved in pulsing, smooth thrusts, never taking his piercing eyes off my face. When he'd sunk to the hilt, I reached for him, dropping my leg from his shoulder and wrapping them around him. He fell over me, hands planted beside my shoulders and lips ravenous against mine.

"You feel fucking incredible," he whispered against my cheek, pulling his hips back and thrusting in again.

"So do you," I told him, locking my ankles at the top of his ass and pressing my heels in, encouraging him to fuck me faster.

He listened, his short thrusts turning deep and rubbing right over my prostate.

"Fuck yes," I gasped, pulling him tighter against me.

He buried his face in my neck, his open mouth panting and pressed against my skin.

I unlocked my legs, lifting and spreading them to get him deeper. Rising up, he slid his hands up the back of my thighs, pressing into the back of my knees and using the leverage to slam into me over and over.

Getting a hand around myself, I stroked fast.

"Come on, Mace. Come for me."

The building wall of pressure broke and I spewed my load over my fist and onto my chest. "You too," I gasped, still stroking the last drops of cum out of myself.

Pax let out a strangled cry, his face contorted in bliss and muscles straining before he collapsed back down, his hands holding his weight.

A long, satisfied exhale slipped through my lips while I rubbed his back, enjoying the little twitches and jerks of his muscles as the aftershocks of his orgasm worked through him.

"Shit," he whispered against my skin a moment later and leaned up enough to reach down and hold the condom as he slipped his softening cock out of me. He tied it off and dropped it over the edge of the bed into the trash can under his side table. "I'll grab a washcloth."

"Hey," I said, pulling him back down on top of me before he had the chance to go anywhere. "Stay for a minute."

Meeting my eyes, he smiled. "I'll stay as long as you like."

I kissed him. "That was amazing."

He hummed against my lips. "Yes, it was."

THE ROAR OF OUR MOTORCYCLE ENGINES BOUNCED OFF THE tall buildings, echoing back and filling my head while the vibration from my Harley beneath me settled into my bones. Typically, we didn't bring a group this large this far into the city for just this reason, but also because we stuck close to our clubhouse on the outskirts, keeping a low profile and off police radar was just a part of our life. Today, however, we were headed to the annual Second Weekend of July charity ride for veterans and their families. There were ten of us in total and I needed to stop by *Spritz Villa*—as Pax had informed me it was called—to pick him up.

The charity ride itself was a good time and always had a huge turnout, but I was also excited because this would be the first time Pax was on my bitch seat.

Calix rode at the head of our column with Riot and myself directly behind him, followed by Axel and Cleave and five other full-patch members.

As we pulled up in front of the apartment building, I saw Pax standing at the base of the steps talking to someone sitting on them. With a closer look, I realized it was Leith and the normally smiling brat had a frown on his face. Pax turned, shooting me a smile as I parked along the curb directly across from him and turned the bike off. The others parked around me and did the same. The silence was almost louder than the group of motorcycles had been. I pulled off my skull cap helmet and smiled back at Pax.

"You ready to go?"

Pax jogged over to me, looking good in his jeans and boots. I insisted he wear the longsleeve protective jacket I'd gotten for him. He whined about it at first because he knew that most of us only wore T-shirts and our vests, but I wanted him to have an extra layer of protection in case I laid the bike over. The jacket itself was light-weight, vented, and cut in a bomber style that contoured to him just right.

"Hey," Pax said quietly, tilting his head down a bit. "Do

you think one of the guys would mind if Leith rode with them?"

I arched a brow, surprised at Pax asking on Leith's behalf. Normally, the redhead grated on my boy's nerves. "I'm sure they wouldn't." I glanced around at the club brothers with me and my eyes landed on Axel, who was funnily enough watching Leith.

"Axel, mind having a passenger today?" When Axel glanced at me, I nudged my head toward where Leith was still sitting on the apartment building steps.

A smile tugged up one side of Axel's mouth. "Hey, Leith," he called. When Leith glanced up, he patted the seat behind him. "Get your pretty ass over here."

Leith was up like a shot, heading toward Axel. He shot a smile at Pax as he went.

With that settled, I dug Pax's helmet out of my saddlebags and helped him get it strapped under his chin. He seemed a little nervous, so I smiled at him and pressed a soft kiss to his mouth while my brothers whistled.

"Just hold on to me, okay? Don't wiggle or put your feet down and it'll be fine."

Pax nodded and climbed on behind me, sliding forward until he was snug against my back with my hips cradled in the V of his thighs. He snaked his arms around my waist and held on tight.

Calix started his bike and we all followed suit, the roar of Harleys filling the street once more. I rested my hand over Pax's clasped ones, giving him a little squeeze and then pulled away from the curb, taking my place a little behind and to Calix's right.

It was so damn good to have Pax behind me that I felt like we were flying as we found some open road on our way out of the city. The charity ride started a big local high school and had a long meandering route through several small towns where people could stop and grab a bite to eat or shop at locally-owned businesses which donated a portion of the proceeds to the ride. In my opinion, there was nothing better than spending the day on two wheels with the cloudless sky above and an open road ahead. Being surrounded by hundreds of like-minded individuals had always made the experience better, but having Pax wrapped around me to share it with was damn near the best thing I could imagine.

There'd been a shift in us that night in his apartment a couple days ago, and more than just the evolution of our physical relationship. I had already felt like we were getting closer than I'd ever gotten with anyone, and from the things he'd told me, it was the same for him. Typically, I never would have reached this point with someone. Warning signs and alarm bells would have been going off long before now—long before I craved him more than having my Harley on the open road.

He'd snuck his way under my ribs, setting up shop there without any kind of permission from me. The hell of it was, that while any of those things would've sent me into a tailspin before, now I wasn't even batting an eye because this was Pax. And for whatever reason, I was determined to make him mine in the same way I was already his. I thought he felt the same way. I knew he trusted me, probably more than anyone save Arden, and I was determined to keep being worthy of that trust. I wanted to show him that he could trust me with all of it—all the things that he hid, all the secrets of his heart —I wanted it all.

As we approached the high school, Pax squeezed my middle when the rows upon rows of motorcycles waiting to begin the ride came into view. There had to be at least five or six hundred bikes already in the parking lot, and we were only one group of several more coming down the road and turning in.

Once we got into the lot, we wove around until we found Lex, Jebidiah, Kade, and Stone. Arden was sitting on the back of Lex's parked bike and waved as we approached. Jebidiah and Kade, members of our Sand Lake chapter, were standing beside their bikes with Lex, chatting. Stone was just getting off of his Harley. We pulled into some empty parking spaces beside them, keeping all of our bikes close together so as to not take up too much room. Once we were parked, Cleave went to sign us in and get the tags to attach to our windshields.

I held my bike steady and offered Pax my hand to help him step off. I knew his legs would be a little wobbly as he'd never been on a motorcycle before, and if you didn't ride them regularly, it was a common occurrence. Once he was stable, I stood and pulled my helmet off my head. "What do you think?"

Pax removed his own helmet with a wide smile on his face. "It was awesome. I'm excited for this ride."

Beside us, Axel had helped Leith step off the back of his bike, and then he met his brother Stone halfway, embracing him in a backslapping hug. Dalton Stone was a couple years older than Axel—both of them hulking beasts, only Stone still had hair on his head. He was also a member of our Nomad chapter. Axel introduced Leith to his brother and the three stood talking.

I took Pax over to where Lex, Jebidiah, and Kade were standing and introduced him to everyone. Arden had climbed off Lex's bike and came to greet us, as well.

"It's pretty great, right?" Arden asked Pax.

"It was badass, but my butt already hurts," Pax said, rubbing a hand over his backside. We all laughed and I stepped in behind him, getting my hands on his ass, giving him a little squeeze. "I'll massage it for you later if it gets too sore," I whispered in his ear. He huffed a laugh and bumped his ass back against me, knocking me back a step.

"Behave," he said with laughter still in his voice.

"Sweetheart, *mis*behave is my middle name, and honestly, you should have known this about me."

Pax narrowed his eyes at me and turned his back on the group, stepping in close. "I just thought of something and I'm kind of ashamed of myself that I haven't asked earlier."

I cocked my head at him, not having any clue what he could be talking about.

Gorgeous brown eyes locked onto mine. "I don't know your full name. Mason is your last name, right? That's all I know."

I chuckled, but it was soft. Seeing as I'd never been particularly fond of my name, I didn't use it outside of legal documents. As with everything lately, though, Pax was welcome to any part of me. "Randall. Randall Elijah Mason."

"Randall Elijah," Pax whispered, sending a shiver through me. He gave me the sweetest smile and the softest kiss. "I like it. Much better than Randall Misbehave."

Snorting a laugh, I kissed him soundly, then turned him around, molding my chest to his back as we re-joined our group of friends.

CHAPTER TWELVE

Pax

It had been a fucking amazing day so far. I didn't really understand how just riding on the back of a motorcycle could feel terrifying, exhilarating, and freeing all at the same time. Maybe it had been so much fun because of the company, or the scenery, or the fact that it was for such a great cause, but I was leaning toward the company. Being snuggled up against Mace's back, my chin resting on the leather of his Iron Heretics vest could be my new favorite thing. When I wasn't making funny faces at Arden or Leith through the side mirrors, I found myself closing my eyes and letting my brain and body empty of all my worries and stress as if the wind rushing over us was whisking them away.

We stopped mid-morning at a café in the second town we passed through. Mace bought me breakfast, and we sat at a table filled with other Heretics and their partners while we finished our coffee. It'd been good to stretch my legs, but I'd been ready to get back on the bike. I wasn't sure how long ago that had been, but the sun was getting high in the sky now, my stomach was starting to rumble, and I was pretty sure my ass had been numb for the last fifty miles.

I'd long ago given up trying to figure out where we were. Our route seemed to loop around and back, but as we crested a hill, my eyes caught on the little green sign on the side of the road that said, *Gnaw Bone.* I perked up hoping that we'd stop at the diner there for lunch. As soon as we entered town limits, our little group started to slow and I let out an internal *whoop!* when Calix clicked on his turn signal and eased his bike into *Harper's Home Cooking's* gravel parking lot. The Heretics seemed to be the only group stopping there as bike after bike continued on through town, the sound of so many engines a continuous roar in my ears.

Once we were parked and Mace had turned the bike off, I said, "I might have to take you up on that ass massage." Mace laughed, unbuckling his helmet and hanging it off the handlebars before offering me his hand. Carefully, I eased myself off the bike, this time expecting the jelly feeling of my legs and groaning at getting to stretch and move.

"Still love it?" Mace asked, watching me with a smile.

"Definitely, but I think my ass needs to build up a tolerance."

At that, he threw back his head and laughed before wrapping an arm around my shoulders and pressing his lips against the side of my head. "If I have anything to say about it, it will," he said, his warm breath ruffling my hair. I turned toward him, sliding my arms around his waist and tilting my chin up, asking for a kiss. He didn't disappoint, cupping my face in his hands and kissing me slow and easy, right there in the parking lot.

"Lord, we aren't going to be able to take them anywhere," I heard someone say, but my brain was too focused on Mace's lips moving with mine to parse out who it was. There were more wolf whistles and catcalls, and Mace finally pulled away with a chuckle and shot a glance around at our companions.

"Y'all are just jealous."

There was some good-natured grumbling at that and some protests from the Heretics with boyfriends of their own, but it was all in good fun. We were halfway to the diner's door when I realized I'd just thought of Mace as my boyfriend. I must've stuttered in my steps because Mace gave my fingers a squeeze and glanced over at me. "You okay?"

"I really am."

Inside, the host pushed tables together for us, and we all took turns making use of the facilities. As I was washing my hands, Leith stepped up to the sink beside me to wash his.

"How are you enjoying yourself?"

It could have been from the sun, but I swore pink bloomed in Leith's cheeks. "I'm having a great time. Thank you for asking if I could come."

"No need to thank me. You were looking awfully cozy on the back of Axel's bike."

"He's great, but before you get any ideas, I'm not in the market for a daddy."

"Understandable, but it's nice to have friends."

"Absolutely." Leith turned off the sink and grabbed a handful of paper towels. "And at least he seems the type that would show up when he says he will."

That morning I'd found Leith sitting on the steps alone, looking dejected. When he'd told me that the guy he was supposed to be going on a hike with hadn't shown, I'd felt bad for him and was glad to be able to offer an alternative.

"Come on, y'all," Arden said, hip checking me out of the way so he could use my sink. "Let's get back out there. I'm starving!"

———

TWO DAYS LATER WALKING INTO WORK, I WAS STILL SMILING. We'd ended the day of the charity ride out at Lex and Arden's cabin with a bonfire and plenty of laughs. Toward the end of the night, Mace had brought a lounge chair down from the porch and set it back in the grass, just on the edge of the firelight. He'd stretched out in it and patted the space between his legs, so I'd sat there, my back to his chest and his arms around me as we listened to the Heretics swap war stories from times out on the road in the soft light of the flickering fire and the stars overhead.

I didn't think I'd ever had a better day in my life. And if teenage me had known that someday we'd have found a family, a real family in Arden, Vivian, and now Mace. I'm sure I wouldn't have believed it.

I stepped through *Spritz's* basement door and made my way through the still empty lounge. I was early, something I hadn't been in too many months, and I waved at the guy setting up the bar as I made my way to the opposite door and the stairs that would take me up to the main level. As soon as I stepped into the club proper, one of the bartenders lifted their head from where they were stocking glasses and waved at me.

"Hey, Pax, Vivian was looking for you. She wanted you to step into her office before shift starts."

Nervous flutters flared up in my stomach, because even with all the warm thoughts. I'd just been having, my first instinct was always disaster. My mind raced with possibilities of what I could have done wrong, but I took a deep breath and told myself that I was being silly, and that jumping to conclusions wouldn't do anyone any good. I made my way to the back and knocked on Vivian's door.

"Come in," she called.

Pushing open the door, I walked inside and was relieved when she smiled at me the same way she always did.

"Hi, Pax, please have a seat." She must've been able to see the trepidation on my face because she added, "You're not in trouble."

A little chuckle escaped me and I shot her a smile as I settled into one of the comfy seats across from her desk.

"How have you been doing Pax? It feels like forever since we caught up."

"I've been good, honestly. Things have gotten easier in the last couple of months."

"I've noticed which I think is excellent, and I've noticed that you've been spending some time with Mace."

I shifted in my seat, not so much uncomfortable as concerned about how I would answer questions if she had them. Because I was certain that I didn't have all the answers myself. "Yes, we've been, uh, seeing each other for a little while now."

"I think that's great. Mace is a standup guy, but that's not what I wanted to talk to you about." Vivian folded her hands together and leaned forward, resting her elbows on the sleek black top of her desk.

"Pax, how would you feel about training to step into the assistant manager spot for the lounge?"

I was stunned. It was like my brain forgot how to make words and I stared at her, my mouth flopping open like a fish, as warmth spread my chest. When my brain came back online, my smile split my face. "I would love to. Are you sure? I've never been a manager before."

Vivian chuckled, but she had that knowing smile on her face. "I know, but I've been watching you for years now and you have the qualities that make a good manager, Pax. You really do. With training, I think you would excel in this kind of position."

Tears stung my eyes, and I said the only thing that I could say. "Thank you, Vivian. I would love the opportunity."

We chatted for a while longer about salary and benefits—both of which blew me away—and about the added responsibilities and type of schedule I would have to keep. When it was almost time for the club doors to open, she and I made our way out onto the club floor, still talking and bouncing ideas about how we could improve the lounge area. The same bartender that had told me Vivian wanted to see me looked up at our approach.

"One of the servers isn't here yet. Leith."

I frowned and a glance at Vivian showed a similar expression on her face. It wasn't like Leith to miss a shift.

"He hasn't called?" Vivian asked as she pulled out her phone to check her messages. I did the same in case he called me. But there was nothing, not even a message from Mace. He was on a different security job for the night and said he'd be on his bike a lot.

"Maybe he's just running late," I offered, even though that didn't feel right.

"Let me know when he gets in," Vivian said to the bartender before giving me a pat on the back and heading back to her office.

I headed back to the dressing rooms backstage and pulled off the T-shirt and track pants I'd slipped on over the gold boy shorts I'd opted to wear that night.

Wednesday nights, the first night of the week *Spritz* was open were never as busy as Thursday, Friday or Saturday. The night still turned out a respectable crowd and kept me busy enough that I wasn't constantly thinking about Leith, but also slow enough that the pit of worry in my stomach kept growing with every hour that he didn't show. By the end of my shift, I was feeling really concerned. I hadn't seen him since Sunday after we got back to Lex and Arden's. He'd roasted a couple of hot dogs with us and had a smore then Axel had offered to drive him home. If something had happened, I would know, because Axel would've told Mace and Mace would've told me.

In the dressing room, I threw my street clothes back on

and then went to find Vivian. She stood as I approached the booth she'd been sitting in.

"He's not answering his apartment door or his phone," Vivian said, crossing her arms over her chest before I'd even asked. "I've got Cleave pulling security footage from the apartment building. Let's go see if he's found anything."

We made our way downstairs to the little room that served as entrance to the lounge beyond. Cleave was behind the desk, his eyes on the multiple screens and his hand on the mouse. He glanced up when we came in before looking back at the screen and clicking several times.

"I was just about to call you Vivian. I think I found the last time he left the building."

Vivian and I walked behind the desk and looked at the screen over Cleave's shoulder.

"You can see here." Cleave pointed at one of the screens. "Where Axel brought him back after the charity ride on Sunday. And then just a couple hours later around three a.m., this guy walks up to the door and Leith comes back out." The angle of the camera showed the man from the back as he made his way up the steps to *Spritz Villa's* door. Then it showed Leith, phone in his hand and a scowl on his face, exiting the building. It looked like they had a short conversation then the man did something quick with his arm—a jabbing motion that we couldn't see very well—and bent down, throwing an unmoving Leith over his shoulder. Then he turned, looked directly at the camera and carrying Leith like a sack of potatoes, walked right back down the stairs.

Cleave clicked around some more on the computer and then zoomed in on the man's face. When the pixelated image came into focus, my heart jumped up into my throat and my blood froze my veins. There was no way, *no fucking way* I was seeing what I thought I saw. Vector was dead. Mace had promised... he'd *promised*, but there he was on screen with that fucking smile on his face.

And now he had Leith.

CHAPTER THIRTEEN

Mace

I stepped off my bike with a groan, pulling the helmet off my head and setting it on the seat. A friend of the club's company was transporting goods, and they had hired us as extra insurance to make sure that those goods arrived at their destination unscathed. That night, myself, Calix, Riot, and Barrett had served as escorts. We got the truck where it was going safely, and had stopped on the way back for gas and to stretch our legs.

Barrett walked over to the grassy area to the side of the gas station where I was standing and waiting on the others. He stopped beside me, sticking a cigarette in his mouth and lighting it before taking a long drag and letting out a plume of smoke. "How do you feel about this truce with the Devil's?"

He never had been one to beat around the bush. After the Devil's new President, Holden, had pulled his stunt showing up to Eben and Cody's housewarming party to apologize for his club's behavior, we'd all been on high alert. After some verification that Holden had spoken true and the Devil's really did want a truce—at least the Devil's who were left—

we'd done exactly as Calix had said we would and taken it to the table for a vote.

Unsurprisingly, it had passed, because no one really wanted a war and a legitimate truce with the Devil's meant quieter days where we could focus our energies on our business.

"I feel like it's a smart move. If they hold up their end and we hold up ours, kinda seems like a no-brainer."

"You really think they'll hold up their end?"

"I don't know, man. All we can do is handle our own business and not change the way we watch our backs."

Barrett shrugged, his frown making the already deep lines in his face look like ravines. "Their new Prez seemed eager enough. I'm more concerned about the members who walked away."

I folded my arms over my chest and cocked an eyebrow at him. "You think they'll seek retaliation?"

He sucked in another lungful of smoke before he met my eyes. "I'm sure they will. The question is, against who, us or them?"

Just like any one, Barrett could be absolutely full of shit, but he had been around for the long haul and seen other clubs fall apart. I tucked his warning away, knowing I'd bring it up to Calix at some point. As it was, there was nothing we could do about it now except toss around opinions and wait to see how it would all play out.

Personally, I was looking forward to some quiet time. Having Pax with me on the charity ride had been something I'd never realized I wanted, and it brought to the forefront just how much I'd come to crave him, to want him in my bed, in my life, on the back of my bike, always.

Calix and Riot exited the gas station and moved toward us. Barrett finished his smoke and tossed the butt on the ground, grinding out the ash with the toe of his boot.

When Calix was only a few feet away, he nodded in my direction. "Have you checked your phone?"

Frowning, I pulled it out of my pocket. I had checked it when we'd first stopped, but there were no messages, so I put it away and hadn't thought about it again. Now, I had three missed calls from Cleave and one from Vivian. I was instantly on alert because either something had happened at *Spritz* or something had happened to Pax. I unlocked my phone prepared to call Cleave when it started ringing silently in my hands, Cleave's name at the top of the screen. *Dammit, I hadn't turned the volume up.* I hit accept and pressed the phone to my ear. "What's going on?"

"We have a problem," Cleave said. "Leith's been taken. It was Sunday night. A couple hours after Axel dropped him off from the charity ride. He walked out onto the front steps of the apartments, talked to some guy, and the guy either popped him in the mouth or injected him with something and just fucking carted him off."

"What the fuck? Did the camera get a good look at the guy?"

"Yeah, I'm sending an image through now."

A second later my phone beeped, so I lowered it and clicked on the text from Cleave. The moment the image loaded, I swore my heart stopped in my chest. If I hadn't been the one looking into Vector's eyes as he died, the one plunging the knife into his heart, I would swear on my life that it was Vector in that image looking back at me. Whoever he was, the bastard had an arm wrapped around Leith's ass as he hung upside down over his shoulder and was looking at the camera with a smile on his face. Like he wanted us to see him, wanted us to know that he'd invaded our territory and taken a hostage.

Vaguely, the rumble of Cleave's voice reached my ear. I

realized he was still speaking to me, even though I lowered the phone. "Has Pax seen this?"

Cleave huffed. "That's what I was just trying to tell you. He was here with me and Vivian when I brought the picture up. He kind of freaked out and ran out of here like his ass was on fire. Vivian's been trying to get a hold of him because it looks like he got into an Uber just before I called you."

"Shit," I breathed. "Okay, this guy that's got Leith, he's got to be connected to the merc I *took out to dinner* a couple months ago."

I could hear Cleave suck in a breath before he spoke again. "The bastard that hurt Pax?"

"Yes. This guy has to be his brother or some relation because they look exactly the fucking same. See what you can dig up. We need everyone working on this. There were no known relations listed on the guy, but obviously this one was hiding under a rock somewhere."

"What are you going to do?"

"I'm gonna go find Pax." I ended the call and turned to the others. "Leith has been taken and Pax is missing." It was taking every ounce of my willpower to not completely lose my shit. I needed to remember my training and keep my head. So, one problem at a time. While Cleave was searching for clues that would hopefully lead us to Leith, I needed to figure out where Pax had gone. Where would he run?

Calix was looking down at his phone having obviously received the image from Cleave, as well. After a moment, he met my eyes. "Those boys are under our protection. I want everyone we have available out looking for this guy, talking to all our contacts, and I'll make a call. If the Devil's are serious about this truce, it's time for them to put their money where their mouth is."

"Agreed. I need to find Pax."

Calix gripped my shoulder with a nod. "Find your boy. Get him to the clubhouse and let's go find this bastard."

Lifting my phone, I hit Pax's number and pressed it against my ear. It rang and rang and then picked up. For a split second, my heart lifted, but it was only his voicemail.

"This is Pax. Leave a message."

"Pax, call me as soon as you get this, okay?" I hung up and clicked back to my contact list, selecting another name. When Arden answered he was breathless, and I had the distinct feeling I'd interrupted something, but I couldn't feel sorry, even for cockblocking my best friend.

"Mace? Is everything okay? You never call me."

"Have you heard from Pax?"

Arden instantly went from puzzled to worried. "No, I haven't talked to him since yesterday. Is he okay?"

I didn't want to freak Arden out, but I wouldn't lie to him, either. "I'm hoping so, but I can't get a hold of him. Leith was taken and the guy who took him looks like he's related to the man that hurt Pax. All I know is Pax left the club in an Uber, but nobody knows where he was going. Is Lex there?" Arden didn't say anything, but there was a rustle, then my friend's voice in my ear.

"What's going on Mace? Arden just went pale."

"Vector apparently has a brother or a cousin that looks just fucking like him."

"Is Pax, okay?" Lex's voice was low.

"The guy took Leith. Pax saw him on the security feed, and they look so much a-fucking-like that he panicked and left *Spritz* in an Uber. No one knows where he was going, and he's not answering his phone. I thought he might be on his way to Arden."

"We can stay here to see if he shows, but then you and I are going hunting."

"Agreed. Calix is already rallying everyone." My phone beeped in my ear. "Lex, Eben is calling me. He's at the club-house tonight. Let me call you back." I clicked over to Eben. Only it wasn't Eben on the other end.

It was Pax.

CHAPTER FOURTEEN

Pax

I'd panicked—heart pounding, brain scrambling— panicked. And the only thought that had broken through my muddled mind was that I needed to get to Mace. Before I knew it, an Uber was pulling up to the curb, and I was climbing into the back seat. The driver had shot me a funny look in the rearview when I'd climbed inside. When he pulled the SUV to a stop in front of the gate at the Iron Heretics' clubhouse, he turned his head and looked back at me over his shoulder.

"You sure you want to get out here, man?" I nodded, pulling a folded twenty out of my pocket to hand him. "Thank you," I said as I opened the door and climbed out.

He didn't hang around, driving off as soon as I walked up to the gate and pressed the intercom button. Eben had answered quickly, and he and Cody both had come out to meet me at the door.

"What's going on, Pax?" Cody asked, pulling me into a hug. I must've looked really shaken.

"Is Mace here?"

Eben stepped to the other side of me, wrapping his arm

around my shoulders and guiding me and Cody inside. "No, he's out on a run with some of the others, but they should be on their way back now. Have you tried to call him?"

Had I? The last hour was such a muddle in my brain that I wasn't sure. Once we were inside, I reached into my pocket for my phone to check, only to find it missing. "Shit," I said, patting myself down, but not finding the familiar shape of my device in any of my pockets. "I think I left my phone in the Uber."

"Okay," Eben said. "Here, use mine to call Mace, and Cody and I will figure out what we need to do to get your phone back."

I accepted the phone Eben handed me and stepped away from them, clicking on Mace's contact and pressing the phone to my ear. Mace answered on the second ring.

"Eben—"

"It's me, Mace."

"Thank fucking God, Pax, are you okay? I just tried to call you."

"I forgot my phone in the Uber." A tremble worked its way into my voice.

"That's okay, baby, we'll get your phone back. The important thing is that you're safe. You're at the clubhouse, right?"

I nodded and realized he couldn't see me. "Yeah, I'm here with Eben and Cody."

"You stay there, okay? Hang out with them or go up to my room if you want, and I'll be there as soon as I can."

"What about Leith?"

"We're going to find him, Pax. I promise you."

"Okay... Mace, I thought that he—"

"It's not Vector, baby."

I closed my eyes. Part of me whispered that he was lying, that of course he hadn't done what he said he would because no one ever really did. Except, I had people in my life that I could depend on now, and the larger part of me knew that Mace was one of them. He'd killed a man to protect me, and I knew in my bones that he was gearing up to do it again—without a second thought.

"Who is he?"

"We're working to figure that out."

"Mace," I said, searching for strength I wasn't sure I had. "I don't want to hide. I want to help." My voice started shaking again and came out in a whisper. "He's already had Leith for two days."

Mace was quiet for a moment, and I knew the same horrible thoughts going through my head would be going through his, too. "We're going to find him and you can help. Cleave will be sending video from around the club and apartments for the last couple weeks. Tell Eben to let you help review it. You'll be able to spot him better than any of us."

"Oh shit. I saw him. That day you found me on the steps. Remember?"

"You said the guy with Leith had reminded you of Vector."

"I didn't get a good look at his face that day." And the small glimpse I'd gotten had sent me spiraling.

"That's okay, it will help us form a timeline. Baby, I need to go make a couple calls and get on my bike. Will you be okay until I get there? Lex and Arden will be coming, too."

I lowered my chin and whispered, "You keep calling me that."

When he answered, his voice was just as low. "You are mine, aren't you?"

"Yes."

A whoosh of air sounded against my ear. It brought a smile to my face. "Mace?"

"Yeah, baby?"

"Be careful."

"I will. I'll see you soon."

I HAD TO LOG ON TO FILL OUT A FORM ON THE CAR service's website to report my lost phone. The driver called me back on Cody's phone, and we made arrangements for him to bring my phone back in a couple of hours. Not knowing exactly when Mace would be back or when Arden and Lex would arrive, I decided to go up to his room and take a shower.

Stepping into the room without him was strange, even though I'd been there a few times and didn't feel like an intruder. It was much the same as I didn't feel like Mace was a guest in my apartment, either. It was more like he belonged there—belonged in my space—and I belonged in his.

Going to his dresser, I dug through until I found a pair of sweats and a T-shirt, then went into the bathroom. It was larger than mine, with an extended vanity counter and a shower stall with plenty of room for two.

I stripped off my clothes, throwing them into the hamper with Mace's and got the spray going before stepping inside. The hot water felt like heaven on my skin, and I stood there, letting it beat against my neck and shoulders in an attempt to loosen and ease my tense muscles.

I told Mace I was okay, but seeing that man's face on the screen had really shaken me up. I'd been afraid plenty of times in my life, but nothing had compared to the totally helpless feeling I'd had when Vector tortured me. I shivered despite the sticky heat filling the shower stall. That night was one I wished I could burn from my memory, and I couldn't let myself dwell on the thought that whoever this man was, if he was anything like Vector, that he'd had Leith for two days. In an instant, the shower stall felt too confining, so I quickly scrubbed my body, washed my hair, and rinsed off. Shutting off the water, I stepped out, grabbing one of Mace's fluffy towels. I was drying myself when there was a tentative knock at the door.

"Pax?" Knowing Mace was so close sent a sharp stab of longing through me. I dropped the towel and rushed to the door, yanking it open before throwing myself into his arms. He caught me, just like I knew he would. I probably should've been worried by the fact that I was still damp and he was fully clothed, but I couldn't bring myself to care. I clung to him, wrapping my arms around his shoulders and burying my face against his neck. His strong arms enveloped me, holding me just as tightly.

"I'm here, baby," he said, his hands running up and down my back.

When I loosened my hold a little, he pulled back enough to meet my eyes. Cupping my face, he pressed his lips to mine. The kiss went from slow and steady to needy within moments. He threaded the fingers of one hand through my hair and gripped hard, tilting my head back and thrusting his tongue in alongside mine. I groaned, kissing him back just as passionately while my hands worked their way under his vest and around his back on down to cup his ass. I thrust forward, grinding us together, just wanting to feel him, but I knew we shouldn't take it any further. One of my friends was missing, and I knew that Mace was only here long enough to make sure I was okay before he'd be out, looking for Leith and putting an end to this nightmare.

"Scared the shit out of me when I couldn't get a hold of you."

I pressed up, leaning my forehead against his and took solace in sharing the same breath—the same space. "Sorry. I lost my mind there for a second. I know I should've called you first."

"It's okay. Now you're here and we're rallying everyone so we can go find Leith."

"Good. I'll help Eben go through the video footage and maybe we'll get lucky and find something."

"That will be perfect."

Mace glanced over my shoulder, a little smile forming on his lips. "Found you some clothes, I see."

"I didn't think you'd mind." Reluctantly, I pulled out of his arms and stepped back into the bathroom, pulling on my borrowed sweats and T-shirt.

Mace leaned his shoulder against the door jamb and watched me. "Hell no, I don't mind. I love the thought of you in my clothes." He cocked an eyebrow. "Especially commando."

I smiled at him and gave my body a little shake, knowing he'd be able to see my dick move behind the material of the sweatpants. Mace groaned and moved into my space, one hand reaching down to cup me through them. He pressed his face right up against mine, so that I could feel his breath on my lips.

"As soon as we get Leith back safe and sound." He gave me a little squeeze. "This is mine."

CHAPTER FIFTEEN

Mace

Walking away from a warm, freshly showered Pax, smelling like my body wash and wearing my clothes took Herculean effort. But I managed it. Somehow. I fixed him a sandwich and got him a soda—because I was sure he hadn't eaten since before his shift—then we both went back down to the main level of the clubhouse to find Eben, Cody, Lex, and Arden standing in the kitchen.

"Pax, oh my God, you scared the shit out of me," Arden said, rushing across the kitchen as soon as we entered and throwing his skinny arms around Pax's neck. Pax didn't protest, only wrapped his arms around Arden and hugged him tightly, nearly lifting the smaller man off his feet.

While they were embracing, I walked over and offered Lex my hand. He shook it before pulling me into a quick hug, as well.

"He okay?" Lex nodded toward where our boyfriends were speaking quietly to each other.

"He's pretty shaken up," I answered just as low. "But yeah, I think he's alright.

Lex nodded and folded his arms over his chest. "Calix and

the rest of the guys are in the garage. Eben's going to hold here, but your Prez wants the rest of us out there looking for Leith. He put in a call to Stone and Warrick, as well, to get them headed this way in case we can't settle this quickly."

I wasn't surprised at Calix calling in reinforcements. If he hadn't done it already, I would have suggested the same thing. There was no way of knowing how long this could take, or even if the guy still had Leith in the city or this state. My gut was telling me that he did. That whoever he was, he was here for one reason and one reason only—because I'd killed Vector and he was going to make me pay for it.

My real concern was why he hadn't come after me directly and why the intel I'd gathered on Vector had made no mention of a relative.

Pax and Arden broke apart and walked over to join us. Arden slipped easily beneath Lex's arm and up against his side like he'd done it a thousand times. Pax pressed against me, and I wrapped an arm around his shoulder, turning my head to press a kiss into his still damp hair.

"We'll keep you updated, okay?"

"And we'll let you know if we find anything." Pax looked up at me and I pressed a quick kiss to his lips.

Lex and I said our goodbyes and headed toward the garage. Once we made it a ways down the hall, Lex looked over at me.

"You think we'll find the boy alive?"

My first instinct was to say yes because my mind didn't want to consider any other outcome, but I knew that time and statistics weren't on our side.

"I think it depends on what this asshole is trying to achieve."

"Retaliation for taking out what we have to assume was his brother?"

I nodded. Nothing else made sense, but I wasn't sure why

he'd taken Leith. Unless Leith had been an easy grab to use as a source of information. We needed to find Leith as soon as possible. If he was only a source of information, and this guy had gotten what he needed out of him... I didn't like our odds at all.

———

WE'D SPLIT UP INTO TEAMS, WORKING OUR WAY THROUGH the areas of the city that lent themselves to higher crime rates and places where screaming might go ignored or unheard. Lex and Axel were riding with me, while Calix, Cleave, and Riot were on the other side of town. Eben was still holding the fort at the clubhouse, and Holden had made good on his word and had his Devil's out searching, as well.

We'd been out searching—talking to snitches and canvassing every seedy bar in our section of town—pushing people for answers and getting the word out that the Heretics were looking for this guy.

My phone rang with Pax's name on the screen.

"Hey, Pax," I said, sitting on my bike in an alley that smelled like trash and other rotting things. We'd stepped back out into the humid July air after talking to a bartender that had proven a reliable source of information in the past. "How's it going with the video?"

"I think we found something. We watched the abduction again, and Leith had his phone in his hand when he came outside, but when the guy carried him away the phone wasn't there. So, Vivian had her guys search in front of the apartment and found it off to the side behind the shrubs. She's going to text you a couple addresses Leith Ubered to in the last few weeks. Two of them are apartments that rent month-to-month."

"That's great," I said, nodding at Lex and Axel when they

both gave me questioning looks." My phone beeped against my ear and I was sure that it was Vivian with those addresses. "Okay, baby. I think Vivian just sent them through. I need to go."

"Be careful, Mace."

A little smile lit my face at the thought of him being worried about me. "Always, baby. I'll talk to you soon." We hung up and I looked at my companions. "They found Leith's phone and pulled a couple addresses that he's visited in the last few weeks. Apartment buildings."

"Hell yes," Axel said. "That's a good place to start, anyway."

I agreed and opened my text messages. The addresses were there from Vivian, but I also had one from Calix telling me which one they were headed to and for us to take the other. I pulled it up in Google maps. It wasn't far at all, so I closed my phone, stuck it in my pocket, and cranked the engine over. With any luck, the bastard would've gotten cocky, after being in our city for weeks without us noticing, and was still staying in the same place.

We flew down the street, weaving in and out of the little traffic there was as my blood ran hot in my veins, ready to put an end to this, ready to meet violence with violence and take back what was ours. To meet out the kind of retribution justified by such an insult.

We slowed down as we approached the apartment building, easing our motorcycles into an empty parking place close to the end of the lot. We stepped off and scanned our surroundings. The buildings were two stories, an ugly mustard yellow in the flickering glow of the security light with brown shutters and weeds growing up around the foundation.

Things were mostly quiet, but there was music coming from somewhere, dogs barking, and a group of guys sitting on the set of steps leading up to the building closest to us. I glanced over at Axel and Lex, meeting their eyes and getting a nod from each of them. Talking to those guys was our best bet, but we needed to approach it right as they were likely as territorial of their house as we were of ours.

We walked toward the stairs. The closer we got, the more I realized that these guys weren't as old as I had anticipated. There were five of them, and none of them looked like they could be much over twenty-one. I hoped that worked in our favor, and that they didn't feel like they had something to prove. I also hoped it meant they knew who we were and that we weren't to be fucked with.

"Evening, gentlemen," I said, infusing my voice with the easy-going tone that led people to believe I was their friendly neighborhood biker.

"Hey, man. What can we do for you?" the guy sitting at the top of the steps asked. He had a patch of acne on his cheek, half covered by wiry scruff, and enough tremble in his voice that I knew he understood exactly who we were.

"You guys look like you keep tabs of the goings on around here. We're looking for a friend of ours."

"A friend?" He sounded skeptical and some of the others shifted around like they were uncomfortable. Good. These guys weren't real thugs and the more intimidated of us they were, the quicker they'd be willing to give us what we wanted so we would leave. It honestly wasn't hard to be intimidating with Lex and his *I will murder you* stare on one side and bald, hulking Axel on the other, arms loose and hands flexing like he was one wrong word away from ripping every one of them to shreds. Sticking my hands in my pockets just deep enough that my vest bulged open and gave a glimpse of the glock riding under my arm didn't hurt either, I imagined.

The leader's eyes slipped down to my gun and quickly back up to my face.

"What friend?"

Holding his gaze, I reached into my back pocket and pulled out the folded picture of the man that took Leith. Cleave had cropped it so you could only see his face and shoulder, but it was clear enough to make an ID.

I held it out to one of the guys closer to me, who took it and passed it back. As the leader was scanning the photo, Axel said, "We're also looking for this guy." He held out his phone with the screen facing them. It was a picture of Leith sitting on the back of Axel's motorcycle. Immediately, one of the guys eyes widened.

I pounced. "You've seen them?"

The guy nodded, eyes still fixed on Leith's picture on Axel's phone.

"Yeah," the guy said, licking his lips. "Seen him a couple times going in and out of 22B."

Axel locked his phone and stuck it back in his pocket. "Where's 22B?"

I took back the photo, folded it, and put it away while they told us that 22B was in the next building on the second floor. We thanked them and moved in that direction, none of us turning around to look when we heard sounds of them going into the building they'd been sitting in front of. I didn't blame them. Axel had looked absolutely murderous when the guy said he'd seen Leith here more than once.

The buildings weren't large. We all slipped on leather gloves as we stepped into the foyer of the second. There were four apartments on the first floor and I assumed four on the second, as well. The hallway smelled stale, a mix of dirt, paint, industrial cleaner, and the lingering aromas from the tenant's dinners.

We moved up the steps quickly, drawing our guns as we approached the door. Keeping close to the wall so as to not be seen out the peephole, I flattened myself beside the door, gun ready, and nodded to Axel. He pushed off the wall, and in a swift move planted his booted foot to the right of the door-knob, kicking it in.

I took point, storming into the room gun up, sweeping the small space and finding no one. Lex and Axel moved in behind me, pulling the broken door closed, and as a team we moved forward, clearing the apartment.

It was dingy with brown carpet and walls that I was sure had once been white, but were yellowed from cigarette smoke and too many years without a fresh coat of paint. After clearing the kitchen and the hall closet, we made our way farther back. Once the bedroom was cleared, we turned back to the only door still shut.

We hadn't heard a sound since we opened the door. The single remaining door had light shining from beneath it. It had to be the bathroom. I took position in front of the door. When Lex pulled it open, I stepped in fast, but immediately lowered my weapon at the sight in front of me.

"Leith?" I said, my voice sounding hoarse even in my own ears. He was on his knees, head bowed with nothing between his bruised knees and the hard floor. He flinched when I'd spoken, but hadn't looked up, keeping his chin pressed to his chest and his hands behind his back. He was also naked, his flaccid cock hanging between his legs and possibly the only part of him that wasn't covered in bruises or cuts. I stood frozen, wanting to go to him and rip the dark leather collar from around his neck and get him out of there, but also terri-fied as to why he wouldn't even look up at me and that I would somehow damage him further.

That's when I noticed the chain. It's heavy links were attached on one end to the back of the collar around Leith's throat and the other to a bracket in the wall.

"Shit." Axel's voice was filled with quiet menace as he pushed past me. He moved around Leith and gripped the chain, wrapping it once around his fist before ripping the bracket out of the wall. The chain hit the floor with a thump. Leith started to tremble. Axel stood breathing heavily for a moment before he said, "Mace. Let me take care of him."

I could only nod. Gripping Axel's shoulder for moment, I looked back down at Leith, my heart aching at the thought of what he'd endured and the lack of reaction which was so far from the bratty boy I knew him to be. I stepped back out into the hall, closing the door until only a crack remained.

Lex was there, a hard look on his face as he stood staring down the short hall to the apartment door, covering our six. With Axel caring for Leith, my mind turned back to what we hadn't found in the apartment—the bastard that had done this to him.

CHAPTER SIXTEEN

Pax

It turned out the worst part of this night would be the waiting. It was fucking brutal to sit there in the club-house—even though I was with two of my best friends—and know that Mace and all the other guys were out there trying to find Leith. After the rush of realizing that Leith's phone must have still been somewhere in front of *Spritz Villa,* calling Vivian, and telling Mace about the addresses, things had been unbearably quiet.

Cody, Arden, and I were sitting in the clubhouse lounge. It was a large room filled with dark leather sofas, its own bar complete with barstools and neon beer signs, a huge flat screen TV mounted on the wall, and a couple pool tables.

"I'm gonna make hot chocolate," Cody said suddenly, rising to his feet. We were all sitting on the same couch, Cody and I at either end with Arden in the middle. "You guys want some?"

"That sounds yummy," Arden said, snuggling further into the plush cushions of the couch and resting his temple against my shoulder.

With a nod, Cody turned his eyes to me waiting for my

answer. In theory, hot chocolate sounded kind of perfect, but then so did a shot of Jack. Spiked hot chocolate sounded even better, but I didn't want to risk getting tipsy or falling asleep; plus, the Uber driver was due back soon with my phone. I hoped that having it back would ease some of the nerves currently rattling around in my stomach, that somehow knowing I was as connected as I could be would help.

"Pax?"

I shook myself out of my thoughts. "Yeah, thank you, Cody. That sounds good."

Cody walked out of the room and into the attached kitchen through a door on the left, and Arden snuggled even closer. I didn't know how he handled Lex being gone all the time, out on the road with Nomad business for the club. Even when Mace had club business, at least he was still there every day. If we hadn't made plans to see each other, which was rare these days, I usually still saw him at *Spritz*.

"You okay?" I asked Arden, reaching for his hand.

He gave a little shrug before pulling himself up to sit straighter on the couch.

"I just keep thinking about Leith." He shook his head and nibbled on his bottom lip. "When my uncle had me taken, I was so scared, and the things he had done to me..." Arden trailed off and I squeezed his hand tighter. "I know you know what it's like, too," he said after a moment.

I shook my head. "No, Arden, I didn't go through half of what you did."

He huffed. "Pax, you don't have to downplay it." My sweet best friend turned to face me, locking his gray eyes on mine, and showing the spine of steel that most people failed to notice at first glance. "You were tortured, Pax. Tortured because of my crazy-ass uncle. I know you don't blame me, so don't even try to pretend that's what this is about. But I do know *you,* and I know you bottle things up. I know you stuff them down, and maybe some things can be dealt with that way, but I'm just worried this isn't one of them." He gentled his tone. "I love you. And I'm pretty sure Mace loves you, and I know that we're both here for you, so you don't have to be ashamed or hide or downplay anything that you're feeling, ever. Okay?"

I pulled in a deep breath, my head spinning and my heart aching, because I forgot how much he *saw me* sometimes and how well he paid attention. Had he really just said Mace loved me? "Arden, I..." I cut off what I was about to say because somewhere inside I knew he was right. I did hide things. I did squash them down until I learned how to breathe through the pressure, until it became my new normal. I didn't want to do that with him, he was my best friend, my brother. And I didn't want to do that with Mace, because whether or not it was true that Mace loved me, I knew that I loved him.

I pulled in a shuddery breath. "I love you, too, and I'll try. I promise, I'll try to do better." Arden squeezed my hand, but whatever he was going to say was interrupted by JJ walking in. His hair was his typical jet black with electric-blue tips, and he was wearing black skinny jeans that looked like they'd been painted on and a *The Doors* tank top.

"Hey, JJ," I said, taking in the disgruntled expression on his face.

"Hey, guys," he answered, walking over to the couch we were sitting on and collapsing on the other side of Arden.

Arden turned so he was facing forward again, then looked over at our friend. "You okay?"

JJ let out a small huff. "Yeah, sorry, I don't mean to be pissy. I just got off the phone with Cleave. He wanted me to come in earlier tonight saying we were on lockdown, but I had a gig. And he was pissed that I didn't rush over here as soon as it was done." JJ swiveled his head toward us. "Is it true that someone kidnapped Leith?"

At that moment, Zach came rushing into the room. "Hey, guys... they wanted me to let you know they found Leith."

Arden and I both stood up, nearly speaking simultaneously as we asked if he was okay.

Zach ran a hand through his hair like he wasn't sure what to do with us. "I think he's busted up some but yeah, he's okay. Doc Joe's coming to check him over, anyway, just to be sure. Anyway, they need the truck, so I've got to go."

He rushed out of the room. Probably afraid we were going to fling more questions at him, but still, even knowing that much made my heart feel lighter. I wondered about Leith's condition. I hoped that Mace and all of them were okay. Surely, if one of the guys was hurt, Zach would have said something. He'd only said the doctor was coming for Leith, so I had to take that as a good sign.

Cody walked in from the kitchen holding four mugs, obviously having heard JJ come in. "Did I hear Zach say they'd found Leith?" He came over, setting the mugs on the coffee table and glancing between the three of us.

"Yes," Arden said, his voice taking on that happy quality when he was excited about something. He reached for his hot chocolate and took a sip, humming appreciatively and looking back at Cody. "Cody, this is delicious."

"Thank you." The sweet shyness Cody had since the day I met him always came out when someone paid him a compliment. I reached for my own mug, taking a long sip. It was smooth and warm, rich and creamy, and tasted like my favorite dark chocolate squares with salted caramel in the middle. It was fucking delicious. "Will you marry me?" I asked, looking up at Cody. He laughed and Eben's voice sounded from the door, "Sorry, but he's going to have to decline that invitation."

Cody smiled and went over to his boyfriend, giving him a quick kiss before they both looked back at us.

"Zach told you all that they found Leith?"

"Yeah, he did, is everyone else okay?"

Eben nodded. "As far as I know, everyone's good."

Cody's phone started to ring. He pulled it out of his pocket and glanced up at me. "The Uber is here."

Feeling relieved, I pushed off the couch and headed toward the door.

"I'm coming with you, Pax," Eben said, moving toward me. Cody's hand was still in his, but he stopped and looked back toward the couch.

"I think I'll stay here." It was obvious Cody wanted to speak to JJ. The two of them had grown close while they'd been roommates, and I was sure that even if he hadn't heard JJ's words, he would have been able to tell by the look on his face that he was upset. Arden must've figured it out, as well, because he sat his mug of hot chocolate down and stood.

"I think I'll walk out with you guys."

With that, Eben, Arden, and I made our way out the front door of the clubhouse. Sitting on the outside of the gate was the same white SUV that had dropped me off earlier in the night.

The July wind was warm, even this late, and the humidity in the air had me feeling sticky before we were halfway across the parking lot. The wind picked up, blowing clouds across the moon, and I had the distinct feeling that it was the kind of wind that blew in a storm.

When we got to the gate, Eben punched in a code and the whirring of gears filled the air as the metal barrier swung open. I walked to the driver side window, Eben and Arden not far behind me, and looked into the darkened cab. The driver that had been concerned about dropping me here earlier was staring back, my phone in his hand.

"Thank you so much for bringing it back."

"No problem," he said with a distinct waver in his voice,

which he then lowered. "Drop the phone on the ground and get into the back seat."

When his words didn't quite register, I met his eyes. Even in the dark, it was plain to see that they were widened in fear. I didn't understand what was happening until a subtle movement from the back seat drew my gaze.

He was there.

The man who looked like Vector was sitting in the middle of the back bench seat with the gun in his hand pressed just beneath the driver's ear. My heart seized up and bile rose in my throat. As I watched, the gunmen leaned forward only slightly and lifted his other hand, pressing a single finger to his lips.

The driver spoke again, "Drop the phone and get in the back seat."

"Is there a problem, Pax?" Eben asked, and out of the corner of my eye, I saw him moving forward.

Fuck. Eben was there. Arden was there. And I had no doubt that the monster in the back seat would not only shoot the driver, but that he wouldn't hesitate to turn the gun on my friends, either. On liquid knees, I shook my head in Eben's direction, unable to push the lie past my teeth and shifted toward the backdoor. I hadn't given Eben enough credit, because he immediately reached for his gun and started forward.

Just as I gripped the handle of the back door, it pressed open and the gunmen leaned out pointing the gun between the frame of the door of the SUV as he grabbed me by my shirt with the other hand.

A gunshot rang out. I heard Arden scream my name, even as I was being wrenched around the door and hauled into the SUV. The gunman yelled for the driver to go. I lashed out at him, the thought of being held against my will again unsticking my brain. I surged up trying to fight him off and scrambling to open the door. I didn't even see the fist coming until it smashed into the side of my face making pain blossom in my head and my ears ring. I gripped my head and at the squeal of tires, squinted open my watery eyes, trying to turn my head to look back, to check on my friends, but we were already gone.

CHAPTER SEVENTEEN

Mace

When Zach arrived with the truck, I stayed upstairs playing lookout, while Lex went down so he and Zach could load Axel's bike into the bed. Once we found Leith, my first instinct had been to text Pax, and I almost reached for my phone until I remembered that he still didn't have his back. Instead, I text Eben, asking for the truck and for him to let Pax and Arden know that we found Leith. I debated whether to have him tell them that we hadn't found Leith's abductor and in the end, decided against it.

I was hopeful we would still catch the bastard, and I wanted to tell Pax myself, if only so that I could be there if he needed me. My phone beeped in my pocket, and I pulled it out. It was a text from Lex, letting me know that they'd gotten the bike loaded and we could bring Leith down. I was glad, for more reasons than one. I was starting to feel twitchy standing around this apartment. We'd been there too long and I wanted to be out there running this guy down.

I walked to the bathroom door and rapped my knuckles against it gently. A moment later, the door pulled open a crack and Axel's face appeared.

"They got your bike loaded. Do you need help getting him downstairs?"

Axel's eyes glanced back into the interior of the room before coming back to mine. "No, I've got him if you don't mind getting the door?"

"No problem. I'll be in the living room." I stepped away as Axel stepped back and pulled the bathroom door open. I didn't look inside, but turned and walked the short distance to the living room. A minute or two later, Axel stepped out into the hall. He was bare chested beneath his vest, and had Leith cradled in his arms with Axel's black T-shirt swallowing his small frame. The only sign of the chain and collar was the red ring around Leith's throat.

As Axel moved down the hall, Leith didn't move or make a sound, only kept his face buried against Axel's neck and his body curled in tight against the bigger man's chest, with his arms cinched around Axel's neck. The dark T-shirt covered him to midthigh and the sleeves hung to his elbows, but there were still far too many bruises on his exposed skin.

Boiling, chaotic rage welled up in me at how small he looked, how dejected, and at the dirty soles of his feet. The look in Axel's eyes told me that he and I were exactly on the same level. The man who'd done this needed to die—slowly, painfully—and we wouldn't rest until he'd met that fate.

Giving Axel a small nod, I turned toward the door and pulled it open. He stepped past me, being cautious not to bump Leith's feet against the door frame. Once he was in the hall, he stood back to let me pass, so that I could go down the stairs before them. We moved slowly as Axel cautiously took the stairs one at a time.

We walked out the front door and found Lex and Zach standing beside the truck—with Axel's bike in the bed—at the base of the steps.

Zach's eyes opened wide as they scanned over Leith, and he clenched his jaw. I glanced at Lex, knowing his expression would mirror my feelings, as well. Our hunt definitely wasn't ending here. Once Axel had both feet on the pavement of the parking lot, Zach pulled open the passenger side door of the truck.

"Open the back," Axel said.

Zach moved quickly to do as he asked. Axel walked past us and right up to the open back seat. He whispered something to Leith, and the boy gave the tiniest of nods before crawling into the seat while keeping one hand fisted in Axel's vest.

Axel glanced over at me. "I need to go with him."

I wouldn't have argued, anyway, but there was absolutely no way I'd deny Leith any comfort he wanted at that moment.

"Of course. Take care of him. We'll let you know if we find anything."

With one more nod to all of us, Axel climbed up into the back seat with Leith and Zach pushed the doors close.

We said our goodbyes to the Prospect and made our way over to our bikes as the truck pulled out of the parking lot and headed toward the clubhouse.

My blood was thrumming through my veins. I both wanted to stain my knife with this asshole's blood and to run back to the clubhouse so I could wrap Pax in my arms. I wanted to feel him alive and well against me, heart steady and arms strong. I'd known I loved him for a while, even if I hadn't been ready to acknowledge the words to myself or anyone else. At that moment, I was ready to tell him. I loved him and if he would have me, he'd never be alone again.

Lex was quiet as we made our way to our waiting Harleys, seemingly as lost in thought as I was.

I needed to call Calix and give him an update. I threw my leg over my Harley and sat down, but as soon as I pulled out my phone, Lex's started to ring. He dug it out of his pocket, accepting the call and pressing it to his ear. The moment the call connected, Lex's body went tense. I couldn't make out the words, but I could hear the frantic edge in Arden's voice from where I was sitting.

"Baby, slow down," Lex said, straddling his own Harley. He listened again for a moment, his dark eyes moving over to hold mine. "Arden, I need you to listen to me carefully. Doc Joe is already on his way. Axel and Zach will be back there soon, as well. When we hang up, call Calix and tell him what happened. Don't worry, Mace and I are going to get him." Lex told Arden he loved him and hung up the phone.

"Just tell me," I ground out, not sure I could handle sugar-coating. That wasn't normally something I had to worry about with Lex, but the look on his face told me that I really, *really* wasn't going to like what he had to say. Lex strapped his helmet on, so I shut my phone, put it back in my pocket, and did the same.

"The guy showed up the clubhouse. He shot Eben and took Pax. They're in a white SUV. Arden thinks it was a Ford, and they were heading west out of the industrial park."

Lex cranked over his bike, and I swore it was only my years of training in the military and my years of dealing with horrible situations as a Heretic that kept me upright. I couldn't think about this new monster having Pax, couldn't think about one of my club brothers being shot, or Arden being basically alone there trying to hold it all together.

I cranked my own engine over, then Lex and I were tearing out of the parking lot. We were ten minutes from the clubhouse, and if we hurried, there was a good chance we would intercept the SUV before it got completely out of the park and back to main roads.

I twisted the throttle, my bike roaring beneath me as I willed the tires to move faster—willed, prayed, begged—any power in the universe that would listen to keep Pax safe and to help me get to him.

We flew down the road, blowing through a stop sign and a red light, uncaring if there was a cop around. They could chase me down and throw me in a cell as long as I got to Pax first. Lex was keeping steady pace with me, holding just a bit behind on my right.

I kept my eyes scanning, heart jumping every time a white vehicle came into view. The wind whipped over and around me, making me feel like I was fighting the current in water that was trying to pull me under. A glance in my side mirror showed a set of headlights coming up fast.

I braced for anything, but as they caught up, what had looked like a single pair of headlights separated into two, and then Calix was speeding up to get beside me. I slowed only a fraction and he lifted one hand motioning to the right before he sped up and got in front of me, turning on his turn signal.

I took the turn at a dangerous speed, leaning into it and feeling that stomach-flipping moment when your balance is hanging on a knife's edge. As soon as we were back on a straightaway, Calix laid into his throttle pulling ahead. I kept myself hot on his heels, just behind and to his right. Cleave had moved up beside me, and Lex rode center behind the two of us, keeping us in a diamond pattern as we raced along.

We were approaching a stop sign, but Calix showed no sign of slowing down. Only moments before we reached it, a white SUV blew through it without so much as tapping the brakes, with a motorcycle riding hot on his bumper.

Without thought, I swerved into the parking lot of the gas station beside us, cutting across the corner of the intersection and storming out the other side. The others with me took the turn, but I was right behind the other biker now.

His bike wasn't familiar, and it took me a second to realize it was Holden from the Devil's Rage MC. The SUV in front of us was erratic, swerving all over the road and still picking up speed.

The windows were tinted, making it impossible to see inside. We needed to get this thing to slow down. The farther we went out on this road, the farther out of the city we moved. The lanes got wider, but light became more scarce as street lamps were fewer and farther between. With Calix, Lex, and Cleave having caught up, I swerved out of the side, getting up alongside the SUV. I got as close as I dared and beat my fist once on the back driver side door.

"Pullover!" I screamed, not even sure that he could hear me. If Pax wasn't inside, I would've already pulled my gun and blown the tires, but he was and I had no way of knowing what shape he was in or if he even had a seatbelt on. A gunshot sounded from within the SUV. I caught the muzzle flash out of the corner of my eye, but didn't see a hole. Panic seized my chest. Two more shots sounded and the SUV careened off the road, hitting the ditch and rolling over once completely, and then half again, before coming to rest on its side.

I brought the bike to a stop, pulling to the side and slamming on the brakes and spinning on the gravel there. Throwing my kickstand down, I leapt off my Harley, Pax's name pouring out of my mouth in a hoarse scream.

I ran to the SUV, sliding down one side of the ditch and jumping up the other.

"Mace! I'm here!" Pax's voice, as a ragged as it was, was the best fucking thing I'd ever heard.

Running to the front of the SUV, I found the driver trying to push out what was left of the busted windshield with his feet. I grabbed the edge and started to pull.

Another pair of leather-gloved hands joined mine. Cleave grunted as we both pulled hard, tearing the mangled windshield away from the SUV.

"I don't know what the fuck was happening," the driver babbled as we helped him crawl out of the vehicle. "That guy got in and had a gun, and he made me drive like a maniac—" Cleave grabbed the driver's arm and pulled him back away from the SUV and around to the exposed underside of the vehicle. Lex joined me, gun drawn and pointing into the darkened interior.

"Pax, are you hurt?"

"I'm okay. Mace get this guy off me!"

I surged in, climbing through the hole where the windshield had been. It was darker in the car, but a small amount of moonlight was coming through the windows that were aimed up at the sky. Pax was lying against the door that was on the ground, looking like he was struggling to get his seatbelt undone. The blond haired man who'd taken Leith and kidnapped Pax was slumped against him.

The man looked stunned, like the wreck had jarred him because he wasn't wearing a seatbelt. Getting my footing, I reached back with both hands, grabbing the bastard and yanking him away from Pax. I managed to haul him into the front seat. Lex grabbed a hold of him, as well, and pulled him outside. With him out of the way, I reached down and pulled out my knife and leaned over the seat. Pax was still trying to get the seatbelt open, and I lay my empty hand over his.

"Baby, let me get it."

He stilled at my touch, dark eyes looking up to meet mine. There were tear stains on his cheeks and his breathing was too fast. Working quickly, I cut his seatbelt and slipped my knife back in its sheath. Getting my hands under his armpits, I helped him climb out of the seat and into the open air. We stumbled a bit trying to get through the windshield opening while still holding onto each other, but we managed.

I held him against me, relief making my body sag. Pulling back, I cupped his face. "Are you hurt?"

"No, I'm okay, I think."

I pressed a kiss to his lips, knowing that we needed to get a move on. There was no way somebody hadn't heard that crash and called the cops. I turned to look at my brothers.

Calix was standing with his arms crossed over his chest, looking down at the blond haired man on his knees. Lex had his gun pressed against the back of the bastard's skull.

I held Pax tighter.

Calix looked over at me. "What do you think Sergeant?"

God, how I wanted the bastard to suffer, but I wanted Pax and Leith to have peace of mind more. I hoped Axel would agree with me. "I just want him gone."

Calix nodded at me, and then gave a single nod to Lex. I lifted a hand to turn Pax's face toward my chest as Lex put his gun back into his holster, grabbed the bastard's head and with a quick twist, snapped his neck.

Pax gasped, but didn't say a word.

Calix took a step back toward where Cleave had taken the driver. "Bring him."

Cleave pulled the man over. Pax started to protest, but I shushed him.

Calix stood in front of the now quiet driver who glanced around at all of us, and then to the dead man lying in the grass.

"What's your name?" Calix asked.

"Matthew Harold."

"Okay, Matthew Harold. That man got into your vehicle and pulled a gun on you. To save yourself, you wrecked. He died in the crash. That's your story. The whole story, and the only one you're going to repeat. Understood?"

Matthew lifted his hands while nodding his head. "Yes, that's exactly what happened."

Calix nodded, satisfied. "Put that filth back in the vehicle, and let's get out of here," he said, just as we heard sirens in the distance

CHAPTER EIGHTEEN

Pax

B eing back in the clubhouse was surreal. As soon as Calix had threatened the driver, Cleave and the Devil's MC guy had picked up the body and thrown it back into the car. Mace had hustled me over to his bike and we'd all rushed away, leaving the scene behind us like it was a bad dream.

It had been a nightmare, but I was proud of myself, too. I'd fought him off when he'd tried to shoot Mace through the window. Grabbing his arm, I'd aimed it at the roof. Matthew had yelled for me to put on my seat belt, so I had, and then he'd run us off the road. I didn't know how, but I was going to find some way to thank Matthew because he'd probably saved my life.

I turned off the water in the shower and stepped out, finding my towel in Mace's hands instead of on the counter where I'd laid it. He held it up for me and I walked into it, letting him run the soft material over my body.

"How are Eben and Leith?"

"The hit took Eben high in the shoulder. It'll take a while, but Doc says he'll be okay."

"And Leith?" Mace looked down, letting me pull the

towel from his hands and finish drying myself. I was so thankful Eben was going to be okay, and I couldn't wait to hug Cody once we'd all gotten some sleep, but I was worried about Leith because no one had been forthcoming with the details of what had happened to him. It wasn't really like these guys to sugarcoat anything.

Mace leaned against the door jamb, watching me while I combed my hair and brushed my teeth.

"All I know is that Doc said his injuries aren't life-threatening and that Axel is guarding him like a dog with a bone. Not that I blame him. I think he just needs some space and Axel is making sure he gets it. Axel did say that Leith told him the guy, who called himself Dustin, apparently, had been asking a lot of questions about the club and our affiliations."

I rinsed my mouth and watched Mace in the mirror's reflection. "Do you...regret that we won't be able to ask him?"

Green eyes stared back at me. "Not for a moment."

I nodded as a wave of exhaustion swept over me. Mace's hands slid up my back, warm and calloused and guiding me out of the bathroom toward the bed. He pulled back the covers and tucked me in before pressing a kiss to my forehead. "Where are you going?" I wasn't even ashamed of the whine in my voice.

Mace smiled. "Just a shower. I'll be right back."

I nodded, settling in, and letting my body sink into the plush mattress. I must've fallen asleep because it seemed like in the next moment Mace was crawling into bed beside me, all his glorious and tattooed skin on display in the gray light of the morning.

He had closed the blinds enough that the rising sun was only muted light beyond the windows. As soon as he settled in, I rolled toward him, molding myself against his side with my head on his chest and my arm wrapped tight around his torso. He held me back just as tightly, pressing kisses into my hair and onto my forehead until I tilted my head back and sealed our lips together. We kissed for a while, slow and steady with an edge of quiet desperation that hadn't been there before.

We broke apart and he turned toward me, pulling me in until my head was tucked under his chin. We lay there for long moments pressed as close together as we could be. I'd never had someone's skin feel so good, so soothing against mine.

When he spoke, his voice was low. "Remember when I told you my dad was an abusive asshole?"

I nodded.

"I'm almost certain he killed my mom, and even if he didn't do it directly, the way he treated her would have done it, eventually."

I held on tighter. "I'm so sorry, Mace."

"She wouldn't leave him. I begged her over and over. Even set up an apartment for her here, but she wouldn't budge." He took a deep breath. "That's why I swore off relationships. Because if that was love, then I didn't want any part of it. I didn't want to end up like either of them—the monster that was killing his wife bit by bit or the prey so far into my delusion that I'd stay even when I could easily save myself."

My heart was pounding in my chest and my eyes filled with tears. I couldn't blame him, not at all, for how he felt about relationships, and I couldn't imagine the pain he'd been through watching helplessly as that scenario played out between his parents.

"Anyway, that's why I decided that I was going to go through life on my own. A lone wolf."

Just as my tears spilled over, he slid down, bringing us face to face.

"I didn't know about the family I'd find in the Marines then, or the Heretics. Didn't know that people that aren't my blood relation could treat me better than my family ever had." His voice lowered to a whisper, his lips brushing against mine as he spoke, "I didn't know about you."

"I didn't know about you, either. Being an orphan, I didn't know anything about love of any kind until I met Vivian and she brought me in off the street. Then I got this skinny roommate named Arden and my life changed." I met his eyes. "But not like this. I've never felt anything like this for anyone. Never had someone take care of me the way you do."

I sniffed, my hand moving up so I could run my fingertips over the wolf running across his chest. *The lone wolf.*

"I'm thinking it's time to get his mate tattooed running beside him."

My eyes snapped up to his.

"I love you, Pax."

I choked out a sob and buried my face in his neck. "I love you, too."

"PAX, YOU'VE GOT A DELIVERY," VIVIAN SAID FROM BEHIND me. It'd been two weeks since the fiasco with Vector's brother and slowly, life was starting to fall back into its normal rhythm.

It was my first official day as assistant manager, and while I was nervous, I felt prepared. The past two weeks had been filled with training and spending every possible moment with Mace.

We hadn't spent a night apart and he told me he loved me every single day. Sometimes, I felt like my heart would burst. It's rusty seams weren't used to that much affection, but I was adjusting.

Some things weren't all sunshine, though. Leith still wasn't up for coming back to work or having visitors. As far as I knew, he hadn't left Axel's room at the clubhouse at all. All of us at *Spritz* had sent him a big bouquet of flowers, his favorite chocolates, and a card signed with well wishes. Of course, it wasn't common knowledge what had happened to him. Most of the *Spritz* employees thought he was ill, and would be back with us before we knew it. I hoped he'd be able to come back, but I wasn't so sure.

"What is it?" I asked Vivian as I turned around from where I'd been straightening the stools at the lounge's bar. I gasped when I saw the vase full of beautiful pink peonies in her hands. I stepped forward, my eyes dropping from the flowers to the satin pink ribbon tied around the vase. There was something wrapped in the knot at its center.

"There's no card. Not that it needs one," Vivian said with a wink.

Rolling my eyes, even as a pleased smile pulled at my lips, I took the vase from her hands and set it on the bar. Carefully, I untied the ribbon and a wooden figurine popped out.

Two wolves. Running side-by-side.

Mace said he was going to get a second wolf placed next to the one already on his chest. It looked like he'd settled on a design. Pulling the little wolves close, I tucked them against my own chest and turned my head to catch Mace's eye.

He was standing off in one corner in his security uniform. He winked at me and lifted his hand to press over the spot where the wolf tattoo lived above his heart—

where I was going to live for the rest of my life.

Thank you for reading!

DISARM

Iron Heretics MC #2

PROLOGUE

Leith

Second weekend of July

Settling gingerly on the end of one of the wooden benches around the fire, I stared, transfixed, by the camaraderie happening all around me. I'd spent the day on the back of Axel's motorcycle as we followed the path of a charity ride to benefit veteran's and their families. I was supposed to have been going hiking and then sharing a scene with the same Daddy I'd hooked up with a couple of times now, Dustin. But he'd stood me up, and when Pax offered, I'd jumped at the chance to escape sitting alone and stewing all day.

I'd needed that scene. Needed to feel taken care of. It hadn't taken me long after my disastrous relationship with Malcolm—and despite the vow I'd made to myself that I'd never be someone's boy again, to figure out that having a Daddy wasn't really optional for me. I craved it. There was a deep-seated, burning *need* in me for a Daddy to please. A Daddy that would spoil me, cherish me, and spank my ass when I needed it. If only I could bring myself to trust someone enough again for that to happen. So far, the answer to that question had been a resounding— *hell no*.

The hook-ups I'd been having didn't come close to meeting that need, but they were better than nothing.

I shifted on the hard bench, my ass a bit sore from being on a motorcycle all day. I'd never ridden a motorcycle before. The first few turns and curves had me tightening my grip around Axel's muscled torso, but I'd quickly grown to enjoy the wind on my face and the sturdy presence of the man in front of me. All in all, it'd been one of the best days I'd had in years.

Everyone had been nice to me—even Stone, Axel's brother, and Calix, the Iron Heretics' MC President, who was the scariest motherfucker I'd ever laid eyes on.

"Soda or water?" Axel asked, appearing at my side with a red can of cola in one hand and a bottle of water in the other.

I looked up at him, my eyes traveling the solid lines of his big body, from the skull belt buckle to his black t-shirt beneath his Iron Heretics' vest to the full, silver-streaked beard before settling on the deep mahogany brown of his eyes. The firelight washed over his bald head, making it shine. He was sexy as fuck. I'd avoided him before today out of sheer self-preservation because I'd always thought he gave off that Daddy vibe. After today, I'd have to avoid him because there wasn't a single doubt in my mind—this man *was* a Daddy, through and through.

"Soda, please." *Daddy*. It was on the tip of my tongue.

He handed me the red can and slid onto the bench beside me, opening up the water bottle and drinking half of it in one go. I opened my can and took a big drink. The bubbles burned my throat going down, and I couldn't stop the small burp after they'd hit my stomach.

My face heated up, and I slapped a hand over my mouth. "Oh my god, sorry, excuse me."

Axel chuckled and patted my back before holding the half-empty water bottle in my direction. "Here. Have some of this, too. It was hot on the bike today."

My face got even more red when he rested his palm on the bench behind me and leaned toward me a little. He wasn't touching me, but I swore I could feel the heat of his hand on my hip through my jeans. We traded drinks. I took an equally big drink of the water and immediately felt some of the sleepiness that had been pulling at my eyelids evaporate. I must have needed that more than I thought.

Axel took a big drink of the soda, burped, and shot me a wink before asking, "Hot dogs or smoked sausage?"

"Huh?"

"Do you want hot dogs or smoked sausage?"

I licked my lips. "Um...what are you having?"

His lips pulled up on one side. He really had the nicest face. His head was that symmetrical round shape that looked amazing and tough for men with no hair. With the fullness of his beard, I wondered if it was an entirely aesthetic choice instead of a necessary one. Down from there, his thick neck and muscled chest, shoulders, and arms were partly intimidating and completely doing it for my libido.

"Sausage, I think."

I nodded. Probably like a bobblehead. "That sounds good to me, too."

"Do you have any food allergies or condiments you don't like?"

"Um, no. I'm really not a picky eater."

He watched me for a moment, head tilted down, those dark eyes roaming from holding mine to my lips and back again. "Okay." He hefted himself up. "You stay right there, and I'll bring you another water before I cook our food."

I nodded, terrified that if I opened my mouth, *Yes, Daddy*, would pop out. Watching him walk up the path to the cabin where all the food stuff was laid out on a long table, I drained the rest of the water bottle then started in on the soda he'd left behind.

Pax, my friend and co-worker, sat down beside me, a huge smile on his face. "I take it you're having a good time?"

I nodded. "It's been a good day. Thanks for asking if I could come." I was pretty sure that up until recently, Pax hadn't been all that fond of me. Not that I could blame him. Morphing into a brat tended to be my default setting, and since Pax and I worked together at the gay night club, *Spritz*, he'd seen plenty of it.

"You're welcome. I'm sorry that guy didn't show up for your date." Pax was a good guy. Taller and broader than me with dark hair, eyes, and olive skin, he was dating the Sergeant-at-Arms of the Iron Heretics, Mace. Mace was also the head of *Spritz's* security team. Truth was, I'd always found him attractive and tried to get him to take me to bed, even though he wasn't exactly my type. He only had eyes for Pax, though.

"It's okay. Really, I don't think there's any way it could have been better than this." I bit my lip before drinking more of the soda, wondering if Pax would understand what an admission that had been for me.

He smiled. It was warm and made my chest feel tight. I really hoped we could be friends. If I wasn't going to have a real Daddy, I'd need friends. Good ones. Pax was a good one.

Axel stopped in front of us, a bottle of water extended toward me and the other hand holding a long metal grilling stick with four sausages on the prongs. He winked at me again as I took the water.

"Thank you," I said as he turned and stepped closer to the fire, holding the roasting stick out over the flames.

Pax nudged me with his elbow, one eyebrow raised.

I lowered my voice. "Like I told you before, I'm not in the

market for a Daddy." It wasn't a lie. No matter how badly I wanted to be someone's boy...I couldn't. Not full time. Not after what had happened last time.

"Doesn't mean you couldn't date him though, does it?" Pax asked, looking thoughtful. "I mean, I'm not personally into the whole Daddy-boy dynamic, so I could be wrong, but it isn't always an *all the time* thing, is it?"

Clearing my throat, I shot a glance at Axel's back, hoping he couldn't hear our whispers. "It doesn't have to be, but..." I didn't know how to finish that sentence without giving everything away. Because I'd only spent eight solid hours with the guy and already knew...if I was with him, he'd be my Daddy. End of story.

Pax nodded. "You don't have to explain. He's a good guy is all I was getting at."

"I know."

Pax excused himself and headed back over to his boyfriend. The bikers were a lively bunch—talking, laughing, eating, and drinking. The sky above was starting to darken. Being July, with the longer days of summer upon us, I assumed it was around nine p.m. I could have pulled out my phone to check, but for the first time in a long time, I didn't want to. Didn't want to worry about the time or if I'd gotten any messages. All I wanted was to sit there and pretend that these were my people, and that the big, beautiful bald man walking toward me with two heaping plates of food, fresh cans of soda stuck in the pockets of his vest, and a smile on his face was really mine.

I'd been home for an hour, and the emptiness was already clawing at me. It was late, after one a.m., and I really should crawl into bed and let sleep soothe the ache in my chest. Instead, I was scrolling through a hook-up app, a blind desperation threatening to choke me. Why hadn't I asked Axel to stay? He would have. I knew he would. But he worked security at *Spritz* too and that meant it couldn't be a one and done. I'd be faced with the temptation of him nearly every day, and if I had him once, there was no way I'd be able to walk away.

So, the apps.

Closing my eyes, I sucked in a deep breath.

I'm okay. I'm home, in my own apartment, and I don't need to have someone to look after me. I can look after myself. I said it over and over in my mind, breathing slowly and deliberately.

A single tear welled up and spilled down my cheek as the same voices that so often drowned out my own were shouting and sneering inside my skull.

You'll never amount to anything, Leith. You can't even take care of yourself.

You know you're not going anywhere. I own you. You'd never make it without me.

My phone buzzed in my hand, shattering the endless, overwhelming noise in my head. The notification on the screen said I had a new message.

I clicked into the app and found a message from Dustin. An apology and a request to see me tonight. It was late, but since it was Sunday, that meant I didn't have to work until Wednesday night. Knowing I'd have plenty of time to sleep off a scene tomorrow, I messaged him back saying I'd meet him out in front of my building, but that I expected that apology in person. I was still pissed that he'd blown me off all fucking day without a word, and pissed that he wasn't who I actually wanted him to be, but he was what I had just then. So I'd make him grovel a little, and then let him take me back to his shitty apartment and give me what I desperately needed.

Ten minutes later, I pushed through *Spritz Villa's* front doors and out into the warm night air. Dustin was standing on the top step. He was a lot taller than me—which wasn't an uncommon thing—and dressed in dark clothes. His head was actually free of the ball cap he was so fond of wearing, and his blond hair shone in the golden glow of the streetlight.

"Hey," I said, coming to a stop in front of him. When he didn't immediately respond, I frowned.

For a moment, he stood completely still, staring at me with his hands stuffed in the pockets of his jeans.

"Um, hello? If you think I'm going anywhere with you before you apologize, you're dead wrong—"

Faster than I could blink, his face split into a wide smile, and he lifted one of his hands, jabbing a needle into my neck. I gasped at the pinch, and my eyes went wide as my heart stuttered out one completely terrified heartbeat before everything went dark.

CHAPTER ONE

Axel

Three Days Later

Someone had taken Leith. Not just someone. The brother of the man Mace had killed for torturing Pax for information a year ago. Somehow, the slimy blond asshole had gotten Leith to come down to meet him on the front steps of his apartment building, drugged him, and carted him off after pausing to smile for the fucking camera. Like he'd wanted us to know exactly who'd taken the red-haired boy that hadn't been far from my thoughts since I'd dropped him off Sunday night.

Only a few hours before his kidnapping, I'd wanted to ask him to come home with me, but decided instead to call the next day and ask for a first official date. I could admit when that call had gone unanswered, it had stung.

None of that mattered now.

Mace, Lex, and I were standing in the hallway of a putrid little apartment. After hours of searching, we'd found Leith. He was kneeling, naked and silent, on the hard linoleum of the bathroom floor. Lex stepped back, leaving Mace and I in the opening of the small room. My eyes kept traveling over Leith's body, unable—unwilling—to compute what I was seeing. Tearing my gaze away from the bruises covering his torso and the cuts on his thighs, my eyes landed on the dark collar around his neck...and the chain running from the back of it to a bracket in the wall.

Something broke inside me.

With a growl, I went straight to the wall and gripped the chain, feeling the metal bite into my skin as I wrapped it around my fist and gave a hard yank. Plaster cracked and gave as the bracket tore out of the wall. I let it fall to the floor with a thud. A bottomless pit of rage opened in my stomach as I sucked in air, trying to get myself under control. Ducking my head, my eyes caught on Leith's slender body covered in bruises and trembling on the floor.

He needed me. That single thought brought me back to myself.

"Mace, let me take care of him." I met my Sergeant-at-Arms' eyes, and we shared a nod of understanding. Someone would pay for this, but whatever Leith needed in that moment came first. Mace backed out of the room, pulling the door closed until only a small crack remained.

Taking a deep breath, I lowered myself down to my knees in front of Leith. "Leith? Can you hear me?"

Fear that he was locked inside his head as a way to cope ran through me. I didn't want to touch him without his permission, but I couldn't leave him here either. After a moment, he nodded. It was a small thing, the barest dip of his already tucked chin, but some of the tension seeped out of my chest.

"Can I help you up off the floor?" He had to be hurting. There was visible discoloration on his knees, and tremors wracked his body. It was taking everything in me to not wrap him up in my arms. "Leith." I kept my voice low and as gentle as I could make it. "Sweet boy, will you look at me?"

Slowly, he raised his head, and the tenuous thread holding my composure together stretched further. His bottom lip was split on one side. One eye was swollen shut, dark red and purple bruising surrounding it. As bad as that one looked, it was the other eye that worried me more. The gaze peering out at me from that single blue orb was distant and clouded with fear.

"Leith, it's Axel. I'm here to help you. You're safe now."

He licked his lips, eye darting from my face to the door and back again.

"The only people here are Mace and Lex. Pax and Arden's boyfriends?" I hoped that mentioning his friends would help jolt him out of his fog.

"Axel?" The cracked, hoarse sound of his voice was at once a complete relief and made me so angry I wanted to tear the goddamn room apart.

"It's me. Let's get you up off the floor."

"Okay."

I reached for him slowly, getting my hands under his armpits as I got back to my feet. He unclasped his hands from behind his back and held on to my forearms. His legs shook as he unbent them. With fingers digging into my skin, he planted his feet, breathing like he'd run a marathon.

"Easy," I told him when he stepped toward the sink and stumbled. "Leith, can I carry you?"

"Yes," he rasped, leaning more heavily on me.

Without hesitation, I scooped him up bridal style and moved the short distance to the sink. It was dingy and devoid of anything other than a single bar of soap. The chain was dragging behind us from where it was still attached to the back of the collar around Leith's throat. I realized it was long enough that he would have been able to reach the sink and the toilet. God, how long had that bastard left him here like this?

Gently, I sat him on the counter. He immediately ducked his chin even as his hands lingered on my arms, like he didn't want to let me go.

"Leith, are you...are you hurt badly anywhere?" I felt like an idiot for asking, but I needed to know. There were bruises all over his body, but I couldn't tell if there was more dangerous internal damage.

He shook his head, eyes still downcast.

"Hey." Slowly, he met my eyes. "If you'll let me, I think I can cut this"—I placed a finger on the collar—"off of you."

The trembling got worse. His fingers fidgeted and twirled in the dark hair covering my forearms.

I took a step closer and lowered my voice. "He can't hurt you anymore. Collar or not, you're leaving here with me tonight. You're safe now, Leith."

Biting his split lip, he nodded and pulled his legs up on the counter as he turned so that I could get to the back of the collar. It was snug against his skin, but I managed to slip a finger between him and the leather. Pulling out my pocket knife and keeping the sharp edge toward myself, I started to saw through it. Thankfully, I always kept my knife sharp. Otherwise, I would have had to leave him to find something else to use, and that really wasn't an option right now. There was no way I was walking out of this room without him in my arms.

Finally, the leather gave way. I quickly flicked my knife closed and stuck it back in my pocket, then carefully pulled the cut collar from around Leith's neck. There was a red circle where the collar had sat, like a heel rubbed raw after walking a day in new shoes. I didn't think my rage could get any hotter. Didn't think the protective—and if I was being honest, *possessive*—instincts rising up in my chest could be any stronger, but seeing the darkened skin where that collar had rubbed him raw felt like tearing open my chest and releasing some wild man that wanted to throw Leith over my shoulder and hide him away in my cave.

Leith let out a big breath and lifted one hand to his neck. He was pale beneath the bruises and looked so small sitting there naked on the bathroom counter.

Pulling off my vest, I laid it on the counter beside him and lifted my black t-shirt over my head. "Here," I said, holding the shirt up for him to slip his head and arms through.

He turned back to me and didn't hesitate to let me help him pull the shirt over his head. A knock sounded on the door. Leith startled, and without thinking, I put my arms around him. He snaked his around my waist and held on tight. It felt like a balm to have him pressed against my bare skin, his breath ruffling my chest hair and fingers digging into the skin of my back.

"It's okay. It'll be Mace or Lex."

He nodded and let me go. I pulled the door open only enough for Mace to see my face while blocking the rest of the room with my body.

"Lex and Zach got your bike loaded. Do you need help getting him downstairs?" Mace asked. I liked Mace. He was a good guy and an excellent Sergeant-at-Arms. It didn't surprise me that he'd called for the truck or that he knew there was no way I was going to be separated from Leith right now. I glanced back to the sink counter where Leith was still sitting, his eyes lowered and his hands in his lap, looking so small and beaten down, and I wanted to break something all over again. I couldn't fucking wait to get him out of there.

"No, I've got him if you don't mind getting the door?"

"No problem. I'll be in the living room." Mace stepped back and turned away as I pulled the door open.

"Leith," I said quietly, coming to stand in front of him and slipping my vest back on. "Our ride is here. Can I carry you downstairs?"

"Yes, please," he whispered and lifted his arms to wrap around my neck.

I got one arm around his torso and the other under his knees and lifted him off the counter. He curled in on himself so tightly that his knees were nearly touching his chest, and I felt like I was carrying nothing at all, let alone a full-grown man. My shirt hit him about mid-thigh. With the hand under his knees, I gathered the hem in my fist so it wouldn't droop and expose him.

"Okay?"

He nodded, forehead moving against my skin where it was pressed against the side of my neck.

"Then let's get you out of here."

CHAPTER TWO

Leith

Silence filled the cab of the truck. Axel had folded his big body into the small back seat with me, letting me press myself against his side. My body ached, and my mind felt fuzzy. I didn't know the guy driving, but he had a Heretics' vest on. My eyes kept drooping closed, making me jerk as I fought to keep them open.

"Easy," Axel whispered, setting his hand over mine where it rested on my thigh. "Sleep if you want."

"Where are we going?" I hadn't even thought to ask. That's how out of it I was.

"To the clubhouse. Our doc is going to meet us there."

I hummed. Resting my temple on Axel's upper arm, I let my eyes drift closed.

It felt like only a moment had passed before Axel's body jolting beside me woke me up.

"What the fuck?" Axel growled at the same time the guy in the front seat said, "Holy shit, that's Eben!"

The truck screeched to a stop, and the driver jumped out. There was commotion happening just outside the vehicle—

panicked voices and someone was crying. *Eben*...that was another member of the Heretics and Cody's boyfriend.

"Stay here, okay?" Axel said a moment before he swung the door open and climbed out too. Scooting to the window, I looked out to find we were halfway up the drive to the Heretics' compound. Arden and the driver were standing over Cody and Axel, who were kneeling next to someone on the ground. A moment later, JJ came running from the building pushing a gurney like you'd see in an ambulance.

Axel said something—I couldn't make out the words, just the deep rumble of his voice—then Arden was pulling a sobbing Cody back, and the driver and Axel were picking Eben up.

"Oh my god," I gasped. Eben's face was ashen and he was awake, but the shirt beneath his vest was soaked in blood. They got Eben settled on the gurney as headlights shone through the truck's cab from behind me.

Axel pointed at the driver, then Eben, and barked, "Get him to the infirmary!" Turning back to the truck, he jumped into the driver seat. "You okay?" He glanced in the rearview mirror at me even as the truck lurched forward.

"Yeah. Is Eben..." I was terrified to ask. Cody had looked absolutely shattered.

"The doc's here. He'll get Eben taken care of. Then he'll see to you."

I huffed. My injuries were so minor compared to whatever I just saw. "What happened to him?"

Axel's voice was grim. "Someone shot him and took Pax."

I pressed a trembling hand against my lips and squeezed my eyes shut. *Oh god.* After Dustin had chained me up, he'd asked me a thousand questions about the Heretics, about security at *Spritz*, and about Pax. And now he had Pax. It had to be him. "I-I think Dustin took Pax. The man that had me. He kept asking me questions about Pax and all of you—" My voice was a reedy, pathetic thing, and I couldn't finish that statement anyway as bile crawled up my throat and dry heaves racked my body.

The truck door opened, letting in a wash of humid air, and Axel reached in, pulling me to the seat's edge so I could spit outside. Throat burning and eyes watering, shame washed through me, leaving me feeling like I was baking inside my skin. Dizziness made my head spin, and the last thing I remembered was Axel's hands grasping onto me as I plunged toward the concrete.

"No, please!" I wheezed, breath taken by fear and pain. He pressed the knife against my skin anyway, as if he hadn't heard me at all. I knew he'd heard me. He just didn't care. "This isn't what we agreed! Red! Red!"

He pulled the knife away from my skin, and I sagged. "My boys take what I give. Your agreement isn't necessary." Sharp, stinging pain lanced through me as he cut a quick, bloody line across the top of my naked thigh. I screamed.

Jerking awake, I grunted in pain. Not the pain of a fresh cut, but the dull throbbing ache from all of them and the bruises combined. Gently, I eased open my one good eye and found a dimly lit room. A blind was pulled down over the only window, and soft gray light shone around the edges. Panic started to rise in my chest until I noticed that both the doors in the room were open—the first open wide revealing a darkened interior, and the second was closed until only a sliver remained, showing the hallway beyond. There was a beer company clock on the wall and a *Lazy-Boy* recliner in the corner. *The Heretics.* Axel had brought me to the Heretics' clubhouse.

The first thing I noticed, after my heart started to slow,

was the smell—clean with a hint of disinfectant. The second was the IV line taped against the back of my hand. A bag of clear fluids was hooked to a stand beside the bed. It looked like a real hospital bed too, with hard plastic risers on the sides and buttons to make it move up and down. I wondered if I pushed the little nurse icon if anyone would show up. Why was I alone? Had they figured out I'd told Dustin everything he wanted to know—or, at least everything I knew—trying to make him stop?

Murmuring voices reached me through the crack in the door, and I tried to brace myself—relief and fear pounding through my veins. Regardless of what they might do to me for having told Dustin what I knew, my traitorous mind and heart didn't want to be alone.

"Oh good, you're awake." An older man with gray hair and a kind face stepped into the room. Axel was behind him. "I'm Doc Joe. How are you feeling, Leith?"

My eyes darted from Doc to Axel. His bald head had a subtle layer of dark stubble and he looked tired, but his dark brown eyes were clear and trained on me. Swallowing against the dryness of my throat, I looked back at the doctor. "I'm hurting a bit, and I'm thirsty."

Doc Joe said to Axel, "Please go grab a couple bottles of water."

Axel looked from the doctor to me before he left the room.

"Now," Doc said, putting the ends of the stethoscope he had around his neck into his ears and gently pressing the other end to my chest. "Big breaths."

I breathed in as much as I could.

"Are you comfortable with Axel being present while we talk about your injuries?"

Once I exhaled, I nodded.

"You sure?"

"Yes. He saved me."

A small smile pulled up Doc's lips, and he pressed the scope back to my chest. "Another breath. I know it seems unlikely, but under all the gruff, they're decent boys. Even if they don't always color inside the lines." He gave me a little wink.

I decided I liked the doc even as I wondered how a sweet man like him ended up being on call for a biker gang like the Heretics. I immediately felt ashamed of myself. The Heretics had been nothing but good to me.

"Here we go," Axel said as he came back into the room. Instead of two water bottles, he had a bottle in one hand and an insulated tumbler with a straw sticking out of the top in the other. "I put one of them on ice."

"Thanks." I reached for the tumbler immediately, only to wince as stinging pain lit up my arm and chest.

"Easy." Axel's voice was a soft rumble. He stepped up beside Doc and held the cup close enough to my lips that I could get to the straw. I took a couple of grateful swallows.

"You don't need me to tell you that you're pretty banged up," Doc started, pulling out a penlight and shining it in my eyes. "Only a few of the cuts needed stitches, but between those and the bruising, you'll be sore for a while. I want you to take it easy, but I also want you to get up and walk up and down the hall several times a day. Have you been to pee yet?"

My cheeks went hot. "No, but I need to."

"Okay, let's get you up then. Do you want Axel to step out?"

I shook my head, and I swore Axel looked relieved. Doc lowered the rail on one side of the bed. Moving my legs was hell. Both my knees were swollen from being on the floor for so long—Dustin had told me he'd cut me again if he found me anyway but on my knees. The cuts on my thighs stung and pulled under their bandages. I grasped the hand Axel held out to me and slowly got to my feet, which I noticed were in a pair of those hospital socks with the grippy things on the bottom. The rest of me was still draped in Axel's t-shirt.

"Slow and easy." Axel stayed with me, holding my hand and keeping his other arm hovering behind me, until the bathroom door. "Will you be okay?"

Taking stock of my body, I found that while I hurt, I wasn't too unsteady on my feet. "Yeah, I think so."

"I'll be right here if you need me."

Looking up into his eyes caused my chest to get all tight and warm. "Thank you, Axel." I gave his hand a little squeeze then stepped into the bathroom, but I didn't close the door all the way.

CHAPTER THREE

Axel

Leith squeezed my hand before he let go. I was glad he left a crack open in the bathroom door. Not because I was trying to creep on him, but I didn't like the thought of barriers between us right now. Not after the night we'd all had and the shit storm the man who'd abducted him had created. I knew we needed to talk about that, which I was dreading. I'd seen the evidence all over Leith's body. I didn't want to know the details.

"He's going to be okay, Axel," Doc Joe said quietly from where he was standing at the end of the bed. Doc had kicked me out while he'd done his initial examination of Leith. I'd been pissed, but I understood. He wasn't mine, and I had no business nosing into his privacy like that. Even though I wanted to. Wanted him.

I nodded. A moment later, the toilet flushed and the sink came on. Leith appeared in the bathroom doorway a little paler than when he went in. He gripped my hand when I offered it, and we made our way back to the bed. Once he was settled, I pulled the blanket back up over him. Before I pulled it away, he reached out and took my hand. I brushed my thumb over his knuckles.

"Leith, I know you're tired, but I need to ask you a couple questions." Doc stepped up to the opposite side of the bed.

Leith turned his head that way and tightened his grip with a nod.

"Did the man who took you, force himself on you? Anally or orally?"

After pulling in a shaky breath, Leith spoke quietly. "No. He did ejaculate on me though, a-after...after he cut me."

Red swamped my vision. The image of that blond bastard taking pleasure in Leith's pain, his fear, sent my bloodlust catapulting into the stratosphere. Leith's thumb stroked the side of my hand like he was trying to comfort me. Fuck. I took a slow breath and smoothed my thumb over his hand in return. I needed to be strong for him, not the other way around.

Doc reached for his other hand. "Okay. I gave you a tetanus shot last night and a shot of antibiotics. I'd like to draw some blood for testing, and in a few days, I'd like a urine sample to test for HIV."

Leith squeezed my hand. "Okay."

"There's something else, too. I'd like you to think about talking to someone about what happened. It doesn't have to be a therapist, but I think you should consider it. My office has connections to several good and trustworthy people. And if you won't consider, then I hope you'll talk to someone you trust." Doc's eyes flicked to me before settling back on Leith.

My heart squeezed in my chest watching his lip tremble as a tear streaked down his cheek. "I'll think about it."

"That's all I ask. I'm going to give you pain medicine in your IV that should let you rest easy. When you wake up this afternoon, they'll have lunch for you, then a short walk. I'll be back to check on you in the evening. Sound good?"

"Yes, thank you." Leith wiped his face with the hand not holding mine.

Doc pulled a loaded syringe out of his kit and injected it into the port in Leith's IV line.

Leith settled back against his pillows, and I lowered the head of the bed a bit.

"That good?"

He nodded at me, but his eyes were already drooping.

As Doc gathered his things, he said, "I'll write out instructions before I leave."

"Thanks, Doc."

Doc gripped my shoulder on his way by. I stood there, holding Leith's hand, long after his breathing evened out and his face relaxed with sleep.

———

IT WAS THE WHIMPERING THAT WOKE ME. MY EYES snapped open when another pained sound came from the bed. I threw off the blanket covering me and kicked in the footstool on the recliner in the corner of Leith's room. He whimpered again as I reached his side. There was sweat on his forehead, and he had one hand fisted in the blanket so hard his knuckles were white.

"Leith." I tried to keep my voice soft because I didn't want to scare him, but I didn't want to leave him in whatever nightmare he was having, either. "Leith, wake up!"

He startled, but his eyes popped open. At first, I thought he was still asleep, still locked inside his head, but then he sucked in a hard breath, and his body went lax against the mattress.

"Hey," I said gently, offering him the water cup. He took it, clasped between both of his hands and took a long, slow drink.

"Thanks." His eyes moved from me to the chair I'd just vacated. "Sorry if I woke you. You don't have to stay if you don't—"

"I'm not going anywhere unless you want me to, but I'd rather stay with you." He looked at me with wide, shiny blue eyes. "Hang on." I headed into the bathroom and grabbed a washcloth, soaking it with cold water and wringing it out. Going back to Leith, I took the tumbler when he handed it to me and gave him the washcloth. He sighed as he dabbed it over his face and settled it on his forehead. "Better?"

"Much better." He leaned his head back. "How is Eben? And Pax?"

I sat down on the edge of the bed facing him. "They're both okay. The shot hit Eben high in the shoulder, and Doc thinks he'll make a full recovery. And Pax is upstairs with Mace as far as I know. He's fine."

"And Dustin? What happened to him?"

My eyes hardened. "You won't have to worry about him ever again."

Watching him examine my face and seeing the exact moment when understanding dawned was hard. I didn't want him to think of me that way. As a killer. As the kind of man who settled his affairs with violence. Even though that's exactly what I was. I'd never had reservations like I did with Leith. Never worried about how a potential lover saw me. Even though it hadn't been me that killed Dustin...I wished it had. I knew my brothers made the only call they could for the situation they were in, but a quick roadside death was so much better than that monster had deserved.

"That's...good," Leith finally said on a long exhale. "He was...he was horrible."

"Was he what you were dreaming about?"

He nodded. "He talked to me the whole time he was hurting me. It wasn't—" Leith cut himself off and looked down at his lap. "It wasn't the first time I'd been with him. I met him through a hook-up app, and we'd gotten together on a couple of different occasions."

We'd gathered as much from his *Uber* history when we'd found his phone after his abduction, but hearing him confirm it—*knowing* that he'd willingly given himself to that asshole was like a kick to the balls. "Is that why you met him outside your apartment Sunday night?"

Leith flinched, and I felt like an asshole. Maybe I should have someone else sit with him. With everything that happened, it felt like the fucking fantastic day we'd had together was a half-forgotten dream.

"He was supposed to have taken me hiking that morning, and then we were going to have a scene after." His face got almost as red as his hair, and his eyes darted to mine. "But he didn't show. That's why Pax asked if I could ride with you. Then that night, he messaged me an apology and asked if we could talk."

"So you went downstairs to meet him."

"Yes. Then I woke up in that bathroom."

"Leith—"

"I'm sorry." He wouldn't meet my eyes. "I wished I'd asked you to stay. I wanted to ask you to stay."

That buoyed my wounded ego some—even though any thought about my ego felt unbelievably selfish on my part—but I still had so many questions. Important questions too, but what came out of my mouth was, "What kind of scene?"

Leith rolled his one good eye at me, although the other was considerably less swollen than it had been twenty-four hours ago. "Like you don't know."

Fuck, was I happy to see some of his sass shining through, and, true, I had my suspicions about what his kink might be, but I'd let him tell me when he was ready. "I don't know what you mean. I'll have you know, it's strictly vanilla around here."

He snorted, and I stood from the bed and offered him my hand. "Think you're up for a walk to the kitchen? It's just down the hall." Licking his lips, he nodded and eased his legs over the side. The swelling in his knees had gone down as well. "I think Pax and Arden might be in there. They've been asking to see you—"

My words died in my throat at how pale Leith had gotten.

"Um, I don't think I'm ready for that. Could you maybe just bring me something in here?"

My forehead furrowed. What had brought that sudden switch? "Of course. Want me to help you to the bathroom before I go?"

He shook his head and slowly got to his feet. "No, I've got it, I think. Thank you."

"Ok, I'll be back in a minute." I'd pulled the door open when he spoke again.

"Axel...I'm just not ready to see anyone. Not yet."

"Then you won't have to, okay?"

His shoulders sagged, and he gave me a little nod before he shuffled into the bathroom and closed the door.

WHEN I GOT TO THE KITCHEN, I WAS SURPRISED TO FIND only Cleave. He was sitting off to one side at the big table where several of us often took meals together or spread out to clean our guns. Like most homes, this room and the big common room with its couches and TV's were where we tended to congregate.

"Hey, man," Cleave said, straightening up from the sandwich in front of him. "How's Leith?" Outside of my brother, Stone, Cleave was the Heretic I was closest to, despite him being a decade younger than me. I remembered when he patched in—quiet and eager for a place to belong. He had that place now. He was by far one of the best men I knew and a damn good enforcer. Our bulk, and being unbothered by getting our hands dirty, often saw us side-by-side with Mace or Lex in the thick of jobs that weren't always easy to stomach.

"Hey." Walking over, I settled in the chair across from him and propped my elbows on the table before running a hand over the scratchy stubble on my head. I needed to shave. "He's...doing okay. All things considered." I shrugged. "He just had a nightmare, but he shook it off quick. I can't decide if he's still in shock or just really good at hiding things."

"Could be keeping it all in. If some fucker had chained me up in a bathroom and cut on me, I'm not sure how I'd be reacting right now either."

I blew out a big breath. "Yeah." It was hard to reconcile that it was only last night I'd carried Leith out of that apartment. "Resilient little shit."

Cleave arched one dark brow at me. "You like him."

"Yeah."

He chuckled. "Is that going to be your answer for everything today?" His blue eyes narrowed in concern. "Have you gotten any sleep? I could sit with him—"

"No." It came out with more force than I intended, and Cleave's eyes got big. "Sorry. Yes, I've slept some, thank you. And, no. You're one of few I'd trust with him, but he doesn't want to see anyone else. Just me and Doc."

"So, I know you two looked cozy as hell on the ride Sunday, and I was serious when I said you like him, but..."

"Yeah. I *liked* him on Sunday, and I like him today...and maybe it was seeing him like that, but he's got me all wrapped up."

"I can see that. You're like full-on Daddy Bear." Cleave smirked.

"Oh, fuck you." I chuckled, glad for the lighter turn in our conversation. "Speaking of wrapped up"—I raised an eyebrow at the dark red mark I could see peeking out at the collar of Cleave's t-shirt—"how's JJ?"

It was amazing how his face softened at the mention of his man.

"He's good. We got into it last night about me asking him to come here for lockdown, but after what happened to Leith and Pax...he understands."

"When are you going to move in with him?" I knew a million people had asked him that question, but I hadn't. Before, I'd figured he'd tell me when he was ready, but I was feeling more and more like maybe we all should be seizing the moment when we could. If I had seized my moment Sunday night, Leith might not be laying in a hospital bed down the hall.

Cleave sighed. "Soon. We talked about it last night or this morning really, after I got in. I was only trying to keep some distance for his protection. To put some space between him and the club, but now...I want to be wherever he is."

A smile spread across my face. "Good. I'm happy for you."

"Thanks." He smiled too, but it faded quickly. "I'm sorry about the way things went down with that asshole. I know he should have been yours."

I nodded as the anger that hadn't dissipated from the night before churned and boiled in my gut. My brothers had been on the side of the road with only their bikes and the cops coming. Their only options had been to leave the bastard that had hurt Leith and taken Pax for the police or to put an end to him right there. As much as I burned to have been the one to do the deed, they made the right call. "Appreciate that, but it's done, and that's really all that matters." Rising from the table, I held out my hand for Cleave to clasp.

Instead, he stood and walked to me, pulling me into a crushing hug.

"Take care of your boy. I'm here if you need me."

"Thanks, man. Let me know if you need help moving your shit to JJ's."

He laughed. "Will do."

CHAPTER FOUR

Leith

Two days after Axel had carried me into one of the infirmary rooms at the Heretics' clubhouse, he carried me back out of it and up the stairs to his personal room. Well, it was more like a small apartment than just a room. There was a sitting area with a big, comfy leather couch and a giant flatscreen mounted on the wall in front of it, a kitchenette, a desk with an *iMac* and an expensive-looking swivel chair, and a big bed over in one corner half-hidden from the rest of the room with a shoji screen.

"This is nice," I said as he set me on my feet. Everything was so tidy I was half-afraid to touch, but Axel gently nudged me farther into his space as he shut the door behind us.

"Thanks. Vivian sent a bag of your things over. I, uh, set it on the end of the bed. The bathroom is through that door. There's towels and things under the cabinet if you want to shower, and I put a box of *Saran Wrap* on the counter to wrap your stitches with."

Could the man be any more thoughtful? For a moment, I felt bad about encroaching on his space. The truth was, I could have gone home. I was still healing, and I hurt a lot, but

I could have looked after·myself. I just didn't want to, didn't want to be alone, so when Axel asked if I'd rather stay with him for a few days...it had been impossible to say no.

"Oh, and this." Axel pulled my phone out of his pocket and handed it to me. "In all the commotion of the last few days, I forgot we still had it."

I felt like I hadn't seen it in years and turned it over in my hands. The glittery case I'd put on it sparkling as it caught the overhead light. "Thanks." The truth was, I hadn't even thought about it. Hadn't missed it. And how crazy was that? Normally, I lived on my phone—checking social media and watching make-up tutorials or playing my games. "I didn't know what happened to it."

Axel moved into the kitchenette and pulled a couple bottles of water from the under-the-counter fridge. "It was in the shrubs out in front of *Spritz Villa*."

Ah. That moment, when Dustin had jabbed the needle into my neck, flashed behind my eyes, making me dizzy for a second as adrenaline flooded my veins. I breathed through it —the same fight or flight response I hadn't gotten to really feel that night because the drugs that asshole pumped into me knocked me on my ass. The next thing I'd known, I was waking up naked and collared on the floor of that shitty bathroom. Before that, I'd thought moments like that were behind me; moments of absolute fear and the gut-wrenching despair that comes with it; moments when I realized that this really might be the end for me. How sad was it that this last round of moments weren't even the worst I'd endured?

"Leith?"

Warm, gentle hands settled on my shoulders. Axel's hands. I gripped his wrists, so strong and thick I couldn't completely encircle them, and dragged my fingers through the dark hair covering his forearms. "I'm okay. Just...still coming to terms, I guess."

"Do you want to talk about it?"

I shot him a tight-lipped smile. "Nope. What I want is a nap. I know you did all the heavy lifting, but I'm already worn out."

He smirked, letting me get away with changing the subject, but his eyes still shined with concern. "You might be a lot of things but heavy isn't one of them."

I laughed, pushing down all the dark swirly thoughts and feelings that wanted to pull me under. For now, I was safe here. "Maybe to you, Mr. Muscles," I said, poking at the bulge of his bicep.

"And you can have your nap, as soon as you eat some lunch," Axel said. Using the hand still resting on my shoulders, he turned me toward the couch. "Go sit, and I'll bring it over to you."

Letting out a sigh, I did as he asked, walking toward the couch and easing myself down on the far end of it. As Axel moved toward kitchenette, I swore I heard him chuckle and the word *brat* escape his lips. With a triumphant little smirk on my face, I pulled my phone from my pocket and turned it over in my hand. I wasn't surprised when the screen stayed black as I attempted to power it on. What was surprising was the lack of disappointment and the absence of an immediate desire to find a charger. Nibbling at the inside of my cheek, I decided not to overthink it and set the phone down on the coffee table.

Settling back against the cushions, I winced as the movement pulled at the cuts on my legs, but the couch comfortable—deep and plush—and I had no trouble letting my eyes slip closed while I waited on Axel to feed me.

A little smile pulled at my mouth. In moments like these, it was hard to remember that he wasn't my Daddy. And if I was being honest with myself, I didn't want to remember. It was much nicer to slip into a little fantasy where this was my actual life—being Axel's boy and enjoying all the love and care that came with it. I could pretend that I'd been in some silly accident and my wonderful man, overprotective as he was, wouldn't let me lift a finger for myself. That wouldn't be our everyday life, though...because as much as I longed to be cherished by a Daddy, I wanted to help take care of them too.

"I thought I said lunch before nap."

I couldn't help it—I smiled and opened my eyes to find Axel standing in front of me—a plate in one hand and a glass of water in the other—with a look of mock seriousness on his face. If I was his real boy, oh, how I would take advantage of that. Pressing his buttons just enough that he would give me what we both wanted. Instead, I sat up and accepted the plate he'd made for me.

"Sorry, Axel." His eyebrows went up, and I could tell he was trying to decide if I was being sassy or serious. I looked at the plate in my hand, finding a turkey sandwich on the wheat bread that I liked cut into quarters and fresh-cut strawberries and pineapple. My mouth watered.

Only a couple days, and without even asking, this man quickly figured out my food preferences, and for some reason, that made tears well up in my eyes. I cleared my throat, willing them back, and looked at Axel with a little smile. "Thank you."

He tilted his head and settled on the couch beside me. "You're welcome."

Instead of sitting on the other end, he chose the seat in the middle, slightly turned toward me with his muscled arm stretching across the back behind my head. I didn't feel crowded, though. Truth was, I liked having him close. Picking up a sandwich quarter, I took a big bite and moaned in pleasure. The turkey tasted like he'd roasted it himself, even though he didn't have an oven. The lettuce was crisp, and there was just enough mayonnaise. Before I knew it, I had half the sandwich gone and was working my way through the sweet strawberries and tangy pineapple. As I lifted the third sandwich quarter, Axel spoke.

"Why don't you want to see your friends, Leith?"

My stomach dove and swooped, caught completely off guard, and it took all my effort not to scowl at him. He'd waited until I was distracted, thoroughly enraptured with my yummy lunch, probably hoping to startle me into giving him an answer. Like the petulant brat I was so good at being, I lowered my eyes to the plate in my lap and started tearing the crust off the bread. "I just don't."

Axel hummed, no doubt giving me the chance to tell him the truth, and then one of his hands sealed over mine, stilling their nervous movement and making me turn to look at him. "I'm not trying to force you into seeing them before you're ready, and anything you say to me will always stay between us, but I would like to know the real reason you're asking me to turn them away."

My heart was beating hard in my chest. I couldn't say that I blamed him. I knew it was strange, at least from an outside perspective, for me not to want to see the people who could offer me the most comfort—that I had the most in common with. I also knew beyond Axel wanting to know the truth— he was asking for my trust, something he absolutely deserved even though I wasn't ready to give it fully. I could share this one truth, though.

"I'm ashamed," I said, my voice sounding small.

Axel flinched. "Leith what happened to you was not your fault—"

"Not about what happened. Although, that is pretty fucking humiliating too. But about what I did...while it was happening." Appetite gone, I placed the plate on the coffee table and took a sip of water.

"And what was that?" Axel asked, his big rumble of a voice the softest I'd ever heard it.

I let out a big breath, only to pull another one in, but it didn't stop the burn building behind my eyes. "I told him everything. Answered every question he had. I know that I didn't know much of what he wanted because of how angry he kept getting with my responses, but I didn't even try to hold back. I just wanted him to stop hurting me." Fresh tears welled in my eyes and spilled over.

Axel's gentle hand settled on my shoulder. "Come here," he said, using that hand to guide me toward him. I went willingly. He pulled me onto his lap, and I buried my face against the side of his neck. One big arm wrapped completely around my waist, holding me secure while his other hand started a steady cadence running up and down my back.

"Oh, sweet boy, I won't tell you how to feel, but I promise you there is no need to feel that shame. You didn't give him anything that he couldn't find out some other way, or that he didn't already know. From the looks of things, he'd been staking us out for a while, and my guess is hurting you was both about covering his bases to ensure he hadn't missed anything and just because he was a sick bastard who would have hurt you regardless. No one blames you. None of this was your fault."

I nodded, my disheveled hair catching in his beard.

"You sure no one blames me?"

"I'm sure."

Swallowing hard, I willed my tears to dry. It must have been my injuries and the stress of everything that happened that let me cry that hard in front of Axel. My old Daddy never minded if I cried while he was hurting me. I knew he liked it, but I'd always found the strength to hold back all my other tears until I was alone because crying like this—without physical wounds to *warrant* it—had been absolutely against the rules and would see me beaten instead of held the way Axel was holding me now. "And if I'm still not ready to see them?"

"Then, you won't see them."

The tension left in my body drained out of me, and my eyes started to droop. I let myself settle more heavily in Axel's embrace, relishing in all of that strength around me and the gentle way he was using it to cradle me against him. If I hadn't been so sleepy, I might have cried again knowing I still didn't have the courage to let my guard all the way down and make my time with him something other than temporary.

———

"THIS IS DUMB," I SAID INTO THE DARKNESS ABOVE THE BED. Axel's answering chuckle was husky and rich from where he was bedded down on the couch. "There's enough room in this bed that we won't even touch, no matter how much space you take up." He chuckled again, and a pleased smile pulled at my lips. The first two nights in Axel's room, I'd still been so tired and sore, I hadn't thought to argue when he put me in his bed and took the couch for himself. Today, I was still tired and sore, but some of my old energy had started to seep in.

"Was that a fat joke?"

"Oh my god," I said, adding that dramatic flair I was so fond of to my voice. "Shut up."

"I don't claim to be an expert, but I'm not sure telling someone to shut up is the way to get them in bed with you. Unless they're into that kind of thing." If he was trying to hide the amusement in his voice, it wasn't working.

"Oh, I'm sorry. Let me try again. Ahem." I cleared my throat and then said in the sweetest voice I could muster, "Axel, will you *please* come sleep with me. Even with all your *huge* muscles, I promise I'll stay on my side of the bed." When he didn't say anything, I bit my lip, waiting to see what he'd do. I'd only had one more nightmare since the first one, but it had been a bad one. Neither one of us had gone back to sleep after, and instead, we'd splayed out on the couch and started to binge watch *Supernatural*. It was easier to think about crazy paranormal demons rather than the very human ones I was contending with.

"Only because you said, please." Axel's voice came from right beside the bed. I jumped, a little yelp escaping my throat and pressed my hand over my heart.

"Shit, Leith." Axel climbed in, scooting all the way over to me and pulling me against his chest. One of his big, rough hands slid up and down over the bare skin of my back, soothing my racing heart back into its normal cadence. "I'm sorry. I thought you heard me moving."

I hummed, pressing my face against the lush, dark hair covering his chest and wrapped my arm around his waist, splaying my fingers over the warm skin of his back. Was I ready to throw in the towel and beg him to be my Daddy? No. Was I a glutton for punishment? Hell, yes. Because this was exactly what I wanted—him holding me. Even if it was going to suck when I didn't have it anymore.

For several long minutes, neither of us spoke. He shifted around, getting his other arm under my neck and adjusting the pillows, but he never pulled back from my embrace.

"Guess that no touching thing is out the window, huh?" His voice was quiet and deep and gentle in a way that made me snuggle closer.

"Is that okay?"

"Yeah, sweet boy. It's more than okay." He pressed a kiss to the top of my head.

I went to sleep with a smile on my face.

I PICKED UP THE TV REMOTE—WANTING TO WATCH
Supernatural, but not until Axel got back—and clicked the
power button. My eyes darted around the empty apartment.
Axel was at church, although why they called their biker
meetings *church,* I had no idea. I sighed. For the last two
weeks, this room had been my sanctuary, and was without a
doubt, the only place I'd ever felt truly safe in all my life. Of
course, I thought with a smirk, that had more to do with the
man it belonged to.

Axel had not only kept his word at every turn, but he'd
also made me feel welcome. I'd been living here with him—
eating his food, sleeping in his bed, and not once had he
asked for a single thing in return. Not once had he made me
feel uncomfortable or like I was out of place. He'd been
exactly the same from day one—kind. No games.

It'd been absolutely amazing, and like all amazing things, I
knew my time here was almost up. My body was almost
completely healed, and I was feeling restless. Despite Axel's
insistence that I was no trouble and always welcome, I
needed to get back to my job and my apartment. Back to
standing on my own two feet...or at least trying to.

The boy in me was not happy about that at all, because in
my bones, I knew if I wanted Axel to be my Daddy—not
temporarily and not just in a fantasy—all I would have to do
was ask. It seemed like such a simple thing, to open my
mouth and ask for what I wanted, but the rest of me remembered all too vividly what could happen when you gave yourself so completely to someone. I still wasn't ready to take that
leap.

As had been happening more and more in the last few
days, I wished for someone to share my fears with—someone
who would let me vent about all these thoughts in my head.

Letting the outside world in was the first step in bringing this little daydream grinding to a halt, but if I was being honest, I needed that. I'd gotten way too comfortable here. I wanted to talk to my friends, and hopefully, they wanted to talk to me. Looking over at the vase full of flowers they'd sent and the balloons that were starting to droop a bit, I thought maybe they did.

I got up and went in search of my phone charger. Vivian had told Axel she'd put it in one of the side pockets on the duffle bag she'd packed for me and that's where I found it. Leaning over, I plugged it into the socket behind the nightstand and laid down on the side of the bed I'd claimed as mine.

Settling back against the pillow, I gave the phone a minute to soak up some juice, then powered it on. It took forever to load before it started vibrating in my hand. And kept vibrating...the number of Facebook notifications alone was staggering. Ignoring all the glaring little red bubbles filled with numbers, I clicked into my messages to text Pax just as a new message popped up. It was dated four days ago.

"Restricted?" Frowning, I clicked open the message and felt my stomach drop. It was only two words.

Found you.

CHAPTER FIVE

Axel

C alix brought the gavel down, bringing my brothers to order and starting church.

"It seems we have ourselves a little Devil problem," our president said, his black eyes sweeping over the room. Calix wasn't a big man; he was cut and hard and ran our club with an indomitable will that had garnered him the respect of every man in the room.

"A former Devil's problem," Riot, our vice president, added from his seat at Calix's right hand.

"The Devil's rejects, if you will," Mace tacked on with a little chuckle. Calix sighed, setting the gavel on its side on the table and shooting a glare at Mace. Our Sergeant-at-Arms only shrugged. "What? You knew someone was going to say it."

Calix grunted as he leaned forward, resting his elbows on the table and clasping his hands in front of him. "Word from the actual Devils is that their castoffs have been causing property damage and harassing businesses that the Devils either frequent or own. Now typically, I wouldn't suggest getting involved in Devil business, but Holden did give us an assist in finding the asshole who took Pax and Leith. So the club is in his debt, and the two former Devils we put a beating on after they busted up our fight last month were in *Mac's Café* yesterday."

"What?" Eben spoke up from his place at the end of the table. Eben's boyfriend, Cody, worked at the café, and all of us Heretics stopped in there regularly. Mac was a friend of the club.

"They went inside and poked around a bit. Bought a coffee each and left, but Mac said he got the impression that they'd be back. If this was all random and uncoordinated, I wouldn't be as worried, but Holden also thinks they've got some new player calling the shots. Nobody knows who he is, and the damage they're causing is starting to escalate."

We all sat and soaked that in for a moment, my mind immediately going to Leith and to *Spritz*. If the ex-Devils were out to cause problems and getting more serious, it was only a matter of time before they made the nightclub a target or started harassing the boys who worked there. Despite the circumstances that had brought him to me, I was suddenly glad that Leith was upstairs in my room, safe and sound. Not that I hadn't been glad about it before. Truth was, I tried to keep myself from dwelling on it because I probably liked it more than I should—having him in my space, getting to take care of him every day, feeling like he was mine to spoil. He'd settled into my life in the last couple of weeks like he'd always been there. I knew he needed to get back to his own life, but I hadn't quite figured out how I was gonna let him go.

"I feel like we need more information," Riot said, the deep base of his voice cutting off the murmurs around the room. He was the only man in the room physically larger than me, and probably the only man quieter. "We need to know who this new player is. See what we can dig up on him."

Calix nodded. "Agreed. I want extra guys on *Spritz*. I want us to be seen in the neighborhood. These Devils need to know that they can't slip into our territory and fuck with our people without consequences." We all tapped our knuckles on the table in agreement. Calix nodded and turned his face my way.

"Axel, how's your boy faring?"

I knew it was semantics and Leith wasn't really mine, but hearing him referred to that way was such a mirror of my own thoughts it had warmth swelling in my chest. I looked at my Prez. "He's good. Healing."

"Excellent. Think you'll be up for a trip to Sand Lake this week? Jeb's got a new fighter I'd like you to vet. He thinks he's about ready for the cage."

As quickly as warmth had come, it fled as the real world pushed its way back in. Had I not just been thinking that Leith needed to go back to his own life? Truth was, I needed to get back to mine as well. I should've made the trip to Sand Lake over a week ago. It was part of my responsibilities—given my history in the cage—to check out all the new fighters before we put them into the rotation. But I'd been putting it off because I didn't want to leave Leith. Hadn't been ready to leave him. I still wasn't, but I took a slow breath and looked at Calix. "Definitely. I'll head out in the next couple of days."

Calix's black eyes stayed focused on me for a moment, intense and scrutinizing. He gave one final nod. "Before we adjourn, I want to say how good it is to see you back at the table, Eben." Immediately, voices raised and hands slapped the top of the table in celebration. Eben had been shot trying to protect Pax from the psycho who'd kidnapped Leith, and it was good to see him upright. His arm was still in a sling, but there was color in his face, and he was looking like he was on the mend. He smiled and nodded.

"Thanks, guys, it's good to be back."

"Meeting adjourned." Calix lifted the gavel and slammed it down once on the table.

I PUSHED OPEN THE DOOR TO MY ROOM, AND THE SMELL OF bacon surrounded me. Closing the door behind me, I turned to find Leith standing at the little two-burner stovetop, bacon sizzling away in the skillet in front of him. His face was a mask of concentration as he used a spatula to flip the slices. The cord for his earbuds was slithering down over the snug deep blue tank top he was wearing, showing off his lean torso, and plugged into the end of his phone where it was partially sticking out of the pocket of his sweatpants.

My heart clenched. I hadn't seen him on his phone once in the last two weeks. He said he hadn't been ready, and its appearance now meant that he was taking a step in that direction. I wanted him healed, and I wanted him confident and happy, but standing there watching him be comfortable in my space and making what I learned was one of his favorite meals—breakfast for dinner—I could also admit that I wasn't ready for him to leave. Wasn't ready for him to go back to his life where I only got to play a minor role. And didn't that just make me feel like an asshole?

"Oh shit," Leith gasped, pulling the earbuds out of his ears and pressing a hand to his chest. "I didn't hear you come in."

I immediately felt like shit for standing there staring like a creeper and scaring him, and for the possessive thoughts I'd been entertaining. Walking over to him, I slid an arm around his shoulders and pressed my nose into the mop of red hair on his head. He smelled like the minty shampoo he liked. "I'm sorry. I didn't mean to startle you."

Picking up the spatula again, Leith stepped out of my

embrace and back to the stove, shooting me a too-wide smile over his shoulder. "No worries. I hope it's okay that I started on dinner. I wasn't sure when you'd get back."

I narrowed my eyes at him, trying to figure out why he seemed so nervous. "Of course. You know you don't need my permission to cook or do anything really. It smells really good, by the way. Which are you doing this time, scrambled eggs or omelets?" He told me once that breakfast food for dinner was his favorite, and that it was the only thing he could cook really well. Something I could certainly attest to, because as soon as he'd been able, he'd jumped at the chance to cook for me. In the last two weeks, I'd been treated to all his prowess at making all kinds of breakfast food.

"Omelets, I think." He glanced back at me, eyes guarded. "If that sounds good to you?"

I frowned. "Everything okay?"

If I hadn't been paying such close attention to him over the last few weeks—learning his likes and dislikes, his facial expressions, figuring out how to tell when he was in more pain than he was letting on—I would've missed it; the slight tensing of his shoulders, the small shift in his stance, the way his eyes flicked quickly my direction and back. Something had happened while I was gone to the meeting. I'd bet my life on it, and I wanted so badly for him to trust me enough to tell me, but I knew before he even opened his mouth that he wasn't going to.

"Everything's fine," he said, shooting another fake smile at me over his shoulder. "Dinner should be ready in about twenty minutes if you want to wash up."

He turned away, focused back on cooking. The deeply possessive part of me—the part that already thought of him as *mine*—wanted to demand that he tell me what was wrong. It was another stark reminder that despite whatever chemistry was between us, he wasn't my boy, and if he truly felt like he couldn't trust me...he probably never would be.

CHAPTER SIX

Leith

I t was impossible not to feel the tension in the air. Nights spent in Axel's bed had become one of my favorite parts of living there. Once I convinced him that I was comfortable sharing a bed if he was, it hadn't taken long to figure out that he was an excellent cuddle buddy and didn't seem to mind that I felt the need to always be snuggled up against him.

All of that only made the foot of empty bed between us seem that much wider, and I hated that I was the one who put it there. Part of me wished I'd told him about the text and what I was afraid it meant when he'd asked if I was alright. This stilted, awkward silence was all my fault because I was lying, and he knew it.

How had everything gotten so messed up? My life wasn't perfect, but I'd been doing okay on my own. I had a job I loved, a place of my own, Pax and I were actually friends now, and for whatever reason, this wonderful man actually cared about me. Me. The fuck up. The one who was incapable of taking care of himself. Axel looked at me, and even though he hadn't said it, I knew he liked me. He'd rescued me. Let me heal in his home.

I'd made a lot of mistakes in my life. Trusted a lot of the wrong people, and I guess I wasn't done paying for it. The hot swell of sorrow settled in my chest. I didn't want to think about what could have been, but it was hard not to with Axel's steady breathing the only thing filling the darkness pressing down on me.

This could have been my life.

Before I could fight against it, a hot lump formed in my throat and the stinging burn of tears started in my eyes. I must've made a sound because Axel reached across the space between us and touched my arm.

"Come here, sweetheart."

I went to him, closing the space between us and tucking myself against his side. I pressed my forehead against his neck, head resting on his shoulder, while the first of my tears slid down into his chest hair tickling my cheek. I wrapped my arm around his torso as he did the same to me, pulling me close and holding me tight.

"Oh, sweet boy." His breath was warm on my forehead, beard tickling my skin as he pressed a kiss there. "I won't ask you to tell me what's going on. I figure if you wanted to, you would, but I'm here, okay? And I'm not going anywhere."

His words made the tears already leaking out of my eyes run faster. He was there and had been there for me in a way no else in my life ever had. I didn't know how to tell him that come tomorrow, he'd still be here, but I wouldn't be. Running didn't get any easier, but this time...this time felt like it might kill me.

Holding on tight, I pressed a kiss to the skin of his chest, relished in his quick indrawn breath, and willed myself to commit the feel of his strong body to memory. I didn't deserve this man, even in this temporary way, and I was jealous of the lucky boy that would someday get to keep him and call him Daddy.

THE VIBRATING BUZZ OF A PHONE WOKE ME. I WAS STILL nestled in Axel's arms, feeling warm and safe. I snuggled in closer, and the chest beneath my cheek rumbled.

"Sweetheart, you're not making this easy," Axel said, voice rough with sleep and...fondness. For a moment, in my half-awake state, I'd forgotten about the text I received and the resurgence of fear that had come with it. I'd gotten away from Malcolm once before, and I wasn't sure I could do it again. I didn't want to do it again. That was why I had to run. Had to leave this man behind, and start over somewhere new. I was exhausted at the mere thought of it.

With enough stretching, Axel managed to grab the phone. He settled back onto the pillow and ran one hand up and down my back, holding me to him while he slid his thumb across the screen with the other and pressed the phone to his ear. "Yeah?" Five seconds later, he went tense beneath me. "What? Fucking hell. We'll be there in twenty."

I pursed my lips. I didn't want him to leave.

"Leith, baby, I need you to wake up. We need to get over to *Spritz Villa*."

That had my eyes popping open. "What? Why?"

"Someone broke into your apartment."

WARM AIR RUSHED OVER ME AS AXEL'S BIKE SPED ALONG the mostly deserted city streets. With my arms wrapped tight around his middle and his broad back to lean against, I'd discovered that being on the bike with him was one of my favorite places. I wasn't as upset about my apartment as I should have been. It's not like I didn't know who had done it.

Malcolm, my former *Daddy*. Not that I thought he

deserved the title, not knowing what I knew now. I sighed, letting the wind whip the sound away and closed my eyes. I should be freaking out. Panic and fear should have been spreading through every cell of my body. Seeing the text had scared me. Knowing that I had to get away again had depressed me. And now this? The fact that the text wasn't a bluff? He'd been in my apartment. If I hadn't stayed with Axel, Malcolm would already have me in his clutches again. Maybe it was everything that had happened with Dustin, and I was just desensitized to terror at this point.

The bike slowed, and Axel dropped his feet to the pavement. I lifted my head and looked over his shoulder. The glow of the red light in front of us glinted off of his helmet. He met my eyes in the side mirror and took one of his hands off of the handlebars to squeeze mine where they were clasped against his stomach. My heart jumped in my chest, and I managed to give him a weak smile.

It was him, I realized as the light turned green, and we continued on our way. He was the reason for my muted fear, like a shield holding the terror at bay. A line of defense I'd never had before. For one fire-bright moment, hope flared in my chest. What if I told him? Would he defend me against this next threat? Sweep in and rescue me like he'd done when I'd been at Dustin's mercy? Would he still care about me if he knew what a broken boy I really was?

The bike stopped again, and I realized we'd made it to the *Villa*. A man in a Heretics' vest was standing on the steps waiting for us. He looked familiar, but I couldn't place him. I must have seen him at *Spritz* before.

Axel dropped the bike's kickstand and held it steady while I climbed off.

"Hey, Zach," he said as soon as he'd gotten off the bike too and stowed our helmets in one of the saddlebags.

"Hey," Zach said, eyes darting from Axel to me. He was a

good-looking guy—clean cut with dark hair and eyes and an obvious love of the gym, if the biceps stretching the sleeves of his t-shirt were any indication. He wasn't Axel-sized or anything, but impressive, nonetheless. "It's good to see you on your feet, Leith."

The driver—that's where I knew him from. He'd been behind the wheel of the truck the night Axel had carried me out of Dustin's apartment.

"Thanks, Zach," I said, giving him a small smile. He smiled back, looking surprisingly awake for three o'clock in the morning.

Axel grunted and wrapped an arm around my shoulders, moving us toward the entrance. "Who's upstairs?"

Zach fell into step beside us. "Riot and Mace. They were on at the club tonight. One of the dancers noticed Leith's door standing open when he got off shift and called them."

"Any footage?"

Zach pulled a set of keys out of his pocket, unlocking and holding the door open for us. "We caught his face coming in, but none of us recognize him."

With another grunt, Axel hit the up button for the elevator and stood so that his chest was pressed against my back. I could tell he was agitated, but I wasn't sure if he was upset with Zach for some reason or just at the situation in general. I let myself lean back against him. He blew out a slow breath and dropped one hand to rest on my hip, giving it a little squeeze.

"You okay?" he asked quietly, as we shuffled forward to get on the elevator.

Once we'd stepped inside, I pressed my side to Axel's and slipped my hand into his. "I'm okay," I answered, looking up and catching his dark eyes. As the door slid shut, he adjusted our joined hands, so that his fingers threaded through mine and gave me a little smile.

The elevator ride was short, and as we approached my open apartment door, I took a deep fortifying breath. As soon as I stepped over the threshold, I was glad that I had. My apartment was a studio; one large room with a kitchenette in the corner and the only other door in the space leading to the bathroom. The whole room was all in an utter state of disarray. My small dinette set was on its side, the cushions of my loveseat had been pulled off and slashed, the TV screen was busted, and all my dresser drawers had been pulled out and dumped. Even the mattress on my bed had been pulled off and tossed against the wall so it covered the window, and there were large slash marks running the length of it.

Mace and Riot were both standing near the kitchenette counter, but I didn't pay them any mind as my heart started to pound and my head went fuzzy. I'd never let myself become super attached to material objects because things could always be taken away, and I'd never had much to call my own to begin with. So I hadn't expected the deep well of sadness that threatened to rise up out of my belly and choke me, or the way it shifted and morphed into a type of rage I had never felt before.

That motherfucker.

I had worked so hard to build a life of my own, and even though that meant slinging drinks or letting the gentleman in the downstairs club buy an evening with me, only to come home to a one-room apartment...

Maybe it didn't seem like much to some, but it was mine. No one had given it to me. No one had made the decision that led me here. This job and this place were the first things I'd ever had that were wholly mine, and Malcolm had ruined it.

I knew without looking that nothing would be missing. Theft hadn't been his goal. He wanted to scare me. Wanted to show me he could reach out and crush me if he wanted to —cut me in ways he knew would make me bleed the most.

Taking a deep breath, I let the anger build and spread until it was permeating every part of me. As much as I wanted to crumble and let Axel take me up into his arms, I needed to confront this on my own two feet.

This was why I didn't trust anyone. Why I'd chosen to never give myself fully to someone again. Even if the man at my side was proving he could be the exception. Axel was a good man, and the way he was looking at me right now—dark eyes full of concern and rage equal to my own—in that moment, I knew that if I told him about Malcolm, he would protect me. But at what cost? He'd already done so much. This was my mess, and somehow, I was going to have to find a way to clean it up.

CHAPTER SEVEN

Axel

L eith stood inside the doorway, his entire body
trembling. At first, I thought he was on the verge of a
breakdown, but then I stepped around him and met his eyes.
His gorgeous blue orbs were filled with the kind of anger I
wanted to make it my mission for him to never have to feel.
He held my gaze for a moment, but as I watched, his face
hardened, features going dark and snapping the connection I
felt to the sweet boy on the inside.

Seeing that look on his face made my chest ache. My
protective instincts were screaming at me to scoop him up
and get him the hell out of there. He'd seen enough. He
didn't need to wade into this mess. I could do it for him—set
everything to rights, and clean away everything that was
broken. It wouldn't be perfect, nor exactly how it was before,
but it wouldn't be this disheveled wreck of the place he called
home.

Stepping further away from me, he went toward the bed,
kneeling down in the small space between it and the wall
where the drawers of his bedside table had been yanked out
and dumped on the floor. I tried not to look too closely, but

felt my cheeks heat anyway at the sight of several dildos and plugs. I couldn't fucking think about that right now—Leith spread out, all his gorgeous, naked, *freckled* skin on display. I'd rather it be me buried inside him than some toy, but honestly, the visual of either was going to have me hard in a matter of seconds. Tearing my eyes away, I moved to the other side of the room where Mace and Riot were still standing in the kitchenette.

"What do we know?" I asked in lieu of a greeting.

"Not much. Guy came in just after one a.m., was up here for fifteen minutes flat, and then back out the door. As far as we can tell from the video, he had some sort of lock picking tool, and it didn't look like he left with anything unless it was small enough to fit in his pockets," Mace answered. The Sergeant-at-Arms, standing with his feet firmly planted and arms crossed over his chest, looked as angry as I felt.

Riot shifted his bulk beside him and glanced in Leith's direction before whispering, "He okay?"

I lifted a hand to scrub over my face because I didn't know the answer to that question. For all that I'd felt like Leith and I had gotten close over the last couple of weeks, it was painfully obvious that there were things he was hiding from me. Hell, he was probably hiding from everyone. "I don't know." I lowered my voice. "First, that asshole Dustin fucking kidnapped and tortured him, and now this bullshit? Anyone would be a mess."

"He doesn't exactly look like a mess," Mace said, with the lift of one brow and his eyes trained across the room where Leith had already begun cleaning up the disaster that was his apartment. "Here." Mace pulled out his phone and brought something up on the screen before turning it to me. It was a picture of a man, bulky but not defined, wearing jeans, a dark t-shirt, and a ball cap. He was walking up the steps toward the front door at *Spritz Villa*. I'd never seen him before in my life.

I took the phone from Mace's hand and crossed the room. Leith was still on his knees beside the bed folding some of his clothes that had been thrown over there. I held out the phone. "Do you recognize this man?"

Leith looked up at me with an indiscernible expression on his face before he dropped his eyes to the phone. His expression didn't change, not even a tick, but the top of his ears went red, and the slightest tremble went through him.

"No," he said before dropping his eyes back to the pile of clothes in front of him.

Maybe we didn't have as strong a bond as I thought, or maybe the feelings for him growing in my chest weren't mutual like I believed, but I knew him well enough to know that he'd just lied to me, and I was determined to find out why.

I LEFT LEITH AT THE LITTLE CORNER TABLE THAT I'D chosen for us. It was just after five a.m., and Mac's Café technically wasn't open to the public yet and wouldn't for another hour. When we'd left Leith's apartment, I knew Mac would already be there and have coffee on. I was thankful he'd answered the phone. I'd wanted to take Leith someplace quiet where we could talk, and I could get some food into him; that wasn't the clubhouse. Plus, I felt like we needed to be on neutral ground.

It had taken us almost a full two hours to clean up the mess that had been made of his apartment. He'd barely spoken a word to me, or anyone, since I'd asked him about the man in the picture. I *knew* that he knew who it was, and it hurt more than I'd like to admit that he didn't trust me enough to tell me. I wanted that trust, badly, but I wouldn't bully it out of him or try to push him into something he wasn't ready for. What I would do was exactly what I'd promised him, I would be there for him.

I couldn't say what was in his mind right now, but there was only one thing on mine—to take care of him and to show him that I would never betray it if he chose to put his trust in me.

I approached the cafés counter as Mac stepped out of the back. He'd been a friend of the club for as long as I'd been a Heretic, and despite his grumpy exterior, he was a good man.

"Here you go, brother. Some caffeine and sugar for your boy over there," Mac said, setting a tray with two steaming coffees, two breakfast sandwiches, and a plate with four iced doughnuts. It smelled heavenly.

"Thanks, Mac. I appreciate you letting us crash your morning."

"No problem. Yell if you need anything." With that, he turned and headed back into the kitchen, and I picked up the tray and went to sit across from the boy I wanted to be mine.

The look of resignation and the dejected slump of his shoulders was so different from the vibrant boy I knew. I didn't think he'd looked this bad even injured in a hospital bed. Something was eating at him, and it was taking all of my self-control not to immediately demand that he tell me what.

"Mac makes an awesome breakfast. Not sure if it's as good as yours, but definitely a close second." That earned me a little smile as I divvied out the food from the tray and set his coffee in front of him.

"Thank you," Leith said as he picked up the cup, inhaling its aroma before taking a slow sip.

Deciding to give it a moment before I posed the question I wanted to ask, I tucked into my food, nearly groaning at the crisp snap of bacon and the welcome warmth of fresh coffee. When we both made it through our breakfast sandwiches, I offered Leith his choice of the doughnuts before picking up an iced maple bar for myself. I watched him take a big bite of the powdered confection and smiled when a drip of raspberry jam ended up on his chin. Before I thought about it, I reached across and swiped it up with my thumb, touch lingering on his skin a moment longer than necessary before I pulled away and stuck my thumb in my mouth, sucking away the sweet and tart flavor of the jam.

Leith swallowed hard, eyes glued to my mouth. I shot him a wink and smiled when pink highlighted his cheeks. Now that his sole focus was on me, I set down my doughnut and folded my arms on the table as I held his gaze.

"I need to head out on a little trip this afternoon."

His shoulders tensed immediately. "What? To where?"

"To Sand Lake. Calix wants me to check out a new fighter at the Heretics' gym there. I'll probably be gone for about a week." He tried to hide it, but I didn't miss the way his shoulders slumped, or the way he didn't want to meet my eyes. "I was hoping that you might want to come with me."

His eyes snapped up to mine. "Really?"

"Really. What do you think?"

He sat for a minute, thinking and licking at some sugar clinging to the corner of his mouth. "Yes. I'd love to go."

CHAPTER EIGHT
Leith

After four hours on the bike, we reached Sand Lake. Axel turned the bike into a gym's parking lot. The low, brick building stretched a long way back from the road, proving it was larger than I'd thought. It was good to stretch my legs when Axel parked the bike around the back near a black metal door. Zach, who'd made the trip with us, parked his bike next to Axel's and climbed off as well. I kept my eyes trained on the building and tried not to dwell on how that was possibly the last time I'd ever be on the back of his bike. I'd clung to him as tight as I could the whole way here.

Axel didn't say anything as he took our helmets and stowed them in one saddlebag before pulling the duffel bag with both of our clothes and toiletries in it from the other. That was an issue. I didn't want to take anything of Axel's—even a bag—so when I found my opportunity to slip away, I'd need to find something else to put my clothes in. There'd only been room for the bare necessities, but I had the money I'd kept stashed in the battery compartments of a couple of my dildos in my wallet. I didn't know this place at all, but Axel had said we were only an hour or so away from Kansas

City. Hopefully, that meant there was a bus station somewhere close. Since I'd left my phone behind in case Malcolm was somehow using it to track me, I'd have to make my way to a gas station and ask for directions when the time came.

I sighed. The phone was another thing on the long list of stuff I'd need to replace. Exhaustion—the bone-deep kind—was already pulling at me, and I hadn't even gotten started yet.

Axel turned toward the building, settling a sure hand on the small of my back and guided me in the direction of the door. I let his touch settle me, even as the thought that I'd soon be purposefully leaving it behind made my eyes burn.

Before we reached the door, someone pushed it open. A man as tall as Axel and just as wide with silver streaks all through his dark hair and beard stepped out to greet us. I'd seen him before at the charity ride and thought his name was Jeb. I knew he was Lex's dad and the president of the club here.

"Axel, Zach, good to see you boys." Jeb's eyes dropped to me. He smiled and held out his hand. "I'm Jeb. I remember seeing you with this lug"—he nodded toward Axel—"at the ride a few weeks ago, but I didn't catch your name."

"Leith," I said, accepting his hand and giving it a firm shake. "It's nice to meet you."

"You too. Now come on in. The rooms are all ready for you, and if you're up for it, Ward is in the cage right now sparring with Kade."

"Perfect," Axel said, taking my hand and leading me along as we followed Jeb inside.

"You know where to go," Jeb said over his shoulder. "Make yourselves at home, and I'll see you out there."

"Thanks," Axel said, turning down a long hallway while Jeb continued forward through a glass door with the gym's name on it.

After we left our bag in the room, Axel led us out into the gym. The entire front of the building was covered in large windows, and there was a short counter off to one side. The rest of the space was dominated by free weights, workout equipment, two full-size boxing rings, and a large metal cage. The whole thing smelled like the dressing room at *Spritz*— sweat-soaked with a hint of disinfectant.

Inside the cage, two men with small black, fingerless gloves on their hands were trading punches and kicks, but it didn't look like they were using their full strength. Zach was standing beside Jeb with his arms crossed and his eyes on the fighters. Axel moved us in that direction, but my eyes lingered for a moment on the counter and the shelves behind it. There were tote bags, water bottles, and some other things with the gym's logo.

Axel stopped outside the cage, leaving a couple of feet between him and Zach. The men in the cage, both sweaty with dark blond hair, tattoos all over, and rippling muscles for days, didn't pay any attention to the audience they'd gathered.

"They both fight for the Heretics?" I asked, keeping my voice low enough that only Axel would hear me.

Axel nodded. "The one on the left is Kade. He's a Heretic and used to fight on our circuit. The other is a new recruit. We're here to see if he's a good fit for St. Louis."

"Oh." I followed the fighters' movements—each a display of brutal grace—and tried not to wince every time one of them landed a blow.

"This is how I got started."

I turned to look at Axel. "Fighting?"

"Yep. Ran away from home. Did a tour of the dive-bar circuit in East Texas. Made enough cash to take me as far as St. Louis. Barrett, one of the older members, spotted me and brought me in. I fought for them, prospected, and then patched in all within a year."

I tried to wrap my mind around that. Axel in a cage or boxing ring, fighting the way these men were fighting now—shirtless and sweaty, full of raw power and sexy, flexing muscles. "That's...um...wow. Did you like it?"

An amused smirk pulled up one side of his mouth. "I was glad to hang up my gloves, but it helped me get out of a bad situation and led me to the club, so I've got no complaints."

His dark brown eyes held mine. He'd been taking such good care of me, for weeks now, and there was still so much I didn't know about him. What bad situation? He'd run from something, the same as me? I couldn't imagine Axel ever needing to run from anything, but it didn't feel like now was the time to ask him to elaborate.

"What do you think, Axel?" Jeb asked as a bell sounded. The fighters stopped their circling and touched gloves in the middle of the cage. The one Axel had pointed out as Kade, stepped over to the side of the cage, undid a latch I didn't even notice, and pushed the door open. He walked out, sweat running down his toned torso, and smiled at Jeb in a way that made me feel like I should avert my eyes.

"Definite potential. I look forward to working with him this week."

"Hear that, Ward?" Kade called back to the man still in the cage. "You're a winner, buddy."

The fighter, Ward, only grunted and walked out past all of us and over to a towel and water bottle sitting on a nearby chair.

"Can he talk?" Zach asked, eyes glued to Ward.

Jeb barked out a laugh. "Yes, he just chooses not to."

"Are y'all hungry?" Kade asked, picking up his own towel and wiping off his face. "We were planning to head over to the diner across the street if you'd like to join us?"

Axel looked at me, and I nodded. "Sounds good."

WE'D GOTTEN BACK TO THE GYM-SLASH-CLUBHOUSE IN THE early evening, full of delicious and totally greasy diner food. Dinner had been a fun affair. We'd sat in the corner booth listening to the guys swap stories about the happenings in both their clubs, talking long after our meals were finished. Well, Jeb, Kade, Zach, and Axel were talking. I mostly listened and let myself lean into Axel's side, enjoying the feel of his arm draped over the back of the booth seat behind me.

It had been nice to forget about my circumstances and relax for a little while.

After we'd walked back across the street, Jeb had offered us a beer, but Axel and I had declined. Neither of us had gotten a ton of sleep the night before—Zach hadn't either, for that matter—but when he noticed Ward sitting in the clubhouse lounge, he'd accepted the beer and made his way inside.

Axel smirked and took my hand, leading me back down the long hallway we'd walked before to one of the club's guest rooms. The room wasn't large, but it was clean and had an en suite bathroom. The bed was a lot smaller than Axel's king-size. Once we'd gotten inside and the door closed behind us, I turned to him.

"I'm not sure we're both going to fit," I said, only half-joking.

He eyed the bed before turning those dark eyes back on me. The heaviness of his stare made my stomach twist in the best way. "I suspect we'll manage. Unless you don't feel like cuddling with me anymore."

"Yeah, that's never going to happen," I scoffed, still feeling that lightness from dinner.

"Then we've got no worries. You ready to sleep?"

I stretched, feeling the lingering tightness from the mostly healed cuts on my legs. All my other bruises and soreness had faded over the last week, and Malcolm's reappearance in my life seemed to have overshadowed the short-lived nightmare Dustin had put me through. "I'm ready for a shower and to lay down for sure."

"Sounds good. You can go first." Axel rearranged the pillows and lay back on the bed, clicking on the small flatscreen TV on the dresser and finding some movie to watch.

I showered and brushed my teeth, standing in front of the sink in only my briefs. They were dark blue and one of my favorite pairs. Forgoing my shirt, I clicked off the light and carried my toiletry bag back out into the room and set it on the dresser next to Axel's. His eyes moved from the TV screen as soon as I came into view, sweeping up and down my body, tracking me as I walked to the side of the bed he was lying on. One large hand cupped the side of my thigh. I pulled in a slow breath as his thumb grazed the edge of the worst of the still-healing cuts there. He'd held my hand a few short days ago when Doc had taken my stitches out.

"These feeling okay?" His voice was soft and deep, the way it only ever got when it was late at night and just the two of us.

"Still tender, but yes."

He nodded, almost to himself, then sat up, pulling me in until I was standing between his spread knees. He had both hands on my thighs now, barely-there touches on the outside of my legs holding me captive. "You'd tell me, wouldn't you? If they were bothering you?"

There was something in his voice...I didn't think we were really talking about my wounds anymore. Not the physical ones, anyway. Since I didn't want to lie to him, I said, "If the cuts started to hurt, I would tell you."

He dropped his eyes with a nod. "Okay." It came out on a

sigh. As he stood, I was forced to step back. "I'm gonna grab a shower."

I could only nod, biting my lip against wanting to call him back. The bathroom door closed with a click, and I curled up in the spot he'd vacated, staring at the TV without really seeing what was happening on the screen. I dozed in and out and felt my lips lift at the corners when strong arms maneuvered me beneath the covers.

When he pulled me back against his chest, I could feel the brush of his hair there and the damp warmth of his skin. I wriggled until I was completely pressed against him, ready to fall asleep held in the safe cradle of his body.

My eyes drooped closed as the heaviness of sleep washed over me. Just before it pulled me under, his lips brushed over the skin of my shoulder. "Good night, sweet boy."

I heard myself whisper back, "Good night, Daddy."

CHAPTER NINE

Axel

The Sand Lake clubhouse lounge was filled with people —club members, old ladies and boys, hang-arounds, and some of the fighters that trained there. Everyone was enjoying a little clubhouse party—drinking, dancing, and getting rowdy. It had been a good week spent working with Ward, who was a hell of a fighter, and spending every spare moment with Leith. He'd been quiet this week, and antsy, seeming to get more so with every day that brought us closer to heading home.

We were leaving in the morning, and he'd been absolutely incapable of sitting still all day. He'd barely said a word, though. I was beginning to think he was trying to mimic Ward, who was as taciturn a person as I'd ever met. My eyes landed on my boy across the room, sitting on a stool and watching Zach lose at pool. Despite spending every night this week sleeping plastered against me, he looked tired. Rundown. We hadn't talked about what he called me the first night in that narrow bed, and I didn't want to push him because I knew he'd been half-asleep when he'd said it. Didn't

mean I could get the sound of his sweet voice calling me
Daddy out of my head, though.

Because, fuck, I wanted that. All the time.

He caught my gaze for a moment, blue eyes so sad that
my eyes narrowed. I pushed myself up off the couch where I'd
been talking with Kade and nursing a beer, determined to
find out what was going on when my phone vibrated in my
pocket.

Pulling it out, I glanced down and sighed at Mace's name
on the screen. Not that I didn't want to talk to my club
brother, but his timing could use some work. I slid my thumb
across to answer. "Hey, Mace."

"Hey, how's things in Sand Lake?"

"Good," I said, stepping over to the wall. "Having a little
club party tonight, and we'll be heading home in the morning.
Everything alright there?"

"That's why I'm calling. We got the name of the guy
rallying the ex-Devil's. Malcolm Sieker."

"Never heard of him." Lifting my eyes, I glanced at the
stool where Leith had been only to find it empty. I stood up
straight from the wall and glanced around the room, not
finding his dark red hair anywhere. A thread of unease slithered through me.

"He's a total unknown, but we're looking into him now.
We don't even know what the guy looks like, so it may take a
minute to run him down. Just stay sharp when y'all head back
this way, and I would appreciate it if you'd pass this on to
Jeb."

"You got it, boss."

"Take care, man."

I strode across the room, approaching the pool table
where Zach was losing to Ward...again. "Where's Leith?"

Zach pulled his eyes away from glaring at the pocket

where Ward had just sunk another ball. "Huh? Oh, he said he'd see me later. I thought he was going to bed."

"Alright. Thanks. I want to head out no later than ten in the morning."

Zach snorted. "In other words, don't get shitfaced. I'll be ready, man."

"Good. See you in the morning. Ward." I nodded at the fighter and he returned it, dark eyes going right back to where he was lining up his next shot. I started toward the door, only for Zach to call me back. When I turned, he'd moved a few feet away from the pool table.

He leaned close and lowered his voice. "Is there something going on with Leith? He's been...off the last few days. And especially today."

My gaze hardened, and my pulse picked up. "I agree, but I don't know what. I'm gonna go find him."

He nodded and clapped me on the shoulder. "Let me know if you need me."

"Thanks, man."

I headed out the door, turning toward the room Leith and I had been sharing all week. The door was closed, but opening it didn't give me any kind of relief. The first thing my eyes landed on was the dresser where our toiletry bags had sat side-by-side for the last five days. Only mine was there now, and the bathroom door was open, light off and empty.

Shit.

I spun around and ran down the hall. Bursting through the back door, I yelled, "Leith!" Not knowing which way to go, I rounded the closest corner, tension releasing from my shoulders when I saw him standing on the sidewalk next to the front of the building. There was a bag over his shoulder, one of the totes with the gym's logo, and tear tracks shining on his cheeks in the light from the streetlamp overhead.

When I was only a few feet from him, his face crumpled and he dropped the bag before launching himself at me. I caught him around the waist, dropping my hands to get a hold of his ass and haul him up so he could wrap his legs around me.

"I'm sorry, Daddy," he cried against my throat, arms wrapped tightly around me as his whole body trembled.

"Easy, sweet boy, it's okay," I whispered against the side of his face, pressing a kiss to his temple and running one hand up and down his back while holding him up with the other. My heart was slamming in my chest, relief and worry clashing together as I held him tight.

Lifting his face, he looked at me from inches away. He leaned in, pressing the smallest kiss to my lips. It was more than enough to snap the tenuous hold I had on my hunger for him. I covered his mouth with my own, licking across his lips and spearing inside when he opened them for me. He moaned, hands loosening their stranglehold so he could run them over my bald head as his tongue met mine thrust for thrust.

With effort, I pulled back, taking in his spit-shiny lips and still damp cheeks. "We're going to go inside, and you're going to tell me what all this has been about. The truth. No more lies, Leith."

He nodded, lowering his eyes.

"Hey, look at me." When I had his pretty blues on me again, I kissed him, slower this time, nipping his lips and only pulling back when his body had gone lax in my arms. "Everything's going to be okay, sweetheart."

He shot me a tiny smile and pressed his face back against the side of my throat. Carefully, I squatted down, grabbing the handle of his bag and turning us back toward the clubhouse entrance. Once we were back in our room, I kicked the door closed behind us and set Leith on his feet.

Sinking down onto the edge of the bed, he dropped his face into his hands. "I'm so sorry, Axel."

I set his bag down beside the duffle our clothes had been in and went into the bathroom to grab a washcloth. Turning on the cold water, I let it run for a moment while I gathered myself. I wetted the cloth and wrung it out, then went to sit beside him on the bed. Gently, I pulled his hands from his face and gripped his chin so he'd turn to look at me. Pressing the cool cloth to his skin, I wiped his cheeks and his nose before tossing it back into the bathroom.

I barely knew where to start. Blowing out a breath, I took his hand in mine. "What are you sorry for?"

He huffed a small breath. "For lying to you and almost just leaving without saying goodbye."

"Where were you going?"

His blue eyes were wet again when he looked at me. "I don't know. I was going to pick a place after I found the bus station."

Something cold and dark settled in my gut. What had scared him so badly that he was running without even knowing where he was going? *Who* had scared him so badly? My Heretics brothers assumed the person breaking into his apartment had either been random or another escalation from the ex-Devils. If they'd been keeping tabs on the place, they'd have known he hadn't been staying there. It was an easy way to encroach on Heretics' territory without physically hurting anyone—something that would have demanded immediate retaliation. But that day in his apartment, I knew he'd been lying to me.

I lifted a finger to his chin, tilting his face up so I could see his eyes. "Who's the man in the picture, Leith?"

He took a fortifying breath. "His name is Malcolm Sieker. He used to be my Daddy."

"Your Daddy?" I heard myself say, while venomous jeal-

ousy and rage so potent I needed to close my eyes before
Leith saw it, dumped itself in my veins. This Malcolm fucker
was supposed to have been his Daddy? But Leith was ready to
run, to leave his entire life behind the moment the man
appeared. What the hell had he done to my boy?

Leith squeezed my hand and brought his other hand up to
sift through the hair on my forearm. "He was supposed to
be." He took a deep breath as I did the same, opening my
eyes and giving him all my attention. "I didn't have the best
home life. Not abusive...not physically anyway, but they made
sure I knew that I'd never succeed being the way I was. So
when I graduated high school, I took all the money I'd saved
from my cashier job and bought a bus ticket. Made it from
South Carolina to Ohio because I had a cousin that lived in
Columbus." He sighed.

"Take your time, sweet boy."

"It's just...I was so stupid. I'd read all these things online
and wanted to try everything. I went to a club one night, and
Malcolm picked me up, told me I looked like I needed a
Daddy...and despite all the shit that came after, the way he
made it sound and the way he treated me in the beginning,
made something *click* into place inside me. It made me realize
that I was a boy, and I definitely wanted a Daddy of my own."

"What happened?" I scooted closer to him, keeping hold
of his hand and moving my other to his back. He leaned into
my side, and I breathed a little easier.

"I think a tabloid would call it a whirlwind romance. We
were inseparable. He moved me into his apartment and basically took over my life." He rolled his eyes. "I thought it was
all romantic at first, like he wanted to take care of me...but
then he decided I should be on his phone plan, and that he
should manage my money, and that I should adhere to the
tightly controlled schedule he created for me. I disagreed,
and that's when I learned how deep in I really was."

"He hurt you?"

He wouldn't meet my eyes. "Yes. Any time he thought I stepped a toe out of line. N-not with knives like Dustin. But he'd beat me and use me and lock me up. Sometimes for days at a time." He squeezed my hand, an earnest plea in his voice. "I can't let him get me again, Axel."

"Daddy," I said, giving him a small smile so he wouldn't see how badly I needed to hunt down and kill the bastard that had hurt him. "If you want. Not that you have to call me that all the time, but I want you to know, Leith, being with me won't be anything like it was with him. We'll be partners, and if you choose to put your trust in me, to give me the honor of taking care of you, I promise you, sweet boy, I will never abuse it. I know what that feels like, too. And how it feels to have to run from someone that should have loved you instead of hurting you."

"Who did you have to run from?"

"My father. He wasn't a good man, and my brother and I always seemed to be the captive audience to his rage. I swear to you, Leith, I'll never raise a hand or anything else to you in anger."

"I know." A sweet smile stretched his lips, and I was so relieved to see it I leaned in and pressed my lips to his. "I've never been afraid of you. Not even for a moment."

"You have no reason to be. Ever. And you don't need to be afraid of Malcolm, either. Cautious, yes. But, sweetheart, whether you wanted to be with me or not, I would protect you. The Heretics will protect you."

"But you do, right? Want to be with me?"

Getting my arm fully around him, I pulled him over until he was straddling my lap. "Yes. I want to be with you. Want to be your Daddy, if you'll have me."

He threaded his fingers through my beard and looked almost shy. "Yes, please."

Wrapping both my arms around him, I pulled him into a slow kiss and let the knowledge that he was finally mine settle into my bones.

CHAPTER TEN

Leith

I woke to an empty space in the bed beside me and the low rumble of Axel's voice across the room. Peeking my eyes open, I found him in the room's only chair, in nothing but a pair of briefs with his elbows on his knees and the phone pressed to his ear.

"I want this fucker found, Cleave. The shit he did to Leith..." Axel growled and rubbed one of his hands roughly over the top of his hand. "Yeah, we'll be heading out in the next hour or so." He was quiet for a moment, nodding his head at whatever Cleave was saying. "Good. Will do. See you soon." He looked up as he pulled the phone away from his ear, catching my eyes. I tried not to squirm.

"Sorry, Daddy."

The smile I got then was as bright as the morning sun coming through the cracks in the curtains. He stood up, dropping the phone on the dresser and climbing back into bed with me. Last night had surprised me. Not the fact that I'd hesitated when I'd heard Axel call my name outside or that he cared about me, but after the talking and the kissing, he'd gotten us both into bed, and then, just held me. All night. Like he'd done every other time we'd shared a bed. No hinting or pushing for more.

I guess I was still a little skittish after everything with Dustin because I'd been nervous. Obviously, without warrant, but it settled something in me when he hadn't automatically wanted to use my body however he saw fit just because I was his boy now. Axel really wasn't like Malcolm, and he wasn't like Dustin. Any nerves I'd still had last night were gone, burned away by the bright sunlight and the affection I could see shining in Axel's eyes.

"Good morning. I didn't mean to wake you." He blew out a big breath as he lay on his side, one arm reaching out to pull me closer. "I'm sorry. You shouldn't have had to hear that."

I nuzzled into him, tucking myself under his chin and rubbing my face over his chest. "I didn't mind. It's sexy when you get all growly."

He hummed, the vibration of it tickling my cheek while his warm hands slid over the bare skin of my back, lighting me up everywhere we touched. "I'll keep that in mind."

"Daddy..."

"Yes, sweet boy?"

"I'm not saying I want to, at least, not yet," I said, suddenly nervous. Why was I bringing this up when I *knew* mentally and probably physically that I wasn't ready for things to get more physical between us? "But, um, you do want to...have sex someday, right?"

All movement stopped. I bit my lip and leaned back enough to meet his eyes. The deep brown of them overlaid with gold in the sun. There was surprise written all over his face.

"Of course. I want you in every way I can have you. I just thought...well, I wanted you to have the space to heal. And there's no need for us to rush. We have all the time in the world."

If I hadn't known that I was falling hopelessly in love with this man, there was no longer any doubt in my mind.

AXEL'S BIKE ATE UP THE HIGHWAY IN FRONT OF US. LEAVING Sand Lake had felt bittersweet. I'd been through so many emotions in the last few weeks it was difficult to get my bearings. The only thing I was sure about was the man in front of me, solid and sturdy in my arms.

Part of me was nervous about going back to St. Louis because regardless of anything else, Malcolm was there, and I had spent so long associating him with fear. It wasn't something I could just overcome in a day. I was finding, however, that I *did* trust Axel, and I believed him when he said he and the club wouldn't abandon me—which was something I'd never had. It felt strange thinking there was a line of defense in front of me now—full of people that had proven I could count on them. For the first time in my life, I was beginning to understand what family should feel like.

Zach sped along beside us, looking cool and sexy in his white t-shirt, Heretics' vest, and aviators. He tilted his head my way, shooting me a little smile. We'd been on the road for a while, and I was finding I truly enjoyed being on the back of Axel's bike—the sun on my face, the wind rushing over us, the vibrating rumble under my butt, and of course, being pressed so close to him.

He tensed in my arms, making me lift my cheek from where I'd had it resting on his back. Two motorcycles were approaching from the opposite direction. They had the kind of full-wrap helmets on that obscured their faces. As soon as we passed them, I glanced in the side mirror. They were brak-ing, and then both of them pulled a U-turn to get behind us.

Just as my heart started to pound, Axel's hand covered mine and gave me a quick squeeze as he shouted, "Hold on tight!" over his shoulder.

I tightened my grip, and the bike below us lurched forward as Axel accelerated. I wanted to clench my eyes shut, but instead, looked over to where Zach had been only a moment ago. He wasn't there now. He'd dropped behind us.

Looking in the side mirror showed Zach was moving his bike back and forth across the lane, keeping the other two motorcycles from getting too close to us as Axel continued to speed ahead. Every time they would try to get around him, he would move to block them. Panic built up inside me as the wind beat harder against my face the faster we went. I was afraid one of the other bikers would do something to hurt Zach or he would lose control.

We passed the sign for a rest area, and Axel slowed the bike a little. As we got closer, I spotted two more motorcy-cles with their riders idling near the rest area exit. A punch of fear shot through me, thinking they'd come to harass us too, but then I caught the insignia on their vests. They were Heretics.

We flew past the exit. The two waiting Heretics pulled out onto the road, quickly gaining speed and getting up behind the two strange bikers and helping Zach to box them in.

After only a moment, the two bikers slowed and turned. Instead of following them, our guys sped up enough to catch up with us. As they got closer, I realized that it was Cleave and Mace on the bikes. Mace passed us, settling into a slightly slower speed right in front of us while Zach and Cleave flanked us—one on either side. I let out a huge breath and pressed my cheek to Axel's back, holding him tight the rest of the way home.

When we pulled into the clubhouse parking lot, I let out a sigh of relief. Axel walked the bike back into his parking spot and killed the engine before holding it steady for me to climb off.

"Any idea who the fuck those guys were?" Zach asked, the moment he'd climbed off his bike next to us.

"No paint on the bikes. No patches on the vests." Mace pulled the helmet off his head and stuffed it into his saddle-bag. "Had to be ex-Devils fucking with us. Probably a very specific one." He turned questioning green eyes on me, voice sharp. "Either of them seem familiar?"

I shook my head. "No, they didn't."

"That's enough," Axel barked, stepping off the bike and getting between Mace and me. "He's got enough shit on his plate without you trying to interrogate him."

Mace raised his hands. "Sorry." He looked around Axel's bulk to me. "I'm sorry, Leith. I'm pissed at those assholes, not at you."

I gave him a small smile. "I understand, it's okay." Sliding my hand into Axel's, I squeezed his fingers. He deflated a bit and took a step back out of Mace's space.

The clubhouse door opened, and a stone-faced Calix stepped out. "Get in here. We've got church in ten minutes."

The guys all nodded and started in that direction. Cleave and Axel clasped hands and pulled each other in for a quick hug.

"Thanks for the assist," Axel said, giving my hand a squeeze as we fell into step beside Cleave.

"No problem," Cleave said, clapping Axel on the shoulder again and shooting me a wink. "How was Sand Lake?"

"Good. Ward's going to be an excellent addition to the circuit here."

He nodded. "What about you, Leith? Jeb and the boys treat you okay? As if this guy would let them get away with it if they didn't." He bumped Axel's shoulder with his own. I knew he was giving his friend shit, but it was nice he was including me. Outside of *Spritz*, I hadn't had much interaction with all the guys. I wanted to change that.

"Oh...yes. They were all really nice."

We made it to the door, and Cleave pulled it open and held it for both of us. Once we were inside, I veered toward the stairs, thinking I'd stay in Axel's room while they had their meeting. Calix's voice stopped me before I'd taken more than a step.

"Leith."

I turned wide eyes to the Heretics' president.

"I'd like for you to join us, if you will."

I swallowed hard, pulling my gaze away from Calix's black-eyed stare to look at Axel. He was frowning, but at my nod, he led us to the meeting room. Pulling a seat up at that table felt surreal, and I tried not to swallow too audibly when the door clicked closed.

I HADN'T BEEN ALONE FOR OVER A WEEK. EVERYWHERE I went, Axel, Zach, or Cleave were stuck to me like glue. At least at home—mostly Axel's room at the clubhouse—I got to lounge around and cuddle with the sweetest freaking Daddy that ever lived. Out in public, it was like having a bodyguard. I was trying to make the most of it, though. Cleave, it turned out, was really easy to talk to, and I'd gotten to know his boyfriend, JJ, more as well. Zach apparently loved ice cream as much as I did, and he totally let me put eyeliner and mascara on him as long as I pinky swore I'd never tell.

There'd been no sign of Malcolm.

Even at work, the guys on duty were sticking close to me. I'd had my first night back on Wednesday. It'd been overwhelming at first, but I'd fallen into my old rhythms quickly. Vivian had greeted me with a hug and only smiled knowingly when I'd told her I needed to only be scheduled on the top floor of the club from now on. Axel hadn't said anything, but I could tell he had been relieved when I'd told him I'd be sticking to serving only.

The way he took care of me, but still gave me the space to make my own decisions—unless I asked him for help—had completely cemented my decision to trust him. And to keep trusting him. Falling in love with him had happened all on its own with barely a passing thought from me. My heart wanted him, and I felt damn lucky every day that he wanted me too. I hadn't told him yet, but I would when the time was right.

Friday night found me at *Spritz*, facing my first weekend shift since Dustin drugged and kidnapped me a month ago. I was feeling good, and ready, wearing tight blue boyshorts—with the legs long enough to cover the worst of my new scars—glitter body lotion, and just a touch of make-up. I was leaning over one of the dressing room vanities, mascara wand in hand, when Pax and Arden appeared behind me.

"Axel's going to shit when he sees your ass in those shorts," Pax said with a laugh. It was still so strange to see him in a vest and dress slacks instead of undies and a halter. Being the assistant manager looked good on him.

I smirked back at him. "I know."

They both smiled.

"Here," Arden said, leaning forward and taking the wand from my hand. "Let me."

I turned around, leaning my ass against the counter and tilting my face up. Arden expertly swiped the black coating on my lashes, and then picked through the other make-up I had spread out on the vanity.

"This color is gorgeous on you," he said, almost to himself while he added some shadow to my eyes.

"Thanks." I grinned at him, then over at Pax who was watching us with a smile on his face.

When Arden was satisfied—he was right, that color *did* look great on me—we headed toward the door together.

"You ready for this?" Pax asked, touching my arm to stop me before we went out onto the floor. "You'll let me know if you need me, right?"

I could admit that I was a little afraid, but I was ready too. Ready to get my life completely back on track. "Promise."

"Okay. Let's do this."

Stepping through the door, I saw Axel at his post midway along the wall beside the dance floor. When he looked my way, I did a slow little spin for him. His eyes went hot and narrow, promising that he'd have some things to say —and maybe do—about my choice of outfit once our shifts were over. I looked forward to it. Our physical relationship hadn't moved beyond kissing and some light groping, in deference to my mental health and my now healed body. I was feeling more ready every day to take that next step with him.

Walking over to him, I leaned up on my toes and pressed a kiss to his cheek. "What do you think, Daddy?"

"You know damn well what I think," he growled, eyes raking over me and looking like he was a second from throwing me over his shoulder and making a break for it. Despite where we were, he pulled me close and kissed me quick. "Be careful tonight."

"I will." I moved to step away from him and toward the bar to pick up my tray and start serving the early crowd, but he caught my wrist. I looked back at him, meeting his dark brown eyes.

"You look beautiful," he said simply, and I was glad my mascara was waterproof because my eyes started to prickle.

"Thanks, Daddy." I squeezed his hand before I let go and made a beeline for the bar. One more second in his orbit and I'd be the one dragging him out of there before our shifts were up.

The night picked up quickly, and once we were in full swing, I didn't have time to think about anything other than balancing trays full of drinks and dodging dudes trying to grab my ass. I loved it—the pace, the flirting, all of it—and I'd missed it. It was so good to be back.

I was on my way back to the bar, weaving between groups of dancing people, an empty tray tucked under my arm, when hands closed over my hips from behind. He pulled me back against his chest, and he ground his erection against my ass. I could see the bill of his ball cap out of the corner of my eye with the way he was hunched around me and made myself swallow down the lump of fear in my throat.

"Hi, Malcolm." I was proud of the lack of waver in my voice.

"Ballsy of him to let you roam around here without a leash," Malcolm said against my ear, still grinding on my ass.

I grimaced, eyes searching for the nearest Heretic. "Ballsy of you to show up here. You know I'm under Heretic protection?"

He laughed. It wasn't a nice sound. "Oh, I've seen you riding bitch on more than one of their bikes. If I'd known you were such a little biker slut, I'd have joined up sooner."

Anger was winning out over fear the longer his nasty hands were on me. "Why did you join? Need a new hobby? You know those assholes you're running with aren't even a real club, and they're homophobic as fuck. What happens when they find out the only ass you like is male?"

Faster than I could blink, one of his hands shot up to my

face, gripping my jaw hard as he hissed against my cheek, "God, I forgot about the fucking mouth on you." He squeezed harder. "Enjoy your little Heretics pals while you've got them, Leith."

He shoved me away hard enough that I dropped my tray and nearly fell. When I spun around, he'd already disappeared into the crowd.

CHAPTER ELEVEN

Axel

"Easy, buddy. Easy. We've got him." Cleave's hand on my shoulder was the only thing keeping me from tearing out into the bar and ripping that motherfucker apart. We'd been watching Malcolm from the moment he'd stepped through the door. Two seconds after he shoved Leith away and hightailed it out, Zach was there, getting a steadying arm around Leith and leading him back to the security booth where Cleave and I were watching all the security camera feeds.

I moved to the door, opening it when they were still ten feet away and striding forward to pull a shaking Leith into my arms. Lifting him up, I kept one hand under his ass and gently squeezed the back of his neck with the other. Zach moved past us and into the booth with Cleave.

"You did so good, baby. So good. Are you okay? Did he hurt you?" I'd protested against this plan from the start. Loudly. Adamantly. But Leith wanted to do it. Wanted to get back to his life, knowing Calix was right and that Leith being back out on the floor working at *Spritz* would dangle him like low hanging fruit and eventually draw the snake out of his hole. The moment Calix had suggested it was the only time in memory that I wanted to punch my president squarely in the face.

Leith had agreed though, and I would never take his choices away.

"I'm okay. He didn't hurt me, but I feel gross. Like I need a shower asap," he said against my neck.

A deep sigh of relief escaped my lungs. Fuck, but I never wanted Leith to be in the same room with that man again. Which was exactly why Calix and Riot were trailing him right now. After tonight, Malcolm Sieker wouldn't be hurting anyone else.

Turning my head, I kissed Leith's neck, his ear, his cheek until he lifted up enough to press his lips to mine. I licked into him, kissing him deeply, and reassuring us both that he was okay and back where he belonged.

When we pulled apart, he met my eyes. "You have to go?"

I nodded. "Yeah, sweet boy. Will you please go to the clubhouse with Zach? I'll be home later."

"Okay."

I set him on his feet, keeping my arm around him, and turned to my club brothers. Cleave was doing something on one of the computers, but Zach walked back over to us. "Do not let him out of your sight."

Zach nodded, glancing at Leith and then holding my stare. "You have my word."

Malcolm and his ex-Devil pals been partying for hours. It was nearly three a.m., and it looked like the card game happening in the kitchen was still going strong. The house was on the edge of a neighborhood that had seen better days. There was an open field to one side of it and a boarded-up house on the other. Calix, Riot, and I had been hiding in the shadow of the empty house's covered back porch since we'd followed Malcolm here from *Spritz*. The beat-up old car Calix and Riot used to follow him was parked two streets over along with my bike.

As far as we could tell, the only people in the house were the three ex-Devils sitting around the table with Malcolm. Finally, he got up and said something that made the others laugh before walking into the darkened interior of the house. I broke away from the shadows and crossed the short yard separating the two houses. Crouching beneath a window along the back, I slowly raised up and peeked over the sill.

Malcolm moved past the window, bumping into a wall as he walked through the living room and entered a hallway. A moment later, a light shone out of a window further down. Staying low, I crept down the side of the house until I was beneath the lit window and listened.

He was moving around in the room, then a door opened, and the creak of water filtering through old pipes reached my ear. Chancing a peek, I found the room empty, and what I assumed was a bathroom door standing open. Pulling my knife out of my pocket, I slit the screen and wedged the blade under the window—not locked. *Perfect*.

As soon as I had the window lifted an inch, I could hear the sound of a shower. Quickly, I slid the window up the rest of the way and hauled myself inside, taking care to keep my balance and brace myself so I didn't land too heavily on the floor and give myself away.

Steam was filling the bathroom when I stepped inside.

Taking a deep breath, I stepped in front of the bathtub and pulled the shower curtain back. Malcolm's startled eyes met mine. He opened his mouth to yell, and I lunged forward, one hand landing across his mouth and the other bringing the knife up and plunging it into his neck. His eyes bulged, arms flailing as he tried to beat me away. Water soaked my arm, the side of my face and vest, dripping down and mixing with the swirling red cloud headed for the drain.

In any other case, I might have felt guilty killing a man like this. Naked. In the shower. With no real means to defend himself, but some part of me—one of the dark, angry places still living in my soul—wanted him to feel helpless. Vulnerable. To hurt even for a moment the way he'd made Leith hurt so many times.

I kept my hand over his mouth as he slid down the wall. Once the light left his eyes, I stood up and rinsed my knife under the still running spray. Then I went back out the window, and let the darkness cover me until I was back with my brothers.

"Daddy?" Leith's sleepy voice came from the nest of blankets he'd made in the middle of my bed.

"It's me, sweet boy." I slid under the sheet, my skin still warm from my shower, and started digging through the blankets until I found his skin. He unbound himself, shoving the throw blankets off the bed and turned into my arms, tucking himself under my chin.

"Is everything okay?"

I buried my nose in his lush red hair, breathing him in until his clean scent filled up every aching part of me. "Everything is perfect, baby."

CHAPTER TWELVE

Leith

One Month Later

The fights were held in an old chicken barn outside the city. It was just one big, long, low metal building with huge sliding doors on either end and a concrete floor. Good for easy cleaning, Axel had said, and I didn't want to think about that. The Heretics had modeled it to their purposes, adding a few interior walls to make up dressing rooms for the fighters, but other than that, the lone metal octagonal cage was the only thing in the space.

Well, that and about fifty people who were buzzing with the drinks some of my fellow *Spritz* employees were serving and the need to see some bloodshed. I didn't really get that. Maybe I'd had enough fists aimed at me in my life that the thought of it as entertainment had lost all appeal. I knew it wasn't the same. This was a sport, or the illegal representation of one anyway, and in no way the same as what I'd experienced with Malcolm or Dustin.

I didn't want to think about either one of them tonight. I hadn't asked Axel what happened the night Malcolm came into *Spritz*. He would tell me if I wanted to know, I was sure of it...but I just...didn't. What I did know was he'd lightened up on having someone on *Leith bodyguard detail* around the clock, and that he'd been uncharacteristically quiet for a few days after.

He'd held me a lot, and I'd held him back.

"You look like you're having a blast," Zach said, stopping beside me. He was working tonight so he was in thick-soled boots, jeans, and his Heretics' Prospect vest over a white t-shirt. I was beginning to think he didn't own anything else.

"Fights really aren't my thing. Anyway, since we both have the night off, Axel and I are going to take off soon. Cleave just needed his help with something." As I spoke, he kept looking around, like his head was on a swivel. "Uh, are you okay?"

"Huh? Oh, I'm fine. Just watching for Calix."

I frowned. "I think he's outside having a smoke with Barrett."

"Cool." He relaxed a fraction.

"Did you need him for something?"

"What? No, no. I don't need him. I'm just trying not to get busted."

My eyes narrowed. "Busted for what?"

He sighed, then scowled and looked at me like he was measuring me for something. After a moment of silent deliberation, he held up his pinky. "If I tell you something, can you keep it to yourself? I mean it, Leith. You can't tell anyone, not even Axel."

"Dude, I haven't told anyone about the other thing, have I?" I batted my eyelashes at him.

He huffed a laugh, clean-shaven cheeks going pink. He really was a nice-looking dude. Like, put him in a football uniform and dump a water bottle over his head so he could glisten in the sun, because he had that all-American, home-grown, heartthrob thing going on. Just, you know, in a motorcycle club vest instead.

"So I," he said, then closed his mouth. Then opened it and closed it again. He glanced around. We were standing back from the crowd, and not one person was paying any attention to us. Finally, he took a big breath and rushed his words out so fast that it didn't sound like there was any space between them. "So I might have slept with Ward while we were in Sand Lake, and I'm supposed to be back there watching the fighters, but it's awkward as fuck between us now."

My eyebrows shot up my forehead. That was literally the last thing I'd expected him to say. "I thought you were straight? I mean—" I threw up my hands "—I don't mean to assume. Sorry. I didn't realize you liked men."

"I don't."

"Huh?"

"Ugh," Zach groaned, scrubbing a hand over his face. "I mean, obviously I do. Apparently? This has never really happened to me before, and I...don't really have anyone to talk about it with."

"Awww, and you came to me!" I grabbed him, hugging the shit out of his arm.

"Oh my god, Leith. Don't be an ass!"

"I'm not!" The giant smile on my face was, admittedly, me being an ass, but was also something so much deeper. Zach was a good guy, and I was proud to get to call him my friend. "Seriously, I'm not. I'm just happy for you, discovering new things about yourself is exciting, and I'm honored that you'd, you know, want to share them with me."

He sighed, looking down, face still red. When he looked back up at me, he smiled. "I'm glad we're friends."

My heart collapsed into absolute mush. "Me too."

"You too, what?" Axel said, stepping in behind me until I

was pressed all along his front.

Zach's eyes went wide, and he shot his hand out between us, pinky extended.

I giggled. I couldn't help it, but I twined my pinky around his, and we shook on it. Right after, his eyes darted up to Axel and he cleared his throat, all manly and gruff. "See you later, Axel. Leith." Then he was striding off in the direction of the fighter dressing rooms.

"Do I even want to know?" Axel asked.

I tilted my head back with a smile. "Nope, which is good cause I wouldn't tell you anyway. We pinky swore."

"Is that right?" He bent down, lowering his face to mine for an upside-down kiss. "You ready to get out of here?"

I thought about the surprise I had waiting for him. "Hell, yes."

Soft, late summer air glided over us as we cruised down some winding back-country road. I had no idea where we were going, and that thought didn't bother me in the slightest. I tightened my hold around Axel's middle and rested my cheek on his shoulder, content to ride along anywhere he wanted to take me.

When the bike slowed and turned, the headlight beam revealed an overgrown, narrow gravel road with trees lining both sides. The ride was bumpy, and we eventually came to a stop on a flat bit of open land with a drop off up ahead. Axel killed the engine, dropped the kickstand, and turned off the headlight.

Once my eyes adjusted, my breath caught. A full, deep black sky dotted with a million stars was shining above, stretching out and reaching down to the lights of the city in the distance.

"How did you find this?" I asked, keeping my voice quiet so I didn't disturb the peace.

"Cleave. He knows all the good spots."

I hummed, sliding my hands down until I could slip them under the hem of his t-shirt. He pulled in a quick breath as I scraped my nails over the solid muscles of his stomach. Unlike some of the guys, he didn't have super cut abs, but he was solid—thick and sturdy and so fucking sexy I couldn't live another day without having him inside me.

Biting my lip, I slid off the bike and pulled off my helmet. The moon was just bright enough that I could see the curious expression on his face.

"Will you take yours off, too?" Nerves made my voice shake a little, so I forced myself to pull in a calming breath. This was Axel after all. My Daddy. I didn't have anything to be nervous about.

He reached up and unclasped his helmet. I took it from his hand and put them in the saddlebag.

"What are you up to, sweet boy?"

"I have a surprise for you."

He started to rise from the bike, but I stepped up to his side and put a hand on his shoulder. "Help me up?"

Still watching me with curious eyes, he wrapped an arm around my middle and lifted me up so that I was straddling the bike in front of him. My legs were draped over his thighs and my ass was half on the gas tank and half on the seat where he'd slid back to give me some room. Tilting my face up, I asked wordlessly for a kiss. He didn't disappoint, drawing my tongue out of my mouth with sweet, seductive swipes of his. I moaned into it, leaning against him and running my hands over his head.

He broke our kiss to nip along my jaw and down my neck, pressing wet open-mouth kisses and sucking just hard enough to make me squirm. Feeling drugged from his mouth on me, I gripped one of his hands where it was holding my hip and started to slide it backward. Lifting his head, he stared at me from inches away, breathing hard.

"Sweet boy?"

I bit my lip, continuing that slow slide until I got his hand positioned beneath the waistband of my pants. Holding his eyes, I brought my hands between us and undid my button and lowered my zipper.

"Make love to me?"

He groaned, mouth sealing over mine and hand sliding further down. His fingers slipped under the material of my briefs and down. His whole body jolted when they brushed the edge of the plug in my ass.

"Fuck, Leith," he panted, tearing his mouth away from mine. He shook his head with a smile. "That is..." His fingers moved gently, circling the base and making me gasp as it shifted and brushed my already sensitive prostate—butt plug plus motorcycle was like the ultimate vibrator. "That is so fucking sexy, baby."

"You like your surprise then, Daddy?"

"Oh yes," he said, claiming my lips again.

I dropped my hands to the front of his pants. "Can I?"

"You can do anything you want, sweetheart."

Reaching into my back pocket, I pulled out the condom and packet of lube I'd stashed there earlier and set them on the small bit of seat between us. He helped me get his pants undone and down enough that I could get my hand inside his briefs and pull his cock out. He was gloriously hard, and my mouth watered at the sight of him. Scooting my ass back, I bent forward and pulled him into my mouth, sucking the crown while I jacked his length.

"*Goddamn*, baby. You keep that up and I won't last. Want you too fucking bad."

Needing to tease him a little more, I circled my tongue

around and pressed it into his slit until his hips started to buck. Sitting up, I grabbed the condom and ripped it open, sheathing him with quick movements. Pulling one leg up, I turned in his lap so both legs were on the same side of the bike and used my toes to kick off my shoes. Pushing my pants down my legs, I bent down, thankful for the arm Axel kept around my waist so I didn't topple over in my hurry and shucked everything—pants, underwear, and socks. While I was at it, I pulled my shirt off too.

He growled, manhandling me back around until I was straddling him again. He reached for the plug, getting a hold of the end, and slowly pulling it out of me. He dropped it over the other side of the bike so it wouldn't land on my clothes, and I shifted closer to him, searching for the lube packet. Once I found it and ripped it open, Axel offered me his hand. I squirted some lube onto his fingers and the rest right on his dick.

Reaching behind me, he pressed one slick digit into my hole, quickly followed by a second. I moved my hips, riding his fingers the way I wanted to ride him.

"I'm ready, Daddy."

He shook his head. "I'm bigger than that plug."

I laughed. "I know, but I want to feel it. Want to feel you." Gripping his shoulders, I lifted myself up with my feet braced on the driver's pegs. He steadied me with a hand on my hip while the other positioned his cock. I loved that he was still fully dressed and that we were out in nature, in the middle of this beautiful overlook he'd brought me to, underneath the stars.

I took a deep breath as he breached me, relishing in the stretch and burn and *fullness* of having him inside. When I'd sunk down all the way, we stopped for a moment, eyes open wide, staring at each other. Leaning in, he rested his forehead to mine, breathing with me and letting me adjust.

"You make me so happy, sweet boy."

I threaded my fingers into his beard. "You make me happy too, Daddy."

He kissed me slowly, raising his hips a little at a time, picking up speed and gripping my ass cheeks to hold me up and open for his thrusts. I wrapped my arms around his neck, bracing myself on his shoulders and using the leverage to press down to meet him. When I was close, he slid his hands up my back and stood up, cupping the back of my head, and holding the weight of my torso on his forearms. I raised my feet to the seat behind him and held on to his biceps as he drove into me over and over.

Pleasure was surging through my body—gathering and building in my balls and ass and the base of my spine. I reached for my dick, stroking myself frantically as his thrusts turned erratic, and I came with a startled cry all over my stomach. Axel tensed a moment later, burying himself in my body with a grunt.

"Oh my god," I panted, basking in the glow of the most glorious orgasm I'd ever had and going limp in Axel's arms. Even cum drunk, I knew he wouldn't let me fall. He sat back on the bike, still inside me and pulled me up into a sensual kiss. I was probably getting cum all over his shirt and vest, but he didn't seem to care, holding me close and running his hands all over my body.

"I love you, sweet boy. I love you so much," he whispered into the space between our lips when we broke apart.

I smiled, so happy I was ready to burst. "I love you too, Daddy."

Thank you for reading!

DISCORDANT

Iron Heretics MC #3

PROLOGUE

Zach

Six Years Ago

"*I don't want to sell myself short.*"

Amy's words played over and over in my brain, bouncing around like a pinball until they were jumbled together along with the brutal fucking ache in my chest. I could admit I'd never been the smartest guy when it came to books, but people? Well, I thought I was a much better judge of people.

Instead, Uncle Mutt was locked up in prison after I'd been foolish enough to believe him when he said it would all be okay, and Amy had decided that instead of sticking to our plans, she didn't want a boyfriend holding her back when she went off to college.

"I don't want to sell myself short," she'd said. Her face had been blotchy and as red as her hair with her tears.

A grimace screwed up my face at hearing her voice again

in my head, at seeing that last image of her face. She'd kissed me quickly before she'd turned and walked away. The college she'd chosen was two states away. She'd been my girlfriend since the summer before our sophomore year of high school and here we were, the summer after our senior year, and I was wondering if I'd ever even see her again. At least we'd come full circle, I guess.

"Zach? You home?" My mom, Sheila's voice broke through my angsty musings. "I've got groceries in the car."

With a sigh, I hauled myself off the couch. It had always been just me and Mom. Well, and Uncle Mutt. Before he'd transferred from the St. Louis Heretics to the Nomad charter, anyway. I'd asked him not to because I knew it meant he'd be gone all the time. Then, not only was he gone for months at a time, he'd done something with the Nomads and ended up with an eight-year prison sentence. He'd already been inside a year. I missed him like crazy...but I couldn't bring myself to go see him. I didn't know what to say.

"Zach?" Mom came around the corner from the kitchen. She took one look at my face and was in front of me immediately, her hands reaching up to cup my cheeks. "Baby, what's wrong?"

I shouldn't cry. I was supposed to be a man now, but I wrapped my arms around her smaller frame, buried my face in her shoulder, and let it all out.

Once I'd settled down and told her everything, we finished putting groceries away. She decided to make my favorite pasta for dinner, and I was sitting up on the counter beside the stove like I'd done since I was little as we talked.

"I can't believe after all the plans we made she could just walk away." I picked at the edge of a rip in my jeans. "I guess I thought she was the one."

"Oh, honey," Mom said, voice laced with sympathy as she

patted the back of my hand. "She was your first love, but she won't be your last."

I knew the thought was supposed to comfort me, but the trepidation those words brought made my already cold stomach twist. Nothing was worth feeling this way, and the only thing I could do now was try to forget her. But I damn sure wasn't about to make the mistake of letting this happen all over again. Amy *was* my first love. If I had anything to say about it, she'd also be my last.

Mom glanced at me and took a deep breath. "I went to see your uncle today."

We didn't talk about Mutt a lot. Not since I'd refused to go with her the first time she'd visited him. Despite myself though, I'd asked how he was every time she did visit, even if I couldn't bring myself to go with her. As a diversion tactic, it was a pretty solid one.

"He doing okay?"

"He is. He said he got a new cellmate a few days ago." She shook her head as she stirred the bubbling pot of sauce. "A young guy. Barely eighteen. Can you believe that?"

I frowned. "What did he do?"

"Mutt didn't know all the details, but I guess he punched a cop."

"Huh." I was barely eighteen myself, and I couldn't imagine being locked up. That had to suck, and with the violent types of inmates in that prison? I'd be fucking scared shitless. Even if I did punch a cop to get there.

"All I know is he's lucky he got put in with Mutt. Makes my stomach hurt to think what could have happened to him if they'd put him anywhere else."

"Yeah." I paused my pity party long enough to send a thought up for some other eighteen-year-old boy that was in a way worse position than me.

Ward
Six Years Later

"You're sure they won't mind?" I asked again, quietly. The concrete of the cell floor felt as unyielding today —my last day in this place—as it had on the first. It still felt entirely surreal. Six years I'd been staring at these walls. Six years of zero privacy as Mutt and I learned to live together in this cramped space. Somehow, I'd managed not to go crazy or get killed. The latter I knew I owed entirely to the man standing in front of me. Probably most of the former, too.

"I guarantee they're already waiting for you out front. Okay? Stop fretting, kid." Mutt, my mentor and only friend, said. He was an inch or so shorter than me and wider, like a bulldozer. He kept his dark hair trimmed short, and I imagined in anything other than a bright orange jumpsuit, he'd probably be handsome. Mostly, he just looked mean. He wasn't, but the look served him well. One of the first things he taught me was that having emotions was fine, but I sure as shit better learn to keep them off my fucking face. I was having more trouble than usual at that moment.

I knew it wasn't logical—my sentence was up—but it felt like such a betrayal to leave him behind.

"Ah, hell, kid." Mutt moved forward and gripped me by both shoulders. Something he'd done hundreds of times, usually to shake some sense into me. "It's a happy day. For me, too. Finally getting rid of your ugly mug is cause for celebration. Hell, I might have a party once they lead you away."

I couldn't help it, I smiled.

"Now listen up, Jeb is good people, and he tells me the club has gone through quite the transformation in the last few years. They won't give a shit that you're gay, and they won't give a shit about your lisp. All they're gonna care about is that you're loyal and that you can knock out the mother-fucker standing across the ring from you. Alright? Pull your weight. Win some fights. You'll be in a Prospect vest in no time. Hell, might be a full patch by the time I'm on the outside with you."

I nodded, trying to rein in the trepidation building in my gut. It was ironic the fear I'd felt the first day walking in here matched the fear I was feeling at walking back out again. I'd come in a scared shitless eighteen-year-old kid, and I was leaving a terrified twenty-four-year-old man. "Doubt it. Didn't you say you have to Prospect for a year? By the time I get the vest and get a full year in, you'll be out, too."

He smirked. "That is true."

Down from our cell, the guard gate buzzed open.

"Alright kid," Mutt said, pulling me into a quick hug. He'd only hugged me a handful of times, but every time I thought if I'd had a father, this is what his hugs should have felt like—solid and strong and like they could protect me from anything. "Watch your back and don't be a pain in the ass."

"I will." I ducked my head to keep him from seeing the wetness gathering in my eyes.

"Ward." A guard barked from outside our cell. "Let's go."

I glanced at Mutt. He gave me a toothy grin. "And kid? Have some fun, okay?"

"I will. Talk to you soon."

"Not too soon, though. I mean it—enjoy some life out there."

I nodded, swallowing down the lump in my throat and schooling my face before I stepped beyond the relative safety of our cell. Just down the aisle from us, I could see Razor, leaning against his door, watching me. He was most of the reason I thought I wouldn't live to see the outside again. He believed that I'd had a hand in putting him in here, and nothing I said would convince him otherwise.

As the guard and I passed Razor's cell, he blew me a kiss. "I'll be seeing you, Ward."

Keeping my face stoically forward, I didn't give in to the cold chill that crawled up my back.

The rest of the walk felt inexplicably long and remarkably short. On the inside, it always felt to me like we were a million miles away from civilization, but it only took passing through a few locked gates to find myself in the processing area.

Once that was done, and I was back in the clothes I'd been wearing on entry—smelling stale and too small now—I stood before the final gate separating me from freedom. Nausea roiled in my stomach. The only person I trusted in the world was sitting in the too-small cell somewhere in the building behind me, and as much as I wanted to be out, in that moment, all I wanted was to turn tail and beg them to let me back in.

The gate buzzed and started to rattle open. I squinted my eyes against the sun and stepped out into a very ordinary parking lot. It was warm, even with my long-sleeved shirt pushed up to my elbows. Two men casually leaning against big black motorcycles stood as the gate lumbered closed behind me. The click of that lock sounded as ominous as ever.

"Ward?" one of the guys said as they made their way over. He was around my height with dark blond hair and, when he took his shades off, vivid blue eyes. "I'm Kade." He held his hand out.

I took it, giving it a firm shake as I nodded. The other man—this one tall and broad with gray in his hair and beard and a President's patch on his vest—offered his hand as well.

"Jeb," he said as he shook my hand. "You ready to get out of here?"

"Yes, sir."

Just like Mutt had said, they didn't flinch at my lisp. Kade smiled at me and patted my back before they led me over to the motorcycles, and we got on the road to my new home.

CHAPTER ONE

Ward

"Here we go," Kade said, pushing a door open in a long hallway at the back of the Sand Lake Heretics business and clubhouse. Mutt had explained that the Sand Lake charter ran a fight gym, *Sand Lake Iron City*. The gym's name was emblazoned on the big glass windows at the front of the long, squat building with the image of a skull biting down on a barbell beneath them. "This will be your room for as long as you need it. Might have to share with a guest overnight here and there if that's cool."

I nodded, taking in the decent sized room—compared to the cell I'd lived in for six years anyway—with its two twin beds and side by side dressers. It looked like paradise.

"Thank you. This is..." Words failed me. The drive from the prison had taken a couple hours and I spent it holding on to Kade's waist with my eyes closed, enjoying the wind on my face. "Thank you."

Kade smiled gently. "You hungry?"

I was, but they'd already done so much for me, I wasn't sure I should let them feed me, too.

"Ward." Kade stepped into my space and placed a hand on

my shoulder, giving it a squeeze. "I just want you to know, I've been standing where you are. I did some time a few years back and without this club...well, I'd probably be dead today. Let us help you get on your feet. Okay? Believe me, you'll be putting plenty of work in soon enough."

I took a slow breath and nodded. "I am hungry."

He chuckled. "Good. Food first, and then we'll rustle you up some clothes that actually fit. Sound good?"

"Yeah, it does. Thank you."

I DUCKED, SLIPPING UNDER THE RIGHT CROSS KADE HAD thrown and dancing back to get out of his range again. I'd always been scrappy—had to be or I would've gotten my ass kicked more than I did as a kid—but the years spent learning technique from Mutt, even though we couldn't actually spar, and the last three months working with Kade had finally brought all the pieces of my fight game together.

Outside the cage, I caught the shadows of several people walking up. *Snap.* Kade caught me with a quick side kick to my thigh. I met his eyes.

Pay attention.

Despite myself, I glanced again—a giant bald man, a much smaller redhead, Jeb, and a dark headed guy about my height. There was something about the last one that made me want to glance again. Instead, I shook off my distraction and we fell back into our spar, trading punches and blocks at half strength while I focused on my opponent and not the eyes staring from outside the cage.

When the bell sounded ending the round, Kade went out to talk to everyone, and I stripped off my gloves. I heard the big bald man say, "Definite potential. I look forward to working with him this week." He must be Axel.

"Hear that Ward?" Kade called over his shoulder to me. "You're a winner, buddy."

With a grunt, I moved past them all to where I'd left my towel and water bottle, hoping the sweat and exertion would disguise the blush I could feel rising in my cheeks. Being exposed wasn't something I was unaccustomed to, but this felt different. I wanted these people to like me. Wanted them to believe that I had value. It was a strange and unsettling feeling. I missed Mutt.

"Can he talk?" The dark haired one asked. I grit my teeth, doing my best not to let my shoulders slump.

Jeb barked out a laugh. "Yes, he just chooses not to."

Blocking out their chatter, I turned my back, picking up my towel and wiping off my face, then taking a long drink of water.

"Hey," Kade said quietly from beside me. "We're going to get dinner across the street. You wanna join?"

I was sure he already knew the answer, and even though it was a definite *no*, I appreciated that he asked. "No, thank you. I meal prepped for the week."

"Chicken and broccoli, again? You can have a cheat day, you know."

I shrugged. "It's food." And honestly, as long as there was some in my belly everyday, I didn't really care what it was. It was nice to be able to go into a grocery store and actually choose things to fix myself—healthy things—but really, food was only fuel.

He kept it quiet, but I heard his sigh. "Okay. We'll see you when we get back. Oh, um, you cool with Zach bunking with you while they're here?"

I knew the big guy was Axel, and with as close as the redhead was standing, I assumed they were together, so they'd be in the double room. That left the dark haired guy—Zach, apparently—needing a single bed, like the extra one in my space. "Of course. It's the club's room."

"It's your room." Kade's face went serious, and I knew I was pushing it with him today. Out of all the guys here, I'd grown the closest to him and felt the most comfortable speaking with him.

"I know. Sorry. I'll see you when you guys get back." I left them all in the gym and went to my room to shower and change. After, I ate my food—chicken with potatoes and salad, thank you, Kade—and settled on one of the couches in the lounge with a beer to watch a movie.

I had no clue what newer movies were good or not, but I stuck to the action and adventure categories on *Netflix* and had been pleasantly surprised so far. Halfway through some secret service movie with the hot guy from *300*, Zach stepped up beside the couch with a beer in his hand.

"Hey, man. Mind if I join you?"

I shook my head, shifting over on the couch so there'd be a full cushion between us. We sat in silence for a few minutes, watching the action play out on screen. Or at least, Zach was. I found myself glancing at him out of the corner of my eye every few seconds. He was gorgeous—olive skin stretched over a muscular body and the kind of classically handsome face that could have been starring in the movie we were watching.

"Listen," he said, not taking his eyes off the screen. "I'm sorry if I offended you earlier with the crack about you being able to talk." He looked over at me then, his warm brown eyes worried and staring intently at mine.

I almost said something then, surprising myself. Instead, I gave him a nod and lifted my beer toward him. He looked confused for half a second, then a boyish grin broke over his face, and he clinked his bottle against mine.

We watched the rest of the movie in a companionable

silence, and once it was over, I stood. Zach followed suit, looking a bit nervous.

"I think I'll turn in, too."

I nodded and led the way to the room I thought of as my own—no matter what I said to Kade.

Zach sat down on the bed opposite mine and reached underneath it to pull out a black duffle bag. He must have stowed it there before he came into the gym to watch me spar with Kade.

I went into the attached bathroom to piss and brush my teeth. A phone started ringing on the other side of the door.

"Hey, Mom," Zach said, his voice slightly muffled by the door and running water. "Yep. How was your day?"

I stuck my toothbrush in my mouth and scrubbed it around. It did something weird to my stomach to hear him talk to his mom—to know that he must have a decent relationship with her. I finished up, but instead of going back out into the room I waited, standing still in front of the sink.

"We'll be in Sand Lake all week. If you need me and can't get me on my cell, call the gym, okay? I will. Love you, too. Bye, Mom."

I waited a couple beats more then stepped back out into the room, stripping off my shirt and sweats, leaving me in just my boxer briefs, before climbing into bed. When I looked up, Zach looked away from me quickly, grabbing his bag and walking toward the bathroom. The door closed, and a minute later, the shower kicked on.

Some tension had invaded the air between us. Could just be the awkwardness of strangers sharing space, but it felt like something else...intrigue, maybe. Like he might be as curious about me as I was about him. Kade said they were staying a week, and I was suddenly glad I'd have a few days with my new roommate to find out.

CHAPTER TWO

Zach

I'd been sharing a room with Ward for four days. The most confusing four days of my life...and *arousing*. Best not to forget arousing. Ward was like a force of nature—a stoic, lean muscled hurricane sent to throw me completely off course. And the no talking thing—not to say he *couldn't* talk, I'd heard a few low exchanges between him and Kade, but he didn't speak often. When he did, it was always quiet and close with the right people who were apparently in his confidence. Something I evidently wasn't. Not that I wanted to be. *Nope.* The point was, it left us maintaining crazy eye contact way too much and me with all these questions.

Why didn't he talk?

What other color was hiding amongst the golden-brown of his eyes?

How did he get into illegal cage fighting?

Obviously, I wasn't going to judge. My club, the Iron Heretics MC, where I soon hoped to become a full-patched member, hosted the fights. Hell, they even let some of the fighters join the club. Axel was a prime example. Kade was another. Although, the way I understood it, Kade had been a

Prospect first and stepped in to pinch-hit when the club was down a fighter for an important match.

Ward thumped his knuckle on the side of the pool table, jolting me out of my thoughts. Looking up, I met his eyes, frowning at his smug grin as he used his stick to indicate he was going to shoot the eight ball into the corner pocket closest to me.

"Yeah, yeah. You're about to kick my ass. *Again*."

That pulled a smirk to Ward's lips, but instead of immediately bending over to take his shot, he walked around the table toward me. The man was frenetic energy on legs— corded muscle containing barely concealed power—whether he was in his fight trunks and gloves or the worn-out jeans and white tank top he was wearing now. I swore to all the *Harley* gods, I could look at a guy and know he was attractive, but I'd never *felt* it the way I did with every shift of Ward's muscle, every tick of his jaw, and every fucking time he locked on me with that golden stare. I felt that shit all the way down to my bones.

He stopped inches from me, the toes of his thick-soled boots bumping into mine. *Fuck*, he smelled good. His short, dark blond hair was messy because he was constantly running a hand through it. I found myself wanting to run my hands through it. I shook myself out of my head and dropped my eyes to his.

Mistake.

His stare was laser-focused on my face. *Huh.* That extra color around his pupils? It was blue. He leaned in, and my heart gave one big thump in my chest.

"You're cute when you pout."

I was so startled he was actually speaking to me that I almost missed his words. His voice was low and not as deep as I expected. He spoke slowly, like he was putting effort into the pronunciation of each word even as the tiniest lisp caught on their edges. His eyes never once left my face, and I suddenly knew this was a test. Truth was, I didn't give a fuck that he had a lisp. I didn't even care that he was a guy. True, I'd never been overwhelmingly attracted to a man before, but I wasn't an asshole or adverse to the possibility. And besides, if Calix thought I had a single homophobic bone in my body, he'd break all of them until he found it.

I smirked. "I'm cute all the time." Yep, I was totally flirting back. "You gonna win this game and put me out of my cute misery or what?"

He smiled, gently bumping my shoulder with his as he passed me on his way back to the other side of the table. Shit, that one touch—his bare arm against mine—had my dick plumping up in my pants and every hair on my body standing on end. I reached for my beer, needing something to soothe my dry mouth. I hadn't been this affected by someone since my high school sweetheart had first given me the time of day. Amy had been a knock-out—perfect body, gorgeous red hair, and smart enough to put me in my place at every turn. She was the first and only serious relationship I'd ever had, and I'd been grateful for every day with her right up until she'd shattered my heart the summer before she went off to college.

I was still grateful—with a few years of distance under my belt—but a lot more cautious. My dick was free-range, but everything farther north I kept under lock and key.

Ward sunk his shot, sending me a wink as soon as the eight ball clinked against the others already in his pocket of choice. Standing up, he hung his stick on the wall, grabbed the rack, and started pulling all the balls back up onto the table. He was moving with purpose so I joined him, settling the solids and stripes back into the triangle. Once we were done, he looked at me and tilted his head toward the door. Without giving me a chance to say anything, he walked that way, out of the clubhouse lounge and into the hall that led down to the room I'd been sharing with him.

My feet felt glued to the floor. If I followed him into that room right now, I had no doubt what was going to happen. We'd been dancing around it all week. Like Ward when he was in the cage—dodgin' and weavin'—waiting for the chance to strike. I glanced around, but no one was even looking my way. I took a deep breath and made up my mind, then double-checked my phone. No new messages from any club brothers needing something from the Prospect.

Walking out into the hall felt surreal. Like it must have been someone else's body heading to that door and what lay beyond. But when I got there and got my hand around the knob, all I felt was the prickle of anticipation along my skin.

The moment I was through the door, Ward was on me, closing it and pushing me back against it with all his lean muscle pressed along my front. Those golden eyes with their circle of blue stared at me from inches away, dropping to watch my tongue when it darted out to wet my lips.

He leaned his hips back, forearm braced beside my head and lowered his other hand to run a finger over the hard line of my dick through my jeans. "Okay?" he asked in the same quiet voice he'd used before.

For a split second, the cocky mask he wore slipped. If I hadn't been standing so close, watching him so intently, I would have missed it. *Fuck it.* I swallowed hard, grabbed the back of his neck, and smashed my lips to his. The scratch of his beard was softly sharp over my clean-shaven chin, and he growled, opening his mouth and pressing in his tongue to stroke over mine.

Fuck me.

Lightning shot down my spine and swooped through my belly, scrambling my brains until the only thing I thought about was getting closer. I hesitated only a second before settling my hands on his hips—groaning at the feel of the firm, flexing muscle there—and pulling him in. He leaned into me, the solid weight of him holding me against the door. Being almost exactly the same height, his gorgeous fucking eyes were right there across from mine, and every other thing about us lined up perfectly as well.

I gasped as the hard ridge of his dick grazed over mine. He broke our kiss, pulling back to watch my face with hooded eyes as he ground his hips forward, rubbing us together.

"Fuck," I said with feeling, tightening the grip I still had on his hips and letting out a shaky breath.

"You seem nervous." His hips stilled, and that lisp was more prominent with the huskiness of his voice. When I didn't answer right away, he started to ease off me, but I held him firm.

"I've, uh...never been with a man."

He arched a brow.

Swallowing hard, I nodded. "I've been attracted to men, but..."

He nudged his cock against mine.

"Never enough to do something about it." I felt breathless. I'd had a lot of hook-ups since Amy ditched me six years ago. Even a few friends-with-benefits arrangements, but I always got out at the first hint there might be something beyond mutual lust starting to form. Surely this hook-up wouldn't be any different. Didn't matter that my partner this time around was a man. Sex was sex. With that thought firmly in mind, I lifted my ass from the door and did some grinding of my own. "We doing this?"

It was his turn to nod. "What do you want?"

A helpless laugh tore out of my throat before I could stop it. "I don't know." I rubbed our jean-clad cocks together again. "This feels pretty fucking good."

He smirked, rocking against me slowly. Leaning in, he ran the tip of his nose along my cheek, hot breath gliding over my skin, and back to my ear. His voice was a low rumble. "It'll feel even better naked." He dropped his hand from where it was braced on the door and turned the lock with a click.

A shudder tore through me. "Then let's get naked."

CHAPTER THREE

Ward

I didn't think Zach noticed the shake in my hands. *Thank fuck*. I knew a twenty-four-year-old me had walked out of prison, but sometimes I still felt like the kid with two months left to wait before my eighteenth birthday aged me out of the system and set me free. Like the last six years of concrete walls, bad food, and jailhouse slippers were just a really terrible dream.

Zach leaned off the door, those rough hands strong on my hips, and pressed his lips to mine. Fuck, he could kiss. Over the last three months of *Grindr* adventures, I'd found kissing was something I hadn't even realized I liked. I'd had a few fumbling kisses with boys I'd messed around with when I was younger, but that was it. The very few handjobs I'd exchanged with a couple guys on the inside didn't leave room for any kind of tenderness. The first man I'd hooked-up with from the app had been older and, thankfully, had taken pity on me. We'd spent half the night with him simply holding my face between his hands while I had my fill of his lips and tongue.

I'd never been more grateful for that as Zach pressed forward, walking us across the room, all the while keeping our mouths sealed together. Sliding my hands down his sides, I found the hem of his shirt beneath his Heretics vest and got my fingers on bare skin. He was hard and smooth, and the edges of my lips curled up when the ridges of his abs contracted as I grazed over them.

"Take it off," I growled out between increasingly hungry kisses. Hot breath fanned over my face as he pulled his mouth from mine. For a moment, our eyes held—warm, honest brown eyes staring avidly into mine.

He huffed a small laugh, and the moment broke. I smiled as he pulled off his vest, laying it carefully over the top of one of the dressers. As he turned back to me, I lifted his shirt. He helped me pull it over his head, then let it fall to the floor.

"You too," he said, reaching for mine. Shoes, socks, and pants followed, until we were pressed back together with only the cotton of our briefs separating us. His skin felt amazing sliding against mine, and just like I thought, his chest and stomach were smooth and completely ripped.

He carded his fingers through the patch of dark blond curls between my pecs.

"Weird?"

He shook his head. "No. Just different." Molding his palm over my pec, he squeezed then rubbed in a circle, perking my nipple up.

I pulled in a slow breath as the sensation stoked the lust building in my gut. While his eyes were still focused on my chest, I ducked my head and latched onto his nipple, sucking and licking until he was pebbled and taut under my tongue.

"Shit that feels good," he breathed, head back while he threaded his fingers into my hair.

I released his skin with a pop and claimed his mouth again. Stepping back, I sat down on the edge of my bed, letting my hands glide back to graze over his ass. I looked up at him and arched a brow before I pressed my nose to the outline of his cock and inhaled. He smelled fantastic, musky and masculine with the faint lingering spice from the soap that was currently in the shower down the hall. Mouthing along the length of him got me a shudder, and when I closed my lips over his cotton-covered head and sucked, he gasped out a moan.

He tasted as good as he smelled. Getting my fingers under his waistband, I lowered his underwear. I was close enough his cock smacked against my cheek as it sprung free. Smiling at Zach's nervous laugh, I sucked him into my mouth while I slid his briefs the rest of the way down his toned legs. He kicked them away. Letting my hands linger among the crinkly hair on his thighs, I took as much of his length as I could, letting him bump the back of my throat before pulling off again. I hadn't mastered my gag reflex in the three months since I'd been out of prison and finally could enjoy other men's bodies the way I'd wanted too since I first figured out I was gay.

Giving head was something I'd discovered I enjoyed a lot —almost as much as receiving it. Some guys were easier than others, for obvious reasons. Zach didn't have the biggest dick I'd ever had in my mouth, but he was long and had a nice girth with a little upward curve. I bet that bend would be amazing at bumping my prostate.

"Hold up," Zach said suddenly, pulling his hips back.

"What's wrong?"

"Wrong?" He gave a self-deprecating laugh. "Not a fucking thing, but I'm gonna blow if you keep that up."

"And?"

"I'm not ready yet." He moved forward, forcing me to scoot back on the bed as he straddled my thighs. "Shit, this is weird. Not bad weird or anything, just...okay I'm gonna shut up now." He chuckled again and pressed his lips to mine.

I'd never smiled so much while kissing someone. It wasn't

the easiest thing, but completely worth it. From the moment Zach walked into the gym earlier in the week, I'd wanted him. He was fucking gorgeous and acted like the boy next door—down to earth and a genuinely good guy—wholesome in a way I hadn't expected to find amongst the biker crowd.

He attacked my mouth as his hands explored from the scruff on my cheeks to the bare skin of my chest and back. I moved, turning to lay on the bed. Zach shifted so that he was kneeling between my spread legs. Brown eyes met mine—a moment's pause—then he reached for my waistband. Together we got my briefs down my legs and off. Bare before him, I let my spread thighs rest against the tops of his while my cock ached from its place flat against my belly.

Zach's eyes didn't leave the juncture of my legs, and for a moment, I thought he'd bail. Instead, he reached out, laying his hand among the hairs of my chest and sliding down over my twitching stomach and the underside of my dick that was so, so hard for him.

A shaky breath escaped him. He bit his lip, cupping my balls and bringing his other hand into play to wrap around me and give me one firm stroke. My hips jumped off the bed.

"Fuck," I whispered. "We might be in a competition for who's gonna blow first."

He huffed another laugh, and the tension in his shoulders drained away. That little grin pulled up the edges of his mouth—a quarter shy and the rest mischief—and deep in my gut, I knew I was fucked.

"Come here," I said, curling up to get my hands on him. He came willingly, settling between my legs and gently rocking his hips while he owned my mouth. I brought a hand up, pulling away from his lips long enough to lick it, and shoved it between us. When I took us both in hand, he shuddered and braced himself a little farther above me. Then he started to thrust.

"Jesus—" I gasped, my whole body lighting up as his dick stroked against mine in the tunnel of my fist.

He thrust harder, balancing on one hand so he could bring the other down to join mine around us. "How does that feel so fucking good?" he asked between panted breaths.

"I don't know." Leaning up, I got my lips on his a moment before my whole body seized up as my orgasm exploded through me, taking me by surprise and emptying my balls all over our joined hands and my stomach.

"*Shit*," Zach gasped, rhythm faltering as his cum joined mine.

Stroking lightly, I breathed through the aftershocks until I was too sensitive to continue. As soon as I pulled my hand away, Zach collapsed on top of me with a sigh.

"That was fucking awesome," he mumbled into my shoulder. I chuckled and stroked his back with the hand not covered in our combined release. He tensed a moment later and started to lift up.

Pressing my hand against his back, I caught his eyes. "Stay...unless you're uncomfortable."

That same little grin stretched across his face. "I'm not." Leaning up, he poured his lips over mine, drawing out my tongue with languid strokes.

We fell asleep like that, tangled together on my narrow bed. I woke at some point during the night to piss and cleaned us up some, but I'd never felt as satisfied to lay back down as when Zach curled himself around me and pressed his lips against the back of my neck.

In the morning, bright sunlight filled the room, illuminating the empty spot in my bed. I'd slept deeper and later than I had in the last six years, and the St. Louis Heretics—Zach included—were already gone.

CHAPTER FOUR

Ward

The sound of the crowd was loud through the thin walls of my dressing room. True to his word, Axel had recommended me for a fight on the St. Louis circuit, and a month later—here I was. Nerves ate at my stomach as I paced the small room, the concrete floor unyielding and strangely comforting beneath the soles of my wrestling shoes. The kicker was, only half my nerves were for the actual fight. Zach was here. In the building. I'd caught a glimpse of him earlier doing set-up with some of the other Heretics, but I hadn't seen him since.

In fact, I hadn't seen or spoken to him since that night in the Sand Lake clubhouse. We hadn't exchanged numbers, and there was no way in hell I was going to ask someone for his. According to Kade, St. Louis' hands had been full dealing with a threat to Leith and another club causing problems. I wanted to ask if that was all settled. The redhead, Leith, seemed like a nice guy and his man, Axel, had been great to spar with for the week they'd been in Sand Lake.

Like I'd summoned him, the door to my dressing room opened and Zach stepped inside. Kade and Jeb were both out mingling—or doing whatever the Heretics did before one of their fights—so I was alone. His dark eyes darted around the room before finally landing on mine.

"Hey," he said, closing the door and coming toward me. "Um, I'm supposed to check in and see if you need anything before the fight."

Supposed to check in—just doing his Prospect duties then. Disappointment like a white-hot blade sliced through my chest, but I made damn sure not a drop of it showed on my face. "I'm good."

He cleared his throat, holding my eyes for a moment before glancing down at his black boots. He looked good in his biker get-up—worn jeans, white t-shirt under his black vest, and those thick-soled boots. "Okay, well..." He moved back toward the door. "We'll be getting started in another twenty minutes or so."

I nodded and watched him go. The ache in my chest was ridiculous. What had I expected? We'd hooked-up and it was great, but that was all it was—a hook-up and nothing more. Considering quick fucks was all I'd ever had, it made no sense for me to be hung up on this one. I had to let it go and get my head on straight. There was a fight in front of me, and I needed to be focused on winning it instead of Zach's brown eyes and wishing I could see that grin again.

Pacing the floor, I tried to empty my mind. I bounced on my toes, shadowboxing the air and warming myself up.

I wished Mutt were here. Despite his insistence that I get out and live a little, I'd written to him at least once a week since I'd been out. I remembered with vivid clarity the quiet joy on his face every time he got a letter when they brought mail around, and my own quiet sadness because there were never any letters for me—because I had no one.

Now I had Mutt, and I'd managed to make friends with a couple of the Sand Lake guys. Especially Kade. He'd confided in me after my first couple of weeks there that he was an ex-con as well. The Heretics had been Kade's place to land and get his life back together after he'd gotten out. There weren't words enough to convey how grateful I was they'd opened their doors to me, too.

I'd been hoping to add Zach to that roster.

I turned to make another pass around the room, and the door opened again. Kade stepped inside, followed by Jeb—where one of them went, the other usually wasn't far behind. They were subtle enough that a lot of people outside the club didn't realize they were together. It had taken a moment for me to pick up on it, too, but now I knew they'd been a couple for years and a hard-fought one at that.

"Feeling good?" Kade asked, immediately reaching out to double-check the wrap on my hands.

My eyes darted to Jeb before I answered, "Yep," keeping my voice low. There was no reason for me to be self-conscious in front of him, and I always felt like shit for it, but I really couldn't help it. I had no idea how my brain chose who it was easy for me to talk to and who it wasn't. Kade, Mutt, and Zach? Easy. Jeb and about a million others? Not at all. I could do it of course, but it took an effort I didn't always have the energy for. The lisp wasn't something I was ashamed of anymore—I was born with it and it was a part of me like any other—but I guess I'd taken enough beatings over it as a child that the need to protect myself had become unconscious.

Kade's blue eyes held mine. "Here's how it'll work. Zach will let us know when they're ready. They'll play some rock song for you to walk out to. Then three rounds just like we've been training." He winked. "And keep the mean mug, the girls are gonna love it."

I rolled my eyes and let a chuckle escape. "You'll be in my corner?"

His smile turned thoughtful. "Always."

He couldn't know what that meant to me. The nerves I'd been feeling got buried under the blanket rush of adrenaline. It was almost time. I didn't have to speak. I didn't have to hold back. All I had to do was step into the cage and fight the guy opposite me. I could do that.

A quick knock sounded on the door a second before Zach poked his head in. He glanced around the room, dark brown eyes catching on me before moving to Jeb. "We're ready."

The walk to the cage was a blur. A rhythmic drum beat from a song I didn't recognize poured from speakers mounted close to the ceiling. A huge crowd of people were gathered around the stage—a lot of them dressed up like this was some country club or something instead of an old chicken barn out in the sticks. They had drinks in their hands, and it seemed half-and-half whether they were booing or cheering for me.

Like Kade suggested, I kept my face formed into the mask that had served me so well in prison—set jaw and a clear *I will fuck you up* stare. Zach was walking in front of me, creating a path through the crowd. Refusing to let my eyes drop to his ass, I focused on the Prospect rocker on the back of his vest. If I didn't fuck this up, I'd be wearing one of those soon.

Kade and Jeb flanked me all the way to the cage. Outside of it, I took off my wrestling shoes, and Kade handed me my mouthguard. Slipping it in my mouth, I gave Kade a nod and turned to step through the cage door Zach was holding open.

"Kick his ass," Zach said as I moved past him.

I paused, meeting his gaze for a moment. Not willing to let my thoughts linger on him, I nodded my thanks and stepped inside. He shut the door behind me.

My opponent was already there, standing against the opposite side. He was taller than me by a couple inches and probably outweighed me by twenty pounds. He looked like a bruiser with a thick chest, tree trunk legs, and dark hair shaved close to his head. With a scowl, he looked me up and down, taking my measure. I stood tall, bouncing lightly from foot to foot to keep my muscles warm and held his stare.

Someone stepped in with a microphone to announce the fight, but I honestly couldn't say who. My entire focus was trapped by the brute staring back at me. This was more than a payday to him. It was in his eyes and written on his face— he wanted to hurt me. He was either shit at schooling his features or he just didn't give a fuck. I was betting on the latter.

The bell rang. Brute immediately lunged across the space between us, swinging his arm in a huge arc, trying to land a haymaker that would take my head off. I darted to the side, getting a solid jab into his ribs as I went. He growled, spinning around and coming after me again. I held my ground, working my feet and ducking my head to dodge his punches while getting in some solid body shots of my own. He caught me once—a glancing blow under my left eye—and I knew I didn't want him to hit me at full strength.

Beneath the sweat, frustration etched itself into the lines of his face. He was getting pissed, but he was moving slower, too. A lot of big guys depended on their strength to win a fight quickly—like he would if I let him land one of those Hail Mary swings—so they didn't give their endurance training the respect it deserved.

Pulling a deep breath into my lungs, I moved in closer to him, watching him closely as I dangled the bait. Within seconds he took it, lunging at me again. Slipping to the side, I let his fist skim past me, twisted my torso, and put every ounce of strength and momentum I had behind the elbow that connected with his cheek. His head snapped away from the contact, blood painting the mat in a shower of red droplets, and he staggered. The crowd was a dull roar in the back of my mind as I jumped at him, sweeping him into a double leg takedown. His back hit the mat with a thud, arms flailing out. I scrambled to straddle his middle and was punching him in the face before I was fully seated. I landed three more blows before hands were pulling me off him.

Kade grabbed my wrist and thrust it up in the air. My chest was heaving as my vision cleared. The room around me came back into focus—the cage, the floor, the crowd beyond, and Zach staring at me. There was something there in his brown eyes that made my stomach flip. Pride. And lust. I let him see mine as well.

I was back in the moment enough to hear the announcer belt out that I was the winner. This time both my arms got raised in the air, Kade holding one wrist while Jeb held the other.

I was still panting, trying to get my breathing back to normal. Now that the fight was over, sweat was pouring off of me. Since we weren't the only fight of the night, Brute's corner guys were getting him up and out of the cage, and Kade turned me that way as well.

When we stepped out, Calix—the St. Louis Heretics' President—stepped into our path. He held out his hand for me to shake. "That was a hell of a first showing. If that's how you always fight, all I've got to say is, welcome to the club."

A smile broke over my face as I gripped his hand. "Thank you."

CHAPTER FIVE

Zach

The Heretics compound was already buzzing by the time I got there. I'd rushed through clean-up, but knowing Ward was at the clubhouse made it feel like it took twice as long. I couldn't get his fight out of my head or the moment we'd had in the dressing room when I'd turned chicken shit and run. I needed to talk to him.

"Hey Prospect," Cleave called from his spot on the front steps. JJ was sitting in front of him with a cigarette between his fingers, and his shoulders leaned back against his boyfriend's knees. There were several other people hanging around in groups, smoking and laughing. Nights were starting to take on that chilly edge of fall, and I couldn't wait for the next bonfire out at Lex's cabin.

"Hey, man. JJ. You guys seen Ward?"

"I think I saw him with Kade and Jeb in the lounge earlier." Cleave chuckled. "Dude is a badass, but he's not much on the socializing front, is he?"

I felt myself bristle and tamped it down. Cleave was a lot of things—an asshole wasn't one of them. He'd never poke

fun at Ward over something like his lisp, so he obviously
didn't know. "Nah, he's more the strong, silent type."

JJ chuckled at that, taking a drag off the cigarette and
exhaling a plume of smoke to the side. "He's more the
gorgeous, silent type."

"Hey!" Cleave protested with a smile, pulling the cig out
of JJ's hand and sticking it between his own lips. "Can't you
gush about your new crush when I'm not sitting right here?"

JJ and I both laughed and rolled our eyes.

"I'll catch you two later." I headed up the steps, leaving JJ
to kiss his man into submission. Following the thump of
music and the sounds of a party, led me to the lounge toward
the rear of the club. Brothers from both the St. Louis and
Sand Lake charters were sprawled all over—talking, playing
pool, making out with whatever hottie caught their fancy. Jeb
and Kade were sitting at the corner of the bar with Calix and
Riot. There were beers in front of all four of them, and they
looked deep in conversation. No Ward in sight.

I started to turn away, but Kade raised his head up, caught
my eye, and waved me over.

"Hey man," he said when I close. "Not going to join the
party?"

"Um, I was actually looking for Ward."

"Oh, he's in the kitchen, I think, getting some ice for his
eye."

I glanced toward the kitchen door. "Thanks, man. I'll
catch you later." I made my way across the room. Pushing the
swinging door open, I stepped inside. The door swung shut
behind me, cutting the noise from the party down to a low
murmur.

Ward had his back to me. He was sitting at the table,
elbows on the top, holding an ice pack to his face with an old-
fashioned glass of amber-colored liquor at his elbow. He

didn't look up to see who'd come in, so I made my way over and pulled out the chair catty-corner to his and sat down.

He didn't say anything, but the golden-brown eye that wasn't currently being iced focused on my face for a moment, then dropped back to the table.

Biting my lip, I rested my elbows on the table as well. "I'm sorry I ran off earlier."

He looked over at me. Even bruised, he was beautiful. Though it was subtle, he had that air of accomplishment about him. He'd pushed his body hard tonight and come out on top. I was proud of him, even if I wasn't sure how or if I should say it.

"It's not the first time."

A jolt went through me. I hadn't expected him to bring up Sand Lake. Running a hand through my hair, I sighed. "Look, I didn't know what to do there. I mean, it was a hook-up, right? I wasn't trying to put us in an awkward morning after moment."

"Alright." He lowered the ice pack and picked up his glass. The skin under his eye was already turning deep shades of blue and purple. After taking a drink, he set the glass back down with a clink.

"That's it? Alright?"

He narrowed his eyes at me. "What else is there? I enjoyed spending time with you. I *really* enjoyed the sex. I guess I was hoping it might be the start of something. You don't feel the same, and that's fine. So, yeah...alright."

"Damn, you're infuriatingly easy-going, aren't you?"

To my surprise, he smirked. "My cellmate used to say that."

A crazy thought occurred to me, turning the pit of my stomach into a pool of green acid. "Were you and he...involved?"

"Lovers?" he asked with both eyebrows climbing up his forehead. "Hell, no. Mutt's more like the father or older brother I never had."

Of fucking course. Mutt. How the hell had I not put that together? Ward had just gotten out of prison a few months ago. Someone had to have hooked him up with the Heretics, and my dumb ass hadn't even thought to ask.

"Mutt was your cellmate?"

"Yeah. He taught me most of what I know about fighting. I wouldn't be alive if it wasn't for him. You know him?"

I picked at a nick in the tabletop. "Yeah. He's my uncle."

Ward leaned back in his chair, the ice pack forgotten on the table and his unbruised eye open wide. "Holy shit. You're Little Z."

"Jesus, no one's called me that in..."

"About seven years, I'm guessing. He talks about you a lot, but in my head, I guess I was picturing a little kid." He watched me for a moment. "You can tell me to fuck off if you want, but...why don't you go see him?"

And the dreaded question had arrived. "I was seventeen and stupid when he went away. I was pissed at him." I shrugged because it sounded lame even to my own ears. "I didn't want to see him in there, and then time went on and now...I don't know how to go see him. Don't know how to bridge that gap."

"I'll tell you—just go. He'd love to see you, and it doesn't matter that it's been years."

I gave him half a smile. "Think he'll be pissed we hooked-up? You probably know him better than me at this point."

"Nah. He'll give me shit for it, but that's it. Although"—he stopped, eyes coming up to hold mine—"if it's never going to happen again, we don't need to tell anyone if it'll make you uncomfortable or out you before you're ready."

Shit. I wanted to lean across the corner of the table and kiss him. "I never said I didn't want it to happen again."

"Do you?"

"Yeah, I do." I licked my lips, his eyes drilling into mine and making my heart jump in my chest. "I'm not good at this. Full disclosure, I got burned several years ago, and I haven't been able to go beyond hook-ups and a couple friends with bennies arrangements since..."

"But?"

Go big or go home, right? "But...I like you. I'm not saying I'm ready to jump in with both feet, but we could hang out. See how it goes. I mean"—I shot him a cocky smile—"the sex really *was* great." He laughed, a deep, husky sound that I felt all the way down in my balls. "So if you want to..."

"I want to. Just let me know where you're at, okay? No need for things to get heavy or awkward. If it's too much, we take a step back or drop it altogether."

I nodded, and feeling brave, I took the soggy ice pack from his hand, letting my fingers graze his, and walked to the counter. We always had a stash on hand, so I tossed the used one into the sink and pulled a fresh one out of the freezer. When I sat back down, I pulled my chair closer to him, leaned an elbow on the table, and held the new pack against the discoloration on his face. "You were badass tonight."

"Thanks."

I guess he was feeling brave, too, as his fingers wrapped around my wrist and pulled the pack away from his face. He leaned in slow, giving me time to run, I imagined, and pressed a kiss to my lips. His cheek against mine was cold, but his lips were warm and just a tiny bit rough.

"Where are you sleeping tonight?" I asked when he pulled back.

"Where do you want me to sleep tonight? Fair warning,

I'm pretty worn out and probably won't be much good for anything other than snoring in your ear."

"I've heard your snore. It's not that intimidating."

He chuckled and climbed to his feet, holding his hand out for me. "Take me to bed, Little Z."

I snorted. "That's so creepy." Grabbing his hand, I hauled myself up and led us up the stairs to my room.

CHAPTER SIX

Ward

"So you and Little Z, huh?" Mutt asked, laughter in his voice and a smile on his face.

We were sitting across from each other in the visitor lounge at the prison. It was weird as fuck to be there in my normal clothes with a *Visitor* sticker stuck to my shirt. "Yeah. We're seeing where it goes."

Mutt looked thoughtful for a moment. "How is he?"

I didn't really want to get in the middle of them, but I knew in some ways, it was unavoidable if this thing between Zach and I grew. My loyalty to Mutt hadn't changed, and I wouldn't betray Zach's confidence. "He's good. Prospecting. He said his full patch vote is coming up soon."

"I knew he'd do well. May not have been the life I wanted for him, but he's always been loyal and a hard worker."

Relief poured through me when he didn't push for more or ask a question I couldn't answer. "How are you doing?"

"I'm fine, kid. Same old, only with less chatter now that you're out of my hair."

I smiled. "That's me. Chatterbox."

"You look good, Ward." His dark eyes swept over my face, glowing with pride. "Strong. Healthy. Happy, even. Keep that up, okay?"

My chest swelled. "I'm trying." The buzzer sounded, giving the warning that time was almost up.

"Listen, before you go." Mutt leaned a bit farther across the table and lowered his voice. "I caught wind that Razor is up for parole soon. Make sure Calix knows. You know he'll be coming for you when he gets out, and probably going after the new leader of the Devils, too. He's made it no secret how he feels about all his old buddies getting ousted from the club he thinks he owns or how much he hates that the Devils and the Heretics have a truce."

Shit. Razor being out was the last fucking thing I needed or wanted to think about. Still, it was better to be prepared then let him catch us with our guard down. "I'll let him know."

"Good."

I stood just as the buzzer rang out again, indicating visiting was over.

"And Ward? Say hi to your boyfriend for me."

I hung my head with a laugh. "Yep. See you next time."

WARD: WHAT'S YOUR FAVORITE FLAVOR?

Zach: Mmm, usually I don't discriminate, but it's hard to beat a good butter pecan. What's yours? Oh god, you're not lactose intolerant are you?

Ward: Lol. Would that be a deal-breaker?

Zach: ...I mean

Ward: That's cold, man.

Zach: Just like my ice cream :)....still can't believe he called me your boyfriend. He didn't even seem surprised?

Ward: Not really. And the boyfriend crack was more about giving me shit than anything. Don't worry about it, babe;)

Zach: You're sassy in text lol. What's on your docket this week?

Ward: Training. Kade wants to keep me fight ready since Calix said there's a spot for me on the next card.

Zach: Good. Wouldn't want to watch my boyfriend get his ass kicked :)

Ward: I like that a little more than I should.

Zach: Getting your ass kicked?

Ward: Haha. What if I told you, your boyfriend doesn't know what flavor of ice cream is his favorite because the only kind he's had in six years is vanilla out of a little styrofoam cup?

Zach: Boyfriend, we've got to fix that STAT.

"OH MY GOD," I SAID, LICKING CARAMEL SAUCE OFF MY LIP. "The *Boozy Banana Rum* is the shit."

Zach laughed, spoon hovering over his own bowl. "Did you try the coffee one? I may have to retract my previous statement about butter pecan."

We were sitting at a little table outside an ice cream shop I hadn't realized existed. The last thing I'd expected when I woke up that morning—a regular Thursday full of training— was for Zach to walk into the gym just before we broke for lunch and declare he was stealing me for the afternoon. For half a second, I'd been afraid Kade would protest, but he'd just laughed, told us to get out of there, and that he'd see me the next day.

I looked down at my double scoop bowl. We'd each gotten two different flavors so we could both try all four.

"Poor butter pecan. It's going to be all offended. Here, have a bite of the triple chocolate."

Zach leaned over, opening his mouth, his hot brown eyes glued to mine as he ate the ice cream off my spoon. "That's pretty fucking good."

"Yeah, it is." Fuck, but my chest was all tight. I couldn't believe he'd driven nearly four hours just to spend the afternoon with me.

He tilted his head. "What's the matter, boyfriend?"

"Nothing's wrong. I think I'm still in shock. I really wasn't expecting to see you."

"Is it a bad thing?"

"Fuck no. It's...unbelievable, but definitely in a good way."

He sat with his head bowed for a moment, scooping up another bite before bringing his warm brown eyes up to meet mine. "Believe it."

"Can I ask you something?"

"Sure."

"What made you join the Heretics?"

He hung his head with a sigh, and I thought I'd fucked up.

"This is embarrassing, but here goes...I had trouble holding down a job after high school. I went through something like fifteen different jobs in a three-year span. Anyway, nothing fit and just when I felt like I'd exhausted every option, my mom says she heard this nightclub was hiring bouncers. So, I went to *Spritz* for an application and the manager interviewed and hired me on the spot." He poked at the ice cream in his bowl. "It wasn't until I'd been there a few weeks that I figured out the Heretics were taking over security there. Uncle Mutt had called in a favor."

"Were you mad?" I couldn't imagine that sitting well with a then twenty-one-year-old's pride.

"Oh, I was pissed. At Mom and at Mutt...but I'd gotten to

know some of the guys, and I fucking loved the job. So, I stayed. The rest is history."

"Well, I'm glad you did."

He smiled, dark eyes meeting mine. "So am I."

CHAPTER SEVEN

Zach

Zach: It was always just me and Mom when I was growing up. And Uncle Mutt.

Ward: Your dad?

Zach: I never knew him. He bailed when Mom was pregnant.

Ward: I'm sorry.

Zach: Thanks, but it's cool. I don't think I would have liked him much, anyway. Did you know your parents?

Ward: I was put in foster when I was five. I have some vague memories, but I'm honestly not sure if they're of my parents or a mash-up of those first few homes.

Zach: I feel like I wish we were together for this conversation.

Ward: Then let's put it on hold until we are.

Zach: Tell me something good.

Ward: I met this great guy a few weeks ago.

Zach: Is he hot?

Ward: Scorching;)

"Did you have fun on your little field trip last week?" Calix asked from behind his desk as soon as I stepped into his office. I knew he was talking about my trip to Sand Lake, and even the thought of it brought a smile to my face. Ward was turning out to be like no one I knew, and I was enjoying the hell out of getting to know him.

Calix smirked. "I'm guessing that smile is a yes. I'm also guessing you won't mind this next assignment."

That got my attention. "What's up, boss?"

"I want you to saddle up and head to Gnaw Bone. Ward's going to meet you at the diner. Accompany him back here. He's going to train with Axel for the next fight."

The next fight wasn't until next weekend. Ward in St. Louis for a week and a half? Hell yes, I was on board with that plan. "When do I leave?"

One of Calix's eyebrows quirked up. "As soon as I'm done with you. Sit."

I settled into one of the chairs across from him.

Leaning forward, Calix rested his elbows on the desk and held me in his black-eyed stare. "Your full patch vote is coming up soon. How are you feeling about that?"

"Honestly? Good. I feel like I've made a home here and earned the respect of my brothers."

"What about my respect? Do you think you've earned that?"

Despite the sweat starting to gather under my collar, I held my President's eyes. "Yes."

For a full minute, Calix didn't say anything, no doubt, watching me to see if I would squirm. Finally, he gave a single nod and glanced toward the door. "Bring Ward in safely. I have a feeling he's going to be a good fit around here, too."

I couldn't stop the smile from spreading on my face or the way my chest puffed up. "You got it, boss."

Harper's Home Cookin' came into view as I rolled to a stop in the center of Gnaw Bone. The town—if you could even call it that—really only had the one stop with the diner on one corner, a bank, and a little grocery store occupying the others. I pulled through the stop and turned into the gravel lot of the diner, a smile breaking over my face at seeing Ward stand up from where he was leaning against a sexy-ass, midnight blue *Harley*.

He approached me as I climbed off my bike and stowed my helmet in the saddlebag. It had only been a week since I'd seen him, but it felt like an eternity. I didn't hesitate to get my arms around him when he walked into my space, relishing the hard planes of his body pressed against mine and pulling him in for a kiss without giving a thought to where we were or who might see.

"That's a greeting I can get used to," Ward said as he pulled back, but didn't step out of my arms.

Warmth rose in my cheeks. "I must've missed you."

"I know I missed you. Texting is fun, but it's not enough."

I nodded. "Calix said you're going to be in St. Louis until the next fight."

"You okay with that?"

"Definitely." I kissed him again. "You hungry?"

"I could eat." From the look in his eyes, I didn't think he was talking about anything from the diner.

WE PULLED INTO THE ST. LOUIS CLUBHOUSE PARKING LOT just as the sky was starting to darken. Ward's bike was a rumbling beast beside mine. It'd been a blast riding along with him at my side, a classic rock station tuned in on the radio, and the cool afternoon wind at our backs. I walked my bike back into my parking spot as Ward did the same beside me when my phone started to vibrate in my pocket.

Killing the engine, I pulled it out and pressed it to my ear. "Hey, Mom."

"Hi, Baby. I mean, this is my baby, isn't it? It's been so long since I've heard his voice, I could be mistaken."

I hung my head and tried not to laugh. The woman was the queen of the guilt trip, but she usually reserved them for special occasions. Ward gave me a questioning look. I shook my head. Might as well plead forgiveness and get it over with. "I didn't call you back. I'm sorry." She'd called me a few days ago and left a message.

"That's better." She laughed. "You want to come for dinner next week?"

I glanced at Ward. "Can we do the week after? I'm pretty booked up with security for some special events."

"Sure, hon. Just let me know what day works for you."

"I promise, I'll call you next week with my schedule."

"I'll hold you to that."

"I know you will," I said with a smile. "Love you, Mom."

"Love you too, Baby. Be good."

I could feel Ward's gaze on the side of my face. "Always am." We hung up, and I turned to meet his eyes. "If you want, I can call her back and tell her we'd love to come to dinner next week"—his eyes widened—"but I didn't want to tell her yes without talking to you first."

He looked stunned. "You really want me to meet your mom?"

Dropping the kickstand, I stood up and got off the bike. "Of course. Even if we were just friends, I'd want you to meet her. I mean, she's Mutt's sister. She'd want to meet you for that alone, but um, and fair warning here, when she finds out we're together, she's going to flip. So, I get it if you want to wait."

"Flip how?"

"Oh, not in a bad way. No way. Mom doesn't have a prejudiced bone in her body. She'll be thrilled that I'm dating. That I'm...happy."

"Okay," Ward said in a big rush of air. "Is it bad that I've got to step into a cage next weekend with a dude who wants to pound my skull in, but the thought of meeting your mom is way more terrifying?"

I threw my head back and laughed. "I'm so telling her you said that."

"You are not!"

"Oh, yes I am."

We grabbed Ward's bags—just the backpack he was wearing and a duffle—and made our way inside. I jogged up the stairs ahead of him and unlocked the door to my room before turning to face him. "Is this good? We do have some empty guest rooms down the hall if you'd rather—"

He cut me off with his mouth on mine, pushing me back into the room and closing the door behind us.

CHAPTER EIGHT

Ward

I loved the feel of his skin beneath my tongue. Zach moaned and lifted his hips, trying to get me to go where he wanted. Smiling against his skin, I rubbed my stubble over his abs and continued to nibble and suck on one side of the perfect fucking V framing his groin.

"Oh my god, you're killing me," Zach panted, and I couldn't help but chuckle. What I wanted was to truly drive him crazy.

Lifting my head up, I found his dark brown eyes focused on me. As soon as we'd gotten into his room, we'd taken turns in the shower, and he'd whipped us up some pasta for dinner. Food was something I'd never had a special affinity for. It was just something you ate so you didn't die, but with Zach, I was learning to really enjoy it. Especially ice cream. Holding his gaze, I slid my hand down, gliding over his straining cock, lightly grazing his balls, and coming to rest on the soft skin behind them. I swept my thumb back and forth over his perineum, watching his eyes grow wide and his nostrils flare.

"Do you trust me?" I asked quietly, trying not to let on

how badly I wanted to taste him and introduce him to some ass play.

"Not the penis, right? At least, not yet. I don't think I'm ready for that."

I smiled at his ramble. "Not the penis, babe."

"Then yeah, go for it."

I shot him a wink, moving down, I licked him from root to tip and sucked his head into my mouth.

"Fucking hell, you're good at that," Zach groaned, and I smiled around him. He groaned again when I released him with a pop and settled lower. His pucker was as gorgeous as the rest of him. Laying flat on my chest, I leaned in, blowing gently on his hole before licking a wide stripe over it and up to behind his balls. His hips jerked, and he fisted the sheet beneath us. "*Shit!*"

"No one's ever touched your hole before?" I asked, so close to him that my lips grazed over him with every word.

He shuddered. "No one. Shit, I didn't know it would feel like that."

I licked him again, letting my tongue catch on his rim. He was tense, so I kept up the pressure, licking and kissing and sucking until I felt him relax. The skin under my mouth was getting soft and pliant as Zach's moans filled the room. I ran a comforting hand up his thigh and used the point of my tongue to press inside.

"Holy shit! Ward," he nearly shouted, hips jerking again. I slid my arms up around his legs, letting his thighs rest on my shoulders and holding him in place as I speared him again. "Oh my god, oh my god..."

"Ward, will do," I said, lifting my head with a smirk.

"You're an ass." His brown eyes were blown wide, and there was a sheen of sweat covering his chest.

Sometimes he was so fucking sexy I swore it hurt to look at him. Pressing my nose against his groin, I inhaled deep, wanting to imprint the musky scent of him into my nose and lungs forever. "Ready for a little bit more?"

"Hell yes," he said with a wiggle of his hips. The movement made my achingly hard cock rub against the sheet. The friction felt so good, I closed my eyes and rocked my hips for a moment just to take the edge off.

I sucked a finger into my mouth, getting it wet. Pressing it to his entrance brought some of that tension back, so I rubbed it in gentle circles around his rim. "Relax, babe."

He nodded at me and took a deep breath. When he went lax again, I pressed my finger inside at the same moment that I sucked his cock into my mouth. His hips jackknifed up off the bed, gagging me. I pulled off him with a cough.

"Shit, sorry."

"It's okay." I pressed my finger back inside, moving in and out, crooking and searching on every plunge.

"Okay, fuck, that feels good," he said, pressing his head back against the pillow as his hips started to chase my finger on every withdraw. I felt like I could come just watching him. Taking him back in my mouth, I sucked him deep and pushed in, holding my finger there and rubbing his prostate. Within moments, he bucked up and shot. I swallowed and gentled my movements as he came down, licking him clean and pulling my finger out of his ass.

Shifting up to my knees between his still spread legs, I took myself in hand, stroking fast and came hard, my cum painting stripes on Zach's spent dick. "Shit," I gasped, slowing my strokes. He reached for me and I went easily, settling between his legs and kissing him deep so he could taste himself on my tongue.

He pulled back, running his hands through my hair and down my back while he looked at me. "That was a lot more awesome than I expected."

"Yeah?"

"Yeah. I almost went back on my no penis rule."

I chuckled, kissing him again. "We'll get there."

"Do you..."

"Do I?"

"Bottom?"

"I've taken fingers and enjoyed it, but I've had a no penis rule myself." I leaned up, bracing on my elbows so that I had his face framed by my forearms. "But only because I wasn't ready to trust someone like that. I think I am now."

A slow smile spread over his face. "You'll have to teach me."

"We'll both learn as we go. I honestly haven't had much experience. Just *Grindr* hook-ups after I got out and learned how to use my damn phone."

His expression softened. "I bet that was tough. I mean, catching up on stuff."

Settling to one side, I propped my head in my hand and ran the other over his chest. "I don't know that I'll ever catch up, honestly. I feel like I missed so much, and I was kind of already behind in the first place. Kade helped me a lot."

"I'm glad he was there."

"You've helped me, too, you know."

"I don't think orgasms technically count as *help*," he said with a laugh.

He did that often—found a way to lighten the mood with humor when things started to get a little heavy. I understood it and even appreciated it a lot of the time, but I needed him to know that the slope leading to this thing between us becoming serious was steep, and I was sliding fast. "All I know is I've never looked forward to anything the way I always look forward to seeing you."

He stilled beside me, bringing his brown eyes to meet mine. Leaning up, he sealed our mouths together, rolling me over until he was stretched out on top of me, all his glorious naked skin sticky against mine. There was nowhere in the world I'd rather be.

CHAPTER NINE

Zach

Spritz was hopping. Even for a Saturday night, it felt like the club was busier than usual. I had my back to the wall, beside the dance floor with a full view of the main room. My eyes did a slow scan over all the activity—Arden was on stage, getting cheers and whistles as he contorted his body in a seductive dance, Leith's redhead was bobbing in and out of sight as he delivered drinks to tables before running back to the bar for more, and for the first time ever, I had a boyfriend sitting at the end of the bar waiting for me to get off shift.

My eyes caught on Ward's tousled blond hair, and I smiled. He was nearly dwarfed from view with Axel sitting beside him, but they seemed to be having a good time, chatting and nursing beers while they waited for Leith and I to get off work.

Speaking of Leith, I saw him raise his hand out and wave in my direction. It was one of the signs our guys used if there was trouble or they thought there might be. I pushed off the wall, heading in Leith's direction and lifted my hand to speak into my comm device.

"Leith's flagging me down on the main floor, table section 3."

It only took a second for Mace's voice to respond in my ear. "Copy. I see him. Looks like a couple guys are having words at one of his tables."

As I pushed through the crowd, I saw Cleave coming from the opposite direction, and out of the corner of my eye, I caught Axel as he climbed to his feet at the bar. I knew he trusted us with Leith, but I wouldn't be surprised if even off-duty he inserted himself into the situation.

I reached Leith's side, and it was obvious there was about to be a fight. The two men had moved to standing, toe to toe as they yelled in each other's faces. I stepped in front of Leith as Cleave's voice sounded in my ear. "I'm on crowd control. Let's move them outside."

"Got it. Axel's moving this way if we need him."

Faster than I could reach them, one of the men grabbed the other by the shirt front and shoved him, sending him careening into a nearby table. I jumped in fast, grabbing the aggressor's arm, pulling it up behind his back.

"Get off me, you motherfucker," he yelled, trying to buck me off and catching me with a solid elbow to the side in the process. I grunted, fighting to keep my breath as my irritation spiked. Suddenly, Ward was there, grabbing the guy's other arm and twisting it back the same as I'd done to the first one.

"I've got it," I snapped, as a new spike of irritation lanced through me.

"I said get the fuck off me!" the man yelled again. I redoubled my grip, securing both arms and clamping down my other hand on his shoulder.

"You're done, sir. I'm going to escort you outside."

"This is bullshit!" he shouted, trying to fight again. A quick twist of his wrist brought him up on his toes while he cursed in pain. "Shit! Okay! Okay!"

I eased up my grip, and glanced at Ward. He'd taken a step back and was watching me with the blankest stare I'd ever seen on his face. I wanted to apologize, but I also wanted to make it clear that I didn't appreciate him stepping in while I was working. This was my job, and one of the only things I'd ever truly taken pride in. One of the only things I'd ever truly been good at, honestly.

Cleave had the other man in hand, and Leith was setting the table to rights. Axel was standing to the side, willing to assist, but letting us handle it. I shot him a nod, and with a last glance at my boyfriend's unreadable face, I towed the belligerent man outside.

COOL AIR SLID OVER MY SKIN AS MY *HARLEY* ATE UP THE highway between *Spritz* and Lex's cabin outside of Gnaw Bone. Leith's arms were a light weight around my middle, and I appreciated the warmth of him at my back even though it felt all wrong. When I came back inside after Cleave and I had sent the fighting men on their way—one in an *Uber* and the other with a non-intoxicated friend—Leith had come up and told me Ward and Axel had decided to go ahead to Lex's and asked if I was cool with giving him a ride. I'd told him of course and went back in to finish my shift knowing that I'd fucked up with Ward.

I slowed the bike with a sigh as Lex's garage came into view. It wasn't a huge gathering tonight, most of the Heretic brothers that weren't working, their partners, and some friends. After I parked the bike, Leith and I climbed off and got into one of the ATVs that had been left to carry people back to the party.

"So," Leith started, pulling his jacket close around him

and turning to look at the side of my face. "I wasn't going to ask, but what the hell did you do?"

I sighed again. "I snapped at him when he tried to help with that guy."

"Ooookay...why?"

I fired up the ATV and pointed it down the path through the woods back to the cabin while I tried to work out my answer. The thing was, I still wasn't one hundred percent sure myself why I'd reacted that way. It had been my knee-jerk reaction, without thought or time to really process. I shook my head. "I'm honestly not sure. It almost felt like he was stepping on my toes, you know? I wouldn't jump into the ring if his opponent was getting the better of him. Working security is my job, and I had the situation under control." I took a deep breath, a dull ache in my ribs reminding me of the hit I'd taken.

"Okay. I can understand that, but I could also understand why he might struggle to just stand by. I mean, you wouldn't think it was strange if some guy got a hit in on me and Axel stepped in."

I huffed. "Of course not. Axel loves you, and I *know* he'd do damn near anything to protect you. The difference is— this is my job." I could feel Leith smirking at the side of my face.

"True, and I like that you didn't deny the possibility that Ward has strong feelings for you." I huffed again before Leith continued. "So, maybe this would be a good opportunity to talk about some boundaries?"

"Are you the relationship guru now?" Leith was one of the few people who knew that I'd only had one real relationship in my life and how it had ended. We'd spent quite a bit of time together when he'd needed around the clock security from a crazy ex a couple months ago. He'd encouraged me to get back out there and really give dating a try again. That it was time to get back in the dating saddle now that I was older and wiser...or at least older.

"No, but I am your friend. And I gotta tell you, for a guy I've always thought was pretty happy, you've seemed especially content since Ward became a fixture in your life."

My stomach swooped. I *was* happy in a way I couldn't ever remember being, but it was more than that. I was...settled, somehow. All the rambling, yearnings in my heart had stilled. Warmth filled me—not fear—when I realized that my heart wasn't protesting because it was right where it wanted to be—falling in love with Ward. A smile tugged at the corner of my mouth. "I am happy."

Leith leaned in closer to my side, laying his head on my shoulder. "And I'm happy for you."

I steered the ATV over the last little hill in the trail, revealing the clearing with the warmly lit cabin and the fire glow coming from behind it. Now, I just needed to find my boyfriend and apologize.

CHAPTER TEN

Ward

I'd never been somewhere like Lex's cabin. It was settled back in a clearing away from the road with hills and trees all around. A porch stretched along the length of the back of it with steps leading down to a gravel path and fire pit. I'd taken a seat on one of the benches around the fire and not moved since we arrived. Thanks to Axel, I had a beer in my hand, but honestly, I'd barely touched it.

As far as fights went, I knew what happened at *Spritz* was mild, and I was guessing it only felt so sharp because of the way part of me had never truly believed that Zach would give this a chance. He'd spooked early, admitted that he wasn't one for relationships, but the truly sabotaging part of my brain couldn't help but throw in that if Zach was going to settle down with someone, there were at least a million better options for him than the ex-con who had no idea what he was going to do with his life.

The Heretics had given me a place and a purpose, which seemed like a lot for a boy who had nothing, but I knew the fights were a short-term gig, and eventually, I was going to have to figure out my own path—as a member of the club or apart from it. I closed my eyes and relished the fire's heat on my face. When I opened them, Zach was standing in front of me.

"Can I sit?"

I nodded. We had this side of the fire to ourselves, thankfully. Most everyone else was up on the porch, talking or raiding the alcohol and food. Zach settled beside me, and a tiny relieved breath escaped my lungs when he didn't shy away from pressing us together, shoulder to thigh.

"I'd never really spent any time in the country before I came out here the first time. I love the quiet," he said after a moment.

It felt like he was gearing up to say something else, so I responded with a nod and let my weight shift a little closer to him. We sat quietly for a little while, the only noise beyond the murmur of the others was the sound of our breathing and the crackle of the fire. I was staring into the flames, mesmerized by the way they writhed and moved and built when Zach turned and pressed his forehead against my temple.

"I'm sorry," he breathed, his lips a whisper of a touch against my cheek.

My eyes slipped closed as a shuddery breath escaped me. I reached over, taking his hand in mine, and threading our fingers together. "I'm sorry, too. I didn't mean to interfere in your work."

He nodded, lifting his face away from mine. "I think that's why it got to me. Because it is my work. It's the only thing I've ever really been good at."

"I understand. That guy hit you and I reacted, but you're right, I shouldn't have gotten involved."

He nudged me with his shoulder. "You don't have to protect me, you know?"

I wasn't sure I agreed with that or that I could help feeling the need to protect him, but I could agree not to step on his toes at his job. "Point taken. I won't interfere when you're on the job."

He eyed me for a moment. "I am sorry I reacted the way I did. That wasn't cool."

I gently squeezed his fingers and leaned over for a kiss. "Apology accepted. You hungry?"

"Starved," he said with a laugh.

"Me, too."

I PACED IN FRONT OF THE DRESSING ROOM DOOR. THE WEEK had flown by in a flurry of training with Axel and getting off with Zach every night before we curled up together in his bed. I'd spoken to Mutt once. He was happy that things were going well between me and Little Z and also that he'd heard Razor's parole hearing had been rescheduled for a later date.

The dressing room door opened and Zach stepped inside, a frown on his face.

"What's wrong, babe?"

His dark brows furrowed as he moved to stand in front of me. "Nothing, really. I guess I'm just nervous. Something feels off."

I smirked at him, leaning in to press a kiss to his mouth. "You just never had to watch a boyfriend fight before," I teased him. While Zach may have caught a case of nerves, I was feeling better than ever—strong, focused, and ready to win.

Some of the tension drained out of Zach's shoulders and he smiled. "You're probably right. It's a different feeling, for sure."

A sharp knock came at the door before Calix stepped in. "You ready?" he asked, looking between Zach and me.

As it often did, my voice dried up at having someone else in the room, so I gave Calix a nod. Calix stepped back out, and I gave Zach one more quick kiss before we headed toward the cage. Axel, who was going to be my cornerman, was already standing to the side of the door. After we went through the motions of checking my wraps and gloves and getting my mouthguard secure, I stepped into the cage and faced the man across from me.

He was leaner than my last opponent and had his long dark hair pulled into a knot at the back of his head. He shifted and bounced on his feet, shaking out his arms; all the while, keeping his dead-eyed stare on my face. He kept nodding his head, and I realized his two cornermen were standing behind him outside the cage, giving him instruction. Taking a deep breath, I ignored him, turning to my own corner and finding Zach and Axel standing there.

"His reach is longer than yours," Axel said. "If you can, try shooting and taking it to the ground. Use your strength to control him and wear him down."

"Or just knock him the fuck out," Zach said, eyes focused over my shoulder toward my opponent.

The announcer started his spiel, so after one last shared look with Zach, I turned and got into position. As soon as the bell rang, Knot Boy and I were moving. He was wiry and fast, keeping me on my toes as we danced around each other, looking for an opening. After trading a few punches, I heeded Axel's advice, lunging in low and catching him in a takedown.

We hit the mat hard, and I wasted no time getting on top of him and wrestling into a position where I could punch him in the face. After three solid strikes, he squirmed, trying to get me off him, but only giving me a better position. I grabbed his arm and spun, falling back with my hands locked around his wrist, his arm between my legs, and my legs over his chest. Locking in the arm bar, I lifted my hips, putting pressure on his forearm, knowing that it would snap if I pressed much further.

I felt his tap of defeat a moment later. The crowd around the cage went wild—some with excitement and some with displeasure, undoubtedly, because the fight hadn't ended in bloodshed. My opponent was up and off the floor before I was. Then Axel was there, hauling me to my feet and lifting my arm in victory. After the celebratory turn around the cage, I accepted a towel from Zach as we headed back toward the dressing room.

"See, boyfriend, nothing to worry about," I said with a grin, as soon as we were past the crowd. He nodded, bumping me with his shoulder.

As soon as I opened the dressing room door and stepped inside, I pressed the towel to my face to wipe the sweat out of my eyes.

"Ward," Zach yelled as hands grabbed my arms from behind, yanking me back just as white-hot pain exploded in my left side. I gasped, dropping the towel to the ground and revealing a man holding a knife directly in front of me. I yelled in shock as the pain spread from my side seeming to eclipse my entire body.

The man rushed forward, knocking me back into Zach and disappearing out of my sight. I was struggling to take in air, and my head was starting to swim. I lost my balance completely, Zach's arms the only thing keeping me upright.

"Axel! Calix! It was that fucker's cornerman! I need the first aid kit! Mace, call Doc," Zach yelled, lowering me to the ground. Sweat and blood were pouring out of my body. Reaching up, I fisted a hand in Zach's shirt, staring at the red smear I transferred there.

"It's going to be okay, baby. You're going to be okay," he

was saying over and over. When he grabbed the towel and pressed it to the center of my pain, I grunted and held on to him, trying to ignore the slick, sticky warmth I could still feel draining from my side.

CHAPTER ELEVEN

Zach

M y hands were shaking and sticky red. The metallic tang of copper coated the back of my throat and the inside of my nose. I couldn't get away from it. The wall outside the infirmary room was hard against my back. I had slid down to my ass, just outside the door, the moment Doc had asked me to wait outside and closed it.

I wasn't sure how long it had been other than long enough for the blood on my hands to dry. My brothers had caught the guy who stabbed Ward in the woods outside the barn. I could go join them in getting the answers we needed, but I couldn't move from this spot. It was probably some form of shock, but all I could feel was the desperate grip Ward had kept on my shirt while I tried to slow his bleeding.

"Hey, Zach," Leith said. I glanced up to find him standing over me with Axel behind him. I had no idea how long he'd been there.

"Come on, let's get you cleaned up."

I started to shake my head, and he squatted down in front of me, his knees bumping against mine.

"Listen, Ward is going to be fine, and when you get to go

in and see him, do you really want to be looking like this? Let's walk down the hall to the kitchen, wash your hands, and change your shirt."

I knew he was right, so I pushed to my feet, only for my knees to start to shake. Immediately, Axel was there, getting an arm around me until I felt a little more steady.

"This was a setup," I said.

He chuckled. "This was the easy option. In the other scenario, I threw you over my shoulder and carried you like a petulant child." He gave me a soft smile. "This isn't the first time I've had to support a brother during something like this. Your man is tough, Zach. He's going to be fine."

With a grateful nod, I followed Leith to the kitchen, Axel trailing behind us. Mace and Pax were there, sitting at the table. Beside them, in front of an empty chair, was a steaming mug of something and a clean, folded white t-shirt. I slipped off my vest, handed it to Leith, and pulled the shirt over my head. Mace stood, holding out a trash bag toward me.

"Thanks, man." I knew that bag would never see the inside of a dumpster and was destined for the burn barrel instead. I scrubbed up to my elbows with soap, and then I washed my face, too. Someone handed me a towel, and after I dried off, I sat in the empty seat. Picking up the mug, I took a long swallow of coffee, sweetened just the way I like it.

I glanced up at the men around the table. "Thanks, guys."

Leith gave me a little smile and reached for my other hand. They seemed to realize that I wasn't up for conversation and talked in low voices about inconsequential things while I sipped my coffee and let the solidarity of their presence soothe me.

My cup was almost empty when Doc walked into the room and looked me in the eye.

"He's asking for you, and is going to be just fine."

I was out of my chair in a flash, following Doc down the hall.

"He got lucky," Doc said. "A stab wound in that area could have been a lot worse. But this was shallow enough that it didn't damage any organs. He will be sore for a while. He'll need to take it easy, keep the area clean, and the bandage changed. Infection is the biggest concern, at this point. What he needs is rest and time to heal."

"He'll have it." I extended my hand. "Doc, thank you so much."

Doc shook my hand and patted my shoulder with a smile. "It's my pleasure." He pushed open the door, and there was Ward, looking surly and a bit rumpled and pale, but alive and warm when my hand found his.

I leaned over his bed, running my other hand through the messy hair at the top of his head. "Hey, boyfriend. How you feeling?"

He huffed a little laugh. "Like I've been stabbed."

I grinned at him, leaning the rest of the way in and kissing him gently. "Doc says you have to behave yourself for a while."

"I think I can do that."

He squeezed my hand as his eyes slipped closed and a little snore escaped him. Relief like I'd never known crashed through me. I settled in the chair beside his bed, one hand still holding his and the other running gently through his hair.

IT WAS FULL DARK WHEN CALIX PUSHED WARD'S infirmary room door open. Pale light from the hallway cut an angled path across the floor and I sat up, wiping sleep from my eyes. I moved to stand, but Calix held out a hand to stop me.

"Don't get up," he said, keeping his voice low. "I wanted to check in before I went to bed and to tell you what we found out."

"He talked?"

"He did." There was a coldness to Calix's voice that made my stomach twist. In truth, there was always something cold about Calix, from his black-eyed stare to the way he didn't flinch no matter how messy things got in this world of ours.

He moved across the room, sitting in the chair on the opposite side of the bed, leaving him mostly in shadow as he watched me from across Ward's sleeping form.

"He's an addict. Razor agreed to forgive the man's debt. The price was Ward's life."

My head spun, and my voice—when I found it—was a furious whisper. "That fucker isn't even out of prison yet."

"Devil's Rage used to have a lot more reach than it does now, and Razor was their President. Even fallen the way he has, he'd still have a lot of connections. I knew that he had a substance abuse problem at one time, but I didn't realize he was also dealing."

"He was more than dealing." Ward's voice cut into our conversation, tired, but steady. "He had a network. I was sixteen when my foster father put a bag of pills in my hand and told me it was my job to sell them. I'm sure that house wasn't the only one. I met Razor for the first time a few months after that. When I'd proved I could move product."

"Shit," I whispered. "All the kids in the house?"

"The ones over fifteen, anyway. When I was seventeen, almost eighteen, I got busted. The cop had a lead on Razor, but not enough evidence to convict. They wanted me to flip on him. When I wouldn't, they hauled him in on some smoke screen charge and paraded me through the bullpen. He went batshit, convinced I'd ratted him out. He's had it in for me ever since."

"That's what put you in prison?"

"That, and I spun around and punched the cop dangling me like fucking bait."

"It seems his agenda hasn't changed," Calix said. "Get some rest, Ward. Zach, I'd like to speak to you outside for a moment." He got up and walked out.

Ward grabbed my hand as I stood. "Is this going to land badly for you?"

"What? No. Why would you even think that?"

"Because I'm a fuck-up, Zach! And now I've brought this shit to the door of the only people that have ever given a fuck about me."

I sat on the edge of his bed, keeping his hand in mine. "Okay, I need to go talk to Calix, but I'm not walking out of this room with you thinking that. You are not a fuck-up. You were a kid and put in a shitty situation, and I won't *ever* be hearing you say that shit again. You got me?"

He made a noise in his throat, and though I couldn't clearly see his face in the dark, I was sure there was wetness shining back at me from his eyes. I braced my upper body over his, careful not to touch his side, and brought our faces close together. "You're hurting and on meds, and I know you've been through more shit in your life than I can even imagine." He breathed out hard. "And I'm going to tell you what else I know—I love you."

"Zach—"

"Just...let me finish." I took a deep breath. "I finally realized it last weekend when we were sitting around the fire, but I swear, I think I've loved you from the first moment I saw you up in that cage sparring with Kade. I called him, by the way. Him and Jeb will be here in the morning because they give *more* than a fuck about you. It started with Mutt. He made you family, and Heretics take care of their family. Do you understand what I'm saying? You have a place here. A real place. Whether you can fight or not, and whether you choose to stay with me or not. I guarantee there is a Prospect vest waiting for you in Sand Lake if you want it."

"You're not in Sand Lake."

I huffed a soft laugh. "I could be. I will be if that's where you want to settle. If you feel the same way."

He scoffed. "Don't be stupid. You know I do. I love you, Zach, and I think I have since the first time I beat you at pool."

My eyes stung, and my heart was racing, and I had a smile on my face. "You're an ass." I kissed him then, slow and deep. "I need to talk to Calix. You'll be okay?"

"I'll be fine, baby."

"I'll be right back." I didn't want to leave him. Not even for a minute, but I pulled myself away and stepped out into the hall.

Calix was there, arms crossed over his chest and shoulder leaning against the wall. "There's a Prospect vest waiting for him here, too," he said, eyes intent on my face, which went red knowing he'd heard everything we'd just said. "Just as soon as you take yours off."

My head snapped up, a flare of panic lighting in my belly.

Calix shook his head and unfolded his arms, revealing the patches in his right hand. He held them out to me. "You're a full-patched Heretic now, brother."

"What?" I took the patches from him, looking at the top rocker and Heretics insignia like I'd never seen them before. "How?"

Calix smiled—actually smiled. "We had a little impromptu meeting and vote while you were watching over your man. I told them you're a Heretic, Zach, and every single brother in this club agreed with me."

"Shit," I said, my hands starting to shake again. "Thank you. I don't even know what to say."

"Say yes, and then sew your new patches on. I'd like the

Prospect rocker when you take it off, and I'd be happy to put it on a new vest for Ward if he wants it. Although, I think you're right, I'll probably have to fight Jeb for him."

"He's a keeper."

"Yes, he is." Calix nodded toward the patches still in my hands. "All that can wait until morning but, Zach, we're going to have work to do." He looked past me to Ward's door. "This can't stand."

"I understand, and I agree." Retaliation for what Razor had done to Ward would be a waiting game, but he'd be on the outside eventually, and I intended for us to be ready for him.

CHAPTER TWELVE

Ward

Being stabbed sucked. Every way I moved pulled at it, and every position I tried to lay or sit made it ache. I felt like a big baby, and I knew I was being a grump, but Zach didn't seem bothered in the slightest. We'd moved me up to his room the next afternoon, and I'd been chilling on his leather couch for days. The room was really like a studio apartment—spacious with a kitchenette and en suite bathroom. I'd been making good use of the flatscreen and trying to put a dent in the long list of movies Zach insisted I needed to see.

The door swung open and Zach walked in, carrying some grocery bags. "Hey, boyfriend," he said, as soon as he closed the door.

"Hey." Gingerly, I lifted myself off the couch and walked over to him. I stopped beside him at the kitchenette counter, taking hold of his chin and pulling him in for a kiss.

He glanced over my shirtless torso and down to the big white bandage taped to my side. "How're you feeling? We need to change that this afternoon."

Zach was militant about every order Doc had given me—

including adding sex to the "no strenuous activity" list, the ass. "I'm fine. Sore and starting to get itchy."

"Good, that means you're healing."

"Healing is uncomfortable."

He moved around me with a chuckle, stowing groceries in the overhead cabinet. "I know, and I'm sorry it sucks. Now go lie on the bed, and I'll get the kit."

"Yes, sir."

He gently swatted my ass as I walked away. Stretching out on what had become my side of the bed, I watched him finish up the groceries and grab the first aid kit. He sat beside me, thigh touching my hip and pulled the tape off the edges of the gauze. The wound itself was low on the left side of my torso, a little jagged, and surrounded by bruising. Apparently, a combination of the knife being a bit dull, and Zach pulling me away from my attacker had saved me from deeper damage but also made the surface damage a little worse. I'd never been more grateful.

As he went about preparing the new bandage, my phone vibrated. I pulled it from the pocket of my sweatpants. The number flashing on the screen gave me a clue who was probably calling—and the fact that I got very few calls. I glanced at Zach and swiped to answer.

"Hello?"

"Hey, kid," Mutt said in my ear.

"Hey. I was hoping it was you. Hang on a sec, I've got something to tell you." Taking a chance and praying Zach wouldn't walk away, I put the phone on speaker and laid it on my chest. "Mutt, you're on speaker."

"Okay. What did you need to tell me? Everything alright?"

Zach's wide eyes zeroed in on the phone, and then snapped up to mine. A million emotions flashed across his face, but I swore *eager* was the prominent one.

"First, I'm okay and going to be okay, but after the fight on Saturday, I got stabbed."

"What the fuck? Did the club catch the guy? Is Zach okay?"

"I'm here, Uncle Mutt," Zach said suddenly. "And yes. We got him, and I'm fine."

Silence filled the room. When he spoke again, Mutt's voice was husky. "Hey, kiddo. Damn, it's good to hear your voice."

Zach leaned closer to the phone. "Yours, too. Look, Mutt, I'm—"

"Don't even worry about it, kid."

After another beat of silence, I said, "Zach has some good news. They made him a full patch this weekend."

A boyish smile bloomed on Zach's face. "Yeah. They let me in, can you believe it?"

Mutt scoffed. "Of course, I can. You'll make one hell of a brother. I'm proud of you."

After he cleared his throat, Zach said, "Thank you."

"Now, I don't have long, tell me about the asshole who stabbed you."

"Razor put him up to it. To clear a debt."

"Shit. That's one of the reasons I was calling. Razor somehow managed to get himself transferred to another facility. I don't know what his game is or where he's going to land."

"We'll pass it along," Zach said, brow furrowed.

"Good. Boys, I've got to go. Don't be strangers, alright?"

"Yep. Bye, Mutt."

"Bye, Uncle Mutt. We'll talk soon."

I hit the end button and took a slow breath. I didn't know what to expect, other than being pretty sure he wouldn't punch me, but I hoped I hadn't just fucked everything up.

His eyes moved from the phone to my face. "Thank you."

An easy smile pulled at my lips. "Sorry to spring it like that."

"No, it's okay." He exhaled hard. "I think I needed the push, but there's no way you're getting out of dinner with my mom now."

IT WAS THE FIRST TIME I'D WORN A SHIRT IN A WEEK, AND I couldn't stop tugging at the collar. It seemed surreal that a week ago today, I stepped into the cage, won my fight, and had gotten stabbed afterward.

"Stop fiddling with it, you're going to stretch it out," Zach said as he stopped the truck in a short gravel driveway outside a one-story brick house in the suburbs. The front of the house was lined with well-groomed shrubs and other flower beds that would probably be bursting with color in the spring.

Zach moved to open his door and I grabbed his wrist, panic seizing my chest. "What if I can't talk in front of her? What if I freeze?"

With gentle fingers, Zach took my hand, rubbing it between both of his and turning to face me. "Then I'll talk for both of us. I know you can't control who it's easy to talk to and who it's not, but I promise you, there's no reason to be nervous. She's going to love you. Just like I do."

"I love you, too."

He leaned over and kissed me before hopping out of the truck and running over to my side. I was perfectly capable of getting out of the truck on my own, but it put Zach at ease to be there in case I lost my footing and slipped. He pulled open my door and offered me his hand. I took it and carefully stepped onto the sideboard, and then down to the ground.

Before we got to the door, Zach's mom was stepping

through it and out onto the little covered porch. She was lovely—slender with dark hair and eyes like her son.

"Hey, Mom," Zach called as we made our way up the walk. Yesterday, he had taken her out to lunch and told her he was bisexual. Like he'd predicted, she'd been completely support-ive, and according to Zach, "crazy excited" to meet me. I tightened my grip on my boyfriend's hand. Even if I felt like freezing up, I'd power through for him. I couldn't bear the thought of being a let-down to him or to this woman who so obviously loved her son.

"Hey, sweetie," she said coming down the steps to meet us. "And you must be Ward. It's so good to meet you." She held out her hand.

I took it. "It's good to meet you, too, Ms. Richards." Zach told me before that his parents had never married, and after his dad split while she was pregnant, there had been no way his mom was giving him the bastard's last name.

"Oh no," she said immediately, with a smile so much like her son's. "Call me Sheila, please."

"Sheila." My lisp felt prominent, but she only smiled and stepped to my other side, taking my arm. Together, they walked me up the steps and through the door.

"Now Zach tells me you had a bit of an accident last weekend, and he couldn't say what your favorite meal was, so I took a chance and made his—stuffed shells—plus bananas foster for dessert because, of course, he knew your favorite ice cream flavors." She rolled her eyes, then shot me a wink.

"That," I started to say, but had to stop and clear my throat. "That sounds wonderful, thank you."

"You're welcome, sweetheart. But you will have to tell me what you love to eat so I know for next time."

CHAPTER THIRTEEN

Zach

Six Months Later

"Welcome home!" everyone screamed as soon as we walked through the lounge door in the Sand Lake clubhouse. Uncle Mutt laughed and was immediately whisked away toward the bar for his drink of choice. The cheers only got louder when a line of shots were poured.

"It's going to be one of those parties, huh?" Ward asked from beside me, a huge smile on his face.

"Definitely." I nodded toward the bar. "Want to get in on that action?"

He contemplated for a moment before turning to face me. "Nah, I think I'd rather beat you at pool, and then let you take me to bed."

Even all these months later, my heart was instantly racing and my dick was already hard. If anything, I wanted him more with every passing day instead of less. "And what makes you think you'll beat me?"

He smirked. "Baby, when have I *ever* not beaten you at pool?"

I pretended to be petulant. Okay, it was less pretend than I was willing to admit. "You don't know, this could be the day my luck changes."

His golden eyes landed on mine as he stepped in close. "Could be. This is definitely where mine did."

I licked my lips. "What if we skipped the pool?"

The glint in his eyes turned wicked. We made our way out of the lounge and down the hall to the same room we'd shared for a week when we'd met. It still had only two narrow beds and two small dressers, but I smiled taking in the sight of it.

Ward closed and locked the door, then pushed me up against it, his mouth falling on mine in a hot kiss. "Have you got stuff with you? Want you to fuck me."

"In my wallet." I kissed him back, pushing off the door and steering us toward one of the beds. He'd bulked up in the last six months with all the fight training and us discovering we enjoyed weight lifting together.

Life was good. Ward had taken to the security business and club business like a duck to water, fitting right in with all the guys and becoming everyone's new favorite Prospect. He called my mom, Mom these days, and that melancholy look he got sometimes when the subject of family came up happened less and less. Now with Mutt out, I knew it would get even better. The only dark spot was Razor. According to public record, he'd been released three months ago and had basically vanished from the face of the earth. Calix thought any one of his numerous enemies had dumped him in a shallow grave. Honestly, I hoped so, but my gut didn't quite believe it.

We pulled at each other's clothes until we fell on the bed, skin to skin. He had the packet of lube from my wallet clenched between his teeth, and a gleam in his eye that told me I was in for a hard ride.

I loved it. Loved every minute that I got to spend with him and loved him more than I'd ever imagined possible.

Tearing the packet open, he coated my cock—we'd been going bare together for a long time—then reached two lube-slick fingers behind himself. As he straddled me, I held my dick still, aiming up to where I most wanted to be. He went slowly, holding my gaze as he stretched around me. When he was fully seated, he rocked his hips, pulling a moan out of me.

"Much better than pool," I said, tracing my fingers over the scar on his side before gripping his hips and starting to thrust up in his rhythm.

"I don't know," he gasped, giving himself away. "Beating you is one of my favorite past times."

"Haha." Reaching up, I got a hand around the back of his neck and pulled him down so I could get my mouth on his. Heat exploded between us as he rode me relentlessly. We came within moments of each other with a shout.

Resting his forehead against mine, my cock still buried deep inside him, and my hands gliding over the bare skin of his back, he looked me in the eye. "I love you. More than anything."

"I know, baby. I love you, too."

Thank you for reading!

DISSENT

Iron Heretics MC #4

CHAPTER ONE

Holden

EIGHT YEARS AGO

T his was probably the stupidest thing I'd ever done. The soles of my boots stuck to the grimy alley pavement as the man in front of me set his hands on my chest and pushed. Jagged brick edges caught at my clothes, scraping the skin of my back beneath the thin layer of my t-shirt.

"Easy, man." I chuckled. "I'm a sure thing."

He leveled the same black-eyed glare that had drawn me to him inside the bar and reached for my belt. The jangle of the buckle coming free was loud in the quiet of the alley. As soon as my pants were undone, he reached for his own with one hand while slipping the other beneath the fabric of my briefs. Hot, calloused fingers wrapped around me and squeezed. My breath caught in my throat at the first stroke.

Still holding his gaze, I reached for him. The taut skin of his stomach met my questing fingers. I brushed down through the trail of soft hair there until I found the thicker curls surrounding the base of him. I hummed in appreciation once I had him in my grip, hot and hard and already leaking at the head.

"Hungry for it, huh?" I asked, voice coming out low and more hoarse than I'd anticipated. He was still working me over, slowly stroking with a squeeze around the head at every pass.

"Shit," I gasped, letting my head fall back against the brick and mimicking his grip with my own hand. That pushed a grunt out of him.

He leaned closer, nearly pressing our chests together as he pushed his nose against the side of my neck. He set his teeth there, and I bared my throat.

He growled—literally growled—and squeezed harder. Tucking my chin, I nudged at his face until I could brush my lips over his. Everything stopped. With his hand frozen on my aching dick, he lifted his head and held my gaze again. I swallowed hard, not sure if that tiny kiss was going to get me punched in the face when he lifted the hand he'd braced against the brick beside my shoulder and placed it on my throat. He didn't squeeze, but the weight of it, of him, sent a shudder through me. A hard breath poured out of me into the small space between us. His fingers pressed against my flesh while the dark depths of his eyes stared into mine. In that moment, I might have let him do anything to me. My body went lax.

He moved like a viper strike. His lips descended on mine in a hungry, demanding rush. That hand on my throat held me captive—pressed against the sharp points of the brick digging into my back and the fiery onslaught at my front. His grip on my cock renewed its urgency, squeezing and stroking me until I was gasping into his mouth. With bites and licks, he owned my lips and tongue, sucking on the latter until my entire body convulsed and I erupted over the iron grip of his fist.

"Jesus Christ," I panted, breathless and trembling.

Without missing a beat, he pulled his hand from my pants and slipped it into his, knocking his own jeans farther down his hips until the full girthy length of him was exposed. The hand still pinning me by the throat slid down, grabbed the edge of my shirt, and hiked it up until the material was bunched beneath my armpits.

He stroked himself, fast and hard, and came with a growl only seconds later. Ribbons of his cum splattered against the clenching muscles of my stomach, and I shuddered all over again.

For a moment, he leaned more of his weight on me, the hand still fisted in my shirt pressing me against the brick. Then he stood up straight, wiped the hand covered in the sticky mess of mine and his cum all against the clean skin of my side, and tucked himself away. I didn't realize I'd been standing there staring until he lifted those eyes to mine again, and the smallest smirk pulled up one corner of his mouth. As soon as he finished buckling his belt, he reached for mine, gently pulling my briefs back up and fastening up my pants and belt. He stepped in close, using both hands to ease my shirt back down my torso.

"What's your name?" I asked, my words coming out a whisper. I could feel his breath against my lips, feel the wet mess we'd created all along my skin, still feel his hand digging into the flesh of my throat.

"Calix."

With one last tug on the hem of my shirt and a nip of my bottom lip, he turned around and walked out of the alley.

I HATED NIGHTS LIKE THIS. PULLING MY DEVIL'S RAGE Prospect vest closer around me, I leaned against the wall of the shithole motel where Razor had the girls working tonight. I was on protection duty along with my old man. My dad, Travis Holden Sr., was one of the founding members of the Devil's Rage MC. I hated him, too.

The sounds of sex, especially a woman moaning like we were on a porn shoot, filtered through the motel room door. Some of the john's liked that, I'd learned. Needed to reaffirm their masculinity or something. The sounds were usually just annoying, but tonight they made my stomach turn. The girls working were Chrissy and Lynn, and for some reason, Chrissy had to bring her son with her. The kid couldn't be more than ten or twelve. He was a scrawny little thing. Chrissy had closed him up in the bathroom with headphones and a book to read. *Jesus.*

I pulled a smoke out of my pocket and lit it, leaning harder against the wall and letting my mind wander to the man who'd pressed me against another wall the night before. *Calix.* He'd said his name was. I'd only ever heard that name once before—the new Iron Heretics President. I snorted to myself. Razor and Travis had all sorts of awful shit to say about him, but there was no way. Although, the way he'd manhandled me...I shook my head. No way was it the same guy.

Travis's phone rang. He pulled it out and pressed it to his ear. "Shit," he said, hanging up quick and banging on the hotel room door closest to him—Lynn's. "Time's up!"

"What's going on?" I asked, knocking on Chrissy's door the same way.

"The fucking Heretics are on their way. Think we're too close to their turf to be doing business here."

"Shit." I banged harder on the door. Two motorcycles pulled into the parking lot, but a glance over my shoulder showed Razor and another one of ours. It wasn't exactly a comfort.

"What! Jesus!" Chrissy yelled, pulling open the door, a sheet barely wrapped around her. Her dark hair was a mess, and her mascara had made dark circles under her vivid blue eyes.

"We've got to move. Heretics on the way."

"Fuck," she said and disappeared back into the room.

I followed, tossing her john the pants he'd left lying on the floor. "Get the fuck out."

He didn't argue, just pulled his shit together and ran. Chrissy was across the room, slipping her short dress over her head and opening the bathroom door.

"Come on. We've got to go."

The kid came out, eyes on the ground like she'd either told him not to look, or he instinctively knew that this was shit he didn't want to see. My stomach rolled again.

I herded them toward the door. Razor stepped into the open doorway, took one look at the kid, and grabbed Chrissy by the arm.

"What the fuck is he doing here?"

"I didn't have anywhere to leave him!" she yelled in his face, trying to pull her arm free.

"Let her go!" The kid said, slipping off his headphones and whacking Razor on the leg with his book.

"You little shit," Razor snarled, letting Chrissy go long enough to smack the kid across the face.

"That's enough," I yelled, getting between Razor and the kid. Razor got right up in my face, but it gave Chrissy the time to get the kid and get out.

"You telling me what to do, prospect?"

"I just meant we need to get a move on," I said through gritted teeth. Fuck, I hated him. Hated my father. Hated how they ran this club. I knew we were criminals. I had no illusions, but that didn't mean we couldn't have a code. Couldn't have some sliver of honor. I remembered when I was younger how trips to the clubhouse used to be fun. I didn't have to worry about someone slapping me around or seeing something I shouldn't have. Then Razor took over, and year after year, everything changed. Including my father. It had taken me longer than it should have to realize he was using. Hooked about as bad as most of the girls were.

The rumble of more motorcycles came from the parking lot. Razor shoved me out of the room. Chrissy, Lynn, and the kid were already in their car and driving away. Travis and the other guy were standing with their backs to us, watching the Heretics roll to a stop. There were four of them, too.

The one in the lead took off his helmet, and my breath caught in my chest. Calix's black eyes zeroed in on me from the parking lot. Guess it really was a small world after all.

CHAPTER TWO

Calix

PRESENT DAY

I sipped the tequila in my glass, watching the movement around me in the mirror behind the bar. The lounge in the basement of *Spritz* was never the busiest place because it was so exclusive—a high-end brothel catering to gay men with a need for discretion and money to burn—but weekends typically saw an uptick in activity. On a weeknight, it was practically a ghost town. Which suited me fine. There were a dozen or so men making use of the grouped couches and chairs, sipping drinks and enjoying the scenery of scantily clad young men roaming about, delivering drinks and flashing charming smiles. Some had pulled a boy or more into their laps, and others were being led to the darkened hallway where rooms were available for private use.

The two-man security team on this floor for the evening —one Heretic and one Devil I'd reluctantly approved—were stationed on opposite ends of the room, ready to move the moment something seemed amiss. Movement directly behind me caught my eye. A dark-haired boy I hadn't seen before moved across the mirror, gathering empty glasses from a side table, no doubt abandoned when something more potent had caught their drinker's eye. He was...lovely—narrow limbed, softly muscled, and pale with ink-black hair. Charcoal gray briefs cupped a soft bulge at the apex of his legs and framed a pert little ass. I had a feeling it would fit perfectly in my hands.

He wasn't my usual flavor, but maybe that was a good thing. It had been a damn long time since I told Holden he wasn't welcome in my bed anymore. Long enough that the stinging bite I always got at the thought, or sight, of him had morphed into a throbbing ache. The kind of pain that settled into your bones. The kind you carried for the rest of your life.

"Just drinking tonight?" Vivian Sinclair, the owner of *Spritz* and Heretics business partner, stopped in front of me, holding a rock glass of amber-colored liquor. I'd popped in tonight for an informal meeting with her. Vivian and Iron Heretics Security, the security company the MC owned, were extending our partnership to include the new club she was opening on the other side of town.

Pulling myself from my maudlin thoughts, I glanced up at her. I honestly wasn't even sure what I was still doing here, and I could tell she was surprised to find me at the bar at all. Drowning sorrows or sitting around feeling sorry for myself had never been my style. If I wanted to drink alone, I should have done it the way I always did—on my own damn couch with a bottle bigger than my head.

Maybe I didn't want to be alone after all.

"The dark-haired boy," I said with a jut of my chin toward his reflection in the mirror.

Real surprise flashed through Vivian's eyes this time. She looked over my shoulder at the boy in question, and it was the first time I'd ever seen her hesitate. "He's...new, Calix. Are you sure?"

Raising an eyebrow at her, I held her stare as I tipped the rest of the tequila into my mouth. The liquor slid down hot into my belly. It wasn't often someone questioned me. I didn't like it, and I especially didn't like being questioned about who I decided to fuck. I'd waged a war and taken over a whole motorcycle club organization the last time someone had.

The cool all-business face she normally wore slid back into place. "I'll send him in."

Setting my glass on the bar, I kept my gaze trained on hers a moment longer before I turned and walked toward the hallway and the room that would give me a closer look at the new boy.

Light and shadow passed over my face in increments as I walked along the hallway from the sconces lining the wall. It wasn't often that I indulged myself here, but I couldn't fault the ease of being able to get off with no strings, no expectations, and no seeking on my part. I detested the pick-up scene and fuck if I was going to use some goddamn app to get laid.

Reaching the last room in the hall, I punched my code into the number pad on the door. It clicked open, and I stepped into what could easily have been an upscale hotel room. Recessed lighting filled the space with a soft glow, letting shadows gather in the corners. Muted gray walls led down to the dark hardwood floor, in the center of which stood a king-sized bed covered in plush silver bedding. The tables on either side of it would be stocked with condoms and lube.

Slipping out of my Heretics vest, I laid it over the armchair in the corner then slipped off my boots and socks. I'd just sat on the side of the bed when a soft knock sounded through the door.

"Come in." I kept my voice low, not wanting to scare off the new boy before I'd had the chance to get a good look at him and feel some of that creamy skin against mine.

The door clicked open and the boy peeked in, long pale fingers gripping the edge of the door. Clear blue eyes met mine. He swallowed and stepped inside, letting the door fall closed behind him.

"Vivian said you...wanted me?"

One corner of my mouth quirked up at the inflection. As I watched him, he clasped his hands in front of himself while soft pink started to color the skin of his chest and migrate north. His gaze moved all around the room, landing everywhere but back on my face. It caught on my vest, eyes widening at the President patch. He swallowed and shifted back a tiny step.

Oh, he'd do very nicely indeed, but I didn't want him afraid of me.

"Take your shoes off and come here," I said, motioning to the spot on the floor between my knees. He walked over slowly, still keeping his gaze anywhere except on me. When he was within reaching distance, I placed my hands on his narrow hips. The barest tremble met my palms as I pulled him closer. Looking up to his face, I rubbed my thumbs in small circles over the jut of his hip bones. "What's your name?"

"Neven."

I hummed. I'd never heard that name before. It suited him. "Do you know who I am, Neven?"

"The President of the Iron Heretics."

"I am. Does that bother you?"

"I don't know. I've heard people say you're...not nice, but you've been okay to me." He paused to lick his lips. "So far."

A chuckle worked its way up my throat. "Well, to be

honest, those people aren't wrong. *Not nice* is probably putting it lightly, though."

He canted his head, hands still held tightly together in front of him.

"Put your hands on my shoulders." He did so, and there was no missing the way they were shaking. Once he'd settled his palms on me, I scooted back, using my grip on his hips to encourage him to straddle me. Humming appreciatively as his slight weight rested on my thighs, I slid my hands around to his back and pulled him closer until the tips of his pink nipples were brushing the cotton of my t-shirt.

The blush crawling up his body deepened, making his cheeks and the tops of his ears match the rosy glow of his chest. He wouldn't meet my eyes. "Neven, look at me."

He lifted his head, crystal blues staring at me from only inches away.

"I'm Calix, and yes, I'm the Heretics President, *but*—and you have my word on this—I'll be nice to you."

He nodded even as the trembling in his body intensified.

"Is it me you're afraid of or what you think is going to happen in this room?"

"Both. This is the first time I've…"

I raised an eyebrow as he trailed off, and that blush got deeper.

"I mean, I'm not a virgin, but I've only been helping on the floor a couple nights. I really didn't think anyone would notice me."

Was this kid for real? With his tight little body and gorgeous face, it was a wonder that I was somehow his first customer. A curl of possessive fire licked up my spine. Squashing that thought before it could take root, I leaned across the short distance separating our mouths and brushed my lips against his.

He opened his eyes wide, surprise written all over his face.

I suppose gentleness was the last thing he would expect from me. The blush covering half of him deepened as I pressed my lips to the underside of his jaw and gave him a little nip. A trembling breath poured out of him.

"Neven," I whispered against the pale skin of his throat. "Do you want this? The choice is yours."

He pulled back completely, pretty blues disbelieving.

"It is. Before we go any further, I need to know that you want to be here."

Swallowing, he looked down, fingers playing with the collar of my shirt. "What happens if I say yes?"

I should've stayed back, given him space, but he was so damn—innocent, *vulnerable*—that I pulled him closer, getting my arms the rest of the way around him and eliminating the tiny bit of space there was left between us. "I'm going to make you feel good." His breath hitched, and I leaned closer still, kissing my way back to his ear. "Can I put my mouth on you?"

He nodded, his dark hair catching on the stubble of my buzzed head. "Yes."

A feral grin spread across my lips. Locking one arm around his waist and slipping the other down to his ass, I stood up and did a quick turn, dropping him onto the bed. He gasped, holding tight until his back hit the mattress. Standing, I pulled my shirt over my head and shucked the rest of my clothes.

Wide blue eyes tracked over my body as I knee walked back onto the bed and sat back on my haunches between his spread thighs. It was gratifying watching his blush get deeper and seeing the answering hardness lifting the material of his briefs away from his body.

Running my hands up the soft skin of his thighs, I took hold of his briefs and pulled them down, encouraging him to lift his legs so I could slip them off his feet. Once we were both bare, I looked him over, enjoying the way he squirmed under my gaze. He was beautiful—delicate—but masculine with compact muscles and trimmed, dark curls surrounding a perfect little leaking cock.

"Calix?"

Laying down on my belly, I shouldered his legs open wider and sucked him into my mouth. He gasped, legs squeezing and hips jerking up. I smiled around him, getting my hands on his hips to pin him to the bed. Lowering my head, I groaned at the salt leaking from his slit and the delicious little sounds coming out of him—like he couldn't stop them. I kept sucking him, moving up and down his shaft, drilling my tongue against his slit, and giving him the barest scrape of teeth on the underside of his crown.

"I-I'm going to come," he stuttered out not a full minute into it, and I was glad I'd chosen this route. My boy really was inexperienced.

My boy. Huh.

His whole body seized up, and he came with a whimper. I swallowed him down and licked him clean, then rose up onto my knees, getting a hand around myself.

Jesus Christ, but he was beautiful—flushed red, mouth open, pupils blown wide. Even cum drunk, he zeroed in on the movement of my hand. Reaching out, he grazed his fingertips along the top of my thighs, rubbing up and down in a whisper over my skin. I was so lost watching his face as he watched me that my orgasm took me by surprise, exploding out in ribbons of cum and splattering all over his belly and spent cock.

When the pleasure ebbed, I collapsed forward, catching myself with my hands planted beside his shoulders. His big, suspiciously shiny blue eyes met mine as I settled against him. I smiled when he spread his legs, lean thighs cradling me, and he returned it with a shaky smile of his own.

"Okay?" I asked, moving to rest on my elbows so I could frame his face in my hands and wipe at the tear tracks running from the corners of his eyes.

"Yes." He brought his hands up, touching my cheeks with that same tentative press before running his fingers back over the stubble of my hair.

I hummed in approval and sealed my mouth over his.

His kisses were as hesitant as his touch, but they grew more confident as I caressed his tongue with mine over and over. He had such a fucking sweet mouth.

Once I got us cleaned up and settled with his head on my chest, he was out like a light. When Vivian said he was new, I assumed she meant *new to Spritz*, not new to sex. He said he wasn't a virgin, but if anyone else had ever taken him in their mouth, they must not have had a clue what they were doing.

I ran my hand up and down the soft skin of his back as a frown settled on my face...for no other reason than I was thinking of hunting down Vivian and telling her that this boy wouldn't be seeing anyone but me. I couldn't stomach the thought of his sweetness in the hands of anyone who might not show him the proper care.

I glanced down at his sleeping face. In truth, there was only one other person I'd be willing to share him with, but I honestly wouldn't even know where to start that conversation. The same way I wasn't sure how things were going to be between Holden and me after church tomorrow. I wasn't happy with the direction the club wanted to move with respect to the Devil's, but I was self-aware enough to know that my feelings on the subject were entirely personal. It was a good decision for the club, even if the thought of having to spend more time in Holden's presence than I already did made my hackles rise. I considered myself to be a strong man, but even my will had its limits. More than that worry, the thought that truly plagued me was what I would do when he figured out that my reason for keeping us apart would be gone.

With a sigh, I closed my eyes. I'd stay for a little while before slipping out into the night and leaving this beautiful boy to rest. The last thing I needed was to get another man's hopes up, only to have to dash them.

CHAPTER THREE

Holden

Calix had been scowling at me since I sat down at the meeting table for church. The truce between my club, Devil's Rage MC, and the Heretics still held strong nearly two years since we'd originally agreed to it. Though, it wasn't often that I received an invite to sit in on their club meetings. Usually, I got a call from Riot or Mace, the Heretics' VP and Sgt-At-Arms respectively, and sometimes even a gruff call from Calix himself. Whatever it was this time, it warranted an in-person conversation, and it was plain from the glare Calix kept aiming my way that he didn't like it.

When the last of the seats around the table were filled and a prospect closed the door, Calix lifted the gavel and brought it down one time on the wooden table top.

"Morning, boys," Calix said, black gaze moving over all his gathered men before landing briefly on me again. "Any news before we get into it?"

Mace leaned forward, resting his elbows on the table. "All is good on the *Spritz* front. We're at nearly six months without a security incident."

A positive murmur went through the crowd.

"Good," Calix continued, turning to Riot. "Fights?"

"All set for next weekend. Jeb tells me Ward is in top shape and more than ready to take on the fighter from Tennessee."

"Good. We'll be all-hands-on-deck over the next two weeks between the club and the fight. Be sure you check the fucking calendar and are at your post when you're supposed to be there." Calix smirked. "It'll be good to have Zach's ass back around here for a few days."

That got several *hell yeahs* and claps to the top of the table. As far as I knew, after Zach had received his full patch last year and his boyfriend, Ward, had healed up from a stab wound, he'd transferred to the Sand Lake Heretics chapter. Jeb Campbell was the President there and a good man as far as I could tell.

"Now," Calix said, bringing me out of my thoughts and moving his gaze to mine. "Holden." A muscle in his jaw ticked. It did the same thing when he was trying to hold back from coming.

"Calix," I answered, letting my eyelids go a little heavy.

He narrowed his eyes as his jaw ticked again. "It's the club's decision in light of our proposed new business venture that we extend the offer of patches over to the Devil's Rage MC."

I sat up straight, stunned. The Heretics had been partnered with Vivian Sinclair for security at her club, *Spritz*, both the legal and not-so-legal parts of it, for a couple years. When Vivian had brought the idea to the Heretics for another club and brothel in the city, I'd been thrilled the Devil's might have a chance to get in on that pie. The Heretics were spread thin between working security and their fight nights. They'd already brought a few of the Devil's onto the payroll of Iron Heretics Security. Apparently, somewhere along the way, they'd decided to take it a step further.

Oh, and their President was not happy about it. He looked like he was barely holding back from gritting his teeth. "If you would, please speak to your club. Next Friday night, after the fight, we'll have a meeting here for the vote, and if all goes well, a patch over party."

That got the loudest whistles and claps of any news shared so far. Calix held up his hand, and the room quieted again.

"What do you say, Holden?"

I let the smile I'd been holding back break over my face— half excitement and half petty joy. "I, for one, am all for it. I'll take the news to the Devil's, and we'll see you next Friday night."

"CALIX!" I CALLED, BREAKING INTO A JOG TO CATCH THE door he'd just gone through before it slammed in my face. I'd planned to talk to him in the meeting room, but he'd booked it out the moment he'd brought the gavel down a final time.

He continued across the garage toward his bike without turning to look at me. His sigh seemed loud enough to echo around the cavernous space. "What is it, Holden?" Finally stopping, he turned to look at me. The furrow etched into his brow was familiar, and it nearly made me smile before I caught the look in his eyes. The usual stubborn resolve looked back at me along with something else. *Exhaustion.*

"You not sleepin', hoss?" Stepping closer, I lowered my voice, continuing my perusal of all the tells on his face. Truth was, I missed his face. Missed him in more ways than I cared to let on. The thought of the Devil's becoming Iron Heretics, of *me* becoming an Iron Heretic, filled me with an excitement I hadn't felt in years.

"I had a late night."

The salacious lilt of his voice told me he was trying to get under my skin. He wanted me to be uncomfortable...probably so I'd leave him alone. *Tough shit.* He was going to talk to me whether he wanted to or not.

"Is that right? Added another notch to the bedpost, huh?" Just because I hadn't been with anyone since he called off whatever was happening between us the last time didn't mean he hadn't. Only one of us had been in love, after all.

"As a matter of fact, I did."

I didn't flinch, but fuck, it was a close thing. Licking my lips, I held his stare, sure he could see some of the hurt that simple statement had caused no matter how badly I wished I could hide it all. "Good." I was proud of how even my voice came out. "Being alone too long isn't good for anybody."

He sighed again. "What did you want?"

I wondered who he'd found to warm his bed—another Heretic? Someone outside the club? Stopping that thought in its tracks, I refocused on the man in front of me. "You going to be able to live with this?"

"It was the club's decision"—he reached into his pocket and pulled out his smokes— "and despite my feelings on the subject, increasing our numbers *is* in the best interest of the club." Without dropping my gaze, he tapped out a cigarette and stuck it between his lips.

"But you voted against patch over?"

"Yes."

When he dropped his eyes to light his smoke, I shook my head. "Jesus, there are hard asses, and then there's you."

"Most of the Devil's aren't Heretics material."

"I'll give you we've got a couple guys that will turn in their vests and black out their ink before they go Heretic." I bit my lip, knowing I should keep my fucking mouth shut but needing to know anyway. "What about me? Do I make the cut? Am I Heretics material?"

He blew a plume of smoke over his shoulder. Feeling a stupid wash of bravery, I reached out and took the cigarette from between his fingers and brought it to my own lips. After I exhaled, he stepped in close, bumping my chest, black eyes staring into mine. He plucked the smoke from my fingers, taking a long drag and blowing it to the side. When he didn't say anything and didn't move, some stupid bubble of hope tried to rise in my chest. I did my best to squash it. He was as likely to bust my lips as he was to kiss them.

"Calix," I finally whispered, unable to stand the tension building between us.

"You've always been Heretics material." His voice was low, face hard as he stared into my eyes. "If I could have figured out a way to get you out of the Devil's without getting you killed, I would have done it years ago."

Fuck, that hope was *singing* now.

"Then why—" Before the words were out of my mouth, his face closed off and he stepped away.

"Goddammit, Calix. If you don't want me, that's fine, but if I'm a Heretic now, what's going to be your excuse?"

He threw his leg over his *Harley* and glared my way. "You're not a Heretic yet." He brought the engine to rumbling life, flicked the rest of his cigarette away and drove out of the garage, once again leaving me to stare after him.

CHAPTER FOUR

Calix

*F**ucking Holden*. Between the blue eyes, slicked-back blond hair, and cocky smirk, I'd been a goner eight years ago, and I was still a goner today. But he'd been a Devil, a fucking legacy, and I was a Heretic. From the moment I'd figured out who he was, I knew there could never be more between us than sex, and even that was risky. So, I'd fucked him in secret for nearly a decade, denying that I felt anything more about it until I'd finally grown some fucking balls and let him go almost two years ago.

That should have been the end of it. I had needed to focus on protecting my guys and keeping us whole as we jumped from one shit storm to another, and he'd needed to grow into the role of President to the Devil's Rage. It hadn't been easy for him, but he'd done a good job of keeping the men loyal to the vest close and cutting loose those that would rather see the whole organization fall than having a truce with the Heretics. And this last year—this peace we'd found since Razor disappeared—was as welcome as it was daunting.

My Heretics had grown into a well-oiled machine, and I'd let myself relax for the first time in a decade.

Mistake.

Given time to wonder, my mind kept bringing me back to the same place—back to Holden. But the excuse held true—he was the Devil's President and I was the Heretic's, and it was a line we didn't need to cross. With that barrier gone, with both of us on the same side of the line...well, I wasn't prepared, or fuck, possibly even *capable* of giving him what he wanted. That shit kept me awake at night.

I rolled the bike to a stop. The building behind *Spritz* had housed offices in another life. When Vivian purchased the club, she'd purchased this building, too, and converted it to apartments for her employees. They called it *Spritz Villa*.

Killing the bike's engine, I pulled out my phone and fired off a text.

Calix: *What apartment is Neven in?*

And here was another conundrum—I couldn't figure out how to let myself love one man. Why the fuck did I feel the need to bring another one into the mix? I didn't know, but he'd been on my mind ever since I left him sleeping the night before.

Vivian: *312...Calix, please be careful with him.*

I sighed. There it was, proof that I should start the bike right back up and ride away. I hit dial on her contact.

"Calix," Vivian answered, ready to placate me. "I didn't mean to tell you what to do. It's just...I get the feeling he's been through a lot."

"What'd his background check say?"

"Same story as a lot of the others. No father listed on his birth certificate, and mother is deceased. His last known address was from a rough part of town."

"Trouble with the law?"

"None. I don't know what it is exactly, but he just seems so—"

"Vulnerable."

She breathed out over the receiver. "Yes. Somehow more so than any I've taken in lately. Maybe any since Arden."

An image of Lex's partner rose up in my mind. That kid had been through some shit. He was also happy and healthy now, protected and loved by one of the deadliest men I'd ever met.

"I'm not going to hurt him, Viv."

"Okay." She went quiet, and I could practically hear her trying to choose her words. "Should I take him off the lounge floor? Honestly, I wasn't sure about placing him there in the first place, but he wanted it."

I pulled in a deep breath. A choice like that shouldn't be made without his input. It was his life, and if sex work was what he wanted to do, who the hell was I to stop him? He stood the chance to make some good money that way, even if I did think he was in way over his head. I wasn't saying all that to Vivian, though. It sounded like she'd already had the same thoughts.

"I'll let you know."

She sighed. "Alright. You know, he doesn't have to work until later this evening in case you were thinking of doing something nice."

I chuckled. "Nice. Yeah, that sounds like me."

She hummed. "Sometimes. Goodbye, Calix."

"Later, Viv."

Getting off the bike, I used my key to let myself in the building and made my way up to the third floor. I still didn't know what I was doing, but I'd gotten on my *Harley* to run away from Holden and ended up here. Ten years ago, I never would have pegged myself for a coward. Maybe I really was getting old. Or maybe I'd just been at war so long that I didn't know what to do with this peace. For the last year, I'd felt unsettled, waiting for the other shoe to drop. It hadn't, and I needed to figure out how to proceed in the new normal.

Stopping in front of 312, I knocked on the door. After a couple minutes, it opened a sliver, revealing a chain and one perfectly blue eye.

Neven stared at me for half a second, then closed the door. He opened it again, giving me the full view of him. His black hair was mussed, and he had on soft-looking plaid pajama bottoms and a gray t-shirt. He was also tiny. He couldn't be more than a buck twenty soaking wet.

For a moment, we stared at each other. Me at a loss for words now that he was standing in front of me, and him looking skittish again. The real truth laid itself out for me in those seconds—I didn't have the first fucking clue how to do this. I wanted to date this boy. Wanted to make him mine. The same way I wanted Holden to be mine. I'd seen several of my Heretic brothers pairing up over the last few years. They made it look easy. They're a bunch of fucking liars. Nothing about this felt easy, but I was there, and if I was really going to do this, I needed to get my shit together.

"Are you hungry?" I finally asked. It came out more like a growl, and Neven's eyes widened.

"Um, I haven't had breakfast?"

Right. Because it wasn't even noon, and he'd been working late last night. "Would you like to?"

"Okay." He stepped back, glancing over his shoulder and then back at me. "Want to come in?"

I moved into his studio apartment, closing the door behind me. Directly to my right was his bed and the door to the bathroom. The other side of the room held a couch, small flat screen tv, and a kitchenette. The apartments came furnished and were nice, but there was nothing beyond the single pillow, one rumpled blanket on the bed, and a small stack of library books on the nightstand to prove anyone even lived there.

"Um." Neven fidgeted with the hem of his shirt. "What should I wear?"

I tilted my head. He looked adorably shy and shorter than he'd been the last time because I was still in my boots. I had the strangest urge to tuck him under my chin. It took me longer than it should have to understand what he was really asking...*did I expect him to be working?* "Wear whatever you want. Whatever you're comfortable in. This is just breakfast, Neven."

"Okay. I'll just be a minute. Make yourself at home." He gestured toward the couch before gathering some clothes out of his dresser and disappearing into the bathroom.

———

NEVEN'S ARMS STAYED TIGHT AROUND ME AS I PARKED THE bike in front of *Mac's Café* beside two other bikes I recognized. It was no surprise to see Eben's bike there since Cody was most likely working, and Axel's ride probably meant he and Leith were heading out to enjoy a day off.

Dropping the kickstand, I slid off and offered Neven my hand. This had been his first ride, and while it'd been short—only a few blocks—his legs would be wobbly. His fingers gripped mine as he stepped off the bike. My lips pulled up at the wide smile on his face.

"What'd you think?" I asked, helping him with the chin strap of the helmet. He'd been nervous when he climbed on and clung to me the entire ride, but if I recognized that look in his eye, *Harley* may have converted another soul.

"It was awesome." Pulling the helmet off, he ran a hand through his hair. "I'm kind of sad it was so short." Big eyes darted to mine and glanced away just as quickly, like he was surprised at himself for sharing.

I chuckled. "I think a longer ride can be arranged." I

stowed the helmet and stepped toward the door, pulling it open for him. "Breakfast first, though." As soon as we stepped through the door, a chorus of voices greeted us.

"Hey, boss," Axel and Eben both called, keen stare brushing right over me to focus on the boy that had stopped two steps inside the door. Leith was watching us from beside Axel's hulking form with a contemplative expression. I caught his eyes, and he dropped his gaze to the coffee cup in his hand.

Placing my hand on Neven's lower back, I steered him to the small table next to their larger one and pulled one of the chairs out for him.

"Axel, Eben," I greeted my men and then nodded at the third in their party. "Leith."

"Hi, Calix." Leith's blue eyes moved from me to Neven. "Hey, Neven."

Neven's smile was small. "Hi, Leith."

"Boss, Cody just took our dishes back." Eben started to stand. "Want me to yell back for Mac to get something started for the two of you?"

"I've got it. Enjoy your coffee." I turned to Neven. "Preferences? Mac makes a mean bacon, egg, and cheese croissant."

He bit his lip, looking from me to the big chalkboard menu behind the pastry counter. "Um, could I have the BLT on toast instead?"

As timid as he looked, I found myself oddly proud that he'd asked for something other than what I'd recommended. "Of course. Coffee?"

"Yes, please."

"You got it." I turned toward the counter, inhaling the rich scent of yeast dough, spices, and coffee. Mac stepped out of the kitchen just as I reached the glass case full of that morning's creations.

"Calix, good to see you." Mac was a bear of a man, tall enough to be a lumberjack with broad shoulders and thick arms. He'd been a friend to the club for many years. "How are you this morning?"

"Fine, Mac. Yourself?" I asked, watching his eyes track over to the other Heretics before settling on Neven alone at the two-seater table beside them.

Mac raised his eyebrows at me in question before answering. "No complaints. Business is good." He shrugged his massive shoulders. "What can I get you and your...friend?"

I huffed a laugh. "Two coffees. Bacon croissant for me. BLT on toast for my *friend*."

Pursing his lips, he nodded once and turned to pour our coffees. "It's good to see you with someone," he said quietly over his shoulder.

I nodded and steered us away from that line of conversation. "You said business is good. No trouble?"

Beneath the heavy line of his dark mustache, his lips pulled into an unhappy purse. "No trouble, but I have seen some of the old Devils passing by." He set the coffees on the counter in front of me along with a little pitcher of cream. "I wouldn't have even noticed them on the street, but they slow down as they walk in front of the door."

I grunted an acknowledgment. "They wanted you to see them."

"Yeah."

"You want me to post someone here during the day?"

"Nah." Mac shook his head and gently patted the counter beside the register. No doubt to remind me of the sawed-off shotgun he kept underneath. "They don't want to come in here looking for trouble."

"Be careful and let me know if you change your mind."

"Of course. I'll have your breakfast out in a few minutes. And I'm thinking some donuts for your friend also."

"Thanks, Mac." I picked up our coffees and the cream, turning back toward the tables. Neven's gaze found mine. There was a question floating in them, and I wondered again what I was doing. Surely this boy would have better prospects than a forty-year-old biker. The thought didn't stop the want curling in my gut. It was more than lust. I wanted to know this boy, to take care of him—protect him—if he'd let me.

I'd had all these feelings before, of course, but I'd squashed them. Regret was a useless emotion, and I usually didn't let myself indulge it. Looking at Neven, bright sunlight highlighting his black hair until it was almost blue, I did have regrets.

I regretted there wasn't a headful of blond hair glowing right beside him.

CHAPTER FIVE

Neven

Calix sat a steaming cup of coffee in front of me. Picking it up, I inhaled deeply and waited for the morning to feel less surreal. Waited for the last twenty-four hours to feel less surreal, if I was being honest. Terror and exhaustion had been my constant companions for weeks. The very last place I'd expected to find a reprieve was in the arms of the ruthless man who led the Iron Heretics.

But I had. He'd been so gentle with me. He'd touched me with care. Put me at ease. It didn't hurt that he was gorgeous despite the dangerous vibes constantly oozing out of every pore. He was tall enough I could tuck myself under his chin if I wanted. Yesterday, given the choice, I would have run from that thought. Today...today, his dark eyes and perma-scowl felt like comfort.

For my first time with a man, I really couldn't have asked for a better experience.

Looking at me over his coffee cup, Calix raised his eyebrows in a question. I'd been zoning out, I guess. Letting the warmth of the coffee and their voices wash over me.

"Neven?" Leith said from across the small space between

our tables. The tone in his voice made me think it wasn't the first time he'd called my name.

"Yes? Sorry...I kind of zoned out." I turned to look at Leith. We worked together at *Spritz*, and he'd been super nice to me from day one. Redheaded and adorable, he was shorter than me, but he had that settled, self-assured vibe all the guys at the club who were paired off with one of the Heretics seemed to have.

He smiled. "It's cool. I was asking if you wanted to join me and Arden for some dance practice." For some reason, he blushed a little and shot a look at the enormous man—Axel, I thought his name was—sitting across from him. Axel winked at him before taking another sip of his coffee. "We've been getting together three afternoons a week before the club opens."

I admitted that I'd been transfixed more than a few times over the last couple weeks watching the guys up on the stage. They were so graceful, so *powerful*. Especially Arden and Leith. Each of them looked so beautiful and strong as they commanded the crowd gathered around the stage each night, and I could admit to being envious at how it must feel. At some point, someone must have noticed my interest. I was honestly flattered Leith thought I might be able to dance the way they did.

"I'd really like that, thank you," I said, trying to keep my voice even as a lump unexpectedly grew in my throat at the kindness of them thinking of me. I imagined teaching a total novice would be hard work, but they invited me anyway. There was no benefit to them. I could count on one hand every instance in which someone had done something for me without asking—*demanding*—anything in return. I treasured every single one.

At the same time, I needed to remember why I was here. Aunt Lynn was counting on me. The same fear and hopelessness that had followed me the last few weeks swelled inside me. How was I ever going to do what I had to?

"Hey, you okay?" Calix's low voice brought me back to the quiet hum of the diner with its soft jazz and dough scented air. He caught my gaze across our small table. In the bright sun, I could see he actually had a burst of deep brown radiating out from around the pupil of each eye.

"Yes, I'm fine." I tried to smile at him, but I'm not sure I pulled it off. A moment later, a young man with vivid brown hair and a scar on his cheek stepped out of the kitchen holding a tray and walked to our table. When he stopped between the two tables, Eben reached out and laid a hand on his hip.

The boy blushed.

"Hi, Calix," he said, setting the tray down. He looked over at me with a nod and smile. "Mac asked me to bring this out to you."

"Thank you, Cody. It's good to see you. This is Neven. Neven, Cody." Calix produced a soft smile for Cody, which only made him blush more.

"Hi, Neven. It's nice to meet you." The hand on Cody's hip got more insistent, and Cody laughed, taking a step back and sitting right in Eben's lap.

"That's better," Eben murmured, kissing Cody directly on the scar on his cheek.

I couldn't help but stare. That surreal feeling was back. Of all the men I'd been around in my life, I'd never seen any that treated their partners with such...reverence. And it was all of them—from the way Mace watched Pax when he was working at *Spritz* to how Cleave kissed JJ's knuckles when he brought him lunch. I'd never met Arden's man, Lex, but with the complete adoration on Arden's face every time he spoke about him, I had no doubt it was more of the same.

"Here." Calix lifted one of the plates off the tray and

placed it in front of me. My BLT was huge, perfectly toasted, and smelled divine. Without preamble, I took a big bite and had to lick a bit of mayo off my lip as I chewed. Calix had taken a bite of his sandwich, too, smiling at me with his cheeks stuffed full and croissant crumbs in the stubble on his chin. The others had gone back to talking amongst themselves. It was all so simple, so easy, and I wanted it to be my reality more than I'd ever wanted anything in my life.

"IF YOU DON'T MIND MY ASKING…WHAT BROUGHT YOU TO work at *Spritz*?" Calix kept his voice low and eyes on the ice cream sundae in his hands. He'd made good on his promise of a longer ride, taking me along winding roads leading out of the city. We'd stopped at a park in some suburb. Now we were sitting side-by-side on a bench, watching ducks play in a pond while we enjoyed ice cream from a shop across the street.

I'd thought about how to answer this question of course, but I found even with the lie being half true, it was still difficult to push past my teeth. "When my mom died last year, I got buried in debt." I shrugged, trying to make it seem like not such a big deal. "I had to quit school, lost my apartment. I'd met a guy in one of my classes who was an escort." I huffed. "I didn't believe him at first when he told me how much money he made."

"And you thought you could too."

"I needed to do something. I didn't want to end up on the street."

Out of the corner of my eye, I saw Calix nod. He stuck his spoon in his sundae and slipped his arm around me. The warm weight of it was welcome, even if I did feel like shit for lying to him. "I'm sorry about your mom."

We hadn't been close, my mom and me. She'd always treated me like a burden. It was Aunt Lynn—not even my real aunt—who'd made sure I stayed fed and clothed. Got to school. Went to the doctor. I'd have probably been dead a long time ago without her. Tears stung my eyes. "Thanks."

Leaning over, he pressed a kiss to my temple. I turned my head to meet his gaze—this big, bad biker who everyone was terrified of. The only things he made me feel were safe and wanted. Tilting my head up, I brushed my cold lips against his. Letting these warm feelings I had for him spread and grow was only going to cause me heartache, but I couldn't stop it. I needed to be close to him, and close meant giving him the only pieces of myself I could.

In the back of my mind, a small part couldn't help but wonder what a man like him did to traitors in their midst.

CHAPTER SIX

Holden

I'd made it a point to avoid Calix all week, but when Mace called asking if I could cover a security shift in the lounge at *Spritz*, I wasn't about to say no.

"Thanks for stepping up, man." Mace offered me his hand to shake over the bar in the downstairs lounge. Even as I took it, I scanned the mirror behind him, keeping an eye on the few people in the room. Since it was the weekend, I knew as the night went on, the various grouping of chairs would fill, as would the couches surrounding the low stage on the far end of the space. But it was early, and for the moment, only a single set of chairs held occupants, both with a boy in their laps. I didn't recognize either of them, but the young men who worked the floor in the lounge were some of the loveliest I'd ever seen.

"Mace?" A shy voice asked from behind me.

Mace released my hand and turned his attention to the owner of the voice—a slim, gorgeous man with black hair wearing nothing but tiny silver briefs.

"What do you need, Neven?"

Neven's blue eyes moved from Mace to me before he

licked his lips and focused back on Mace. "Um, Pax wanted me to tell you he needs help in the beer cooler."

"Thanks, I'll be there in a minute."

Neven nodded and turned, heading back the way he came. Mace and I both watched him walk away for a moment before Mace leaned closer to me.

"Keep a special eye on that one, will you?"

I nodded. "Am I looking for anything in particular?"

Mace moved to the end of the bar, lifted the pass-through, and walked around the side until he stood beside me. "He caught Calix's eye, and I think boss-man and Vivian are both worried the lounge floor may not be the best place for him."

My attention immediately shot to the retreating boy one more time, a jolt going through me. Was Neven who Calix had been with? Honestly, I never would have guessed that, but then, I didn't know all that much about Calix's preference in sexual partners...other than me.

FROM MY CORNER OF THE ROOM, I WATCHED AS THE NIGHT wore on. Leith was on stage for the second time, gracefully twirling around the pole like he'd been doing it all his life instead of only within the last year. Arden was apparently not only a skilled dancer himself, but a good teacher, too. I wasn't super close with any of the Heretics, Calix included, unfortunately, but I'd been around enough that I'd gotten to know them and their partners. Just from the little I'd seen, Leith was flourishing, and Axel couldn't be prouder of his boy.

Neven's dark head caught my eye. He stood across the room with a small tray on one hand, delivering a glass to a gentleman whose eyes were trained on every movement of Leith's supple body.

As I pulled my gaze away to sweep the room, Leith's song ended. There was applause from that side of the room as Leith stepped off the stage. I glanced back at Neven to find him with wide eyes, watching the man he'd just been serving advancing on Leith. I moved in that direction. I was the closest with Mace stationed beside the bar and Cleave in the foyer where guests were screened before being allowed to enter. That was a security step the Heretics had implemented when they took over the club's security. Considering Pax had once been assaulted with a hidden knife, I thought it was fitting.

As I approached, the guest moved in close, grabbing Leith's hips and pulling him back so his crotch pressed against Leith's ass. Leith twisted his body away, keeping his hands in a placating gesture.

"I'm very sorry, sir, but I'm only a dancer. If you'd like some company for the night, I'm sure we can—"

"How much?" The guest said loudly, speaking right over the top of Leith and reaching into the inner pocket of his suit jacket.

"He said no." Neven moved to stand beside Leith until they were shoulder-to-shoulder.

The man's eyes narrowed on Neven. I was so close I knew what he was going to do before he did it and sped up. Like a snake strike, he hit Neven across the face. Rage bloomed hot in my chest. Leith shrieked and stumbled back, taking Neven with him.

Lunging forward, I tackled the guest to the ground. We hit the floor with a thud, and the guest groaned. Gripping his shoulder, I flipped him to his stomach and gathered his wrists in one hand to keep them secured behind his back. Looking up, I found the boys pressed together, Leith's arm around Neven's shoulders, and two sets of blue eyes trained on me.

"You okay?" I asked them quickly, keeping my weight on the asshole squirming below me.

Leith nodded, but Neven's gaze only moved from mine to the man who'd struck him.

Mace and Cleave appeared on my other side.

"Let me have him," Cleave said, leaning down and replacing my hand on the man's wrists with his own and hauling him to his feet.

The man was red-faced and spitting curses. "With the money I pay, these whores should drop to their knees the moment I ask for it."

"Mr. Fenten," Mace said, calm authority cutting off Fenten's words. "We're going to escort you from the premises. Your membership is revoked."

Fenten sneered and started to say something else, but Cleave flexed, twisting Fenten's wrist and whatever other hate he'd been about to spew was lost in a plea not to break his arm.

Mace smiled, and it was chilling. "You'll want to come quietly."

The fight seemed to drain out of Fenten. Cleave moved him toward the door. Mace looked over at me. "Cleave and I will escort Mr. Fenten outside. You'll take care of them?" He glanced over at Leith and Neven.

"Of course."

With the drama over, the room mostly went back to what it was doing. I looked at the boys. Leith seemed to be okay, but Neven still had the fingers of one hand pressed to the place Fenten had struck him and the other hand in a white-knuckle grip on Leith's forearm.

"Um," Leith said quietly, looking from Neven's pale face to me. "Dressing room."

I nodded, letting Leith lead Neven while I walked closely behind them. Once we were inside the room, Leith sat Neven down onto one of several stools lined up at the vanity counter. The dressing room door opened again behind us, and Axel strode into the room.

"Daddy," Leith breathed, relief sweeping over his face, and moved to meet the big man halfway. Axel pulled Leith up into his arms within the next breath, holding him tight and murmuring low. Attempting to give them some privacy, I turned my back to them and knelt in front of Neven.

"Hey, I'm Holden," I said gently. He met my eyes. His were clear and lucid and the prettiest blue, but they were also filled with fear. Slowly, I lifted my hand and slid it into his. He immediately gripped it the same way he'd done with Leith's arm. "You did a good thing, sticking up for Leith. I'm sorry I didn't get to you in time."

"It's not your fault." He finally lowered the hand from his face. The lower part of his cheek and half his chin were bright red, and there was a small split on that side of his bottom lip. He dropped my gaze and started to tremble.

"It's not yours either. You know that, right?"

He nodded without looking up. I couldn't stand it. It didn't matter at that moment if he was sleeping with Calix; all I wanted was to comfort him. Rising up on my knees, I leaned closer and wrapped my free arm around him. He slumped forward into my half embrace, and relief rushed through me. We moved at nearly the same time, him releasing my hand and wrapping both arms around my neck, and me getting one arm around his back and the other under his knees. I picked him, sat myself on the stool, and placed him sitting sideways on my thighs. He kept himself pressed tightly to my chest, face buried against the side of my neck. I ran my hand up and down his back.

When I looked up, Leith's feet were back on the ground. He said something to Axel. Axel nodded and turned for the door as Leith moved until he was sitting on the stool beside me, facing Neven.

"Axel went to get an ice pack and some water," Leith said, looking at Neven. "You doing okay?"

"Yes," Neven answered, voice small. "It just startled me. I'll be fine."

Following Leith's lead, I kept quiet as we sat with him and waited for Axel to return. Which he did a few moments later, only he wasn't alone. Calix stood beside Axel with an ice pack in one hand and a murderous expression on his face. I was glad Neven wasn't looking at him. Even as I thought it, Calix's expression softened in a way I'd never seen before and he moved toward us.

"Come on, baby," Axel said, still standing just inside the door.

Leith patted Neven's knee and climbed to his feet. He went to Axel, and they left without another word.

Calix positioned himself on the stool Leith had just vacated and scooted forward, bracketing his knees on either side of Neven's, close enough they were pressed against the side of my thigh. Some unknown emotion was burning in his eyes when they met mine. He lifted one hand and gently slid it along Neven's jaw, brushing against my chest in the process, as he placed the ice pack against the wounded spot on the other side.

Neven started to move toward Calix, and I loosened my arms, prepared to let him go, but Calix gave a small shake of his head.

"If you're comfortable, you can stay there." He paused for a moment before adding softly, "It doesn't bother me to see you with him."

For a moment, uncertainty wrapped around the three of us like a cloud. That tiny interaction confirmed something was happening between them, so what did Calix mean he didn't mind seeing Neven with me?

Eventually, the silent conversation they were having made Neven relax, melting against me more than he had been. I continued to rub his back, confused, but strangely pleased that he'd chosen to stay where he was.

"What happened?" Calix asked, voice low.

"I didn't get there in time."

Raising his head up, Neven squinted his eyes at me. "Stop saying that. You tackled him and kept him from doing something worse."

Even though he'd basically scolded me, I couldn't help the smile that pulled at my lips. It was nice to see some fire from him. "Yes, sir."

He moved his gaze to Calix and let out a slow breath. "I really am fine. It just scared me."

Calix nodded, pressing the ice pack back to Neven's face. "I think you're done for the night. Why don't Holden and I walk you to your apartment or..." He trailed off, looking down before he glanced up at me, then met Neven's eyes again. "You could come back to the clubhouse with us."

"Us?" The word was out before I gave a thought to stop it. Just like that, my heart was pounding in my chest.

The dressing room door opened as a couple dancers from the club upstairs walked in. Their chatting stopped as soon as they spotted us. Neven tensed up, and Calix stood. I did the same, keeping Neven cradled against my chest.

"Excuse us," Calix said, opening the door and holding it for me.

Once we were through and enveloped in the quiet, dim hallway, Neven spoke. "I can walk."

I set him on his feet, keeping one arm around his back. He leaned against me for a moment, then stood on his own. It surprised me how much I missed the weight of him once he stepped away. He looked up at Calix, and it was bizarre to watch them have the kind of silent conversation Calix and I had had over the years. Jealousy wanted to start percolating again, but I pushed it down. Calix had said *us*, and Neven wasn't shying away from me, hadn't leapt from my arms to be in Calix's. I wanted to see how this played out.

"I think," Neven said, taking the ice pack from Calix's hand and holding it to his own face. "That I wouldn't mind some company tonight."

CHAPTER SEVEN

Calix

Conscious of the fact Holden was staring at us, but needing to get my hands on Neven all the same, I cupped his face, bringing his bright blue eyes to meet mine as I gently ran my thumb over the bruise already forming on his jaw. Something hardened in my gut. I wanted to hurt the man who'd put that mark there.

"Why don't you change? Then we'll get out of here."

He nodded, eyes darting to Holden before he looked back up at me and leaned closer. There was no way I'd deny him, so I bent down to get my lips on his. Just a soft press. He gave me and Holden a little smile and disappeared back into the dressing room.

The door had barely closed behind Neven when Holden stepped into my space and hissed, "What are you doing, Calix?"

I glanced at the door. Even though I knew there was no danger to him in that room, I'd almost followed him back in anyway. I'd been in Vivian's office upstairs going over plans for the new club when Mace had radioed to let her know there'd be an incident in the lounge. The moment he'd said Neven's name, I hadn't been able to get my legs under me fast enough to get to him. Then to find him in Holden's arms? My insides had lit up like a bonfire. I'd never imagined wanting this, and I had no idea if it would work, but if they'd give it a chance. I wanted to try.

Holden was still staring at me, close enough that I smelled the lingering traces of his cologne mixed with the leftover sweat of adrenaline.

"The other day you asked me why," I said, shifting closer as he nodded. "Beyond the divide between our clubs, I don't have a good reason for you. I've been the Heretics President since before the first time I had my hand on your dick, and you were still a pissant Devil's prospect."

He snorted, a smirk pulling up one side of his lips. "I still think about that alley sometimes. You know, the hand job was great. I'm sure it was, but that's not what I remember."

I couldn't do anything but stare. I'd seen him only days ago, but somehow, I'd forgotten how fucking beautiful he was when he wasn't on the defensive, when I had him in close and all that attention was focused on me. "What do you remember?"

"I remember the kiss. You grabbing me by the throat and kissing me like you'd rather be punching me in the face. I'd never been kissed like that before. But then...I don't want to say you got gentle, because that'd be fucking a lie, but something happened. Shifted. You let me in. It was just a few seconds, but—" He looked down, shaking his head. "I was addicted. Just like that. And I see that same part of you when you look at Neven. And fuck, I gotta admit, I'm feeling a little jealous."

Jesus Christ, I wasn't ready for this conversation. He fucking deserved to have it, though. "I wasn't expecting him, but you...I've always felt that way about you. You make me feel *soft*. There was a time I wouldn't allow that."

"Like today?"

"Yes, smartass. Today. The last eight fucking years. My whole goddamn life." I pushed a big breath out of my nose. "This shit with patch over has me twisted up because I want you that close Holden, but I don't know how to fucking deal with it and still be who I am."

"You don't have to change. Just...let me in every now and then. Treat me like I'm one of your guys instead of like something you stepped in."

"I don't feel that way about you."

"You got a funny way of showing it sometimes. Your guard doesn't always have to be up around me, you know? I'm no danger to you, Calix."

Disbelief pulsed through me. How could he not know? *Because I've never fuckin' told him.*

He was the bullet with my name on it.

Stepping forward, I pressed him back against the wall. His blue eyes went wide, pupils dilating even before my lips sealed over his. I kissed him hard, full of all the love I'd spent the last eight years burying. He groaned, gripping my hips and letting me take him over. When I pulled back, he was panting.

"You're the most dangerous thing in my life."

Confusion furrowed his brow, before understanding lit his eyes and his face went slack with the same disbelief I'd been feeling. "Calix," he whispered into the space between us. "Are you? Do you?" *Love me?* He left it unsaid, and I was grateful.

I kissed him again. "I'm working on it."

Still holding my gaze, he licked his lips. "What about Neven?"

I smirked. "He reminds me of you."

Holden tilted his head. "I don't think I've ever been that cute."

Chuckling, I shook my head. "You were, but that's not

what I mean. He's trying so hard to be tough, but there's a vulnerability there that makes me want to protect him. To take care of him."

All the humor disappeared from Holden's face. He may have been a vulnerable boy all those years ago, but the man I had pressed against the wall now was every bit the hardened biker President that I was.

When he didn't speak, I lifted a hand and traced my fingers across the blond stubble on his jaw. "I didn't get that right with you. I can't help thinking that maybe you and I together could get it right for him."

"How's he feel about that?"

I leaned a little closer. It'd been way too damn long since I'd had his body pressed to mine. "I haven't brought it up to him yet. He looked good wrapped up in your arms, though."

He finally smiled again. "He felt good there, too."

NEVEN

If it was possible, I thought my heart was beating harder now than when that asshole had hit me in the face. For a split second, I'd been a little kid again, terrified of the next blow. Then Holden had been there.

Just like before.

It was obvious he didn't remember me, but that was okay. I'd thought about him often enough in the last eight years. Back then, everyone mistook me as younger than I was because of my size. Thanks to my mother's drug addiction, I'd been a preemie and, it seemed, forever trailing behind other kids my age, both in size and schoolwork. I'd managed, though. Thanks to Aunt Lynn, I'd discovered a love of reading, and while other subjects had been a struggle, my English classes had been a joy. It was why I'd set myself on a path to get my English degree.

Going to the locker I'd been assigned, I twirled out my combination on the lock and stripped out of the shiny underwear that was my uniform. Thoughts of Aunt Lynn and school sobering the nervous excitement that had been fluttering in my belly. I wanted this. Wanted Calix. Wanted Holden. What I didn't want was the real reason I was here.

The urge to tell them the truth before anything went further warred with everything that was on the line. My face throbbed. No. I'd do what I came here to do, and someday, I'd get my life back. My only hope was the price wouldn't be too high.

With a sigh, I pulled on my clothes—jeans, a soft t-shirt, and my worn-out chucks—and dropped the used ice pack into one of the dressing room sinks before heading back out into the hallway. The sight that greeted me stopped me short. Calix had Holden pressed up against the wall so they were chest to chest. They were nearly the same height, and a jolt of arousal hit my belly at how their bodies lined up.

They'd been staring at each other, but as one, they turned their heads until their eyes were focused firmly on me. For a moment, we all stood still, seemingly connected by an invisible string. Despite them being pressed together and several feet away from me, I felt them like I was touching them, too.

Calix turned his head and Holden did as well, accepting the chaste kiss Calix gave him, much the same as he'd given to me before I went to change. Lifting away from Holden, Calix stood up straight and held his hand out. I didn't need to think—I stepped forward and slid my hand into his.

"Holden needs to stay and finish his shift, but he's going to join us after if that's okay with you?" Calix looked down at me, those dark eyes as open as I'd ever seen them.

The truth almost spilled out of me right there. *Don't*, I

wanted to tell him. *Don't let me in.* But I couldn't. Both because I wanted to be close to him and Holden more than I'd ever wanted anything in my life and because it wasn't just my life that was depending on me getting that close before it was too late.

I nodded. Biting my lip and still holding Calix's hand, I stepped toward Holden. "I'm more than okay with that. Thank you for coming to my rescue tonight."

"My pleasure," Holden said, closing the short distance between us. He slid his hand along my jaw and tilted my head back, blue gaze locked on mine. The first press of his lips landed softly to the side of my mouth, in the middle of the dull ache that had settled there. A low breath trembled out of my lungs as he slid his lips over, a feather across my skin until they settled on mine.

His kiss was the gentlest I'd ever had, plush lips tender, not pushing or demanding, but coaxing and tempting until I opened enough to let him in. Calix's hand squeezed mine, his rough calluses against my palm and the scrape of Holden's goatee against my chin, tightening everything below my belly in an almost painful clench. I whimpered, and Holden pulled back with a gentle chuckle.

"If I don't stop now, I don't think I'm going to be able to."

Calix's voice was gruff. "If you don't stop now, I'm not letting you go back to work."

Holden looked at him with a smile. "Mace would have both our asses." He turned back to me, running his thumb along my cheek from where he still held my jaw. "I'll see you soon." With one more quick kiss, he released me and leaned in to kiss Calix, too. "See both of you soon."

CHAPTER EIGHT

Holden

Wind whipped around me as I sped the bike down the industrial road where the Heretics clubhouse was located. I was already an hour later than I wanted to be because I went to my house first for a quick shower and overnight bag. It probably would have made more sense for me just to stay there and see Calix and Neven in the morning, but like hell was I falling asleep tonight somewhere other than where they were.

I pulled up to the Heretics gate. It buzzed and slid open before I had the chance to push the intercom button, and warmth filled my chest. Calix must have told them I was coming. I parked my bike, and with my pack still snug on my back, made my way to the door. Calix stepped through it before I got there.

"Hey," I said as I ascended the cement steps.

"Hey."

When I reached the top, he grabbed me by the backpack straps and pulled me into a fierce kiss. I wrapped my arms around him, slipping my hands beneath his shirt and vest to squeeze at the shifting muscles of his back. He pulled back, breathing hard, and pressed our foreheads together.

"Fuck, I hadn't realized how much I missed your damn mouth."

I chuckled. "You say the sweetest things."

He shot me a playful glare. Well, playful for Calix. I'd seen very similar looks from him send grown men scurrying for cover.

"Sit with me." He pulled back and settled on the top step, reaching into his inner vest pocket and pulling out his smokes.

I took off the backpack and sat down beside him, leaving very little space between the two of us. "Where's Neven?"

Calix stuck a cigarette between his lips and lit it. "He's out. He wanted to wait up for you, but his eyes were drooping, so I put him to bed. Fell asleep about two seconds after his head hit the pillow."

I nodded and let the image of Neven asleep in Calix's bed —somewhere I'd never been before—wash over me. A companionable quiet fell over us; our shoulders pressed together while Calix smoked, and I enjoyed the cool night air.

When Calix broke the silence, his voice was low. "This time next week, you'll be a Heretic."

"You still against it?"

He blew out a cloud of smoke and flicked the ash off the end of his cigarette, looking down at his boots. "I was never against you. You think your boys will vote yes?"

"Most of them will. I've got a dozen really solid guys, and then I've got three or four who will probably drop off. And that's probably for the best."

Calix hummed his agreement. He turned his head and pressed his nose beneath my ear. "You smell good. You could have showered here."

"I assumed so, but...you'll have to give me a minute to

adjust. I'm not trying to beat a dead horse, but it's not like I've ever been invited to your place before."

He nodded, keeping his head bowed and attention on his boots. "I don't believe in regret, Holden. I did things the way I did them, and no amount of words from me can change that." Lifting his head, he met my eyes. "Doesn't mean I don't recognize that I fucked up. So I get that you might need some time. I can't say for sure how this is going to play out, but you've got my word I'm going to do better."

Shit. I had to clear my throat when a burning lump settled there. Nudging his shoulder with mine, I reached for his smoke and took a long drag. After I'd exhaled, I handed the cigarette back and met his eyes again. "I'm going to hold you to that."

"Good." One corner of his mouth crooked up, and he stubbed out the cigarette and lobbed it into the big stone planter the Heretics used as an outdoor ashtray. "Let's get in there and cuddle our boy."

I chuckled as I climbed to my feet. "Is it bad that you using the word *cuddle* in a sentence is maybe the most bizarre thing that's happened to me in the last couple days?"

"What?" he said, all affronted. "I cuddle."

A snort escaped before I could stop it. "Sure you do."

He paused with a hand on the door. "*We've* cuddled."

"Uh-huh." I smirked at him, eating up how offended he was pretending to be. We'd been having sex off-and-on for the better part of a decade, but I'd never had this much fun with him. There were times we'd been playful—little glimpses of the pieces of him I wanted so badly—but this? Him kissing me before I even made it through the door, talking, and bantering? Goddamn, but I could get used to this.

He narrowed his eyes. "I may be changing my stance on believing in regret."

That made me laugh out loud. I swooped in and planted a

kiss on his lips. "Somehow, tough guy, I think you'll pull through. Now, I believe you said there's a boy who needs cuddled."

NEVEN

When the apartment door closed behind Calix, I pulled my exhausted eyelids back open. I wanted nothing more than to pass out, but I'd felt my phone vibrate several times in my pocket while Calix was driving us to the clubhouse. Since I had a feeling I knew who was texting me, I didn't dare pull it out and check it with Calix still in the room.

Sitting up, I threw the covers off my legs and went to the jeans I'd folded with my shirt on top of Calix's dresser. His apartment was nice and bigger than I'd anticipated. He'd led me through the darkened open living area with its eat-in kitchen and spacious living room, down a hall with three doors. He'd pointed out the bathroom and guest bedroom before showing me into his bedroom. It was the size of my whole apartment, and the king-sized bed at its center was so comfortable and smelled like Calix that it had taken all my strength not to sink in and fall asleep for real.

Pulling my phone out of my jeans pocket, I unlocked it and opened my message app.

Aunt Lynn: *You know how I worry when you don't check-in.*

Aunt Lynn: *Neven, is this any way to treat your aunt?*

Shit. Licking my lips, I quickly replied.

Neven: *Sorry, I wasn't alone. Everything is going very well.*

Almost immediately the message showed as read, and three little dots appeared to indicate someone was typing.

Aunt Lynn: *Good. I'll expect to hear from you soon. Don't make me wait again.*

The same rush of hopeless fear I'd been feeling the last couple weeks poured over me, grabbing at my heart and throat, threatening to take me to the floor. I stumbled back a step and collapsed on the side of the bed. Tears burned a path down my cheeks, and a sob spilled out of me. I slapped a hand over my mouth to quiet myself and winced when I hit the sore spot where Fenten had slapped me.

What was I going to do?

Down the hall, the front door opened and hushed voices met my ears. Calix and Holden. Jumping up, I stuffed the phone back into the pocket of my jeans and spun around, heading for the en suite bathroom. I was halfway across the room when they walked through the bedroom door.

"Hey," Calix said, coming straight for me. "I didn't expect you to be up until noon tomorrow."

I stopped where I was and quickly wiped at my face. The light was dim in here so maybe they wouldn't realize I'd been crying.

Feigning sleepiness, I cleared my throat. "Just have to pee."

Calix stopped right in front of me, dark eyes scanning my face. He lifted his hand and ran the backs of his fingers down the middle of my cheek. I could feel the wetness still there lift off my skin and onto his.

"Try again."

The words weren't harsh, but there was an authority in his voice that made my insides flush hot with shame. Fuck, I didn't know how I thought I was going to lie to this man. New tears welled up and spilled over while I squirmed under his gaze. Sucking in a harsh breath, I decided to give him a truth, just not the one I'd been crying over.

"It just scared me." My voice came out raspy and smaller than I'd felt in a long time. "M-my mom used to have this boyfriend that slapped me around all the time." I touched my face where the dull ache of my jaw was quickly morphing into a much worse headache.

"You don't have to hide, Neven," Holden said, dropping a backpack to the floor and walking around us. He pressed his chest against my back, wrapping his arms around my waist. "That's what the growly one is trying to say."

Calix shot an irritated glance at Holden then gave a little shake of his head. "He's right."

Closing the little distance between us, Calix wrapped his arms around both Holden and I until I was sandwiched between them. I turned my face, resting it on Calix's solid chest and slid my arms around his waist. The scent of leather, cologne, and smoke filled my nose. I drew it in, holding it in my lungs, savoring it, and for a moment let myself believe that the four strong arms around me would still want to protect me from harm—would still want me at all—when they learned my real truth.

CHAPTER NINE

Calix

Warm yellow light filtered through the blinds, and Neven's dark hair tickled my nose as I woke up the next morning. For a moment, I let the warmth of his slim back against my chest and the feel of Holden's side pressed against the arm I had around Neven's waist soak in. When I actually opened my eyes, I couldn't stop the smile from pulling up my mouth.

Neven lay on his side in front of me, little ass pressed against my cock and his nose planted nearly in Holden's armpit where he was sprawled out on his stomach beside us with his arms tucked up under the pillow. Holden's chin-length blond hair glowed where it fanned out covering his face and against my gray sheets. We'd knocked the sheet down in the night until it was barely covering the swell of Holden's ass. I was comfortable with it draped no farther up than my waist, and Neven felt warm enough, so I left it.

It should have felt odd waking with someone beside me, let alone two people, but it only felt right. With a smile still on my face, I slipped out of bed to shower and dress. Stopping for a moment before I left the room just to look at them once more. I rubbed at my chest, thrilled and terrified at the enormity of what was growing there, of acknowledging what had been there for Holden all along and the rapidly expanding feelings I had for Neven.

The look on his face when we'd walked in the room the night before had nearly sent me back out to hunt down Fenten. Knowing he'd been stripped of his *Spritz* membership and not wanting to leave Neven were the only things that stopped me. For a single moment, I'd entertained the dark thought of making the phone call that would end the man. But the truth was, he wasn't a threat beyond being an asshole and wasn't worth any of our Nomads' time to come and deal with. Maybe if Lex had already been in town...

I shook my head, pushing all thought of the incident from my mind, and made my way downstairs. I could've started coffee in the apartment, but I didn't want to wake Neven unnecessarily, and I wanted to check in with my men. We all had our own places in and out of the clubhouse, but we tended to have coffee together several mornings a week and especially on Sundays.

True to form, I smelled coffee as soon as I hit the hallway leading to the kitchen, and when I turned the corner, Riot was seated at the table, long dreads pulled back and banded together, a cup in his hand, and the morning paper spread out in front of him.

"Morning," I said, walking straight to the pot and pouring my own cup before joining him.

His dark gaze met mine as he didn't even attempt to hide a smirk behind his cup. "A good morning for you, I hope. Otherwise, you may be doing something wrong."

"Jesus Christ," I groused, already chuckling. "Can a man get half a cup in before the shit starts flying?"

"Hell no," Mace said, coming around the corner, hair dripping from his shower and a shit-eating grin on his face. "You brought home two men last night. *You!* And you really expect us to keep our mouths shut?"

I sighed, hanging my head. Why I loved these assholes, I'd never know.

"At least we can all stop pretending we don't know you're tapping Holden." Riot took a big drink of his coffee and continued to read his paper.

That brought my head up fast. "The fuck do you mean, pretend?"

"C'mon, man." Mace grabbed his own cup and slid into the seat across from me. "I mean, before he showed up at Eben's housewarming, we really weren't sure, I'll give you that. But that appearance pretty much sealed it."

I huffed. "I broke it off after that."

They both paused in lifting their drinks to look at each other and then back at me.

Riot broke the silence. "No shit?"

"No shit."

"Wait...so how long had you been together before that?"

I thought back over all the shit that had happened in the last decade. The times I'd allowed myself to be with Holden were some of the brightest spots. "We started sleeping together off-and-on, roughly eight years ago. It wasn't serious."

Mace outright laughed. "Eight years, and it wasn't serious?"

"How long did you sleep with Lex and it wasn't serious?" Before Mace and Pax had settled down together, Mace had been notorious for his string of fuck buddies and "no relationships" attitude. I wasn't about to let him bust my balls over Holden.

That shut Mace right up, but now Riot was laughing. "You two are a mess."

Of course he had all the room to talk. The man had had the same partner for as long as I'd known him.

"Yeah, yeah," Mace said, eyeing me warily. "Well, however it happened, all we're saying is it's nice to see you with someone. Two someones."

"How did that happen?" Riot asked, setting the paper aside and leaning his elbows on the table.

I frowned down at my coffee. "I don't know. From the minute I met Neven, I felt like he needed me, and maybe I needed him, too. As for Holden...well, that whole *not serious* thing was really me kidding myself."

These were two of my closest friends, my second and third in the club. They'd both lay down their lives for me in a heartbeat, but I still expected to see ridicule when I lifted my head and met their eyes. What I found instead was understanding. Mace broke out in a grin and nodded his head as he offered me his fist to bump over the table.

"Happy for you, brother."

"So am I," Riot agreed. "Mace and I were talking last night. You've been working your ass off for years to get this club into the position it is today. Why don't you let us hold the fort for a few days while you take your men and get out of the city?"

A vacation? My initial reaction was to say hell no—we had a fight coming up and the new club opening to finish planning and about a million other things on the list—but when didn't we? More importantly, these guys could handle all that and more for a couple days without me. We didn't have to go far. And just like that, the idea settled into my mind and took root. Just the three of us off on our own for a few days to figure out this dynamic and spend some time relaxing together? Hell yes.

"Calix?" Neven's voice came from the hallway. We all turned to the kitchen door in time to see a sleepy Neven poke his head around the corner. His eyes opened wide at the sight of the three of us, and a deep blush bloomed in his cheeks.

"Hey, baby. Come here." I held out my hand to him, and he scurried over to my side of the table. He was swimming in one of my Iron Heretic t-shirts, bare legs sticking out under it and feet stuffed into untied chucks. Fucking adorable.

When he took my hand, I pulled him closer, maneuvering until he settled on one of my thighs with my arm snug around his waist. He reached out and picked up my coffee, taking a sip and glancing at the other two men at the table.

Leaning up, I kissed his cheek. "I know you know Mace, but have you met Riot? He's my VP."

Neven shook his head. "Hi, Riot, I'm Neven." He gave Riot a shy smile.

He'd always been a stoic man, kept his business to himself and rarely teased me like he had today. The smile on Riot's face now told me just how happy he really was for me.

"It's nice to meet you, Neven."

Movement in the doorway made me look up. Holden was leaning there, shirtless, with one shoulder against the jamb and arms crossed over his tan chest. His hair was as messy as Neven's and eyes still squinted from sleep. They'd both just woken up, and they'd both come looking for me. My heart was doing all kinds of fucking gymnastics in my chest. These two would be the fucking death of me.

"Morning," Holden said, looking us over.

I met his blue eyes, my chest warming when one corner of his mouth lifted. He looked happy—*content*—and I realized two things. I'd never seen him look so relaxed, and I'd never been so relaxed. Something settled in me with Neven's warm weight in my arms and Holden's eyes holding mine.

"Morning," I managed to say back, belatedly enough that Mace snorted into his coffee. "Alright, that's enough out of both of you." I looked from my Sergeant to my VP. "I think I'll be taking you boys up on that offer."

Neven turned his face to look at me at the same time Holden tilted his head and raised a questioning eyebrow.

I looked from one to the other. "And I'll fill the two of you in as soon as I finish this cup." I lifted my cup to my lips, smiling to myself, only to scowl at Neven's giggling face when I found it empty.

CHAPTER TEN

Holden

Contentment welled up in my chest, cresting up and out through my skin and down my arms, propelling my rumbling *Harley* forward like it was tethered to the one bearing two passengers in front of me. Neven's slim arms were wrapped tight around Calix's middle, his head turned sideways, cheek resting on his shoulder, eyes closed, and trust written into every line of his face.

The smile on my face in response was impossible to wipe off.

We'd been gliding along backcountry roads for over an hour now with the sun warm and big puffy clouds overhead. It was a beautiful day for a ride, and I honestly wasn't too concerned about our destination. After we'd finished our coffee and a light breakfast with Riot and Mace, Calix had told both of us to pack a bag.

Neven had been hesitant at first, but Calix promised the place wasn't far and he'd have Neven back for his dance practice with Arden and Leith on Wednesday afternoon. Which meant we'd have three nights together away from the city and everyone in it. Anticipation curled in my belly. I thought I'd never want anyone the way I'd wanted Calix from the moment I met him, but him and Neven together? I craved them both.

Calix flicked on his turn signal and put on his brakes. I slowed, barely seeing the dirt turn off before we were right on it. I steered the *Harley* carefully, following directly behind Calix and watching for holes. The drive was packed down well, narrow, and flanked by overgrown woods on both sides. I couldn't see where it was headed until we rounded a bend and the trees thinned, opening to a clearing with a cute little cabin sitting in the middle of it.

The drive went around the cabin and ended with a wider parking area covered by a carport off to one side. I parked the bike beside Calix's and climbed off, looking around. The cabin was sided with dark wooden planks and topped with a dark green metal roof. A gravel walkway led up from the carport to a screened-in back porch. A fork off the walkway made a path farther out to a small fire pit.

"Is this yours?" I asked, taking off my helmet and pulling the sunglasses off my face.

"Yep," Calix answered, helping Neven with his helmet.

"This is awesome." Neven reached for me, looking a little unsteady after Calix had stepped away to put the helmet in one of the saddlebags and to grab his overnight bag out of the other.

Sliding my arm around Neven's shoulders, I pressed a kiss to his dark hair. "How's the legs?"

"Like jello." He laughed. "And my butt is numb."

That got a chuckle from both me and Calix. I reached down and squeezed one ass cheek. Neven yelped, but he was laughing, too, swatting at me before refocusing on our new surroundings.

"Well, come on," Calix said, herding us forward. "Don't you want to see the inside?"

"I definitely do." I released Neven to gather up his and my bags out of my own saddlebags. We followed Calix up the walk. He pulled open the screen door for the porch and led us to the back door of the cabin. The porch was nice, a four-seater table sat to one side of the door, and a couple loungers with thick cushions occupied the other side. There was a ceiling fan overhead, and I had no trouble picturing an afternoon nap sprawled out on one of those loungers.

"It's so quiet here," Neven whispered while Calix unlocked the door.

Calix glanced back over his shoulder, looking at each of us. "I think that's my favorite part."

A LIVELY FIRE CRACKLED IN THE PIT, WARMING MY SHINS and face. Neven was crouched beside it, roasting stick in hand and big puffy marshmallows about to catch fire. Calix, the sneaky bastard, had given us the grand tour of the cabin when we'd arrived—a simple three-room affair—open living area and kitchen, one bedroom, and one bathroom. All of it nice and still smelling like new paint. Not twenty minutes after we'd walked through the door, a couple Heretics prospects had shown up in a truck with groceries and supplies. I'd shaken my head at Calix's smirk and Neven's wide eyes at having people on-call to make deliveries out to the middle of nowhere.

Sometimes, it was good to be king.

The afternoon passed with more quiet—a movie on in the background while Neven read one of several paperback thrillers Calix had laying around, and he and I took naps on the big sectional in the living room. Eventually, Neven decided he wanted to explore outside. That led to him sweet-talking Calix into a fire. Not that it'd been hard. We'd cooked our dinner over the open flames, and as the night got darker, the tension simmering between us threatened to roast my bones.

"Boy, if you don't like your mallows crispy, you'd better raise that stick up." There was laughter in Calix's voice, but Neven had startled like Calix had yelled.

I frowned, leaning forward in my chair and resting my elbows on my knees.

Neven chuckled, but it was strained. He pulled the stick away from the fire and looked at the golden-brown marshmallow on the end. After a moment, he held it out to me. "Do you want it?"

"You don't?"

He shook his head.

I pulled the sweet treat off the stick and popped it into my mouth, licking the sticky residue off my thumb. Neven's gaze followed my every move. Taking the stick from him, I leaned the cooking end on the stones surrounding the fire pit and shifted forward in my seat, getting a hand around the back of one of his thighs and pulling him to stand between my knees.

He swallowed audibly but came willingly, resting his hands on my shoulders. I tilted my head back. A small smile lit on his lips a second before he lowered them to mine. He licked at the sweetness lingering around my mouth, and I groaned. With both my hands cupping just beneath his ass, I drew him closer, stretching up to lick into his sweet little mouth.

When he pulled back, my voice came out hoarse against his lips. "Sweeter than marshmallows."

His blue eyes looked black with the fire glow behind him. Licking his lips, he lowered his gaze and a tremble went through his body.

"Neven?"

Calix appeared behind him, arms sliding around Neven's

waist as he pressed himself against the boy's back. "What's the matter, baby?"

"I lied to you." It was barely a whisper. My attention shot to Calix, expecting to see emotion of some kind exploding across his face, but he only looked steadily back at me and pressed his cheek to Neven's with a nod. Neven took in a big shuddering breath and leaned back against Calix's chest. He still didn't look at either of us. "That time at *Spritz*? That's the only time."

Calix closed his eyes and pressed a kiss to Neven's temple. "Do you remember what I told you that night at *Spritz*?"

Neven nodded. "The choice was mine."

"And that hasn't changed." Calix's voice came out harder, authority coating his words. "Do you understand? Holden and I would never do anything that you didn't want."

The questions swirling around my head came to an abrupt stop. Neven was a virgin? A pulse of pure outrage shot through me. This beautiful, *innocent* boy had been on the lounge floor at *Spritz*? Calix's big hand landed beside Neven's on my shoulder, gripping tight. Pulling in a deep breath, I looked up to find Calix staring down at Neven and me with Neven's gaze still on the ground and a deep blush on his cheeks.

"Hey," I said, squeezing gently on the back of Neven's thighs. "What do you want, huh?" When he lifted his head and met my eyes, I grinned. "Whatever it is, you can have it."

Calix had an eyebrow cocked at me, but the smug look on his face told me I'd said the right thing. He took his hand off my shoulder and placed it on Neven's belly, sliding it up under his t-shirt, revealing pale skin and caressing his flat stomach.

"Anything?" Neven's breath hitched.

"Anything, but if it's okay with you, I wouldn't mind being let in the loop about what you've already done with our old man here."

"Old man?" Calix growled.

A smile split my face at the same time Neven let out a giggle.

"Come on, C. It's a figure of speech."

"I'm going to *figure of speech* your ass."

He wasn't even being dirty, but the thought of Calix doing anything to my ass had a shot of pure lust tugging at my balls. "Shit." My voice was breathy, and I wasn't even going to try to hide it. "You can do whatever you want to my ass. It's been too fucking long."

"How long?"

I met his stare. "You know how long."

He growled again, taking his hand out from under Neven's shirt and fisting it in the collar of mine. "Get up here." He hauled me to my feet, barely moving him and Neven back a step so I was plastered to Neven's front. Warm, tentative hands slid around my waist at the same time Calix leaned over Neven's shoulder and licked into my mouth, moving his hand from my shirt collar to grip the back of my neck. I met his tongue with mine, letting him own my mouth for a long minute. When I pulled back, I found Neven watching us with heat in his eyes.

"How long?" he asked. "I know you two were together before, right? But how long has it been since you broke up?"

Clearing my throat, I looked between them. Calix's face wasn't giving much away, but I knew he wouldn't want to talk about it. I also knew that if the three of us had any hope for building something out of the mutual attraction we all shared that we needed to keep shit open and honest.

"It's been almost two years since the last time we slept together. Before that—"

"Before that," Calix cut in. "I never let it be more than just sex. Which was a mistake."

Neven bit his lip, and then he slowly slid out from

between us, taking a step back and turning so he faced us both. "Have you had the chance to, um, reconnect?"

I almost chuckled, but he looked so sincere that I held it in. I looked at Calix. He was watching Neven with a thoughtful gaze. "Beyond what you've seen?" I shook my head. "No, not really. Not physically, anyway." I looked down, reminding myself what I'd just been thinking about how openness and honesty were the only way this thing was going to work. "Though, I'd argue that the conversations we've had over the last couple weeks have brought us closer than we've ever been."

Now Calix's gaze was on me. "Agreed."

"I know what I want," Neven said, voice sounding stronger than it had all night. Calix and I both looked at him. "I want to watch."

CHAPTER ELEVEN

Neven

Holden took my hand and led me inside while Calix put out the fire. We barely made it into the bedroom before he reached for my shirt, pulling it over my head while he kicked off his boots. My skin was hot and cold in waves, feverish one moment, frostbitten the next as Holden stripped down to nothing but his golden-toned skin before me.

A small smile pulled up one side of his mouth as he reached for me, big, rough hands gliding from my shoulders down to my ass, pulling me in until our chests pressed together.

"Tell me," he whispered into my hair, pressing kisses against my temple, then down my forehead and nose until he reached my mouth. "Tell me what Calix did for you at *Spritz*."

My breath hitched. I pressed my fingers into the meaty sides of him, muscles hardly yielding while still offering me something to hold on to. To ground myself with. Leaning forward, I kissed Holden's chest, lips caressing the screeching head of a phoenix tattooed over his heart. "He took me in his mouth."

Holden groaned like those six words were the best thing he'd ever heard. "Did you like it?"

My face was on fire. "Yes. A lot."

He hummed, palms gliding over the skin of my back, letting me keep my face hidden against him. "He used to be pretty good at that."

"High praise." Calix's gravelly voice came from the open doorway.

Holden chuckled. "For all I know, you may have lost your touch."

I jerked my head up just as Holden glanced back over his shoulder, a playful smile on his lips. Glancing around Holden's arm, I looked at Calix. He narrowed his eyes and started pulling his leather Heretics vest off his shoulders.

"Get the rest of his clothes off," Calix growled. He tossed his vest over the top of the dresser across from the foot of the bed. Grabbing a hold of the blankets on the bed, he yanked them down, scattering pillows over the light blue sheet. "And both of you get on the bed."

A shiver went through Holden's body, vibrating against my skin. I reached for my pants at the same time Holden did, and we both huffed a little laugh. Holden leaned down, pressing kisses against the side of my neck. I pulled my hands back, resting them on his shoulders instead and letting him get me undressed. As he knelt, pulling my pants down my legs, Calix came into view, still standing at the foot of the bed. Only now he was naked, all his beautiful, tattooed skin on display. I gasped, watching him stroke himself to hardness as his gaze followed Holden down to where he was lifting my feet one-by-one to remove my pants and underwear.

Calix's gaze met mine. "Neven, get on the bed. Gather up the pillows and make yourself comfortable. Holden, get the lube out of the drawer and put it on the nightstand."

I moved without thinking, crawling up onto the big bed

and gathering two of the pillows. I placed them against the headboard on the far side so I could lean against them. The third I put beside them, where Holden and Calix would hopefully be laying. A bolt of lust went through me. My dick had already been hard at the mere thought of seeing them together, but now, being in the room with both of them naked and Calix growling orders at us both? My skin was buzzing with how badly I wanted this.

Holden pulled open the nightstand drawer, reaching inside and setting a half-empty bottle of lube on the top before pushing it closed. He turned and looked at Calix, waiting. Calix nodded his head at the bed. Holden climbed up, on his knees, facing Calix.

Looking from one of us to the other, Calix gave his cock a final stroke and then crawled up the bed. When he was in front of Holden, he bent his head down and sucked Holden into his mouth. An electric shock raced up my spine as Calix bobbed his head, making me and Holden both gasp. Calix pulled off with a slurp, wet mouth smiling and rose up until he was standing tall on his knees the same as Holden.

"Still think I've lost my touch?" Calix asked, knee-walking forward until they were pressed together from thigh to lip.

They began to kiss—deep open-mouthed kisses—and I fisted my hand in the sheet to keep from touching myself. I'd never felt like this, even when I'd been on the receiving end of Calix's ministrations. They were just so *beautiful* together, devouring each other and clutching like they'd been apart for far too long. I knew the moment I touched my dick, I'd go off like a rocket.

Calix pulled back with a gasp, keeping his face resting against Holden's. "On your back, baby. Need to be in you before I go off like a teenager." He glanced over at me with a smile. If it were possible, I'd have blushed harder.

"Hey, I'm twenty!" I laughed.

As Holden laid down, Calix leaned over toward me. He palmed my dick, pressing it up against my belly and making me squirm as he caught my mouth with his. "Comfortable, baby?"

I had to suck in a ragged breath before I could answer. "Yes."

He brushed his lips against mine. "Ready to watch me fuck our man?"

Something hot and bright exploded inside my chest, searing me with its intensity and making my eyes burn. I wanted this so badly. Wanted them. Wanted this to be real. And it was—for them. They cared about me. I could see it in Calix's eyes, feel it in the hand Holden reached out and ran gently over my chest. I should tell them the truth, call this whole thing off.

Calix tilted his head, face only inches from mine, watching me. "You okay, baby?"

Holden slid his hand down my arm, making me shiver, and laced his fingers through mine.

I nodded at Calix. "You're just both so beautiful. I"—I licked my lips—"I've never seen anyone else having sex before either, you know."

A predatory grin slid onto Calix's face. He kissed me one more time before he pushed himself back, settling on his haunches between Holden's legs. Without missing a beat, Holden handed him the lube, and Calix popped it open.

"Wish I could say this was going to be slow and sweet," Calix said, spreading some lube on his fingers of one hand. He stroked his cock with that hand, added more lube, and then did it again.

"But that's never really been our style," Holden finished. He squeezed my fingers one more time and pulled his hand away. Lifting his legs, he grabbed his own thighs, pulling his legs toward his chest and opening himself up to Calix completely.

Calix rubbed his lubed thumb over Holden's entrance. With heavy-lidded eyes, he watched Holden squirm before he slipped one finger inside. "You been doing this for yourself, sweetheart? Riding your own fingers and thinking of me?" Calix pressed another finger into Holden, making him groan and throw his head back on the pillow. A dark flush bloomed in his cheeks and spread down his neck.

"Shit," Holden panted, fingers turning white with how hard he was gripping his own flesh. "It's been a while for that, too."

With his other hand, Calix gripped the back of Holden's thigh farthest from me and pushed it closer to Holden's chest, opening him up even wider as he pumped his fingers in and out.

I was transfixed. Holden's rim dragged over Calix's shiny digits, and each plunge pulled a moan from Holden.

"Fuck, I've missed you," Holden gasped when Calix added another finger. A tear slid from the corner of Holden's eye. I wasn't sure if Calix had seen it until he slowed his hand and leaned over Holden, bracing his other hand on the bed, until they were face to face.

"I missed you, too." That gravelly voice was just a whisper before Calix kissed Holden, slow and sweet despite both their protests that they didn't operate that way. Calix slid his fingers from Holden and gripped himself. Without breaking their kiss, he lined himself up and pushed forward.

Holden's hands scrambled over Calix's back, one sliding down to squeeze his ass and the other up to hold the back of his head.

Calix rolled his hips, feeding himself deeper and deeper into Holden's body until he was plunging in and out in long strokes and they were both gasping into each other's mouths. Raising up on both hands then, Calix started to thrust in earnest, making that dark flush spread farther down Holden's chest while he held himself open, eyes never moving from Calix's.

So caught up in watching them, it took me by surprise when my dick jerked against my stomach, smearing pre-cum and jolting a little moan out of me. The noise made them both look over at me.

"Neven, come here. Stroke his dick," Calix grunted.

"Fuck yes." Holden reached for me, getting his hand around the back of my neck as I scooted closer. He pulled me into a kiss at the same moment as I got my hand around the hard, thick length of him. "Harder."

I adjusted my grip, squeezing as I stroked him. He undulated beneath me, gasping against my lips and thrusting into my fist every time Calix slammed into him. Just as Holden's cock pulsed in my fist, hot cum spilling over my hand and onto his chest, a rough hand wrapped around me. Two quick, firm strokes of Calix's hand and I was gone, spilling myself all over Holden's hip and the bed between us. Calix's hand tightened up. I pried my eyes open, watching him thrust deep into Holden one more time and still, groaning as he came, too.

"Shit," Holden said with a laugh.

Calix smiled, leaning down to kiss us both. "Together?" he asked, laying on top of Holden with an arm draped over me, keeping me held close to them.

"Yes," Holden answered without a pause. "Together."

I looked from Calix's black eyes to Holden's blue ones and prayed they wouldn't hate me for not being strong enough. "Together."

CALIX

I woke to a wailing alarm. Disoriented, I wrenched myself up from the bed, eyes burning and pressing my forearm against my mouth and nose as I choked on smoke. A flaring orange glow shone through the bedroom doorway from the direction of the kitchen.

"Shit," I gasped, grabbing my jeans up off the floor and stumbling into them. "Holden!" I yelled, through fits of coughing. I heard him swear as the sound of fire consuming the cabin turned into a roar nearly drowning out the high-pitched smoke detector. Running across the room, I squinted my eyes against the heat coming from the living area and quickly slammed the bedroom door shut.

"Neven! Come on, baby, get up!" Holden shouted, shaking Neven's shoulder and pulling his own pants on.

Trying to think past the burn in my throat and eyes, I grabbed up the bags we'd each brought with us and went to the window. Pushing it up, I kicked the screen out of the frame and tossed the bags out into the yard before turning back to my men. Holden was right behind me, pushing a shaking, wide-eyed Neven at me.

"Out the window, baby." I grabbed his hand and helped him through. Turning back, I already had my hand out for Holden, but he wasn't there. "Holden!" He popped up from the floor on the other side of the bed with our boots and Neven's sneakers in his arms. A loud crash sounded from beyond the bedroom door. "Move your ass!"

He ran for me, tossing our shit ahead of him and scrambling out the window. I followed right behind him, the cool grass welcome under my feet. Holden and I grabbed up the bags and shoes off the ground and moved farther away from the cabin. Looking up, I found Neven standing close to the woods, moonlight shining down on him and tears streaming down his face. One of mine or Holden's t-shirts swallowed his slim frame, but it couldn't hide the way he was trembling. As much as I wanted to go to him, there was something I needed to do first.

"Give me my boots," I said to Holden. He handed them to me. I pulled them on and dug into my bag, pulling out my holstered 1911. I slid the gun out, pointed it at the ground, and released the safety. Then I looked at Holden. "Stay with him."

He looked like he wanted to argue but wisely kept his mouth shut. He'd managed to get his boots on as well, and I knew he'd have his gun in hand within moments. I scanned the woods surrounding us. There were plenty of shadows to hide in, but if someone had set the fire to flush us out, why hadn't they made a move before we'd regrouped? We'd have made damn easy pickins when we stumbled out that window.

Moving in a wide arc, I did a quick jog around the tree line surrounding the clearing the cabin sat in. Visibility was shit, but I alternated between looking for vehicle tracks and scanning the trees for anything out of place. I made it back around to the side Holden and Neven were on. Holden had his back to the burning building, watching the woods beyond.

A thunderous crack hit the air, and the roar of flames got louder. I turned to the cabin, refusing to let the heartsick feeling taking over my chest show on my face. The roof had caved in, and the flames were getting hotter and reaching toward the stars. Holden and Neven moved up beside me. Holden had Neven's back pressed to his front, blocking him from anyone who might be lurking behind us and gun naked in his hand.

"You think this is an attack?" Holden asked quietly.

"I don't know." I swallowed hard. "No one outside the club knows about this place."

Smooth, cool fingers touched my hand. I looked down, turning my wrist so Neven's fingers could slip between mine. His tears had dried, but he looked devastated. "It's okay, baby." I lifted our joined hands to kiss the back of his. "It's just wood and metal. It can all be rebuilt."

With a sniff, he nodded his head.

I met Holden's gaze. "Did anyone's phone make it out?"

"Yeah, mine's in my pocket," he replied, taking his arm from across Neven's chest to dig out the prepaid flip phone he carried. He handed it to me, and I considered who I wanted to call for a moment.

"I'm going to call Mace and the fire department." I turned so that we were facing each other because I knew he wasn't going to like what I said next. "I want you to take Neven and head back to the city. To the clubhouse."

They spoke at the same time.

"Calix, no…"

"Hell no, I'm not leaving you here alone."

I sighed, looking from one set of blue eyes to the other.

"We're in this together," Holden said, one arm back around Neven and eyes hard. "If you meant that, then we're not going anywhere. We're with you."

"Calix, please." Neven gripped my hand tighter.

I pulled my gaze away from Holden's to look down and meet Neven's. He still looked terrified, but his face had the hard edge of determination. "I just want to keep you safe, baby."

"I'm safest right here. With both of you."

The fire warming the entire side of my body said otherwise. Of course, if this was purely an accident, then I was overreacting for no reason. I took a deep breath. It was true my club had made plenty of enemies over the years, but most of those beefs had been put to bed. We were patching over the remaining Devil's in less than a week. No one knew we were here or that I even owned this land outside of the club.

"Okay," I finally said, leaning in and pressing my forehead to Holden's then Neven's. "We stay together."

CHAPTER TWELVE

Neven

Later that week, we were still sticking together. Monday after the cabin burned down had been the longest day I could ever remember having. We'd stayed at the cabin long after it was nothing but smoking rubble because the fire department and police found it difficult to believe that an Iron Heretics President had been the victim of an accidental fire. They asked Calix, Holden, and me a million questions.

By the time we'd gotten back into the city and to the Heretics clubhouse, it had been late afternoon. I'd eaten a sandwich someone handed me, collapsed into Calix's bed with my men on either side of me, and slept until Tuesday.

The rest of the week had gone much the same. The guys did whatever they needed to do. When I went to *Spritz* to work in the evenings, one of them brought me back to the clubhouse, and then the three of us fell asleep together. It was...nice. So nice in fact that aside from the silence from *Aunt Lynn*, I spent every waking moment wishing this could be my reality. With only a couple minor adjustments, it'd be perfect.

Setting the box I was carrying into the back of the van, I turned to find Holden standing beside the open bay door of the converted chicken barn where the Heretics hosted their fight nights. It had been my first time at one of the fights, and it had been both scary and awesome. It was my understanding that tonight had been even livelier than usual because of the patch over vote happening tonight, too. When I'd asked what that meant, they'd explained that the Devil's Rage MC, which Holden was President of, would vote to see if they wanted to become a charter with the Iron Heretics MC instead. Making all the Devil's Rage members who stayed into fully patched Iron Heretics members.

My MC knowledge was limited, but from the experiences I'd had with both—the Iron Heretics had my vote. I knew Holden didn't run the Devil's Rage as it had been in the past, and even though neither of them had said it out loud to me, it felt like my men were relieved that club name would be going away when Holden and the others patched over.

Holden walked toward me with a small smile on his face. I went to his arms willingly, wrapping mine around his waist and pressing my face against his chest. He kissed the top of my head and held me close.

"Calix and I are heading back to the clubhouse for the vote. You want to ride with me or him?"

Lifting my head, I pulled back just enough to meet his gaze. "I actually thought I'd ride back to *Spritz* and help unload the van. We all want to shower and change and then Arden's going to drive us all to the clubhouse."

"Who's all of us?"

"Me, Leith, and Pax."

Holden blew a long breath out of his nose. Ever since the fire, he and Calix had both been skittish about letting me out of their sight. The fire marshal's report wasn't finished yet, so we still didn't know if the fire had truly been an accident or arson.

"You'll be careful?"

"Of course."

He pressed a lingering kiss to my lips.

A wolf whistle sounded from the barn, and Holden smiled against my lips. Breaking the kiss, we looked up to find Leith, Arden, and Pax heading toward the van. Leith was carrying a box of empty bottles the same as I had been, and Arden and Pax each had a hand on the rim of an empty keg dangling between them.

"Mace is looking for you whenever you're finished, Holden," Pax said with a big smile on his face.

"But feel free to make out with your cutie a little more if you want," Arden said with a laugh, helping Pax hoist the keg up into the back of the still open van.

With my cheeks warm, I pressed one more quick kiss to Holden's lips. "Good luck with the vote. I'll see you later."

"Alright, *cutie*," he said, pinching my ass and getting a laugh out of the guys.

After he'd walked away, I turned to them. "You guys are terrible." It was impossible to keep a straight face, and I found myself chuckling before I even got the last word out.

"Baby." Calix's growly voice brought us all to attention. I turned, finding him silhouetted in the barn's doorway. He stalked toward me, eyes looking over at my companions. "Boys," he said, with a nod. I knew they were all comfortable with Calix, but where they'd been ready to joke with Holden, they all said a polite goodbye, closed up the van, and got in. Leaving me to speak with him in private. I couldn't help the small smile that pulled at my mouth.

In his Heretics vest, jeans, white t-shirt, and thick-soled black boots, he didn't look different than any of the other guys, but there was something about him, some edge that made people wary of him. Maybe it was the President patch on his chest. Maybe it was the coldness of his eyes. My smile got bigger. Only Holden and I would ever know how warm those black eyes could be.

"What are you smiling at?" he grumbled as he pulled me to him.

"How sexy you are." I'd never really said anything like that to him. My blush deepened, but I didn't regret it. He was sexy, and I wanted him to know I thought so.

He watched me for a moment, eyes tracking over my face. Bringing a hand up, he ran one fingertip over the hottest part of my cheek. "I love that you're getting more comfortable, but I hope this never goes away."

"You want me to blush forever?"

He smiled then. "I really do." His lips pulled back into a straight line, serious again. "Stay with the others and stay alert. Okay?"

"Of course."

"You have your phone?"

I patted my pocket. "Yep."

He sucked in a breath and gave me a nod. "Okay. Have fun, and we'll see you after the vote."

I licked my lips. "You are...happy about the vote, aren't you?"

"I'm happy Holden will be wearing a Heretics vest before the night's over."

"Okay." Popping up on my toes, I kissed him, opening up and letting him in when he pressed his tongue against the seam of my lips. There were no wolf whistles this time.

"Go," he growled, hands roaming over my back and down to my backside. "Before I change my mind."

I giggled when he patted my ass and stepped back. "I'll see you soon." When I climbed into the van, three pairs of wide eyes turned to me. "What? I know that was PG compared to some of the scenes I've heard about out of the rest of you."

Arden shrugged. "We've just never seen Calix be playful before. It's nice."

"You know, I'm not sure I've seen Lex be playful either," Leith said from the seat beside me.

"I haven't even met Lex yet," I chimed in, as Pax started the van and got us heading down the long gravel drive to the road.

Arden, in the passenger seat, turned as far sideways as his seatbelt would allow. "He called me earlier and is on his way back. He's hoping to make it for some of the party tonight." A big grin split his face.

I didn't know exactly what Nomad members did for the club, just that they were always spoken about in respectful tones and spent a considerable amount of time traveling. "Is it hard with him being gone a lot?"

Arden tilted his head, some of his fine, blond hair coming untucked from behind his ear. "I always miss him. We've got a bit of a routine now, though. And anyway, him coming and going is how our relationship started."

I'd heard that story—Arden working the lounge floor at *Spritz* and Lex paying for exclusive access for a couple years before they'd gotten together for real. It honestly gave me some small measure of hope. I knew I'd been playing with fire, getting as close to Calix and Holden as I was, letting them trust me as they did. I could only hope that when I figured out how to tell them why I'd really come into their lives that they'd somehow forgive me. Maybe even still want me. The dark, inescapable pit of dread I'd been ignoring for days opened in my stomach. A much more likely scenario involved Calix's eyes colder than I'd ever seen them. Dread turned to despair because, in my heart, I knew the truth—

he'd banish me or kill me. Despite the reason, my deception was too big for anything else.

Turning to look out the van's window, I let the others' chatter wash over as I stared up at the cloudless night sky. Headlights flashed from a side road. I pulled my eyes away from the canvas of twinkling stars in time to see the front end of an SUV smashing into the side of the van.

CHAPTER THIRTEEN

Calix

Looking around the table, pride swelled in my chest. All of my Heretics were present and accounted for along with members from our Sand Lake charter. They wouldn't be participating

in the vote to bring the remaining Devil's members into the Iron Heretics, but it was good to have members from other charters present to witness the historic event. Jeb, Kade, Zach, and Ward were off to one side, sitting in chairs lined up against the wall. Ward was already sporting a shiner on his left eye. The only decent hit his opponent had gotten in on him during the fight earlier. It was too bad Lex hadn't been able to complete his job in time to get there. Having a Nomad charter presence would have been a welcome edition.

Directly across from me at the other end of the table, Holden had the same glow of pride on his face. Between us, filling our normally full table to overflowing, were the Heretics and all the men soon to be joining our ranks. Despite my misgivings about letting the Devil's wear the Heretics patch, the significance of the occasion was burrowing under my skin. Seeing the hope for better tomorrows written on the faces of Heretic and Devil alike, even after all the shit we'd been through the last few years, melted the stubborn resolve I'd been clinging to. This was the right choice. I knew that now. As surely as I knew the relationship between Holden, Neven, and I was it for me.

I brought the gavel down. The room went silent as every eye turned my way. "When my club brought the idea of patch over to this table, I was firmly against it. Mine was the only *no* vote in the room." I sighed, looking down at the gavel resting on the table in front of me. "Since I took over eight years ago, I've done everything in my power to keep this club healthy and whole. To grow us to a place beyond the label of outlaw. In my mind, the only thing welcoming our historically most vicious rivals with open arms would accomplish was killing us from the inside out." Looking back up, I let my eyes meet each Devil's gaze up and down the table, ending with Holden. "I was wrong. Together as two Heretics clubs, we're going to be stronger than ever."

Several men released breaths they'd been holding. Holden smiled.

"All those in favor of the Devil's Rage MC members present tonight becoming fully patched Iron Heretics members and forming their own Heretics charter, Yea or Nay." I paused, brow scrunching when I caught Holden looking down at this phone on the tabletop instead of at me. "Yea."

To my left, Mace said, "Yea." And all down the side it went, each man, Heretic and Devil alike putting their vote in the yes column. Axel gave his vote, and the room went silent again, waiting for Holden.

A beat passed.

"Holden?"

He looked up, face gone pale, and met my eyes. "No." His eyes never left mine as the room around us erupted with questions and protests. "Razor has Neven and the other boys."

"What?" I pushed to my feet, white-hot rage swirling with bone-chilling fear. Mace and Axel were on their feet, too, demanding answers and looking stricken.

Holden held up his phone. "He texted me from Neven's phone. Wants you to call him and put him on speaker."

The room got quiet again. I pulled out my phone, laying it on the table after I clicked to Neven's contact, pressed his number, and the speaker icon. The sound of ringing filled the air.

"Calix," a voice I'd thought I'd never hear again drawled. I hadn't seen Razor in years, but I could imagine the viciously smug expression on his face. "It's so good of you to call."

Around the table, every Devil went pale. Razor had been a nightmare before he'd finally been put away. I glanced at Ward, finding him three shades paler than the rest, making the deep red and already purpling bruises on his face stark against the pallor of his skin. Razor had been made to believe —thanks to a cop playing with a then eighteen-year-old Ward's life—that Ward was the reason Razor had been thrown in jail. That Ward had ratted on him. Ward hadn't, but the kind of grudge that accusation brings didn't go away quietly. When Razor had failed to show his face after he'd been released from prison, we'd all been hopeful one of his many enemies had buried him in a shallow grave. That had been over a year ago. A year of peace.

"Where are they, Razor?"

Razor tsked. "Why jump into business right away? Don't you want to catch up? Find out all the fun I've been having while you try to steal my club out from under me?"

Rage won the struggle still happening in my chest. "If you were so goddamned concerned about losing your club, you would have been here all along. So, no, I don't give a shit what you've been up to. Tell us where the boys are and what you want in exchange for their freedom."

The motherfucker sighed like I was wasting his time. Gritting my teeth, I braced my fists on the table to either side of the phone and bit my tongue to keep from lashing out.

"Fine," he snapped after a moment. "Tomorrow. Noon. I want three hundred k and the deed to your clubhouse." An outraged noise swept through the room. "You wanted to take my club, and now I'm going to take yours."

"I want to talk to Neven. Confirmation and assurance."

Silence again.

"Not Neven. Here's the blond one."

"Calix?" Arden's shaky voice came through the speaker. Jesus fucking Christ, Lex was going to lose his mind. Mace, Axel, and Holden all leaned closer over the table.

"Arden, it's me. Are you okay? Has he hurt any of you?"

"No, um, except in the van. They hit it with an SUV. Pushed us off the road. We're all a little banged up, but okay. Calix, will you call Lex?" Arden's voice broke on Lex's name, and I wanted to put my fist through the table.

"Of course. You're doing real good, Arden. We're going to get you out of there."

He sniffed. "Okay."

Razor's voice was back a moment later. "Happy?"

I growled at him. "If you hurt them, if you fucking touch any of them, there is no deal. Every man in this room will make it his personal mission to hunt you down and gut you like the filth you are. Am I making myself clear? You want this deal, fine. I'm demanding that assurance. They remain unharmed."

"Fine. The Heretics boys will stay in the condition they're in now. Slightly bruised, but otherwise unharmed and unspoiled. I'll send you the location for the meet in the morning."

The call clicked off.

NEVEN

Arden came back into the bedroom where we were being held. It was dingy with brown carpet and old, peeling wallpaper. The window beside me and the one in the attached bathroom had been boarded over. The only other things in the room were two bare mattresses and a twelve-pack of bottled water.

Leith pressed closer to me when the door opened, letting out a little whimper. I curled my arm tighter around him. We were sitting on one of the mattresses with our backs to the wall. Arden came through quickly, heading for the other bed where Pax was sitting, still holding a washcloth to the bleeding wound on the side of his head. We'd all gotten banged up in the accident—*accident, ha*—but none of us were seriously injured. I'd been afraid Pax had a concussion, but he wasn't dizzy or nauseous, and his pupils were both normal. He'd just sustained a free-bleeding split to the skin on the left side of his head when he'd cracked it against the window on impact.

Instead of the door closing and being bolted behind Arden, Razor stepped inside and glanced around at all of us. He still had the same mean glint in this eye that I remembered from when I was little, but the new scar on his face, bisecting his cheek and turning into a gnarled mass midway down his throat, made him seem even more vicious.

"Good news, gentlemen." He sneered with the last word. Between him and the two men working with him, they'd already called us every homophobic word in the book. "You're worth something to your bullshit bikers after all. As long as you behave and Calix keeps his word, you get to go home in the morning." He met my eyes with a smirk. "Well, three of you do."

"What?" Pax said, exploding up off the other mattress and swaying as soon as he was upright. Arden and Leith both leapt up, too, getting on either side of Pax to steady him.

"You mean, you haven't confessed yet?" Razor said to me. All three men, standing united in front of the man that was my nightmare come back to haunt me, turned wounded, bewildered eyes on me. "Better make use of the few hours you have left until daylight because, after that, I've found a new way for you to work off your debt," he snarled and took a step toward me, hand reaching out.

Flinching, I pressed my back hard against the wall, wishing I could somehow go through it and run away out into the night.

Stopping short of actually touching me, Razor took a deep breath. "I guess it all worked out in the end. Subterfuge never was really my style, and I should have known you'd be shit at it. Enjoy this night, Neven. Even if they beat the shit out of you like you deserve, I imagine it'll still be better than what's waiting for you tomorrow. You must have embarrassed Mr. Fenten terribly for him to be willing to pay the price I asked for your scrawny ass."

He backed toward the door.

"What about Lynn?" I yelled, getting to my feet. If I was dead anyway, I wanted to know she'd be safe. As safe as any of us could be with him in our lives. "If you're getting the money for my debt, you have to let her go!"

"You're so stupid, boy. She's already back to work, and that's exactly where she'll stay as long as she keeps making me money. You stay alive and go to Fenten without a fuss tomorrow, and she gets to keep doing what she does best." He backed out of the room, and we all watched the door, listening to the heavy locks on the outside of it clicking into place.

"Oh god..." I gasped, Razor's words sinking in. I wilted back down onto the dirty mattress, all the strength draining out of my body. Hot, useless tears spilled down my cheeks. Despite the shame burning over my body, a small pulse of relief bloomed in my chest. Tomorrow I would suffer, but at least, after that, it would all be over. No more lying. No more living in fear. I'd never see Calix and Holden again. More tears spilled at the thought, my face crumpling in on itself. I had wanted the chance to at least tell them I was sorry. For everything.

"He's been blackmailing you?"

I was startled out of my thoughts and jerked my head up. Leith was kneeling in front of me, hand stretched out like he wanted to place it on my shoulder. To comfort me. Why would he want to comfort me? Hadn't he just heard what Razor said?

"Yes." My voice came out in a hoarse whisper. I looked past Leith's kind eyes to Pax and Arden, both of them watching me with sympathy instead of the disgust I'd expected to find. I cleared my throat. "My mom was one of his working girls. When she died last year, I thought..." A wave of shame washed over me. "I thought I'd be free of him and all of it for good. And I was for a while, but he showed up at my college a few weeks ago and told me I was responsible for her debt. He said she still owed him thirty grand for drugs, and if I didn't want him to hurt Aunt Lynn, I'd do exactly what he told me to."

I looked down, remembering how terrified I'd been that day. Even after he'd gone to prison, Razor had haunted my nightmares. Mom had still worked for the Devil's until

Holden had taken over and put a stop to a lot of the shadier parts of the Devil's business—including keeping the girls so strung out that they'd do whatever they were told as long as they got their next fix. She went independent then, despite Aunt Lynn and I begging her to stop, to get help. I'd been eighteen by then and already out trying to build something for myself. I tried so many times to get her to walk away and go to rehab. She refused every time.

I swallowed hard. "He wanted information on the club. Wanted me to get close to one of the members. Find out about the new brothel, get any information I could. Anything he could use to hurt the Heretics."

"And you set your sights on Calix?" Pax asked, sounding both impressed and incredulous. He and Arden moved as one, coming to sit on either side of me. Leith still knelt in front of me. He reached out and took my hand, giving it a squeeze.

I squeezed back and shook my head. "No. He chose me." Looking up, I met each of their eyes in turn. "I'm so sorry. I didn't want to hurt anyone, but I didn't know what to do. I hadn't even given Razor anything. That's why we're here. I told him I needed more time. That I didn't know anything yet." I huffed. "Obviously that wasn't good enough."

"Hey," Arden said, sliding his arm around my shoulders. "Believe it or not, we've all been in situations similar to this before. Kidnapped and worse." He grimaced. "The guys have always come to our rescue. There's no way Calix is going to let Razor have you."

I wanted to believe him, but I knew once Calix learned the truth, the only reason he'd save me from Razor and Fenten was so he could kill me himself.

CHAPTER FOURTEEN

Holden

I hadn't slept more than a fitful doze, sitting at one end of the couch in Calix's living room between bouts of pacing. I didn't think Calix had slept at all. Neither of us had touched the bed, and aside from one brief hug once we'd broken away from the meeting and gotten behind a closed door, we hadn't touched each other either. The rage was too close to the surface in each of us. Blood running too hot and with no target close at hand. Not to say anything of the fear neither of us had acknowledged out loud.

It was an ice pick in my chest. Fear that Razor wouldn't keep his word. Fear that Neven or the others were hurt worse than Razor would let Arden say. Fear that even if we got Neven back whole, he'd do what any sane person should and run. That we'd lose him either way. Fear that he was already gone.

Across the room, Calix was still as stone, standing with his arms crossed and watching the pale gray dawn climb over the horizon. He hadn't said a word in hours. Once Razor had hung up, everyone in the meeting room clamored to get a word in—predictions, tactics, plans. It had all hit my skin and run off like water because all I could hear was Razor's voice in my head, *Not Neven*, he'd said. *Here's the blond one.* Neven's name didn't belong anywhere near that bastard, and it chilled me to the bone that he'd chosen to say it when he couldn't be bothered with Arden's.

He knew exactly who Neven was to me and Calix. Three hundred thousand dollars and a piece of land didn't seem like nearly enough ransom for that kind of leverage.

"I should have insisted on speaking to Neven." Calix's voice was unusually small. "Arden's not a liar. But to protect Pax and Leith? To save his own life? I would expect him to say whatever they told him to."

I clenched my eyes shut. *Shit.* I'd been hoping the thoughts swarming my brain were off base—my own paranoia and plan for the worst mentality. My voice came out flat. Any other inflection and I was pretty sure I'd lose the composure I was so desperately clinging to. "You think he's already dead."

"I think Razor hates the both of us, especially you for growing the Devil's into something worth a damn, and would not pass up the opportunity to gut either one of us." Turning from the window, Calix walked to the couch and sat down beside me. He pressed his thigh to mine and reached for my hand. I gripped his willingly, taking comfort in the warmth of his palm against mine. "We need to prepare ourselves. Nothing can get in the way of getting the others back safely."

I nodded, looking down at our joined hands. "I love you." He turned his head toward me, but I didn't look up. "I've loved you for a long time. Maybe it just comes easy to me with the right people because I'm pretty sure I love Neven, too. I wish I would have told him already." Lifting my head, I finally met his startled gaze. "I didn't want to go out there today without telling you."

"If he's alive, we're getting him back." His voice had gone rough. "Either way, Razor dies today."

I nodded.

"And I love you, too." He leaned in quick, pressing a hard kiss to my mouth. Then he was up and moving toward the door.

———

NEVEN

The only indication that morning had arrived was the thin strip of pale light beneath the bedroom door. We'd all decided we should sleep in shifts so there was always someone awake to listen for Razor or his goons coming back, but it'd been a quiet night. The others had each managed some sleep. I'd barely been able to shut my eyes. The one time I'd dozed off, I'd jerked back awake from a half-remembered dream of Calix pointing his gun to my head, betrayal written into every line of his face. My want to see him again warred with the relief that I wouldn't have to see that look on his face in person. I had no idea how Holden would react beyond knowing he'd be the calmer of the two.

"What time is it?" Leith asked, looking up at me from where his head was pillowed on my thigh. Of all of us, he'd taken our imprisonment in this room the hardest. Not that I could blame him after Pax had explained in whispered words how some psycho had kidnapped Leith and chained him up in a bathroom for days.

I brushed my fingers through Leith's red hair. "Not sure. Early morning probably."

He closed his eyes with a nod.

"You okay?" Pax asked me, but before I could answer the door rattled as someone unlocked it. We all tensed as it opened a crack and an unopened box of *Poptarts* was unceremoniously tossed inside. The door shut again, locks clicking into place. Pax heaved himself up and leaned forward, grabbing the box before settling back on the mattress. He checked it over and apparently didn't find anything amiss because he tossed a couple silver packets across for Leith and I, then opened the third for himself. "Hope you guys like blueberry."

Leith pulled himself up to sit beside me, keeping our shoulders pressed together and opened his packet only to stare at the pastries for a long moment before he took a bite out of the corner of one.

I frowned when I realized there had only been three packets in the box. Pax hadn't even offered Arden one. "Arden, do you want one of mine?"

Arden gave me a small smile. "I can't eat them. Celiac disease."

"Oh."

Pax smiled at me, too. I should have known he wouldn't just let Arden starve.

"I can ask for something else. That way when they get mad, they'll take it out on me."

"Please don't," Arden said quickly. "Let's not draw attention to ourselves. Anyway, I'm fine. Just ready to get out of here." His face paled as soon as the words left his mouth. "Shit, Neven, I'm sorry."

The bite of pastry in my mouth turned to ash. "It's okay. It's not your fault."

Pax stood up, a determined look on his face, and sat on the small bit of space on the other side of me. "Listen," he whispered in my ear. "Just stay alive, okay? Do whatever you have to, and don't fucking feel bad about it for a minute. As soon as we're back with the Heretics, we'll be coming for you."

Turning my head, I met his eyes from inches away. "But I'm a...a *rat*. The only reason I was at *Spritz* to begin with is because Razor made me be there."

"You're telling me that if Razor had let you off the hook, you'd have walked away from Calix and Holden without a backward glance?"

I felt my face heat. "Of course not!" My whisper turned furious. "I love—" My eyes went huge as I bit my lip to cut myself off.

Pax lifted an eyebrow. "Listen, I've never seen Calix act with anyone the way he does with you. And even if he's pissed, which he probably will be, I can't imagine him leaving you like that. And Holden? No way. He's coming for you, with or without Calix. And I can guarantee that we"—he motioned at himself then Leith and Arden—"are going to be coming with him."

A hot lump grew in my throat, and I had to look away. "I can't ask any of you to do that."

"You're not asking. I'm telling you. Heretics take care of their own, and so do we."

Leith nudged me from the other side. "And you're one of us."

"Just stay alive," Arden said, moving to squeeze in between me and Leith. "That's the important thing."

I nodded, terrified and tucking their words close to my heart—stay alive. I knew how to do that. "I will. Thank you all for being my friends."

We all sat huddled together, quietly sharing warmth and strength until hours later when the door opened again.

CHAPTER FIFTEEN

Calix

At noon, Holden, me, and the Heretics stepped off our bikes at the end of a gravel drive. The location was a good one for shady business—back off a county road and surrounded by trees. The area we were parked in was cleared like someone was planning to build a house there but had only gotten as far as putting the driveway in.

Across from us, Razor with an ugly new scar on his face and three of the old Devil's Rage members, were standing in front of a windowless black van.

"Calix, Holden," Razor smirked. "So glad you could make it."

Beside me, Holden tensed.

"Easy," I said, under my breath before turning my attention back to Razor. I scanned the trees. Lex hadn't answered my call the night before, but I'd sent him a message with the coordinates for the meet. I had every faith in the guys at my back—Cleave, Eben, Riot, Axel, and Mace. The last two were as ready to tear Razor apart as Holden and I were. I'd left Jeb at the clubhouse with his crew in case Razor tried to pull any nasty surprises while we were away. Still, it would have been nice to have an ace in the hole. "Razor. I see your face has had better days."

Fire lit in Razor's eyes. "A souvenir from my little prison vacation courtesy of the rat I heard has weaseled his way into your ranks."

I sighed. "Ward didn't rat you out. Even if he had, he was an eighteen-year-old boy. Not really his problem you like to use children to do your dirty work."

Razor bared his teeth then broke into a laugh. "Trying to rile me up, huh? Make me get sloppy? That's an old trick, Calix."

"What can I say? Old habits, die hard and all that." I smirked at him. There was a lot of history standing in this field between us. A lot of bloodshed. "Where are they, Razor? You don't get anything from us until I know they're okay."

"You brought what I asked for?"

I pulled a folded file folder from the inner pocket of my vest, holding it up to show him, then gestured back at Cleave, who held up the bag containing the money. "All here and accounted for."

"Open the bag," Razor said. "I want to see green."

We stared at each other. It was on the tip of my tongue to tell him to go fuck himself. That he wasn't seeing shit until I had Neven safe in my arms, but I swallowed it down. I nodded at Cleave. He stepped forward, putting him on the other side of me from Holden. Kneeling, he placed the bag on the ground in front of him and unzipped it. Tilting it, he flashed the bills on top in Razor's direction.

"Your turn, Razor."

He signaled his guys. They went to the rear of the van and opened the doors. Leith was the first to step down, duct tape over his mouth and wrapped around his wrists held together in front of him. One of the Devil's grabbed him by the upper arm and spun him, so Leith's back was to the Devil's chest, with the Devil's beefy arm banded around Leith's torso. Leith's eyes were wide with fear and focused over my shoulder.

Axel sucked in a hard breath behind me.

"Easy, brother," Riot said, keeping his voice low.

Arden and Pax were next. Both trussed up the same way Leith was. The other two Devil's grabbed Arden and Pax, holding them the same way the first one was Leith. They all looked rumpled, and there was a bit of dried blood visible on the side of Pax's neck, but they were lucid and upright. Mace cursed under his breath. My heart picked up speed for every second Neven didn't appear. The Devil's closed the van.

"What the fuck?" Holden growled.

"Where is he?" My voice rang loud in the clearing.

"Who?" Razor asked, all innocence. "Oh, you mean, the other rat that's been hanging around your crew?"

"The fuck are you talking about?"

"My sweet little ratty boy Neven, of course." Razor chuckled, and the other Devil's laughed along. Then his face went serious as stone. He stared at me. "He was working for me the whole time, Calix." He moved his gaze over to Holden, a dark sneer twisting up his lips. "I always told your old man what a little faggot you were, but I'm glad he isn't alive to see you now. Moaning like a whore while you take it up the ass!" Razor spit on the ground in front of him. "It really was a nice cabin. Shame the three of you didn't burn up with it."

Holden was rigid beside me, face red and eyes blazing like wildfire. My heart lurched and stuttered in my chest, trying to reconcile the words Razor was spitting with the man I knew. Neven had played us? Behind Razor, Arden's gaze caught mine. He stared at me hard, blue eyes intense. He shook his head—one solid move from side to side. I focused on Razor again and somehow found my voice. "Still using boys to do your dirty work, huh? Where is Neven, Razor?

The deal was for all of them, and I'm not leaving here without him."

"No, the deal was for all the Heretics boys, and they're right here." Razor motioned to Leith, Arden, and Pax. "Neven was never yours. He's belonged to me since his whore mother pushed him out twenty years ago. He forgot that for a moment while I was gone, but I imagine right about now he's remembering."

The inflection of his voice made my stomach shrivel up. "What did you do?"

"Found someone willing to give Neven a reminder of who he works for. You really should be more careful who you let into that little brothel you protect for Vivian. Rich men don't like to be slighted."

In one smooth motion, Holden pulled his gun and leveled it at Razor's face, arm steady and face harder than I'd ever seen it. "Where is he?"

The Devil's reached for their guns, but a hand raised from Razor stopped them. I could feel the tension ratcheting up in the men at my back. Mace and Axel were restless, wanting to get to Pax and Leith. And we were all ready to put an end to this farce of an exchange and put Razor down for good.

"Grew some teeth after all," Razor murmured, like he wasn't staring down the barrel of the gun. "But I don't think you want to do that."

The crack of a gunshot hit the air, and for a split second, I thought Holden had fired. Then the man holding Arden jerked, blood splattering onto the side of the van behind him. A circle of red shown in the middle of his forehead as he slumped to the ground. The clearing erupted in chaos.

Arden threw himself forward onto the ground, head turned toward Pax and Leith, yelling indiscernible words behind his duct tape gag. It didn't take a genius to figure out what he was trying to say—*get down*! Pax and Leith both lurched forward, using the confusion to break the hold their captors had on them. Two more shots thundered through the clearing in rapid succession. Two more Devil's fell.

Razor was alone.

I lifted my fist to shoulder height, knowing Lex would cease fire. With Holden still holding Razor at gunpoint, he and I moved across the grassy space between us. Razor sneered at me as I reached under his vest, pulling the gun from his shoulder holster and quickly patted him down for other weapons. Moving behind him, I kicked the back of his knee and sent him down into the dirt.

Beside us, the other Heretics had rushed forward. Axel was cradling a shaking Leith to him while Cleave cut the duct tape from Leith's wrists. Riot and Mace were taking care of Arden and Pax, but Arden's eyes were fixed firmly on the opposite tree line. A moment later, Lex strode out, long rifle on a strap over his shoulder. With duct tape still on his wrists, Arden side-stepped Riot and ran, throwing himself into Lex's arms.

I took a deep breath and brought my attention back to the man on his knees between Holden and I. "You're done, Razor. Tell us where Neven is, and we'll make it quick. Don't, and I'm going to start cutting pieces off."

"I ain't telling you shit." Razor laughed, the sound of a man that knew he had nowhere left to run. "By the time you find him, there'll be nothing left but bloody pulp."

Gripping the pistol I'd taken off him by the barrel, I swung hard and caught him high on the cheek. He grunted and fell over, blood pouring from the side of his face. Tossing his gun aside, I reached down and grabbed two handfuls of his vest, hauling him back to his knees. "Save yourself some fucking pain here, Razor. Tell me where he is."

"Calix," Pax said, making me turn to look at him. "It's not far. We can get you back there. You don't need him."

I held Pax's gaze. "You're sure?"

"Yes, and we need to hurry."

"Bullshit!" Razor yelled, teetering on his knees like he was going to try and get up. Blood still oozed from the wound I'd given him, and his eye was already swollen shut.

I looked at Holden. He gave me a nod and stepped to the side of Razor so the blowback wouldn't land on any of us. He fired two shots, straight into the side of Razor's head. The body slumped, falling over on its side with a thud.

For a second, we all stood with the echo of those shots ringing in our ears.

Looking up, I glanced over my men, the newly returned partners, and finally to my lover. "Let's go."

NEVEN

Quiet settled over the house after Razor took the others to meet the Heretics. I knew he'd left one guy, because he'd told me, but wherever that guy was, he wasn't making a sound. With the others around me the night before, I hadn't let myself dwell on what was going to happen to me today, but now, in the stillness, my mind could barely focus on anything else.

Except when it turned to Calix and Holden, which was honestly worse. The deep, aching hole of regret that opened in my chest every time I thought of them, kept tears burning along the edges of my eyes. I told myself it didn't matter, that regardless of how I felt, they wouldn't feel the same as soon as they knew the truth about me. Pax was right. Holden would come for me, but how could I face him? And Calix...I was glad we'd had a nice goodbye after the fight. Clutching tight to the memory of being held in arms so sure might somehow hold me together.

I just needed to stay alive. Whatever Fenten planned to dish out, I needed to find a way to escape or endure. Gravel crunched outside, and my heartbeat ticked up. Voices carried through the walls but not loud enough for me to hear what they were saying. Two men. Perhaps Fenten had come alone.

"He's in here," the Devil said, and one of the locks on the outside of the door clicked.

I climbed to my feet, standing between the two mattresses. If there had been a door on the bathroom, I'd have run in there, tried to barricade myself in, but there wasn't, and I was out of time. Whatever they had planned, I'd meet them head-on.

For a long, horrible second, all I could hear was the clicking of the locks being undone. The final one gave, and I took a deep breath. *I love you, Calix*, I thought. *I love you, Holden. I'm sorry, Lynn.* Somehow, I hoped they knew.

The door flew open, and the Devil came straight for me. I screamed, trying to duck away from his reaching hands, but he grabbed me by the back of the shirt and yanked until I lost my footing and went down hard on my side.

"Your visitor's here, boy," the Devil sneered, meaty hands turning me onto my back despite my struggles. He was bent over me, face full of maniacal glee. He had orange-red hair and a bushy beard the same color. His breath smelled like cheap beer. He looked up at the man still standing in the door. "This is him, ain't it?"

"Yes," Fenten said. He looked the same as he had in *Spritz's* lounge—sharp gray suit, neatly styled salt and pepper hair. He looked at me with a dark sort of lust in his eyes that sent a frisson of true terror up my spine. "Now, Neven, is it?" He stepped into the room, removing his suit coat and draping it over one of the bare mattresses before unbuttoning the cuffs of his shirt and rolling his sleeves to the elbows. "I plan to get what I paid for."

I screamed again, adrenaline coursing through me as I dropped into a sheer panic. I grabbed at the arms holding me down, slapping and clawing. Reaching up, I went for the Devil's face, catching his cheek with my nails.

He yelled and brought one hand, closed fisted, down hard right on my nose. The blow hurt, bringing tears to my eyes, and making me blink black dots out of my vision. When I looked up again, Fenten was nearly on top of me, the button of his pants open as he dodged the clumsy kick I aimed at his leg.

"Will you hold him still?" Fenten barked.

"Maybe we should tie him up, huh?" Devil said, hands like steel bands pinning my shoulders to the floor.

"No!" I yelled, some instinct kicking in. I didn't want to be tied down. "I'll be good." My voice came out shaky and raw. I must have been screaming more than I realized. I settled, pressing my head back against the floor. I just needed to stay alive. My eyes caught on the hilt of a knife, a big knife, the Devil had attached to his belt. In his bent-over position, it had gotten pushed forward from where it normally rode on his side.

Fenten grabbed my ankle, stepping between my legs and reaching for the waist of my pants. I had to time it right. I shot my arm up, making the Devil flinch like I was going for his face again, and grabbed the knife. Using my whole body, I twisted around, sitting up and dragging the blade out of the sheath and along the Devil's arm. I caught him, because he yelled and reflexively let me go. I didn't think, I just stabbed as hard as I could into his thigh, on the inside where I knew there was an artery. Blood gushed, pouring all over my hand and arm and face. I stabbed again.

The Devil swung wildly at me, catching me high on the

side of my head. The impact knocked me over onto one of the mattresses and Fenten's fancy coat. Scrambling up, knife held at the ready, I watched the Devil take one lumbering step toward me, blood running between the fingers on the hand he'd pressed to his leg before he dropped to one knee and face planted on the floor.

"Shit!" Fenten yelled from the doorway.

I shifted my attention to him, knife pointing in his direction. There was blood all over me, my skin was slick with it, and the smell was overpowering everything else. The Devil groaned, face down in the bloody brown carpet, while Fenten and I stared at each other.

The rumble of motorcycles sounded outside.

I lunged for the door—knife first.

CHAPTER SIXTEEN

Holden

The gravel driveway was a bumpy, pot-holed mess. Mace, with Pax on the bike behind him, was leading us down toward the old farmhouse at the end of it as quickly as possible. I was seriously considering getting off the bike and running the rest of the way, when a side door on the house burst open and Neven, covered in blood, ran out into the yard.

My heart stopped beating.

Throwing the kickstand down, I jumped off my bike and ran toward Neven. Calix had been riding beside me, but I didn't stop to see what he was doing. I couldn't peel my eyes from Neven's slight frame. He choked out a little sob and moved into a stumbling run in our direction.

Jesus, how bad was he hurt? There was so much blood. I ran up the drive, weaving around holes and trampling the thick weeds growing in a swath down the center. Ten feet away from me, Neven's eyes went wide, and he went down hard on his front with a grunt.

"Neven!" I landed on my knees beside him, grabbing him

up in my arms and rolling him over. "Where are you hurt, baby?" The frantic voice that came out of me didn't sound like my own.

He gasped, one hand clutching at my vest and saying in a raspy whisper, "It's not mine. It's not my blood." Then he closed his eyes and went limp in my arms. I pressed my fingers to his neck, and breathed out hard when his strong pulse beat against my fingers. It was then I noticed the giant fucking hunting knife laying a couple feet from us, coated in blood the same way Neven was.

"Neven." Calix's broken voice startled me.

Looking up, I found him standing over us, hands spread out like he didn't know what to do and a look of absolute devastation on his face.

"Hey," I said, reaching one hand for Calix. "It's not his blood." When he didn't move, I raised my voice. "Calix! He's alive. It's not his blood."

Neven squirmed, blue eyes opening and shutting several times.

"We need some water!" Calix yelled, dropping to his knees on the other side of Neven and taking the hand closest to him like he was afraid to touch him.

"He's still in the house," Neven said, voice nothing more than a raw scraping sound. "I got one of them."

"Who's in the house?" Calix asked.

"Fenten."

"I've got it, boss," Mace said, turning toward the old farmhouse.

"No," Calix's voice was clear and strong—full of growl and gravel again. "This one's mine." He leaned down, pressing a kiss to Neven's bloody lips and climbed to his feet. He met my gaze a second before he bent down and picked up that hunting knife and strode toward the house.

"Watch his back," I said, looking at Mace. Mace nodded, and he and Cleave pulled their guns and jogged after Calix.

Looking down, I pulled Neven closer to me, gripping the hem of my shirt and trying to use it to wipe the blood off his face. It was already turning tacky, and I wanted it off of him. He watched me with dazed eyes. "You're gonna be okay, baby. You're safe now."

His face crumpled, and tears spilled down his cheeks. "I'm sorry."

"None of that." I ran a hand through his hair, rocking him gently. "Everything is going to be okay."

A blood-curdling scream cut through the air from the direction of the house. Neven flinched, and I gripped him tight, tucking him against my chest. Some dark, spiteful part of me rejoiced in that sound. I was glad Calix had made it hurt, but I didn't want anything else ugly to touch Neven today.

"Holden?"

I looked up to find Arden kneeling where Calix had been moments ago. He had a camping canteen in one hand and a crumpled white t-shirt in the other. Probably from Lex's saddlebags. For the first time since I'd seen Neven, I looked around at the others. All the bikes were parked in the middle of the driveway, and the Heretics that hadn't followed Calix had positioned themselves, guns drawn and facing out, in a loose circle around us. Pax and Leith were sitting on the ground between two of the closest bikes. It wasn't much, but with our current location, the bikes were the only cover available.

"Neven, do you think you can sit up, baby?"

He nodded, dark hair brushing my chin. Maneuvering us around, I got one arm under his back and the other under his knees and carefully climbed to my feet. I walked us back over to my bike and threw my leg over, so I was sitting normally and he was sitting sideways, half on my thighs, half on the tank. I kept one arm wrapped around his back and reached out with the other toward Arden. He handed me the damp t-shirt.

Neven gripped one end of it too, and together we got most of the blood wiped off his face, neck, and arms. He was still red around the edges, but it was much better than when he'd come out of the house. Getting rid of the blood also revealed bruises forming beneath each of his eyes and around his nose.

"He hit you?" I asked quietly, letting my fingers trail along his jawline.

"The Devil guy. Punched me once." His voice was still destroyed. Letting the t-shirt fall to his lap, he leaned hard against me, resting his cheek on my chest.

Looking over at Arden, I handed him the now stained shirt and motioned for the canteen. He handed it over, and I held it in front of Neven's face. Gripping it with both hands, he took a long drink then passed it back to me. Arden took it back, then reached out and squeezed Neven's hand. Neven looked up at him with a small smile.

"You're all okay?"

"We're good," Arden said. "Glad to see you're okay, too."

Neven nodded and closed his eyes. I held him close, thinking we were going to have to tie him to one of us on the back of a bike to get him home if he couldn't stay awake. The same side door on the house Neven had come out banged open again, and Calix, Mace, and Cleave made their way back toward us.

Neven jerked up, eyes watching them get closer. He started to tremble. The others stopped and positioned themselves with the rest, but Calix kept walking straight to us. When he was standing beside the bike, he reached down and got his hands under Neven's armpits and picked him up off my lap.

"It's over, baby."

Neven let out a sob, arms and legs clenching tight around Calix. He buried his face in Calix's neck and hung on. Calix pressed his nose into Neven's hair behind his ear and ran a hand up and down Neven's back, keeping the other under his ass to hold him up.

I let out a slow, shaky breath and met Calix's eyes. It was time to take our boy home.

CALIX

Glancing over my shoulder, I looked at the clock on the nightstand. Midnight. We'd been in bed for six hours. Neven was a warm weight pressed all along the front of me with his face pressed into the hollow of my throat. Holden was behind him, cocooning Neven between us with one of his strong arms draped over both of us. They were both gone to the world.

With a sigh, I kissed the top of Neven's head. He'd been completely wiped out—fear and adrenaline draining him dry —by the time we got back to the clubhouse. We'd gotten him showered, fed him some scrambled eggs and toast, and poured him into bed. He kept trying to apologize to me, but I insisted we could talk about it after he'd rested. The only thing he wouldn't let go was that we had to find his Aunt Lynn. Apparently, she'd been a working girl along with Neven's mother under Razor years ago. She'd gotten out, though, and Razor had forced her back into the life—threatening her in the process—to get Neven to do what he wanted.

Holden knew who she was immediately, from his time prospecting while Razor was still in charge of the club, and sent his Devil's out to find her. He'd gotten a text a couple hours ago that the Devil's had broken up a little impromptu brothel some of Razor's cronies were running. Lynn had been there, and now she was safe downstairs in one of the infirmary rooms.

Neven stirred against me. I held still hoping he'd drift back off. He needed sleep, but his mind seemed determined not to let him rest. He'd woken a couple times already.

"Calix?" His voice was still raw. I wanted to kill that motherfucker all over again.

"I'm here, baby."

"Did you sleep?"

A small smile pulled at my lips. "Some. How are you feeling?"

"Okay. Sore. I need to pee."

Chuckling, I eased back from him and slipped off the bed. He took my offered hand and pulled himself over to the edge. Holden smacked his lips and rolled over onto his belly, burying his face in his pillow. I held onto Neven while he climbed to his feet in case he was unsteady, but he seemed fine.

While he went to the bathroom, I walked out to the kitchen and got a bottle of water. Bringing it back to the bedroom, I put it on the nightstand and sat on the edge of the bed, waiting for Neven.

He came out of the bathroom a moment later still wearing nothing but a pair of black briefs. The dim light from the windows softened the bruises from the crash and the asshole who punched him in the face. He walked right into my space, standing in between my thighs and resting his forearms on my shoulders, fingers gliding up and down the back of my neck.

He smiled. "This feels familiar." Leaning down, he kissed me gently.

I settled my hands on the backs of his thighs, just under the gentle curve of his ass. "You okay, baby?"

Biting his lip, he looked down. "I killed a man today. I keep seeing his face when I close my eyes. Not when he was dying, but when he was trying to hold me down. He looked... excited. Excited to hurt me."

Pulling him closer, I wrapped my arms completely around him. "And you made sure he won't ever do it again." I kissed the middle of his chest. "No one's ever going to hurt you again."

"Am I going to have bodyguards?" He made it sound like a joke, letting out a little laugh, until he saw the serious set of my jaw. "Calix..."

"You're the partner of two Iron Heretics Presidents. Two. I'm sorry, sweetheart, but you're never going anywhere without a patch watching over you."

"Maybe I should have my own patch."

I smiled. "You want a prospect vest? A *Harley*? After today, if you wanted one, I'd sponsor you."

He hummed. "A *Harley*...yes, actually. I'd love to learn to ride, but you can keep the vest. I think I'd rather just be your boy if that's okay."

A wave of love so big it filled my chest to the brim rose up in me. "You *are* my boy," I told him, my voice coming out a growl.

"I'm sorry for what Razor made me do." He swallowed hard, eyes shiny in the dim light. "I didn't want to. I can't believe he burned down your cabin."

"Did you know he was following us?"

"No. I swear. He put some location app on my phone before he sent me to *Spritz*. He must have used that because I didn't even tell him we were going."

"I believe you."

"He's really gone?"

I squeezed him to me, his belly flush with my stomach. "He's really gone. Your other man back there took care of business."

"Damn right." Holden's voice was scratchy with sleep. He slid across the bed and wrapped himself around me from behind, pressing his sleep-hot skin all along my back. Sliding his arms around my waist, he reached for Neven, letting me be the man in the middle for a change. "And Calix is right about that patch. You could have one if you wanted, but you're definitely not going anywhere unprotected."

"Okay."

"Aunt Lynn is downstairs," Holden said. I was grateful to him for changing the subject. Neven was shaken enough. I doubted he'd fight us on whatever security measures we deemed appropriate until he was a little more settled again.

Neven's head snapped up. "What? Is she okay?"

"Yes," I said, meeting his gaze. "She's fine. She was worried about you. The guys put her in one of the infirmary rooms to sleep."

"Can I go see her?"

"Of course," I said, leaning in to kiss him. He met me eagerly, opening up and letting me lick into his mouth. I kept the pressure light, not wanting to press on his bruised nose and cheeks. "Find some clothes baby, and I'll walk down with you."

"Me too," Holden said, leaning forward for a gentle kiss of his own.

"Okay." Neven slipped out of my arms and went over to the dresser, pulling open a drawer and grabbing one of my t-shirts.

I snorted a laugh at the way it hung on him, but nothing

could have made me happier in that moment than seeing him so at ease in this space.

Turning my head, I kissed Holden and was rewarded with a smile. We slid off the bed together and found sweats and shoes to pull on. Neven also cabbaged a pair of my boxer shorts to go along with his borrowed t-shirt.

The clubhouse was quiet around us as we made our way downstairs in the dim security lights that stayed on around the clock. Moving down the hallway toward the infirmary rooms, we stopped outside the one with the closed door.

"She's probably sleeping."

"That's okay." He reached for the door handle. "I just want to see her."

I nodded and stepped aside. Holden moved with me. Neven slipped into the room, but left the door open a crack. Inside the room, the attached bathroom light had been left on leaving the space more brightly lit than the hallway. Lynn was laying on her side, turned away from the door, but she stirred as soon as Neven reached the side of the bed.

"Neven? Oh honey, your face..." Lynn sat up, reaching for him.

"I'm sorry, Aunt Lynn," Neven said, going into her arms and voice clogging with tears.

Holden nudged me with his shoulder. I met his gaze—as suspiciously shiny as I imagined mine was—and together we stepped back from the open door to give them privacy. We could meet Aunt Lynn tomorrow.

Holden leaned his shoulders back against the wall across from the door, and I went to him, like a moth to a flame, pressing myself along his front and wrapping my arms around his shoulders. He sighed into my hold, slipping his arms around my waist and kissing the side of my head.

"We made it, boss."

I huffed a laugh. "You're still not a Heretic." I pulled back enough to hold his gaze. "We need to remedy that."

"We will." Holden pulled me closer. "I'm so glad we got him back."

Pressing my forehead to his, I let out a slow breath. "Me too. When I saw him fall after he ran out of that house..."

"I know. Believe me I know."

I'd never been so scared in my life. Holden and I stood quietly after that. Just holding each other, and it was one more thing that I'd never allowed to happen in all the years before that I was so grateful for now. I needed this man and his steady strength.

Behind us, Neven slipped out of the infirmary room and pulled the door softly closed. "She's asleep again."

Without comment, Holden and I put Neven between us, arms overlapping where we each wrapped one around him and made our way back up to our apartment. Once we were back in the bedroom, we stripped back down to our underwear. I helped Neven pull my shirt over his head while Holden slipped the too-big shorts Neven'd borrowed down his legs. We sandwiched him in a hug between us, taking turns pressing kisses into his hair.

Letting out a big breath, Neven sagged in our hold. "Thank you so much."

Holden's voice was rough. "You don't have to thank us for anything." He swallowed hard. "We love you, Neven. We're always going to be here for you."

He looked at Holden, eyes wide, before sweeping that blue gaze to me.

"We love you," I said, simply. All my life, I'd been fighting letting myself feel this. Holden had made it nearly impossible, but I'd held on, determined that I wouldn't let something as silly as *love* weaken me. Turns out, I was the silly one. This thundering cadence in my chest wasn't weakness. It was power and the food my soul had been begging for. I loved them. I was a better man because of them. And I'd take care of both of them, protect both of them, until it was my turn to go into the ground.

"I love you both," Neven whispered. We climbed back into bed, sharing kisses and warmth. We'd sleep tonight and deal with the rest of the world tomorrow.

Simple.

EPILOGUE

Holden

FOUR MONTHS LATER

I had a feeling I knew where we were going. Although, I had to hand it to Calix, if he'd somehow managed to pull this off while keeping it a secret for the last four months—I was going to be damn impressed. The last time I'd been out this way, it'd been warm and Neven had been wrapped around Calix on the back seat of his bike. So much had changed. Neven was back in school, and the three of us were solid—settled and in love in a way I didn't know was possible. The breeze was cool, the trees were just starting to change shades, and Neven was on his own bike cruising along between Calix and I.

He'd taken to riding like a duck to water, and I knew for a fact he was going to pout through the short winter months when it was too cold or icy to be out on a bike. Calix and I ribbed him all the time about needing a vest and patch of his own, but he still insisted he was more than happy just being our boy.

On cue, Calix turned on his turn signal, and we all slowed to pull into the cabin's packed dirt driveway. When we made it around the curve and the trees cleared, where the pile of smoking rubble had been the last time I'd been there, stood a house twice the size of the old one. It wasn't exactly a cabin with dark brown brick covering the outside, but the metal roof was the same shade of green. There was an attached garage with a matching green double bay door that started to rise after Calix stuck a hand in this pocket.

He rode his bike right into it, so Neven and I followed suit. There was plenty of room for us all to park side by side.

As soon as the engines cut off, Neven pulled off his helmet, hair sticking up everywhere. "What! How?"

Calix chuckled. "You like it?"

I got off my bike, stowing my helmet and heading for the door that led inside the house. I shook my head at Calix, smile so big it was hurting my face. "I can't believe you kept this a secret."

He shrugged, meeting me at the door and putting his hand on my chest to get me to stop. He brushed his fingers over the Iron Heretics MC and President patches on the right side of my chest. "I'll never get tired of seeing those."

The transition had been a fairly smooth one, and my charter of Heretics were happily working security at Vivian's new club and getting in on Calix's fight nights every chance we got. I gripped his fingers with mine and leaned in for a kiss. "Same here."

"Are we going in?" Neven asked, watching us with happy eyes and a smirk on his face. Calix and I had really enjoyed learning all the facets of Neven over the last few months, but we'd also built the kind of bond between the two of us that I'd never believed would happen outside of my dreams.

Calix chuckled. He pushed the door open and stepped back with a sweep of his arm, offering for us to go first. "Welcome home, sweethearts."

Thank you for reading!

The Iron Heretics will return.
For updates on future books, please subscribe to my newsletter and receive, Decadence, a free Lex and Arden prequel short story.

CONNECT WITH MICHELLE FROST

For updates, sales, and freebies sign up for my **newsletter** at:
www.michellefrostwrites.com

For teasers and fun join my **Facebook group**
The Frost Files.

For first look at works-in-progress, behind-the-scenes access
to my writing process, exclusive short fiction, and more,
check out my Patreon.

facebook.com/michellefrostwrites
patreon.com/MichelleFrostWrites
bookbub.com/profile/michelle-frost
pinterest.com/michellefrostwrites

ALSO BY MICHELLE FROST

Iron Heretics MC Series

(Contemporary MM Biker Romance)

Free Short Story: Discord

Disrupt

Disarm

Discordant

Dissent

Iron Heretics MC Prequels

Cold Light

Make No Mistake

Metal & Magic

(MM Urban Fantasy)

Metal Heart

Kingdoms of Pelas

(Gay Harem Fantasy Romance with Michele Notaro)

Zyon

Open Wounds Series

(Contemporary MM Romance)

Carry and Drag

Take Down

Matched Intensity

Vidar

Made in the USA
Middletown, DE
14 September 2021